# THE
# MANDIE
# COLLECTION

## VOLUME TEN

# MANDIE MYSTERIES

Mandie and...

...the Secret Tunnel

...the Cherokee Legend

...the Ghost Bandits

...the Trunk's Secret

...the Abandoned Mine

...the Mysterious Bells

...the Shipboard Mystery

...the Foreign Spies

...the Silent Catacombs

...the Mysterious Fisherman

...the Windmill's Message

...the Invisible Troublemaker

...the Courtroom Battle

...Jonathan's Predicament

---

The Mandie Collection:

---

Mandie: Her College Days

*New Horizons*

# THE MANDIE COLLECTION

## VOLUME TEN

## LOIS GLADYS LEPPARD

BETHANYHOUSE
Minneapolis, Minnesota

The Mandie Collection: Volume Ten
Copyright © 2003
Lois Gladys Leppard

Previously published in three separate volumes:
  Mandie and the New York Secret © 2003
  Mandie and the Night Thief © 2003
  Mandie and the Hidden Past © 2003

MANDIE® and SNOWBALL® are registered trademarks of Lois Gladys Leppard

Cover design by Dan Pitts
Cover illustrations by Chris Wold Dyrud

Published by Bethany House Publishers
11400 Hampshire Avenue South
Bloomington, Minnesota 55438

Bethany House Publishers is a division of
Baker Publishing Group, Grand Rapids, Michigan

Printed in the United States of America by Bethany Press International, Bloomington, MN.
July 2011, 1st printing

ISBN   978-0-7642-0933-8

The Library of Congress has cataloged Volume One of this collection as follows:
Leppard, Lois Gladys.
    The Mandie collection / Lois Gladys Leppard.
        v. <1–  > cm.
    Summary: A collection of tales featuring Mandie, an orphan, and her friends as they solve mysteries together in turn-of-the-century North Carolina.
        Contents: v. 1. Mandie and the secret tunnel ; Mandie and the Cherokee legend ; Mandie and the ghost bandits ; Mandie and the forbidden attic ; Mandie and the trunk's secret—
        ISBN-13: 978–0–7642–0446–3 (pbk.)
        ISBN-10: 0–7642–0446–7 (pbk.)
        1. Children's stories, American. [1. Family life—North Carolina—Fiction. 2. Orphans—Fiction. 3. Christian life—Fiction. 4. North Carolina—History—20th century—Fiction. 5. Mystery and detective stories.] I. Title.
    PZ7.L556   May 2007
    [Fic]—dc22
                                                                                          2007023752

# ABOUT THE AUTHOR

LOIS GLADYS LEPPARD worked in Federal Intelligence for thirteen years in various countries around the world before she settled in South Carolina.

The stories of her own mother's childhood as an orphan in western North Carolina are the basis for many of the incidents incorporated in this series.

Visit her Web site: *www.Mandie.com*

# MANDIE

## AND THE NEW YORK SECRET

For
CAROL JOHNSON,
who accepted the first Mandie Book twenty-one
years ago, and who has held Mandie by the
hand all these years.
And to all the wonderful people at
Bethany House Publishers who accompanied
Mandie on the way.
With much love and many thanks.

# CONTENTS

## MANDIE AND THE NEW YORK SECRET

"To thine own self be true,
and it must follow, as the night the day,
Thou can'st not then be false to any man."

—William Shakespeare,
*Hamlet* (Polonius) Act 1, Scene 3

# CHAPTER ONE

# NEW YORK AT LAST!

The train pulled into the station in New York and stopped with a sudden lurch. Mandie Shaw straightened up in her seat and recaptured her white cat, who had managed to escape her with the motion.

"Snowball, you have to behave now. We're going out there into a noisy, overcrowded street," she said as she secured his red leash and bent to pick up her small bag.

"I'll help you with him," Celia Hamilton said as she stood up.

Mrs. Taft, Mandie's grandmother, looked back as she started down the aisle of the train car and said, "Amanda, be sure you hold on to that white cat now."

"Yes, ma'am, I will," Mandie replied, following Celia.

Joe Woodard and his parents, Dr. and Mrs. Woodard, came along behind them.

"Yes, I don't want to have to search for that cat in this big city of New York," Joe said with a grin as Mandie glanced back at him.

As they all got off the train, Dr. Woodard led the way out of the depot and hailed a public carriage. While everyone waited inside the carriage, he went back to pick up the luggage.

"It won't be long now until I find out what the secret is that Jonathan said he had found," Mandie said to her friends.

"It must be something important for him to send you a message by wire to the depot back home," Celia said.

"Remember he said in the wire to hurry up and come on up to New York, that he had found a secret," Mandie told her. "And he doesn't know how close he came to missing me with the message."

"He knew you were coming on up to visit while your mother and the others were at his house," Joe said.

"But he didn't know when we would get back to my house from visiting my Cherokee kinpeople," Mandie replied, rubbing Snowball's fur to calm him down as he tried to get away from her again.

"I hope my mother has already been shopping when we get to Jonathan's house so I won't have to spend so much time buying clothes," Celia said.

"Yes, and my mother, too," Mandie agreed. She glanced at her grandmother, Mrs. Taft, and Joe's mother, Mrs. Woodard, sitting across from them, but they were deep into their own conversation and were not paying any attention to the young people.

Finally Dr. Woodard and the driver came back with all their luggage and loaded it, and then they started on their way to Jonathan Guyer's house. Even though Mandie had been to the big city of New York once before, and that was for Thanksgiving in 1901, it was now June of 1903, and everything seemed new to her again. The carriage driver drove as though he were going to a fire and ignored the pedestrians who scampered out of his way as they crossed the streets before them. She held tightly to Snowball as the vehicle swayed.

When the carriage turned into the driveway of the Guyer mansion and stopped under the portico, Mandie remembered seeing it that first time and being absolutely speechless to learn that Jonathan lived in such a huge stone building. And as it had happened the other time she came to visit, the door opened and the butler came out to assist with the luggage, only this time she knew the man's name.

"Good morning, Jens," Mandie greeted the man as he assisted Mrs. Taft out of the carriage.

Without even looking at her, the proper butler replied, "Good morning, Miss Amanda." After Mrs. Taft was safely out, he turned to help Mrs. Woodard alight.

As Mandie waited for everyone to go inside the house, Mrs.

Yodkin, the Guyers' housekeeper, appeared at the doorway. "Please come in," she told Mrs. Taft and Mrs. Woodard. Looking back she added, "All of you, please come into the house."

Mandie looked around as they stepped into the parlor that opened off the portico. There was no sign of Jonathan or his father, or Mandie's mother and the others who had come to New York ahead of them. Then she realized the others were also wondering where everyone was.

"Is Jonathan at home?" Mandie asked the housekeeper.

Mrs. Yodkin stopped and looked directly at Mrs. Taft and Dr. and Mrs. Woodard, who had been following behind her. "I regret that there is no one here at the present. Everyone has gone to visit friends in Long Island. Since we did not know your arrival date, Mr. Guyer left the message that if you arrive in his absence you are to make yourselves comfortable."

"Gone to Long Island?" Mrs. Taft repeated, frowning. "Probably to see the Fredericksons."

"Yes, madam, that is where they went," Mrs. Yodkin replied. "Now, if you will all come with me, I will show you to your rooms." At that moment Monet, the French maid, came into the room. "And Monet here will show you young people to your quarters," Mrs. Yodkin added.

Mandie thought, *What a difference in our servants and the Guyers'*. The ones in the Shaw household were treated with friendliness and love. These people seemed to be cold and detached from the world.

When Mrs. Yodkin started toward the door, Mrs. Taft just stood there, frowning. "When is everyone coming back?" she asked.

Mrs. Yodkin stopped and looked back. "Mr. Guyer said they would return tomorrow," she explained. "They only left yesterday." She continued walking out into the huge hallway. The others followed.

Mrs. Woodard looked at Mrs. Taft and said, "That will at least give us time to recuperate from that long train journey."

"Yes, but we don't have that much time to stay here," Mrs. Taft replied.

Monet finally spoke to the young people. "If you will come this way, I will show you your rooms," she said, turning the other direction in the long hallway.

The girls and Joe looked into the rooms they passed along the way. Mandie remembered seeing the huge library they passed, the music room with two baby grand pianos in it, a formal drawing room, and another parlor. Huge double doors set in the mahogany wainscoting were closed.

They reached the carved stairway, split in the middle and rising on either side to meet a balcony above. At the bottom of the stairs, Monet stopped and, pointing to a door with glass windowpanes in it, said, "I remember you do not like the lift. Do you still not like it?" She waited.

"Let's walk up," Mandie and Celia said at once and then grinned at each other.

Joe spoke up as they continued up the stairs. "I should just ride up and let y'all walk. What are y'all going to do when you find a place that only has elevators and no steps?"

"Oh, Joe, there won't ever be such a place," Mandie replied, holding on to Snowball as he tried to get down.

"I wouldn't guarantee that," he replied.

Monet went ahead of them, threw open the door to a room on her right, and said, "Here is the room for you." She looked at Mandie and then added, "Box of sand for cat is here."

"Oh, thank you," Mandie replied, looking into the room.

"And you will be next door," the maid told Celia, pushing open the door to the next room. Then quickly stepping across the hall, she opened another door and said, "And this will be your room." She looked at Joe.

"Thank you," Joe said.

Jens and another servant came along the hallway with their luggage, and Mandie, Joe, and Celia stepped out of the way while it was deposited in their different rooms. Monet stood there waiting until this was accomplished. Then she said, "We will have luncheon ready in thirty minutes." Then she turned and walked back down the hallway, following the other servants.

"Thirty minutes," Mandie repeated. Turning to Joe, she said, "I'll meet you back out here in fifteen minutes."

"All right," Joe agreed, going into the room he had been given.

The girls found their rooms had an adjoining bathroom, and each bedroom had a huge four-poster bed. Mandie put Snowball down at last, and he immediately found the sandbox.

"Why don't we just share one room?" Celia asked. "Then we can talk."

"Yes, I was going to suggest that," Mandie agreed. "We can use this one because Snowball's sandbox is in here. Now, let's hurry and change clothes so we can go talk to Joe." She looked at the small china clock on the mantelpiece.

At that moment there was a slight knock on the door, and Zelda, the other maid, stuck her head in. "I come to unpack zee clothes," she said in her foreign accent.

"Oh, hello, Zelda," Mandie greeted her. "Let us just get something out right now to change out of these traveling clothes, and then you can hang everything up."

"Yes," Zelda agreed, going to open the trunk the men had put in the bedroom.

"They put my trunk in the other room, and you can hang everything up in the wardrobe in there, but I am going to sleep in here with Mandie," Celia explained.

Zelda looked at her, smiled, and said, "I know. House too big, dark, empty." She began unpacking Mandie's dresses.

While Zelda was doing that, Mandie went into the other room with Celia to help her open her trunk and get something out to change into.

The girls actually made the change and were out in the hallway within fifteen minutes. Joe was already sitting on a settee near his doorway. Various pieces of furniture and lamps were placed all along the corridors of the Guyer mansion.

"Y'all made it," he said, standing up and grinning.

"Let's just sit here a minute," Mandie told him as she and Celia sat down and he sat beside them.

"It's a long way back to the parlor, so we can't sit too long," he reminded them.

"I know," Mandie replied. "I just wanted to ask, without anyone around to hear, do y'all think we could start trying to find out what this secret is that Jonathan said he had found?"

"Oh, Mandie, how can we look for something when we don't even know what we are looking for?" Joe asked with a loud sigh.

"Well, in the message Jonathan said he had *found* a secret, so it must be something you can see," Mandie explained.

"But this house is so big we'll never be able to *see* any secret that Jonathan might have found without his help," Celia reminded her.

"Anyhow, how can you *find* a secret?" Joe asked. "A secret is usually something someone knows or does that they don't want you to find out about."

"Joe, now you are getting complicated," Mandie argued. "You know Jonathan doesn't exactly use the same English we do, since we're from the south and he's here in the north. So he says things in a different way from us sometimes."

Joe suddenly stood up and said, "Anyhow, I think we'd better get started back to the parlor." Grinning at Mandie, he added, "We sure don't want to keep your grandmother waiting for her meal."

"Joe, that's mean," Mandie said, pouting as the three started down the hallway.

"Well, I could include my parents in that, too. They like their meals when they are hungry, and I imagine they are all awfully hungry by now," Joe said.

"I am hungry myself," Celia told them.

"Me too," Mandie added, walking faster down the long hallway. "And I have to bring something back for Snowball. I hope nobody lets him out of our room while we're gone."

"All of the servants know you brought him, so I imagine they'll be watching out for him," Celia said.

Suddenly Mandie stopped and asked, "Where are we going? No one told us where to go." She looked at her friends with a frown.

"Hmm," Joe said, running his long fingers through his unruly brown hair. "I suppose we should go back to the parlor where we came in."

"There will probably be someone in there to tell us where we are expected to eat," Celia added.

"This house is just too big," Mandie complained as they walked on down the huge staircase they had come up before.

"Now I believe we go down this hallway," Joe said, motioning to the left.

The girls stood there looking at the different corridors branching off from the bottom of the steps.

"Yes, I believe you are right," Mandie agreed.

With Joe leading the way, they eventually found the parlor again. Mrs. Taft and Mrs. Woodard were sitting there talking as Dr. Woodard roamed the room looking at the fine objects on shelves and in cabinets, which had evidently been collected from various countries and which looked very expensive.

"We finally got back," Mandie said, going to sit on a settee near the two ladies. Joe and Celia joined her. "Grandmother, I thought your house was big, but this one is absolutely too big. You have to walk miles to get from one place to the other."

"Yes, I know," Mrs. Taft replied. "I see no reason to display one's wealth in that way."

Before Mandie could reply to that, Dr. Woodard settled down in a nearby chair and said, "But it is good exercise, especially after eating all the rich food served in such households."

Mandie smiled at him and said, "But I like to get my exercise outdoors where I can walk and walk. And as far as I remember, New York is not very walkable."

Joe grinned at her and said, "Is there such a word? Walkable?"

Mandie blew out her breath and said, "Oh, you know what I mean. It's so crowded here in New York, you can't walk down a street without getting bumped into and having to get out of someone's way." And then grinning at him, she added, "But I do love New York. I'm just not used to it."

Mrs. Yodkin came to the doorway just then and said, "Ladies and sirs, if you will all follow me, please. We have the meal ready."

She led them to a small dining room at the back of the house that had French windows overlooking an enclosed garden. As everyone sat down at the table, she explained, "We did not open the windows because Master Jonathan's dog is out here in the garden and he would be likely to come into the house."

Mandie quickly leaned forward to look out one of the windows. "Yes, there he is, sitting there watching us," she said. "So Jonathan still has him." The big white dog was looking at her.

"Yes, miss, and he has become one of the family," Mrs. Yodkin said with a smile. "Now, if you are all ready, we will serve the food," she added to Mrs. Taft and Mrs. Woodard.

Mrs. Taft nodded, and Mrs. Woodard said, looking around the table, "I believe we are ready and probably hungry, too, after that fare on the train."

Mrs. Yodkin stood back, watching and supervising the other servants as they poured coffee, brought steaming food to the table in expensive china bowls, and checked to see that everyone had napkins and the proper silverware, all of which was already on the table when they sat down. Mandie smiled to herself as she realized the servants were only going through a memorized ritual for serving meals.

Finally, as everyone began eating, Mandie looked down the table at her grandmother and asked, "Do you have plans for us today, or are we just going to sit around and rest?"

Mrs. Taft laid down her fork and replied, "Mrs. Woodard and I have been discussing that, dear, and we have decided that we will just recuperate from our journey today." Smiling at Dr. Woodard, she added, "And the doctor thought that was a good idea."

"A good idea except that I need to get some exercise," Dr. Woodard replied. Looking at the young people, he said, "Thought maybe you all would be interested in a long walk this afternoon."

"Oh yes, sir," Mandie quickly replied with a big smile.

"Yes, sir," Celia nodded.

"Count me in," Joe told them.

"Then we'll just get out and go," Dr. Woodard replied. Turning to his wife and Mrs. Taft, he added, "Are y'all sure you don't want to come with us?"

"No, I'll get enough exercise just walking around this huge house," Mrs. Woodard replied.

"And I will get my exercise tomorrow when we all go shopping," Mrs. Taft said. Looking at Mandie, she said, "Now, Amanda, you are not to go off out of this yard without an adult with you. Is that understood?"

"Yes, ma'am," Mandie replied. Then she asked Dr. Woodard, "Do you think we could take Jonathan's dog with us for that walk? As far as I remember, Whitey loves exploring streets and sidewalks."

"Yes, I suppose we could. But, Joe, you will have to be responsible for the dog and see that he doesn't get away from us," the doctor answered.

"Yes, sir, Whitey will remember us, I think, and there won't be any problem controlling him on the streets," Joe said.

Looking at her grandmother, Mandie said, "I should take Snowball with me so he can get some exercise. I can put him on his leash!" Then smiling, she added, "And Whitey will behave with Snowball around. He's afraid of the cat."

Everyone laughed. Even the prim servants smiled.

Turning back to her friends, Mandie said, "Maybe we could explore the garden to see if we can find Jonathan's secret."

Joe blew out his breath, frowned, and then smiled as he said, "Amanda Elizabeth Shaw, how are we going to find Jonathan's secret when we don't even know what it is we're looking for?" He spoke so loudly he caught his father looking at him.

"Joe, let's keep this a secret among us three," Mandie whispered. "We don't want grown-ups messing in our business, do we? We'd never solve a mystery with them in on it."

Celia smiled at Mandie and asked, "And what are we going to do when we get to be grown-ups? I'm already fifteen, and you soon will be."

"Oh, that's a long time away before we get to be grown-ups," Mandie quickly told her. "And tell me one thing. Why should we stop tracking down mysteries and secrets when we do grow up? I'm sure I'll have the same curiosity about things that I do now."

"That's the truth," Joe said, grinning. "You'll never outgrow it, Mandie."

Celia thought about that, frowned, and then said, "I'm not sure what I will do when I am grown. It might be fun to act like the dignified young ladies that Miss Hope and Miss Prudence are trying to make out of us at their school."

"No, that would be too restrictive," Mandie protested. "I want to do whatever I want to do, not what someone else thinks I should do."

"Wait till you get to college," Joe said, looking at both girls. "Then you will have to settle down, at least a little."

"Oh, Joe, you go to college and I can't see that you have changed any," Mandie told him. Then, lowering her voice so her grandmother wouldn't hear her at the other end of the table, she added, "I am still thinking about asking Grandmother to take all of us back to Europe next summer for our graduation from the Heathwood's School. We could at least have one last fling." She grinned at Celia and Joe.

"Well, I suppose, if you call that a fling," Joe said.

"I would call it very educational and a whole lot of fun," Celia added.

"When I catch the right time and place to ask Grandmother about this, I'll let y'all know," Mandie promised. She hurried to finish eating. She was anxious to walk the streets of New York right now.

CHAPTER TWO

# PLANS

The weather was warm for June in New York. Mandie was glad Dr. Woodard led them over to Central Park to walk beneath the trees. Dozens of people sat in the shade there, reading, talking, or just relaxing and watching strollers go by.

Dr. Woodard, always the friendly gentleman, nodded, tipped his hat, and smiled as they passed several ladies who smiled at them.

As soon as they were out of hearing, Joe quickly asked, "Did you know those ladies?"

Dr. Woodard grinned at him and said, "Why, no, never saw them before in my life. It doesn't hurt anyone to smile, does it?"

Joe looked at Mandie walking by his side, with Celia in step with Dr. Woodard. "You don't smile at anyone in this park," Joe warned her with a frown. "This is New York and you never know what reaction you might get from a stranger in this town."

"I can assure you, if someone smiles at me first I'll smile right back," Mandie replied with a frown. Looking at Dr. Woodard, she added, "Just like your father does."

"But you are a pretty young lady, and it's dangerous for young ladies to be friendly with strangers," Joe said. He held the end of the leash for Whitey as the dog trotted along and smelled everything.

"If you couldn't protect me and Celia, then Whitey can," Mandie replied. She set Snowball down to walk at the end of his red leash.

"Oh, Mandie, this is getting to be a silly conversation. Let's change the subject," Joe told her.

"Like Jonathan's secret," Mandie said, making sure Dr. Woodard couldn't hear her.

"All right, then, Jonathan's secret," Joe agreed with a shrug. "But there's nothing we can do about that until Jonathan comes back home."

Slowing down to let Dr. Woodard and Celia walk a little ahead, Mandie whispered to Joe, "I have decided we ought to search his room to see if we can find anything relating to a secret."

"Oh no, not me," Joe quickly told her. "I am not searching anyone's room for any reason, much less for something that we don't even know what it is. Besides, I think it would be dishonest."

"We wouldn't be doing any harm," Mandie argued. "And he will never know we did it."

"Harm?" Joe exclaimed. "It would not be right to go through another person's personal things."

Dr. Woodard and Celia both suddenly stopped and looked back. They were a few feet ahead of Mandie and Joe.

"Are y'all tired already?" Celia asked.

"Tired? Oh no," Mandie quickly replied, walking faster. "Just dillydallying." She smiled at her friend.

They had come to the edge of the park. Dr. Woodard looked ahead, then glanced back to say, "I see a place over there that looks like it might have coffee. What do y'all say?"

Mandie quickly said, "I say yes, sir." She could see a small sidewalk café across the street. She picked up Snowball as he tried to run ahead.

"Yes, sir," Celia added.

"Coffee would be nice. Maybe they have some chocolate cake, too," Joe said.

They crossed the street and sat down at one of the little tables on the sidewalk, in the shade of a huge awning. Mandie held Snowball in her lap.

"I believe coffee is all we should have, and that rather quickly,"

Dr. Woodard told the young people. "I imagine those servants back at the Guyers' house will insist we have afternoon tea when we return."

"Yes, sir, and they'll have something sweet with it," Mandie agreed.

"Then let's hurry and get back," Joe said. He held the end of the leash as Whitey sat by his chair.

The waiter came and Dr. Woodard ordered. He quickly returned with four cups of hot coffee and placed them on the table.

"Dr. Woodard, when are you going to see Dr. Plumbley?" Mandie asked as she sipped the hot coffee.

"I'll have to see if Lindall Guyer has anything planned for us first before I contact Dr. Plumbley," the doctor replied.

"I'd like to see him, too, but Jonathan may keep us busy whatever time we aren't shopping with our mothers," Mandie said.

Dr. Plumbley was from back home in Franklin, North Carolina. He had come to New York years ago to get his medical education and had stayed to build up a well-known practice.

"I hope my mother has done a lot of the shopping already and that we don't have to spend too much of our time in the stores," Celia remarked.

"Maybe my mother has already bought whatever we need," Mandie said, picking up her cup of coffee. "That is one thing I love about my grandmother. She doesn't waste time shopping. She can always go directly to whatever it is she's looking for and that's it."

Dr. Woodard pushed back his chair and stood up. "If everyone is finished, I believe we should get back to the house now," he said.

The three young people quickly rose. Joe held Whitey's leash and Mandie carried Snowball.

"I am really surprised that your grandmother agreed to come to the Guyers' house," Celia remarked as they started down the sidewalk behind Dr. Woodard.

"I am, too, but it was the only solution to our being able to go visit my Cherokee kinpeople first and then come up here," Mandie said. "If Grandmother hadn't agreed to come with us to visit the Guyers, then we would have had to come on to New York with my mother and your mother and Uncle John. I was surprised, too, that she agreed to come."

"I'm glad you finally got that quilt mystery solved," Joe told Mandie.

"So am I," Mandie agreed. "My grandmother figured out why I wanted to visit my Cherokee people, and she was anxious to know what it was all about. I explained it all to her the night we got back home."

Dr. Woodard slowed down to look back. "Now, y'all must get a move on. Otherwise it's going to be suppertime before we get back to the Guyers' house." He smiled at the three.

"Yes, sir," Joe replied, walking faster and holding on to the dog's leash as Whitey suddenly decided to rush ahead.

"Oh, we have to get back for tea," Mandie agreed. She and Celia caught up with the doctor.

They did make it back just in time for tea. Mrs. Yodkin was waiting for them in the parlor. She spoke to Dr. Woodard. "The ladies are still retired. Shall we send word up that tea is about to be served, sir?"

Dr. Woodard hung his hat on the hall tree just outside the doorway and replied, "Yes, please, that will save me a journey through all those hallways to tell them." Then he stepped back inside the parlor.

"Yes, sir," Mrs. Yodkin replied as she turned to leave the room. "We will have tea ready in fifteen minutes, sir." She went out into the hallway.

Mandie, Celia, and Joe found seats around the parlor and sat down to await the afternoon tea. Mandie set Snowball down, and he jumped up onto a stool and curled up.

Joe reached down to unclip Whitey's leash and said, "Maybe I should put Whitey back out in the yard now." He looked at his father, who had sat in a large upholstered chair.

"Yes, I believe you ought to do that," Dr. Woodard replied. "I think it would be better if he was not present when the tea and goodies arrive."

Joe stood up, smiled at the girls, and said, "I'll be back as soon as I can find my way through all the hallways to the back door." He left the room with Whitey following.

Dr. Woodard looked across the room at the girls and asked, "And what do you young ladies plan on doing with the rest of your vacation after we go home next week?"

"Are we going home next week, then?" Mandie asked.

"Yes, your grandmother is not too anxious to stay here very long, and it seems she is expecting her friend Senator Morton to come to your house in Franklin late next week. And of course I have to get back to my patients," Dr. Woodard explained.

"Yes, sir," Mandie replied. "Grandmother had told me she was expecting Senator Morton and that maybe we would visit the Pattons in Charleston. I'm not sure what my mother is planning, but I do know that my grandmother is usually the boss."

"What about you, Miss Celia?" Dr. Woodard asked.

"My mother always says it's better not to plan too far ahead because something else may come up that we would rather do. As far as I know, she will go on home when we return to Franklin and allow me to stay and visit at Mandie's house for a little while." Glancing at Mandie and smiling, she added, "So I suppose it's up to Mandie as to what we will be doing. She usually has some good plans."

"It would be nice to visit the Pattons. I love the ocean down there," Mandie said. "However, I may resist, because I don't want my grandmother always leading everyone around on a string." She grinned at the doctor.

Joe stepped into the parlor at that moment and heard the comment. "And how long is that string?" he asked, grinning at Mandie as he sat down nearby.

Mandie laughed and said, "Not very long when my grandmother begins pulling it."

Mandie suddenly realized she did not know what Joe's plans were. She frowned as she asked, "When do you have to return to college?"

Joe sighed deeply and said, "I am going back early, probably in about two weeks. You see, I'm still trying to catch up and get ahead with my studies since I did not have the exact requirements for entrance to the college."

"Joe!" Mandie exclaimed.

Joe frowned and said, "I'm sorry." Then he quickly added, "But you'll have Tommy Patton to help you solve mysteries if you go to his house in Charleston. And if you don't, you can always get Polly Cornwallis to help you." He grinned mischievously at her. Polly

Cornwallis lived next door to Mandie in Franklin and was forever chasing Joe when he came to visit.

"Polly Cornwallis! Never!" Mandie declared. "Besides, she's always afraid of everything. And Tommy Patton is not dependable. Soon as we find a mystery, he wants to run off to something else before we even solve it."

"But you always have Celia," Joe said, winking at Celia with a smile.

Before Mandie could reply, Celia quickly said, "Yes, I always follow Mandie through her mysteries and right on into her troubles sometimes."

"We haven't been involved in any bad trouble really," Mandie said. "Think of all the good we've done by solving a lot of our mysteries."

At that moment Mrs. Taft and Mrs. Woodard came into the parlor.

"Oh dear, don't tell me you are all off on another mystery," Mrs. Taft said as she sat in a nearby chair.

"That's what it sounds like," Mrs. Woodard added with a smile at Mandie as she sat near Mrs. Taft.

"No, ma'am, we haven't found a real mystery. Maybe when Jonathan comes home we'll find one," Mandie said. She didn't want her grandmother to know about the secret Jonathan had wired that he had uncovered. She had hidden the message in her purse.

Monet, the parlormaid, came in with the tea tray on a cart. Mrs. Yodkin followed closely behind, overseeing the serving.

Joe stretched to see what was on the trays. "Ah, there's lots of goodies," he whispered to the girls.

"Including chocolate cake," Mandie added.

As soon as everyone was served, Monet left the room.

"If you should want something else, please ring the bell. The rope is over there," Mrs. Yodkin told the ladies as she motioned toward a heavy plush rope hanging at the side of one of the draperies.

"Thank you," Mrs. Taft said.

Then Mrs. Yodkin went on out into the hallway, and the adults began their own conversation among themselves.

The young people ate for a few minutes as though they were starved. Then Mandie asked her grandmother, during a lull in the adult conversation, "Will we be going shopping in the morning, or will we wait for Mother and Celia's mother to come back and go with us?"

"I thought we'd just run down to a couple of stores in the morning and get whatever we need, and then when Elizabeth and Jane and John return, we won't have so much shopping left to do," Mrs. Taft replied with a smile at the girls. "What do you young ladies think?"

"Oh, that's the very thing to do," Mandie agreed.

"Yes, ma'am, I'd like to go with y'all since we don't know when my mother will be back," Celia replied.

"Then you girls plan on it," Mrs. Taft said.

Looking at her son, Mrs. Woodard said, "And, Joe, you might as well come with us in case we find something for you to wear. You're growing so fast I'm not sure I could fit you."

Joe shrugged his shoulders, sighed, and finally said, "Yes, ma'am."

Mandie knew Joe did not like to go shopping.

"Remember what I said about my grandmother," Mandie whispered to her friends. "She won't waste time in the stores like my mother does."

Dr. Woodard spoke up. "Since you ladies are going shopping tomorrow morning and we don't know when the others will come back from Long Island, I suppose I should just go on and look up Dr. Plumbley." He grinned at his wife. "I'm certainly not going shopping with you ladies."

"Yes," Mrs. Woodard agreed. "That is a good idea."

"I was hoping I could go visit Dr. Plumbley while we're here," Mandie said, looking at her grandmother.

"We'll shop first and get that out of the way," Mrs. Taft said. "Then I will see that you get an opportunity to visit with Dr. Plumbley before we go home." She smiled at her granddaughter.

"Thank you, Grandmother," Mandie replied. "Please remember you said that when my mother gets back and wants to spend all our time in the stores." She grinned at her grandmother.

"I'm sure Elizabeth will understand," Mrs. Taft replied.

As soon as tea was finished, Mrs. Taft and Mrs. Woodard decided to sit in the back garden for some fresh air. Dr. Woodard joined them.

The young people followed them outside but drifted away toward the far end, out of hearing of the adults. Mandie fastened Snowball on his leash to a stake in the garden.

Sitting on a long stone bench by the fence, Mandie said, "Remember I suggested searching Jonathan's room for clues to his secret?"

"Yes, and I refuse to do that," Joe reminded her.

"Oh no, Mandie, I couldn't do that," Celia protested.

Mandie blew out her breath and argued, "But we won't disturb anything. He won't ever know we've been in his room."

"No, and I mean the answer is no, so just count me out of that," Joe emphatically told her.

"And me, too," Celia added in a whisper.

Mandie jumped up and paced around the bench. "All right, all right," she said. "I'll do it by myself. However, y'all could help me look through some of the other rooms."

"But, Mandie, what are we looking for?" Celia asked.

"Well, something concerning his secret. I don't know just what, because I have no idea as to what the secret is," Mandie said, frowning as she thought about it. "However, we might find something mysterious somewhere or other."

"Mandie, Jonathan will be back home tomorrow," Joe reminded her. "It's best if we just wait and talk to him."

"In the meantime we don't have anything to do," Mandie complained.

"Just for the rest of this day. Tomorrow we go shopping," Celia said. "And I'm sure when Jonathan gets home we won't have a spare moment, because he is on the go all the time."

"Remember Dr. Woodard said we would be going home next week," Mandie reminded her friends. "Therefore, we shouldn't waste a minute of our time here in New York."

"I'm not wasting any time. I'm just plain tired after that long train trip," Joe said, stretching out his long legs in front of him.

"And tomorrow we'll feel as though a cyclone has hit us when we get into that shopping district, all those women snatching and grabbing everything in the stores and pushing and shoving you out of their way. Makes me tired just thinking about it," Celia said, shrugging her shoulders.

"Oh, Celia, that won't happen with Grandmother in charge," Mandie said. "She knows how to handle all that. Besides, we won't be going into very many stores. She has certain ones that she prefers and never wants to go exploring into the others."

"You two country girls need to get out of the country more often," Joe teased them.

"Joe Woodard, I am a country girl and proud of it," Mandie said. "As far as I am concerned, an occasional trip to New York is plenty."

"And since we live close to Richmond, an occasional trip to Richmond is plenty for me," Celia added.

"You girls need to think about your future," Joe told them. "You can't live in the country forever. You'll have to get out into the world and go to college. In fact, that is not too long off. Next year when you graduate from that boarding school in Asheville, you are both going to have to spread your wings." He grinned at them.

"Just because you picked that college in the big city of New Orleans is no sign I'm going to pick one in such a big city," Mandie replied. "I'm sure there are smaller colleges and some in country towns, too."

"Your choice will depend on what exactly you want to study," Joe reminded her.

"You know the answer to that very well," Mandie said, getting up to walk around the flowers. "Grandmother keeps reminding me that I have to have an education to handle all the business that I will inherit someday from her and my mother and Uncle John." She stopped to look at Joe and added, "Unless I could figure out some way to get disinherited." She laughed loudly.

"I'm glad I have no such burden to bear," Joe quickly told her, also laughing out loud.

Celia looked at her two friends and said, "Well, I hope to someday marry a man who will take care of all that for me, because I, too, am the only heir right now."

"That's the solution," Joe teased. "Mandie, you should just get married and let your husband handle all the business matters."

Mandie stomped her foot as she stopped to look at him. "I certainly don't want a husband who would be handling my life for me."

Joe sobered up and said, "I agree. A marriage should be a partnership." And then whispering to Mandie, he added, "And that's just what we'll make ours."

Mandie felt her face flush, and she turned to Celia and said, "Let's go to our room and rest awhile." She stooped to pick up Snowball.

Celia stood up and Joe joined them.

"That sounds like a good idea," he said. "We need a little rest before dinner."

Mandie led the way back into the house. When the three found their way upstairs to their rooms, Joe went inside his and closed the door. Mandie took Snowball inside hers and Celia followed. The cat jumped up onto the bed.

"I do believe I am a little tired," Celia said, plopping into a large cushioned chair. Then she stood up. "In fact, I think I'll go into my room and lie down for a few minutes," she added.

"All right," Mandie agreed. "Just in case I fall asleep, I hope you don't and will let me know when it's time to go down for supper."

"Of course," Celia agreed, going through into the next room and closing the door.

Mandie quickly looked around her room. She didn't intend lying down. She was going snooping into Jonathan's room if she could find it. Who knew what she might find.

# CHAPTER THREE

# A DISCOVERY

Mandie left Snowball curled up asleep on her bed and quietly opened the door and slipped out into the hallway, making sure she closed the door behind her. Holding her breath and hoping that Joe would not come out of his room, she quickly tiptoed down the long hallway. Pausing at the top of the curved staircase, she asked herself, "Now, which way would Jonathan's room be?"

When she had visited the Guyers for Thanksgiving in 1901, she didn't remember Jonathan ever telling her and her friends exactly where his room was. He had said the wing in which they were staying was the guest wing. She looked ahead and saw a turn in the corridor, which meant there must be another wing around the corner.

The hallway was dark even though there were lamps lighted along the way. The mahogany wainscoting covered the bottom half of the walls, and a dark flowered wallpaper reached from there to the tall ceiling. Small settees, chairs, and tables were scattered along every hallway in the mansion that she had been in. Every time she thought about that, she smiled to herself and said, "They have so much furniture it won't all fit into the dozens and dozens of rooms."

She quickly walked on down to the corner in the hallway. Looking down another corridor, she could see there was a cross hallway intersecting this one. This place was like the streets outside in

New York: corners, intersections, and no directional signs to tell her whether she was headed toward the front or back of the house. All the doors along the way seemed to be closed. She stopped and decided to open a door and if possible look out a window to see where she was.

"Please don't squeak," she whispered as she turned a knob and slowly pushed a door open, revealing a bedroom. The draperies were drawn, making the room dark and musty smelling.

"This must be a guest room," she muttered to herself as she stepped inside. She walked over to a window, found the pull for the draperies, and gave it a yank. The draperies opened, revealing a large window with the outside shutters closed, which made it impossible to see out.

"Oh, shucks!" Mandie said, slightly stomping her foot on the thick flowered carpet. She turned to glance around the room. It looked similar to the one she had been given, with a tall four-poster bed, wardrobe, bureau, washstand, and several chairs, all of which must have cost a fortune.

Stepping back into the hallway, Mandie tried to remember how many turns she had made since leaving her room in order to figure out which side of the house she was in. But then she realized she had not even looked out the window of her room. Therefore, she did not know what was below it.

"Well, I suppose I'll just keep going," she decided. Continuing down the hallway, she finally came to a large open area with a skylight overhead and steps going down in the middle of it. Walking around the circular hallway, she searched for doors and found one huge double door halfway around from the head of the stairs. She paused to look at it.

"That looks like a door to a parlor or something, not a bedroom," she said to herself.

Stepping over to the door, she turned the handle and gave a push. It wouldn't open. Then, looking closely, she found it was a sliding door and not one that could be swung open. Grasping the handle, she gave a shove and the door slowly moved on its track. As the opening widened, she squeezed through into the room.

"Well!" she said in surprise as she gazed at the skylight in the ceiling and the dozens and dozens of chairs and tables placed in rows about the room. Walking on into the room, she saw a large stage at the far end, with a huge maroon-colored velvet curtain drawn across it. Looking around she added, "Not a single window in this room."

Suddenly realizing she had been gone from her room for quite a while, she decided she had better work her way back before someone missed her. She stepped into the hallway, closed the sliding doors, and started back the way she thought she had come.

She had not gone very far before she realized she was in a corridor that she had not come through. Stopping to think, she said to herself, "Oh well, I suppose if I just keep going I'll eventually get back to my room."

She continued down the dimly lit hallway. Some of the doors here were slightly open. When she stepped inside a room to look around, it was evidently being used, but no one was there at the moment. There were toiletries on the bureau, the wardrobe door was slightly open, revealing clothes hanging inside, and the room smelled of perfume.

"Probably one of the servants' rooms," she whispered to herself as she started to step back out into the hallway.

Suddenly someone came rushing in, and they collided in the doorway.

"Oh, I'm sorry," Mandie muttered, moving back to straighten her skirt and then look at the other person.

"Excuse me, miss," the girl standing there said in surprise.

It was Leila, the young German maid who took care of the bedrooms in the mansion. She smiled as she pushed back her white cap on the top of her reddish blond hair.

"Please forgive me. This must be your room. I was looking for Jonathan's—" Mandie began.

Leila interrupted. "Master Jonathan's room. Come, I show you." She stepped back out into the corridor.

Following the girl down the long hallway, Mandie was trying to compose herself after being caught in someone's room. Evidently the girl did not think it strange that Mandie wished to see Jonathan's room.

Leila seemed to be going around in circles through the hallways, and as Mandie followed her she wondered what she would say to the girl when they finally came to Jonathan's room. Would the maid go on her way and leave her there to go into the room and explore? What would she say to Leila for an explanation as to why she wanted to see his room?

Suddenly Leila stopped in front of a door halfway down one of the hallways and turned to Mandie and said, with an indication of her hand, "Here is Master Jonathan's room." She smiled at Mandie and stood waiting.

Mandie frowned as she looked at the door and said, "So this is Jonathan's room." She was nervous and wouldn't look directly into Leila's eyes.

"*Ja,* miss, is his room," Leila replied.

Mandie glanced up and down the long hallway and asked, "Where are we? Is this the front of the house, or where?"

Leila replied, still smiling, "*Nein,* miss. Back of house, it is."

Mandie did some quick calculations. "Oh, so it is above the back garden," she replied thoughtfully. "Can we look out and see?"

Leila shook her head, still smiling, and answered, "Nein, miss. Master Jonathan, he locks the door when he goes away."

Mandie was surprised at that. "Locks the door?" she repeated.

Leila pulled a large key ring full of keys out of her apron pocket, held them up, and said, "But I have key."

"In that case, could you unlock the door so we could look out the window in there?" Mandie asked.

Leila shook her head again and said, "Nein, miss. I open only to clean, and it has been cleaned today."

"Well, I suppose I had better find my way back to my room," Mandie said with disappointment, wondering how she would ever remember where his room was. She turned back the way they had come.

"Miss, we go this way," Leila quickly told her, pointing in the other direction.

"But we came from that direction," Mandie said, pointing back.

"Ja, but you not at your room when we start," Leila explained. She started walking as she said, "We go this way."

Mandie followed the girl. After three different turns at cross halls, they ended up in front of Mandie's room. Celia was standing there looking out the open door.

"Oh, Mandie, I was beginning to believe you must have been lost," Celia told her. "And it's time to go back downstairs."

As Leila went on her way, Mandie explained, "I was just walking around the hallways and got lost. Leila showed me the way back." She went on into her room. Celia followed and closed the door.

"Mrs. Yodkin has already been by to say it's time for us to go back down to the parlor. Dinner will soon be ready," Celia explained.

"All right. Soon as I wash my hands and brush my hair I'll be ready," Mandie said, going toward the bathroom door. Then looking back, she noticed Snowball was no longer on the bed. "Where is Snowball? I hope he didn't get out." She started looking around the room.

Celia laughed and said, "No, Mrs. Yodkin wanted to take him to the kitchen to feed him, but she seemed to be afraid of picking him up. So I went across the hall and asked Joe to take him down."

So Joe had gone down to the kitchen with the cat. Mandie hurriedly freshened up. She closed their door behind Celia.

"Did you go back in the other part of the house and get lost?" Celia asked as they hurried toward the staircase.

"Yes. I don't know exactly where I was. All the doors are closed. I looked in one room, but then all the outside shutters seem to be closed, so I couldn't tell where I was," Mandie hurriedly explained as they descended the steps. She cleared her throat and added, "I just wanted to see what else is in this house."

"Well, I'm glad that we have memorized the way to the parlor from our room and won't get lost when we're in a hurry, like now," Celia said.

At the bottom of the staircase, Mandie stopped and asked, "Did you tell Mrs. Yodkin I was not in our room but out wandering around somewhere?"

Celia laughed and said, "Of course not, Mandie. In fact, I didn't even mention your name to her. She just said it would soon be time for dinner and that she would like to take Snowball to feed him. She didn't come inside our room. Joe came in and got Snowball, and he didn't ask about you, either. He was in a hurry. He said he wanted to speak to his father about something if he got a chance before dinner."

Mandie blew out her breath and contined on down the hallway. "I'll sure be glad when Jonathan gets back home."

Celia looked at her as she walked fast to keep up. "Because of the secret he said he discovered. I'm getting more curious myself, wondering what would be important enough for him to send a wire to you."

Mandie laughed and replied, "Oh, but you forget. Money means nothing to Jonathan. There's always more in his father's bank. I just hope he hasn't forgotten about the secret by the time he comes back home. You know how he flits to one thing and then another. He's always busy with something going on."

"I know," Celia agreed.

As they turned the last corner in the hallway and came into the part where the parlor opened off it, Joe and Dr. Woodard were coming along from the other end.

"Just on time," Joe teased as they all stopped at the open door to the parlor.

Dr. Woodard went on inside the parlor, and Mandie and Celia caught up with Joe.

"You are almost late yourself," Mandie teased back.

"Y'all come on or we really will be late," Celia said, leading the way into the parlor.

Mrs. Taft and Mrs. Woodard were sitting near the fireplace, and Dr. Woodard had joined them.

When Mandie saw the fire, she was amazed that the Guyers would have one going in the month of June. But then she realized the huge mansion seemed to be cold, and she was glad she had on a long-sleeved dress.

"Did y'all have a nice rest after your walk?" Mrs. Taft asked as the three young people sat down on a settee near her.

"Yes, ma'am," Celia said.

"Grandmother, you should have gone with us," Mandie said. "We had coffee in a sidewalk café, just like those we saw when we went to Europe."

"Probably the one across from the entrance to Central Park, was it?" Mrs. Taft replied, looking at Dr. Woodard.

"Yes, ma'am, that was the one," he agreed.

At that moment Mrs. Yodkin came to the parlor doorway. Looking across the room directly at Mrs. Taft, she announced, "Dinner is served, madam."

Mrs. Taft immediately stood up as she replied, "Thank you, Mrs. Yodkin. We're ready."

As they all followed Mrs. Yodkin from the parlor, Mandie thought about her grandmother. Mrs. Taft always seemed to command respect and was always the one consulted in such cases. Somehow people got the impression that Mandie's grandmother was the boss. She grinned to herself as she thought, *They just don't know how much of a boss she is.*

After they were all seated at the table in the dining room and were served, Mandie decided to tell Joe and Celia what she had done that afternoon. She made sure the adults were engaged in their own conversation.

Sitting between Joe and Celia, Mandie whispered, "I have something to tell y'all."

Joe and Celia both immediately looked at her and then leaned forward to listen to whatever she had to say.

Glancing from one friend to the other, Mandie whispered, "I found Jonathan's room this afternoon."

"You did what?" Joe exclaimed, loud enough that Mandie saw her grandmother look down the table in her direction.

"Please don't talk so loud," Mandie told him.

"What have you been up to now?" Joe asked.

"I said I found Jonathan's room," Mandie repeated in a whisper.

"Mandie!" Celia exclaimed in a whisper.

"I hope you are not planning to search his room," Joe said, frowning at her as he bent closer to speak.

"It's locked," Mandie said.

"So you couldn't get in," Joe said, smiling at her. "That's good."

"Leila, the German maid, has the key to it. She carries a key ring just full of keys," Mandie explained.

"How do you know that?" Joe asked.

"Because I asked her where the room was and she showed me and said it was locked because she had already cleaned it today," Mandie explained, still speaking in a whisper.

"So that's where you went this afternoon," Celia said.

"If I can find out her schedule for tomorrow, I'm going to be around there when she opens the room to clean," Mandie told them.

"Remember we are going shopping in the morning," Celia reminded her.

"And Jonathan is coming home sometime tomorrow," Joe added. "Why don't you forget about this crazy idea of searching his room, Mandie?"

"I want to know what the secret is he has discovered," Mandie said.

"I don't think you'll find the answer to that by searching his room," Joe told her. "And he will be home tomorrow."

Mandie realized her grandmother was watching her and that she had not eaten one bite of food during the secretive conversation. She picked up her fork and dug into the mashed potatoes on her plate. She glanced at her friends' plates and saw that they had been consuming their food.

Mrs. Taft spoke from down the table. "Amanda, Mrs. Woodard and I have decided we will begin our shopping journey immediately after breakfast tomorrow morning, which I understand is served at eight o'clock. So you should all be ready to leave as soon as we have finished breakfast. We plan to be back by noontime."

"Yes, ma'am," Mandie replied, quickly swallowing her potatoes.

"Yes, ma'am," Celia added.

"And I'll be ready, too," Joe told her, looking at his mother.

"And I will be leaving then to go visit Dr. Plumbley and should return in time for the noon meal," Dr. Woodard added.

"Does anyone know yet when my mother and the others will be back from Long Island?" Mandie asked.

"Mrs. Yodkin knows the transportation schedules to and from Long Island and thinks they should return by noon," Mrs. Taft replied.

Celia and Joe both immediately glanced at Mandie. She sighed and said under her breath, "Oh well!"

The three of them knew Mandie would not have time to catch Leila and get into Jonathan's room.

"That will keep you out of trouble," Joe whispered, grinning at Mandie.

"Well, at least if he's here when we get back we can find out about this secret he discovered," Mandie said, frowning at her friends.

When the meal was finally over and everyone stood up to leave the room, Mandie suddenly remembered Joe had brought Snowball downstairs to eat.

"Where is Snowball?" she asked Joe as they followed the adults, who had walked out into the hallway and were going into the parlor for coffee.

"I took him to Mrs. Cook in the kitchen," Joe explained. "She said she would feed him."

"But, Joe, where is he now? Someone may have let him out," Mandie said, getting excited.

"I don't think so," Joe said. "You see, I fastened on his leash, and Mrs. Cook hooked the end of it to her cabinet door in the kitchen just in case he tried to get out."

"I think I'd better go get him," Mandie said and then added, "if I can find the way to the kitchen. I don't know why anyone would want such a monstrous house."

"I know the way," Joe said. "Go this way." He turned down the hallway in the opposite direction from the parlor.

"I hope you know the way. Wait a minute," Mandie stopped him. "I suppose I should tell my grandmother where we are going if we are not going to have coffee with them."

Joe stopped and said, "I almost forgot about that. No, let's go have that coffee first and then we can get Snowball."

"I suppose he can wait," Mandie agreed. Grinning at Joe, she added, "I don't think the possibility of chocolate cake can wait."

"Never," Joe replied.

"Yes, let's have our coffee and cake first," Celia said, smiling at them.

As soon as everyone settled down in the parlor, Mrs. Yodkin came in with Monet rolling the tea cart behind her. Joe stretched to glance at the contents on the tray, smacked his lips, and said, "I was right. That's chocolate cake on there."

"You must have given Mrs. Cook a hint when you took Snowball back to the kitchen," Mandie teased him.

"Let's see, now. Come to think of it, I do believe she asked me if we like chocolate cake," Joe said, grinning at her.

Mrs. Yodkin watched as Monet served the coffee and cake. When they were finished, she turned to Mrs. Taft and asked, "Do you wish Monet to stay and replenish your cups, madam?"

"No, no, thank you, Mrs. Yodkin. We can take care of that," Mrs. Taft replied.

"Yes, madam. We will return later for the cart," Mrs. Yodkin replied. Then she followed Monet out of the room.

Mandie noticed again that Mrs. Yodkin had spoken to her grandmother for instructions, and she smiled.

"What is so funny?" Joe asked, watching her.

"Mrs. Yodkin treats my grandmother like she is the lady of the house," Mandie said, beginning to giggle and setting her coffee down as it sloshed in her cup.

"I noticed that, too," Celia said.

"I suppose your grandmother just looks like the lady of the house," Joe teased.

Mandie thought about that. Her grandmother had her own mansion and servants and was used to being the lady of the house.

# CHAPTER FOUR

# MANDIE'S ESCAPADE

After everyone had gone to bed that night, Mandie tried to stay awake until Celia fell asleep. She intended exploring the hallway to see whether Jonathan's room might possibly be unlocked. Celia seemed to be in a talkative mood, and Mandie pretended to be sleepy.

"What do you intend buying tomorrow?" Celia asked after they were in bed.

"I don't know," Mandie mumbled.

"If I see something I really want, I suppose I can go ahead and buy it. I think that will be all right with my mother," Celia said.

"Ummm," Mandie replied.

"Of course, I'll have to go shopping with my mother, too," Celia said. "And I have no idea as to what she will want to buy."

"Ummm," Mandie again mumbled.

"You sound half asleep, Mandie, so I'll shut up. Good night," Celia said, turning over on her side away from Mandie.

"Night," Mandie muttered as she turned over on her side of the bed. She kept listening for Celia to go to sleep. Celia seemed wide awake. And Mandie had to keep blinking her eyes to keep from falling asleep herself. She waited and waited.

The next thing Mandie knew, she suddenly sat up in bed. She had been sleeping. And Celia by her side was evidently sound asleep.

She wondered what time it was. How long had she slept? Did she dare creep around the dimly lit hallways in the huge spooky mansion in the middle of the night by herself? And would she be able to find Jonathan's room?

Mandie pushed up in the bed to look around. The room was dark, but faint light filtered in through the sheer curtains from the moonlit sky outside. Snowball was sound asleep at her feet. Celia was still turned over facing the other side of the room, so Mandie couldn't tell whether her friend had opened her eyes with the movement or not.

Suddenly she heard the faint chimes of the tall clock down the corridor outside and learned that it was actually five o'clock in the morning. Therefore the servants were probably up and around already, so she must hurry if she was going to look for Jonathan's room.

Slowly sliding down from the tall bed, Mandie stood up, grabbed her robe from a nearby chair, put it on, and without taking time to put on her slippers, she hurried barefooted over to open the door to the hallway. She looked up and down the corridor. There was no sign of anyone. Quickly stepping out of the room, she quietly closed the door and then crept down the hallway, being careful not to collide with any of the furnishings sitting about in the dark.

Mumbling quietly to herself, she tried to retrace the way she had gone to the room yesterday, or rather the hallways Leila had brought her down, because that was the shortest distance to Jonathan's room.

Suddenly, turning the corner into a cross hall, Mandie spotted Leila going down it ahead of her. She quickly ducked behind a small settee sitting nearby and peeked over the back of it until she finally saw Leila turn left at the next cross hall. She watched a few minutes and then continued on. She went in the opposite direction from that taken by Leila.

As she silently walked on, the hallway grew darker and darker, and then she realized the lamps along the way were not burning. With the doors to the rooms all closed, the corridor didn't get any light. And she almost passed a room that had the door open. She stopped and looked. *This must be Jonathan's room,* she thought as she slowly, quietly stepped inside. The shutters on the windows were closed, and the room was so dark she could barely see the furniture.

She could tell there were objects on the dresser and the desk in the corner. Someone was using this room. She bent to look closely at whatever was there. She found cuff links in a glass dish on the bureau.

"At least I know this room is being used by a man," she decided to herself.

Opening the wardrobe door, she saw clothing hanging inside that confirmed that. Even in the darkness she could tell there were pants there.

Suddenly the door to the hall was quietly closed and she could hear a key turning in the lock. Her heart almost jumped out. She could not get out. And whoever locked the door had only paused to do that and was probably long gone down the corridor.

"Oh, why didn't I yell when they locked the door?" Mandie moaned to herself as she paced the floor of the room. "How will I ever get out of here?"

The room seemed to be darker than ever with the hall door closed. She had to feel her way around, touching furniture and stumbling into things. She tried the door but it wouldn't budge. And this room was probably so isolated that no one would ever hear her if she tried yelling. However, Celia would miss her. But on the other hand, Celia would not have known where she had gone. And this house was so big it would take someone a long time to locate her. She stumbled into a footstool in the dark and sat down on it to think.

Her grandmother was going to be furious with her if she didn't show up for breakfast. Mrs. Taft had told them all to be ready to go shopping right after the morning meal. And since no one knew where Mandie was, they would all waste time trying to find her.

She sat there for a long time thinking about what she could do. Then she heard a key being inserted into the lock of the hall door. She stood up and rushed to the far side of the room, trying to hide. She bumped into furniture, and putting her hand out to keep from falling, she felt what must be a doorknob. Quickly running her fingers over it, she realized it was actually a door. Hastily turning the knob, she pushed and was amazed to find it opening. She almost fell into the next room. Or whatever was beyond. Stepping inside, she quietly closed the door just as she heard the door to the hallway being opened.

Blowing out her breath for a moment, Mandie glanced around in the darkness and was surprised to see this was a bathroom. Feeling around the wall, she searched for another door. Finally her hand touched another doorknob. Pushing that door open, she found herself back out in the main hallway.

Her knees trembled and she almost lost her breath as she tried to hurry down the hallway before whoever had gone into the room came back out and saw her. She didn't look back until she reached the cross hall.

Leaning against the corner of the wall, she finally caught her breath. Trying to stay behind a chest standing there, she looked back. Then she almost lost her breath again as she saw Jens, the butler, come out of the room, lock the door, and continue down the hallway away from her.

"Oh, how awful!" she exclaimed to herself. "That must be Jens's room! If he had caught me, I just would have died right there on the spot." She blew out her breath, straightened her long robe, and silently stomped her bare feet.

Pushing back her long blond hair, she took a deep breath and hurried back in the direction of her room.

As she opened the door, Celia, already dressed, greeted her. "Oh, Mandie! Where have you been? It's time to go downstairs for breakfast." She frowned as she looked at Mandie.

Mandie threw off her robe and raced to the wardrobe to pull down a dress. "I just went . . . for a . . . a walk," Mandie muttered as she began hastily dressing. "And . . . got lost."

"I hope your grandmother is not furious with us for being late," Celia told her. "Remember, she told us to all be ready to go shopping right after breakfast."

"I know, I know," Mandie replied, buttoning her shoes and rushing over to the bureau. She picked up her brush and brushed her hair. "I'm ready, I'm ready," she said, looking around the room. "Where is Snowball?"

"Leila came and got him to take him downstairs to feed," Celia replied, hurrying over to the door and opening it. "Come on, Mandie. Let's go." She paused to look back.

"I'm coming," Mandie replied, rushing behind her into the hallway. Glancing at the door across the way, she asked, "Have you seen Joe this morning? Has he already gone downstairs?"

"Yes, he knocked on our door to say he was going ahead a while ago," Celia said, leading the way down the corridor to the staircase.

Mandie couldn't decide whether to tell her friends about her escapade. She wasn't sure what their reactions would be, due to the fact she had intruded into the butler's room, of all places. Joe would probably give her down the country about it. And it kinda hurt when he scolded her. Others' criticism just floated away, but his mattered.

"Come on, Mandie," Celia called from the bottom of the steps. "What's wrong with you being so slow? Are you all right?" She watched as Mandie caught up with her.

"Oh, I'm all right, Celia," Mandie replied, hurrying on down the corridor with her friend. "I'm just thinking about something."

"Well, I can tell you, that something had better be breakfast, because I don't want to incur the wrath of your grandmother to start off the day," Celia replied.

Mandie grinned at her as they walked on and said, "Oh, Celia, my grandmother is not that bad. All you have to do is smile at her and make her think you are agreeing with everything she says."

"Mandie!" Celia exclaimed.

They met up with Joe coming into the main hallway from a side corridor. "Well, well, you girls finally made it," he teased. "I was beginning to think I'd have to go get y'all." He walked along with them.

"That won't be necessary. We were looking for you," Mandie teased. "Why did you have to come downstairs so early?" She remembered Celia had said he had gone down earlier.

"So early?" Joe replied, grinning back. "Well, for one thing I had to go check on that white cat for you to be sure he was being fed and that no one would let him outside while we are gone shopping."

"That's nice of you to be so concerned about my cat," Mandie said, smiling at him.

"Oh, it's not your cat I'm concerned about. It's me. I don't want to waste my time chasing after him if he runs away," Joe replied, still smiling.

Mandie stopped in the hallway and said, "Joe Woodard, you

don't have to chase after my cat. I can always find him myself," Mandie told him.

Joe also paused to look at her. Before he could reply, however, Celia looked back and said loudly, "Will y'all please come on? I'm hungry."

Joe grinned at Celia and quickly followed her to the parlor door. "Yes, and I'm hungry, also."

Mandie, reaching the door with him, said, "You are always hungry. However, I am hungry myself this morning. And I would advise you and Celia, too, to eat everything you can find on the table because, knowing my grandmother, when she goes shopping, that's all she does, shop. She never takes time to stop and eat. Therefore, I'd say we won't get another bite until we return here for the noon meal."

As they entered the parlor, Mrs. Taft and Dr. and Mrs. Woodard were rising from their chairs. Mrs. Yodkin, standing inside the doorway, had evidently just announced breakfast.

"We made it," Mandie whispered to her two friends.

"Just barely," Celia whispered back.

"Let's go," Joe whispered as they followed the adults to the dining room.

The three young people sat together down toward the other end of the table from the adults. Mandie was silent, trying to decide whether to tell Celia and Joe about her adventures that morning.

After they were served and had begun eating, Celia looked at Mandie and said, "You never did tell me where you went so early this morning."

Mandie swallowed a mouthful of coffee and said, "I just . . . walked around the hallways."

Joe immediately looked at her and said, "Now, I'd say that's not exactly an explanation. Have you been snooping around this big house?" He grinned at her and then added, "Like I have?"

"Oh, so you have been snooping," Mandie said, smiling at him. "And what did you see during your travels around the hallways?"

"Practically nothing but closed doors. These people really believe in keeping all the doors closed," Joe remarked, drinking his coffee.

"I know, and they are locked, too," Mandie agreed.

Quickly looking at her, Joe asked, "Locked? How do you know

they are locked? Have you been trying to open all those closed doors?"

"No," Mandie quickly replied, sipping her coffee. "Not all of them, anyway."

"So which ones have you been able to open?" Joe asked.

Mandie frowned, looked up at him, and said, "Only one."

"One?" Celia repeated. "Mandie, you didn't go inside any of those closed rooms, did you?" She laid down her fork and looked at Mandie.

"Well, yes, but only one," Mandie replied. Then smiling, she added, "All the others were locked."

"And what room was it that you were able to go inside?" Joe asked.

"I don't know. It was dark and no one was in there," Mandie replied. "And it was a long way around the hallway from our room."

"Why didn't you turn on the light in it and see what kind of a room it was?" Joe asked.

"Turn on the light?" Mandie asked, puzzled.

"Of course. This house is lighted by electricity," Joe explained. "You know your room is, and all the rest is, too. It's not like back home, where the electricity has not been extended into the country yet."

Mandie quickly said, "Well, I knew that, of course, but I just didn't think about it." She was secretly thinking she would do just that next time.

Mrs. Taft spoke from up the table. "Amanda, you need to hurry up and finish so we can be on our way."

"Yes, ma'am," Mandie replied and quickly began eating the food on her plate.

Celia and Joe also finished their food.

Shortly thereafter, as everyone rose from the table, Joe asked, "And where exactly was this room you went in? I didn't find any unlocked doors along the way when I went down to the kitchen."

"I'm not positive," Mandie replied as the three of them followed the adults out of the dining room. "I just walked down the hallway from our room and then turned into a cross hall, I think. This house is so big and so confusing to find my way around in it." She had quickly decided she would not tell Joe exactly where she had gone lest he figure out it was the servants' rooms, as it must have been.

Mrs. Taft looked back and said, "You all be at the front door in the parlor in fifteen minutes. We will be leaving then." She continued down the hallway.

"Yes, ma'am," the three replied.

When everyone gathered in the parlor a few minutes later, Hodson was there, ready to drive them in Mr. Guyer's carriage.

"Leave me at Dr. Plumbley's first," Dr. Woodard was telling the man.

"Yes, sir, that I will," Hodson agreed. "And when shall I return for you, sir?"

"Don't worry about that," Dr. Woodard replied. "I will ask Dr. Plumbley to drop me off here after our visit together."

Mandie heard that and said, "Oh, Dr. Woodard, if Dr. Plumbley brings you home and we have come back from shopping, please ask him in so I can see him."

Dr. Woodard smiled at her and replied, "Of course, Miss Amanda. In fact, I have cleared it with the housekeeper for Dr. Plumbley to have the noon meal with us here if everyone is back."

"We will be back by then," Mrs. Taft spoke up. "We don't have much shopping to do."

"Maybe my mother and the others will be back by then, too," Mandie said.

Everyone piled into the huge fancy carriage, and a little while later Hodson stopped in front of a small brick building downtown in New York. Mandie was not familiar with the city and had no idea where they were exactly. But there was a shingle hanging over the doorway: *Dr. Samuel Hezekiah Plumbley.* She smiled as she read it, proud of her old friend from back in Franklin, North Carolina.

After Dr. Woodard left the carriage, Hodson continued traveling downtown into the shopping district. Once in a while Mandie would see something that she remembered from her previous visit to New York, but it was mostly a busy, jumbled-up mess of buildings, carriages, pedestrians, and now and then a motorcar. And once again she thought, *How could anyone live in a place like this all the time?*

Suddenly Mrs. Taft spoke as the carriage slowed down. "Here we are. Hodson is going to wait for us around the corner. We won't be long, but we need to look for a new steamer trunk for you, Amanda."

As everyone stood up to get out, Mandie asked in surprise, "A new steamer trunk for me, Grandmother? But what will I do with it?" She followed her grandmother to the door of the carriage.

"Amanda, you will need a new trunk the next time we go to Europe," Mrs. Taft said. Looking back at Celia, she added, "I'm not sure whether your mother would want us to get one for you, too, Celia. I know Mrs. Woodard is getting one for Joe."

The three young people stopped and stood there, looking at the lady.

"To Europe? Grandmother, are we going to Europe again?" Mandie asked.

"Of course," Mrs. Taft said, looking back as Hodson assisted her and Mrs. Woodard in descending from the carriage.

The three young people hurriedly followed.

"But when are we going to Europe, Grandmother?" Mandie asked as she managed to stay right behind Mrs. Taft.

"I didn't know we were going back to Europe," Celia said.

"Neither did I," Joe added. "I wonder when this decision was made."

"We have had plans to return to Europe for a visit ever since you all went with me before," Mrs. Taft explained as everyone assembled in a group on the sidewalk.

"But when?" Mandie insisted on knowing.

"We'll have to make a decision on that soon, but while we're in New York we can go ahead and purchase the new trunks," Mrs. Taft turned around to say.

Mandie waited for Mrs. Taft and Mrs. Woodard to move ahead of them, and then she turned to her friends to whisper, "I have not asked her yet about going to Europe for our graduation present next summer. Therefore, she must be making plans of her own, plans that involve all of us, and we need to find out what it's all about."

"Yes," Celia agreed. "However, she has probably already talked to my mother or she wouldn't be buying a trunk for me today."

"And my mother evidently knows about it, too," Joe added.

Mandie glanced at her friends and said, "You know my grandmother. She is always in charge. Now all we have to do is find out what her plans are and decide whether we want to go along with them or not."

Her friends agreed.

# CHAPTER FIVE

# THE STORM

The young people followed Mrs. Taft and Mrs. Woodard into a huge store that seemed to sell everything. The ladies went straight to the section that sold trunks. And there were trunks of every shape and size and price.

Mandie and her friends looked over the assortment, and when Mrs. Taft made a choice Mandie noticed that it must have been the highest-priced trunk in the collection.

"I think this one will do very well, as far as handling on and off the ship, and will also hold enough clothes for every occasion while we travel," Mrs. Taft said, examining the construction of the trunk she had selected. Turning to Mandie, she said, "Amanda, would you like this one? What do you think?"

Mandie had never been asked for her opinion before on such a purchase, and she frowned as she looked at the trunk. Then, smiling at her grandmother, she replied, "Grandmother, you are the expert. Whatever you decide will be all right with me."

"Fine, then we will order this one," Mrs. Taft replied. Turning to Celia, she asked, "Do you think you would like one just like Amanda's? I could go ahead and order it for you. This store will ship the trunks to our homes, of course."

Celia didn't seem to know what to say. She looked at Mandie

and then back at Mrs. Taft. "I'm sorry, Mrs. Taft, but I don't know what my mother would want to buy. As far as I am concerned, that one would be all right."

"Then we will order it for you," Mrs. Taft decided. "And I'm sure your mother will be pleased with it."

As Joe stood there listening and watching, his mother turned to him and said, "You will need a trunk of your own if you go to Europe, because I will not be going and I don't want you to take the only trunk I have at home in case I decide to go somewhere else while y'all are gone. Now, tell me what you would like."

"But I'm not sure I will be going with Mrs. Taft's group," Joe replied.

"Oh, but, Joe, you must go with us," Mrs. Taft said.

"Yes, I think you should go," his mother added.

"I don't know when they are planning to go, and I may be in extra classes at college and won't be able to leave," Joe said.

"Well then, Joe, we'll just arrange the journey for whenever you can go," Mandie spoke up.

"Yes, we'll take that into consideration when we make our plans," Mrs. Taft told him.

"All right, then," Joe finally said. Turning to his mother, he said, "Why don't you just pick out whatever I should have. I know nothing about steamer trunks." He glanced at Mandie and grinned.

Mandie grinned back and said, "It's time you learned."

Mrs. Woodard turned to Mrs. Taft and asked, "Could you give me some advice on what to purchase for Joe?"

"Of course," Mrs. Taft replied and then walked across the room to another stack of trunks.

The young people listened and watched as Mrs. Taft made recommendations to Mrs. Woodard and then Mrs. Woodard selected a trunk for Joe.

"Now that we're finished with the trunks," Mrs. Taft said, "we need to look at shoes. They have a much larger selection than we can find anywhere else."

So they followed Mrs. Taft onto another floor of the building and then into a section of nothing but shoes. Mandie had never seen so many shoes in one place. There were different styles, different leathers and fabrics, and also different colors.

And this department held shoes for everyone. So the young people had to try on shoes after shoes until the right fit was found in something they wanted to buy.

"Amanda, you are old enough now that I don't think your feet will grow any more, so I'd say it's safe to buy a few pairs to last until next year," Mrs. Taft told Mandie. "What would you like? We'll limit it to six pairs."

"Six pairs? Grandmother, what would I do with six pairs of shoes?" Mandie asked in amazement.

"You need shoes for different occasions," Mrs. Taft insisted, motioning to shelves holding every variety. "You need shoes to wear to school, school socials, walking shoes, slippers for formals, shoes for bad weather. Let's start over here with these plain ones for school." She picked up a black pair.

Mandie sighed as she followed her grandmother around the shelves. She had never seen so many shoes. And she could remember when she had only one pair of shoes, back when her father was living and she had not even known she had a living grandmother. They had lived in a log cabin at Charley Gap, and her father had worked hard on the farm for a living. *Oh, if he could only share in all this now.* She turned her back to her friends and wiped a tear from her blue eyes.

"I do believe it's raining outside," Mrs. Woodard said, looking out through the plate-glass window.

Mrs. Taft turned to glance out. "Indeed it is," she said. "And it looks awfully dark. This rain may last awhile. Luckily this store has a restaurant attached that we can go into for our noon meal if we have to."

"But weren't we expected back to dine with Dr. Plumbley at noon?" Mrs. Woodard asked.

"Yes, but I think we have a good enough reason to be excused from that," Mrs. Taft replied. Turning back to the young people, who were listening, she started naming other departments they needed to shop in while in that store.

Mandie didn't like not being able to see Dr. Plumbley as Dr. Woodard had promised. She caught up with her grandmother as the lady led the way across the floor. "But, Grandmother, we have the carriage. We wouldn't get wet, not much, if we got in the carriage and went back to the Guyers' house," she argued.

Mrs. Taft looked at her and said, "Amanda, this could turn into a storm, and I don't want to be outside if it does." She continued on across the store.

Mandie walked fast to keep up with her. "And also, Mr. Guyer, Jonathan, and my mother and Celia's mother and Uncle John are all expected back about then, aren't they?" she asked.

"I believe so, Amanda, but they may have trouble getting back in the ferry if it storms," Mrs. Taft replied, still hurrying on to another part of the store.

Mandie dropped back with her friends and said, "My grandmother always has to have her way." She frowned.

"But in this case she may be right," Joe said. "We don't want to be caught out in a carriage in New York if a real storm comes up. Traffic can get jammed up and wrecks could occur."

"Oh, Joe," Mandie said. Glancing toward the large window across from them, she said, "It's only a little rainstorm out there, and besides, it may quit."

At that moment a deafening roar of thunder and a blinding flash of lightning outside caused them all to stop and look.

"Guess you're right," Mandie finally conceded as she hovered near her friends.

Mrs. Taft turned back to say, "Hurry on, now. We need to get to another part of this store where there's no window." She rushed on through the other shoppers who had also stopped to look outside.

Mandie overheard her grandmother and Mrs. Woodard talking as they walked on.

"I need to find the telephone in this store. I can call and let the servants know we are stranded and will be much later getting back," Mrs. Taft said.

"Yes, and I should leave a message for my husband," Mrs. Woodard agreed.

They finally found the office of the store, and Mrs. Taft used the telephone there to call the Guyer residence. Mrs. Woodard also added her message for Dr. Woodard. The young people stood by and tried to listen.

"Now that that's taken care of, we need to go to the restaurant. The lady at the desk explained which way to go," Mrs. Taft said.

Mandie suddenly remembered Hodson was sitting outside in the Guyer carriage, waiting for them in the storm.

"Grandmother, shouldn't we send word for Hodson to come inside out of the storm?" Mandie asked as she caught up with her.

"Yes, the lady at the desk will send someone out to speak to him. She said there is a small place where he is parked for him to get something to eat," Mrs. Taft explained. "Then when the storm has passed over he will come in here for us."

Mandie was relieved to hear that her grandmother had thought of the carriage driver.

The restaurant was not very crowded when they got there, but as soon as they were seated crowds started coming in. Evidently all the shoppers in the store had decided to eat at once.

The storm lasted for almost two hours, and by that time they had eaten and Mrs. Taft had finished shopping. Hodson came and got them after parking the carriage at the front door.

When they returned to the Guyer mansion, Mrs. Yodkin informed Mrs. Taft that Mr. Guyer had called from Long Island and said the ferry service was temporarily delayed because of the storm on the waters there.

"Mr. Guyer said they would try to get a ferry as soon as the storm is over and that you should all make yourselves at home in the meantime," Mrs. Yodkin told Mrs. Taft as they came into the parlor.

Mrs. Woodard looked around and asked, "And did Dr. Woodard return?"

"No, madam," Mrs. Yodkin replied. "The doctor called to say he would be staying with the other doctor for the noon meal and would return later this afternoon."

Mandie heard that and said, "And I missed seeing Dr. Plumbley."

Mrs. Taft and Mrs. Woodard had both walked across the room and sat down in front of the fire.

"The fire feels good after being out in all that wet," Mrs. Woodard remarked.

Mrs. Taft looked at Mandie and said, "We'll arrange to see Dr. Plumbley while we're here, so don't worry about it, dear."

Mandie smiled at her and said, "Thank you, Grandmother."

Mrs. Yodkin, waiting by the door, looked across the room at Mrs. Taft and asked, "Since the weather has jumbled up plans, should we serve tea early, madam? Perhaps it would be refreshing after traveling through the wet outside."

"Oh yes, thank you, Mrs. Yodkin," Mrs. Taft replied. To Mandie she said, "Amanda, if you and your friends want to get freshened up before tea, hurry and do so. I don't have the energy. I'll stay right here."

"Yes, Grandmother, and I need to see if Snowball is all right, too," Mandie replied, turning to leave the room. "Celia, Joe, are y'all coming? I'm going to the kitchen first."

"Yes, Mandie," Celia replied.

"Since I was the one who left him there, I'd better go, too," Joe said, and then grinning at Mandie, he added, "just in case he has managed to get loose and run off somewhere."

"Oh, Joe, that's not a laughable matter. I'd never find him in New York," Mandie replied, leading the way into the hallway.

"Or in this house, either," Celia added.

"You're right. He could get lost in this house and never be found," Mandie said seriously.

"Oh, you'd be able to find him. When he got hungry, he would meow loud enough to wake the dead," Joe said, laughing. "You'd hear him."

As they walked down the long hallway, Mandie said, "I'm glad that shopping with Grandmother is over with. Maybe my mother won't want to do much."

"I don't know what else your mother would want to buy. Your grandmother bought everything anyone could possibly need, or want, for that matter," Joe said.

"I'm glad she purchased things for me, too, so I won't have to spend a lot of time shopping with my mother," Celia said.

Joe found the way to the kitchen and pushed open the door. When he did, Snowball, tied behind a counter, immediately sent up a howl. Looking back at Mandie, Joe laughed and said, "I do believe he's in here."

There was no one in the kitchen. Mandie hurried behind the counter, untied Snowball's leash, and picked him up. "Oh, Snowball, just be glad you didn't have to go through what we've been through today," she told the white cat.

Joe went over to look out the window. "Whitey is on the back porch, so he wasn't out in the storm, either," he said. Looking at the girls, he asked, "Do you think it might be permissible to bring Whitey inside?"

"Oh no, Joe, not right now," Mandie quickly replied. "Remember we will be having tea, and that's food that he might want."

"Yes, you're right. I'll get him later," Joe said, turning back to the girls.

"Mandie, I'm going to our room to leave my hat and purse and wash my hands," Celia told Mandie.

"All right, I'll go with you. I suppose I'd better leave Snowball in our room until after tea, too," Mandie agreed.

"I need to freshen up, too," Joe said.

The three went upstairs to their rooms.

As Mandie hurriedly washed her hands and then brushed her hair, she wondered when she would get a chance to investigate the hallways again. According to Mrs. Yodkin, Jonathan had been delayed, so Mandie should have time to look around again if she could get away from her friends—or, on the other hand, maybe they would go with her up and down the corridors of the mansion.

Celia, using the other side of the bureau mirror to brush her hair, asked, "Mandie, when will we be able to settle things with your grandmother about that journey to Europe? There are other things I'd like to do."

"Other things? Like what?" Mandie asked, looking at her in the mirror.

"I'd like to go back to Charleston and visit the Pattons, and I know my mother has said she would like to, also, and maybe Robert would go, too," Celia explained. Robert was a friend who went to the boys' school near their school in Asheville.

"Oh, I see," Mandie said with a big grin. "Yes, I'd like to visit the Pattons again, and I believe my mother intends doing that, but I don't know when. But I suppose since my mother and your mother and the Pattons are old friends, we could probably go just about any time and be welcome."

"What about your grandmother? She said that she expected Senator Morton to come to your house in Franklin when we return," Celia said. "Do you think Mrs. Taft intends taking him with us to visit the Pattons?"

"I don't know, but I do know my mother will have some say-so about some things we are planning," Mandie replied. "And Uncle John won't let my grandmother boss everyone else." She grinned at her friend.

Mandie's mother, Elizabeth, had married John Shaw after Mandie's father, Jim Shaw, had died. John was Jim's brother, and Mandie looked to him for support against any unwanted plans made by her grandmother, who was Elizabeth's mother.

"I sure am glad you have someone to look out for you," Celia remarked, grinning back.

Mandie threw down her brush and said, "Come on, we'd better go. I'm going to shut Snowball up in here." She looked at the white cat, who had curled up on the big bed and gone to sleep.

When they opened the door, Joe was waiting for them in the hallway.

"What have you two young ladies been doing all this time?" he asked teasingly.

Mandie led the way down the hallway toward the staircase and said, "Only necessary freshening up." Looking up at Joe, she added, "I'll be glad when Uncle John gets back. My grandmother seems to be making her own plans, plans that include everyone else."

"I realize that, but I also know how your uncle John can change some of her plans," Joe said laughingly as they descended the stairs.

"Joe, if we don't go to Europe until next summer, couldn't you go with us then?" Mandie asked.

"I suppose so, but I can't say for certain until later when I see what my academic schedule is for next year," Joe replied. Then, smiling down at Mandie, he added, "Of course, I'll do everything I can to arrange things so that I will be able to go with y'all. You can count on that."

"What about going with us if we visit the Pattons in Charleston after we get back home? Can you go with us then?" Mandie asked as they came to the bottom step and paused there.

"Mandie, I'll have to sit down and talk things over with my father. I believe he and my mother have some plans of their own," Joe replied. "However, I will go with you if there isn't a conflict in plans with them."

"Then we'll just ask your mother and father to go with us to Charleston, too. They are friends of the Pattons, also," Mandie said. "What I'm trying to do is figure out what we want to do and stay ahead of my grandmother with her plans."

"I know, I know," Joe agreed. "Come on. I'm hungry." He started on down the hallway.

"I believe I am, too, even though I did eat quite a lot in that restaurant," Celia agreed.

"And I would guess that Mrs. Yodkin has ordered chocolate cake for us," Mandie said with a big grin.

"In that case let's hurry," Joe said, walking faster down the long corridor.

When the three entered the parlor, Mrs. Taft and Mrs. Woodard were discussing future plans.

"Of course you and the doctor would be most welcome to go with us on our journey to Europe, you know," Mrs. Taft was saying to Mrs. Woodard.

The three young people sat down on a settee nearby and listened.

"Yes, and I thank you, but you know how doctors' work is. I don't know how much time the doctor can be away from his patients unless he gets another doctor to agree to look after them while he's away. And that new young doctor over at Bryson City expects sick people to come to see him rather than he go visit them."

"Yes, times are changing," Mrs. Taft agreed. "However, we ought to be able to work something out."

Mandie whispered to her friends, "Grandmother hasn't said when we would be going to Europe."

But then Mrs. Woodard was saying, "I certainly don't want you to plan anything because of us. If we are able to, we'd love to go, but on the other hand, go ahead and make your plans and we'll see what happens."

Mrs. Taft happened to glance up and saw the young people. "Of course you know I will have to get together with my daughter to settle on final plans for that journey to Europe. And I hope to be able to do that soon."

"Yes, I understand," Mrs. Woodard said.

At that moment Mrs. Yodkin came in with Monet following her, pushing the tea cart.

"Well, here's food," Joe said.

"Yes, and we can always discuss plans later," Mandie agreed.

Mandie was trying to decide if she would have time to explore the upstairs hallways or if her friends would agree to go with her before the Guyers and the others returned.

# CHAPTER SIX

# *WAITING*

As soon as tea was finished, Monet came back for the tea cart, with Mrs. Yodkin along to supervise. Mrs. Taft and Mrs. Woodard decided to stay in the parlor, since Dr. Woodard would probably be back shortly.

Mandie looked at her friends and asked, "Would y'all like to go for a walk around the upstairs hallways since it's all wet outside?"

"If we don't take too much time, because my father should be back sometime this afternoon, and I'd like to discuss a few things with him," Joe replied.

"Yes, I need the exercise," Celia said, rising from the settee.

The three left the parlor and headed for the huge staircase at the front of the house. Mandie led the way as she tried to figure out which way they should go in order to pass by Jonathan's room. Even if the door was open, she didn't think she would stop to investigate with her friends along. She was sure they would object. However, if the door was open she could go on and have some excuse to backtrack.

"I've been thinking about that ferry from Long Island, and I'm wondering if my mother and the others will be able to get back here today," Celia said as they climbed the long, curved staircase.

"I'm sure they will," Joe told her. "I think the ferry just got off schedule and the passengers are pretty well jammed up because of it. I would think the ferry will just keep on running back and forth to catch up."

"I hope they will get back today," Celia said.

"I do, too," Mandie said. "I want to get that shopping over with that I have to do with my mother. And I want to see Dr. Plumbley sometime or other before we go home."

"Yes, and I have to do some shopping with my mother," Celia reminded her as they came to the top of the staircase. "Now, which way do we go?"

"As far as I can tell, this hall goes clear around the house, with all these little cross halls off it," Joe remarked as they stopped to talk.

"I wonder what part of the house the family lives in, Mr. Guyer and Jonathan," Mandie said. "And also, where do the servants stay?"

"I have an idea the servants have rooms at the far end of the house on the inside hallway, which I found circles around the flower garden below. In other words, it's like a courtyard beneath their section," Joe said. "There's an inside stairway there that goes straight down into the back hallway where the kitchen is."

"That sounds complicated," Celia said with a laugh.

"There is also a huge ballroom of some kind at one end of the house," Mandie said.

"Yes, I found that, too," Joe said.

"Well, just what part of the house are our rooms in?" Celia asked.

"I believe we are just about in the middle. This house is very long," Joe explained. "And it also has a small third floor and a huge attic above that."

"I tried looking out a window in my room and also in Mandie's, and all I could see was trees and a rooftop below," Celia said.

"Oh, so that's what the view is from our rooms," Mandie said thoughtfully as she tried to envision where Jonathan's room was. "I've been meaning to look out to see where we are."

"Come on. I thought y'all wanted to walk," Joe told the girls as he started on down the hallway.

They walked up and down hallways and came to a balcony, beneath which was the glass room filled with plants and flowers.

"Oh, that's the room we found last time we were here, remember?" Celia told Mandie and Joe.

"Yes, I remember. Snowball loved that room because he could get in all those huge pots of plants," Mandie said.

"I just thought of something," Joe said. "I don't even know where my parents' room is, or your grandmother's, Mandie. Remember the housekeeper took them one direction and we went the other."

"You're right," Mandie said, walking over to a window on the outside wall and looking out. There was a small building below.

Joe followed and said, "That's where the butler lives now."

Mandie turned to look at him and asked, "Jens, the butler?"

"Yes, don't you remember Mr. Guyer gave him the use of that place down there because of his little girl?" Joe told her.

"Oh yes, that's right," Mandie agreed. She remembered seeing Jens come out of the room that she had been trapped in that morning. So that was not his room, after all. But whose was it? It definitely belonged to a man, because what she had found in the wardrobe were men's pants. And if Joe was right about the servants' rooms being in the cross hall, then whose room was it? Could it possibly be Mr. Guyer's? He would probably have a whole suite of rooms somewhere.

"I think I'd better go back downstairs. My father might have returned by now, and I do want to speak to him about something," Joe told the girls, turning to go back the way they had come.

Mandie looked at Celia and asked, "Do you want to walk on around a little more?"

"I suppose so, but I am also wondering whether my mother and the others might be coming back soon," Celia replied.

"Just a couple more hallways," Mandie told her.

"All right," Celia agreed.

"Then I am going back. See y'all downstairs," Joe told the girls, and he walked back down the hallway.

The girls walked slowly on down the corridor they were in and then turned left into a smaller hallway. Then they made a few more turns into other hallways.

"I hope we aren't lost," Celia said with a smile. "We may never find the way back downstairs in time for supper."

"Oh, we can find our way back. We'll just go round and round, up and down these hallways, and we'll eventually get back to the staircase," Mandie said.

"But remember there is more than one staircase in this house," Celia reminded her.

"Well, if we go down any one of those, we will at least be on the main floor and then we can find the way back to the parlor," Mandie assured her. "The next staircase that we find we'll just go down it."

"I just can't imagine why anyone would want to live in such a mixed-up house," Celia remarked as they walked on.

Finally Mandie spotted steps going down ahead. "There is a staircase right there," she said, pointing as they came closer. "Come on. We'll see where it goes."

Mandie noticed this staircase was plain and narrow and steep as they descended. Looking ahead, she said, "I believe we are coming down right by the kitchen."

"You're right," Celia agreed.

When they reached the hallway below, Mrs. Cook was just coming out of the kitchen and stopped to speak. "We will be having a big dinner tonight. Two doctors."

"Two doctors?" Celia asked.

"Dr. Woodard and Dr. Plumbley," Mandie said with a big smile.

Mrs. Cook nodded and said, "Yes." She went on down the back hallway.

Mandie looked at Celia and said, "Now, if I can remember the way to the parlor from here . . . I should have asked Mrs. Cook."

"Let's just keep trying different doors and halls real fast," Celia said, opening a door on their left. "Oh, I'm lucky. I do believe this is the main hallway to the parlor."

"Yes, it is," Mandie agreed, leading the way down it.

They finally came to the door to the parlor. Mandie quickly looked as they stepped inside the room. There was Dr. Plumbley sitting in an armchair and talking with Dr. Woodard, who sat nearby. No one else was in the room.

"Well, hello, Miss Amanda," Dr. Plumbley said, quickly rising and coming to meet her.

Mandie rushed forward, grasped his hand, and said, "Oh, Dr. Plumbley, I'm so glad to see you." She smiled up at the tall black man whose education her grandfather had paid for many years ago. He was also the doctor who had saved her mother's life a long time ago when she had the fever and Dr. Woodard had exhausted his knowledge.

"It's a delight to see you, Miss Amanda."

Dr. Woodard spoke from his chair. "It didn't take much coaxing to bring him back with me for supper since we had missed out on lunch because of the storm."

At that moment Joe came into the parlor, saying, "I've been looking everywhere for you, Mandie, to tell you Dr. Plumbley was here." He sat on a chair near his father.

"We came down the back stairs," Mandie said. "I'm sorry. Let's sit down, Dr. Plumbley." They sat on chairs nearby. Mandie looked around the room and asked, "Where is my grandmother? And your mother, Joe?"

"Oh, they had gone to their rooms when I got back down here," Joe explained.

"They'll be back in time for supper," Dr. Woodard said.

Mandie turned back to Dr. Plumbley and asked, "How is Moses?"

"He's just fine," Dr. Plumbley replied. Moses was Dr. Plumbley's nephew.

Just at the moment Mandie opened her mouth to ask another question, the front door opened and Mr. Guyer came into the room. He paused, staring straight at the door to the hallway, and Mandie turned her head and saw her grandmother standing in the doorway. They both seemed to have frozen as they looked at each other.

Then suddenly Mr. Guyer moved aside and apologized to Mandie's mother, Elizabeth, Celia's mother, Jane, and Mandie's uncle John as they came into the room. "I apologize for blocking the doorway," he muttered.

Then Jonathan Guyer more or less pushed his way through the crowd into the room, glanced at Mrs. Taft, and came straight to Mandie, whispering, "Watch and listen."

Mandie and everyone else seemed at a loss for words as Mrs. Taft still stood in the doorway. Then Lindall Guyer hastened across the room, holding out his hand to Mrs. Taft and saying, "Welcome. It's been a long time." He smiled at her.

"Yes, but we don't have to dig up the in-between, do we?" Mrs. Taft replied as he continued holding her hand.

"Of course not," Mr. Guyer replied. "And I think we should all sit down and relax."

Jane Hamilton, Elizabeth Shaw, and John Shaw immediately went on through the parlor into the hallway, saying they needed to freshen up.

"Why don't we go outside for a little walk?" Dr. Woodard asked Dr. Plumbley, and they immediately left. Dr. Woodard nodded at Joe, motioning that he should also leave the room.

Joe stood up and said, "Come on, Jonathan, show us the way around this great big mansion."

Jonathan grinned at him and said, "Of course."

Mandie left the room with her friends even though she didn't exactly want to. She was dying to find out what was going on between her grandmother and Jonathan's father.

Out in the hallway, Jonathan said, "Come on. I'll tell you about the secret I found."

Mandie immediately forgot about everything else and quickly followed her friends.

Jonathan took them down the main hallway to a cross hall on the left and then opened a door on the right. "Come on. Let's go in here," he told them.

Mandie looked around as Jonathan turned on lights. The room was a library, and the books all looked very old.

"Just have seats there and I'll show you something," Jonathan said, motioning to chairs around a long mahogany table.

When everyone was seated, Jonathan turned to the bookshelves behind him and said, "These are all very old books and have been in here probably since before I was ever born. You see, my father inherited this house from his parents, and their furnishings are still in some of the rooms. This room, for instance, has never been changed as far as I know, and I'll show you the reason for my thinking that."

Mandie and her friends watched as Jonathan turned to a small ladder and climbed up it to reach the top shelf. He took out several books in the tightly packed shelf, laid them across some other books, and then reached inside the emptied shelf. He pulled out an envelope, came back down the ladder, and sat down at the table with the others.

"Now, I believe you are all going to be shocked by what I found in this envelope," Jonathan said, grinning at them as he slowly pulled out a handful of newspaper clippings and laid them on the table.

Mandie quickly leaned forward to look. "What is that?" she asked.

"Just some articles out of an old newspaper. Read what they say," Jonathan said, grinning again as he spread out the clippings.

Mandie and her friends leaned closer to read.

"But what could be so special about old newspaper articles?" Celia asked.

"Looks like gossip columns to me," Joe said.

"But read the names," Jonathan told him.

" 'The latest twosome on the town, Mary Elizabeth Ashworth—' " Mandie stopped, about to lose her breath as she recognized the name. "That's my grandmother's maiden name, there with your father's name!"

"Yes indeed," Jonathan said, watching everyone. "Read on."

" 'The beautiful heiress Mary Elizabeth Ashworth, with her steady escort, Lindall Guyer II, at the St. Patrick's Day Ball,' " Mandie read. She quickly flipped through the other clippings, which were all the same gossip column that seemed to follow every move her grandmother and Jonathan's father made. Looking at Jonathan, she said, "My grandmother and your father! But what happened to this romance?"

"I'm sorry, I don't know," Jonathan told her. "This is all I've found so far. Evidently it broke up, because my father married my mother."

"So that is why my grandmother acts like she doesn't like your father whenever his name is mentioned," Mandie said, still shocked at the news.

"Maybe she was jilted by Mr. Guyer," Celia suggested.

"Or maybe Mrs. Taft jilted Mr. Guyer," Joe added.

"I don't know, but you all saw the looks on their faces when they met down there in the parlor a while ago," Jonathan said.

"But, Jonathan, didn't your father know my grandmother would be here when y'all came home?" Mandie asked.

"I don't know. I never heard anyone mention her name while we were gone," Jonathan said.

"Everyone certainly hurried out of the room," Celia remarked.

Mandie nodded and said, "Yes, like they knew something was going on." She tried to figure out their reactions.

"My father could possibly have known about this," Joe said. "He has known your grandmother, Mandie, for years and years and years. And—"

Mandie quickly interrupted as she took a deep breath and said, "I just remembered something. Uncle Ned said Mr. Guyer used to come visit at my grandmother's house when my grandfather was living. My grandfather died right about the time I was born, and I don't know if your father ever came back to visit after that, Jonathan." Uncle Ned was Mandie's father's old Cherokee friend.

"I don't suppose he did, because he had married my mother probably two or three years before your grandfather died," Jonathan figured.

"That solves some of the mystery, but why does Mrs. Taft always act like she doesn't like your father, Jonathan?" Joe asked.

"I haven't found out yet, but give me time. There's bound to be more information somewhere," Jonathan said.

"I overheard a remark that gave me the impression that my mother doesn't even know why my grandmother doesn't like your father, Jonathan," Mandie said.

"I was surprised that she agreed to come with us to your house," Celia said.

"I think there is some important reason," Jonathan said.

"This is going to be a strange situation while we're here together," Joe said. "What do we do now? Go back to the parlor together? We have to go to the dining room together to eat."

Mandie straightened up and smiled as she said, "We don't have to do anything. We can just act like nothing has happened."

"That's going to be hard to do," Celia said.

Jonathan gathered up the clippings, inserted them back into the envelope, and stood up. "I'll just put these back up there where no one will find them, and we can all come back in here and search the rest of this room. I didn't have a chance to do it before we went to Long Island." He climbed the ladder, replaced the envelope, and then hid it from view with the books he had removed.

All of a sudden Mandie started giggling, and everyone looked at her.

"Are you all right, Mandie?" Joe asked.

"I just think this is funny. I wish I could walk right up to my grandmother and say, 'I know all about you and Jonathan's father,'" she managed to say between giggles.

Jonathan laughed and said, "We'll do just that before you all go home. In the meantime, maybe we'll find something else that will give us more information."

"Do y'all think Mrs. Taft may still be in love with Mr. Guyer?" Celia asked.

Everyone laughed. Then Mandie said, "I think it would depend on whatever broke up the romance in the first place. Just imagine my grandmother and your father, Jonathan."

"Yes, we were almost kin to each other," Jonathan replied with a grin.

"I intend staying away from both of them while I'm here," Joe said. Then he added thoughtfully, "In fact, I'm going to speak to my father and ask him if he knows why Mrs. Taft seems not to like Mr. Guyer."

"But, Joe, please don't give away our secret until we can look for more information," Mandie reminded him.

"I won't, but as you know, almost everyone will tell you that Mrs. Taft doesn't seem to like Mr. Guyer," Joe replied.

"And I'm also wondering why she agreed to come here with us to visit in Mr. Guyer's house," Mandie said. "And I intend finding out."

Everyone nodded in agreement.

And Mandie suddenly realized that if she had found Jonathan's room, she would not have found even a clue to his secret. Now that Jonathan had come home, they would all be able to help him in his search for more information regarding her grandmother and his father.

# CHAPTER SEVEN

# *DECISIONS*

Jonathan led the way to the parlor, where everyone gathered before mealtime. No one was in there except Dr. Woodard and Dr. Plumbley, deep in a conversation at one end of the room. And Lindall Guyer came in right behind the young people as they sat down near the doctors.

Mr. Guyer spoke to them. "I do hope you young ladies had something to do while we were gone." He sat in a chair by Dr. Woodard.

"Yes, sir," Mandie replied with a big smile. "My grandmother took us shopping this morning."

"And did you buy lots of pretty clothes?" Mr. Guyer asked.

"No, sir, we bought steamer trunks," Mandie explained.

"Steamer trunks? Then you must be going on a long journey," Mr. Guyer said.

"Grandmother says we're going back to Europe, but I don't know when," Mandie explained.

Dr. Woodard spoke to Mr. Guyer, "Dr. Plumbley here has been filling me in on some new treatments he has learned."

"Dr. Plumbley, that would be most interesting to hear about," Mr. Guyer said, turning all his attention to the two doctors.

"Dr. Plumbley, before you get deep in conversation, Aunt Lou said if I saw you to tell you she sent her love," Mandie quickly said.

"Now, that's the best news I've had today. And how is that nice lady?" Dr. Plumbley asked.

"She's just fine," Mandie said. Aunt Lou was the housekeeper for her mother and Uncle John.

"I must get down to see all those friends, Abraham, Jenny, and Lou," Dr. Plumbley said, then turned back to talk to the other men.

Jonathan leaned over near Mandie, as they sat across the room from the adults, and said, "Do you suppose there's a romance going on between Aunt Lou and Dr. Plumbley?"

Mandie started giggling and put her hand over her mouth as she replied, "Oh, Jonathan, I had not even thought about that. They are about the same age, I believe, and they have known each other since way back years and years ago."

"And neither one of them is married," Joe added.

Celia whispered to Mandie, "I wonder where your grandmother is. I see Mrs. Yodkin headed this way, to announce supper I would imagine."

Mrs. Yodkin came to the door of the parlor and looked inside. Then without saying a word she turned and went back down the hallway.

"I hope she is not delaying supper," Joe said.

"She can't announce dinner until all the ladies have come back to the parlor," Jonathan explained.

"I wish they would come on back here so we can get this all over with," Celia remarked. "I think I'm hungry."

"Yes, so we can see how my father and your grandmother, Mandie, are going to behave in the same room," Jonathan said.

At that moment Jane Hamilton came into the parlor, followed by Mrs. Woodard, Elizabeth and John Shaw, and Mrs. Taft. The men stood up as the ladies entered.

Before anyone could speak Mrs. Yodkin came to the doorway again and announced, looking straight at Mr. Guyer, "Sir, dinner has been served."

"Thank you, Mrs. Yodkin. We'll be right in," Mr. Guyer said. As Mrs. Yodkin went back down the hallway, he added, "Ladies, shall we go dine?" looking directly at Mrs. Taft, who avoided his glance.

As Mr. Guyer led the way to the dining room, Mandie watched

her grandmother. Mrs. Taft had immediately started talking to Dr. Plumbley and ignored Mr. Guyer. She seemed flustered, and Mandie had never seen her that way before.

With Mr. Guyer seated at the head of the table, the adults sat near him and the young people were placed down far enough that they could carry on their own conversation in low voices without being overheard.

"Your grandmother won't look at my father," Jonathan whispered to Mandie after everyone had been served.

"I noticed that," Mandie replied. "I wonder what they had to say to each other after everyone left the parlor when y'all came home, Jonathan."

"I'm afraid we'll never know," Jonathan said.

"Your grandmother seems to be awfully nervous," Joe said.

"She is not acting normal," Mandie decided.

"No wonder," Celia said. "Coming face-to-face with an old beau from long ago would be unsettling."

"Well, I can't imagine how it would be," Mandie said. "Do you suppose we will have lots of old friends when we are as old as Grandmother?"

"Probably," Jonathan said.

Mandie was looking at her grandmother and saw her speak to Elizabeth. "I have bought the new steamer trunk for Amanda," she was saying. Turning to Jane Hamilton, she added, "I also purchased one for Celia."

Mrs. Woodard said, "I purchased one for Joe, also, just in case he is able to go with y'all."

Elizabeth looked at her mother and asked, "Steamer trunk for Amanda?"

"Yes, for our journey to Europe," Mrs. Taft explained.

"Mother, we haven't settled anything on that yet," Elizabeth replied.

"Neither have we, but I suppose Celia does need a new trunk," Jane Hamilton said. "I will reimburse you for it, Mrs. Taft, and thank you for saving me the trouble."

"So you are all planning to go to Europe," Mr. Guyer said.

"I certainly wish I could go with y'all, but I see no free time anywhere in the near future," Dr. Plumbley said.

John Shaw had been listening and now he said, "This journey may not be in the near future. It depends on when everyone will be free at one time." He turned to look down the table at Mandie and winked at her as he smiled.

Mandie smiled back. She knew what he meant. He was not going to let her grandmother make plans for everyone unless everyone wanted to go along with whatever it was.

"When did you plan on going to Europe, Mother?" Elizabeth asked.

"It would certainly have to be during the summertime because of school," Mrs. Taft replied. "And I was hoping we could make it this summer. I don't see why we couldn't."

"As far as Joe is concerned, the journey would depend on how long you plan to be away," Mrs. Woodard said. "He may have to return to college early because of the makeup courses he's trying to finish."

"And I will have to sit down and discuss plans with Celia before I would make any commitment," Jane Hamilton said.

"We could leave immediately after we return to Franklin and be back before their summer vacation is gone," Mrs. Taft said.

"We should get everyone together and sit down and decide whether we will all be going on the journey," John Shaw told her. "And we need to do that before we leave here in order to include Jonathan."

"Yes, that's what we should do," Mrs. Taft agreed. "I'll leave it up to you to arrange this, John."

"Yes, ma'am," John Shaw said. "As soon as I find out when everyone will be free at the same time for a few minutes."

"After we finish here and have coffee in the parlor would probably be a good time," Lindall Guyer told John Shaw.

John Shaw smiled at him and said, "You're right. And that may be the only chance we'll have everyone together in one room."

Mandie heard that arrangement and was disappointed. She had hoped they could skip coffee in the parlor and go back to the old library and search for more information on the long-ago romance.

"Looks like our secret work will have to wait a little while," Jonathan whispered to her.

"Maybe we can make quick work of the meeting," Joe suggested.

"Quick work?" Mandie questioned.

"You know, we could all just say we have something else to do at whatever time they decide to go to Europe, that is if y'all really don't want to go," Joe explained.

"I would like to go back to Europe," Mandie said, "but not until we graduate next year."

"Yes, that would suit me just fine, too," Celia said.

"Well now, I'm all for the journey anytime you people decide to go," Jonathan said, grinning at the others. "I don't have any plans made that can't be changed."

"We really do need to get together on something before we go in the parlor," Mandie said.

Celia leaned forward to whisper, "Mandie, I just thought of something. Your grandmother said Senator Morton would be coming to your house after we go back. Do you suppose he will be going with us if we go to Europe this summer?"

"I just thought of something, too," Mandie whispered back. "Why can't Grandmother just take Senator Morton with her and go on to Europe without us?"

"Mandie, that would not be proper," Celia replied. "They wouldn't have a chaperon without us along."

"Maybe they will get married and move to his house in Florida, and then Grandmother wouldn't be around trying to make all the decisions for everyone," Mandie said, grinning.

"But then we would be stuck in the school all this next year without having her to go visit on weekends and all," Celia reminded Mandie.

"Y'all sure can come up with problems," Joe teased the girls. "Why not just say yes or no about going to Europe and forget about all the other problems? Or better still, why not just tell your grandmother that you would like to wait until graduation next year to go, Mandie?"

"I suppose I could," Mandie agreed. "We could go visit the Pattons in Charleston when we go home, and if Grandmother wants to go with us she could."

"And take Senator Morton," Celia added with a grin.

The young people had finished their food and looked up the table as the adults prepared to go to the parlor. Mandie and her friends stood up.

Mandie's mother, Elizabeth, spoke to her. "Come along to the parlor with us for a few minutes whether you want coffee or not. We need to settle this European date."

"You too, Joe," Mrs. Woodard said.

"And you, Celia," Jane Hamilton said.

As the young people stood up, Jonathan looked at his friends and said in a whisper, "My father didn't ask me to go to the parlor."

"You have to go with us, Jonathan," Mandie insisted. "Not only to help decide about Europe, but you just can't go back to that library and start searching without us. Please." She smiled at him.

"I suppose I could go with you all, but I warn you I won't be staying in the parlor long," Jonathan replied, grinning at her as the four moved out and followed the adults.

As soon as everyone sat down in the parlor, Mrs. Yodkin came in followed by Monet with the coffee on a cart.

Mrs. Yodkin walked over to Mandie and said, "Miss, the cat has been fed and is in the kitchen."

"Oh, thank you, Mrs. Yodkin," Mandie said. "I just plain forgot about him when I left him in my room. I'll get him after we finish with our coffee in here. Thank you."

"He will be fine in the kitchen until you have time to get him," Mrs. Yodkin told her and went across the room to check on Monet, who was serving the coffee to the adults.

"I wondered where that white cat was," Jonathan said.

"We took your white dog for a walk with us yesterday," Mandie told him.

"Well, I appreciate that. Where did you go?" Jonathan asked.

Mandie told him about their walk in Central Park.

Then, as Monet approached them with the coffee, John Shaw spoke from the other side of the huge room. "Why don't all you young people move over this way so we can discuss the possibility of a journey to Europe?"

"Yes, sir," Mandie said as she and her friends went over to sit on a small settee near the adults. Monet served their coffee there.

Turning to Lindall Guyer, who was sitting next to him, John Shaw then asked, "Why don't you conduct our discussion since you most likely will not be involved in our plans, Lindall?"

"I'd be glad to, John," Mr. Guyer replied and sat up straighter in his chair next to Dr. Woodard and Dr. Plumbley. "I suppose the first thing to ask is, who would like to go to Europe?"

"I would, Mr. Guyer, but—" Mandie said immediately.

Her friends interrupted with, "I would, too." The adults nodded in agreement.

"Now that everyone seems interested in traveling over there, let's start around the room from my right and ask when you would be free to go," Mr. Guyer said, indicating Jane Hamilton next.

"I could arrange our affairs and go just about anytime, but of course the date would have to be agreeable with Celia," Jane Hamilton said, looking across at Celia.

Celia smiled at her mother and said, "Whenever you would like to go would be just fine with me, Mother."

Joe was next and said, "Don't let me change any of your plans. Just let me know when you settle on a date and I'll see if I can make it then."

Mandie was sitting next to Joe and said, "I'd like to go to Europe next summer."

Everyone turned to look at her. Mrs. Taft was surprised with this date and asked across the room, "Amanda, why wait until next year?"

"I've been thinking about going back to Europe, and I would like to go, but I've also been thinking that a journey to Europe would be the most wonderful graduation present I could think up. You had asked me what I wanted for graduation next year. And that's what I would like," Mandie replied.

"Oh, I see," Mrs. Taft said as everyone looked at her.

No one said anything for a minute or two, and then Mrs. Taft spoke again. "But, Amanda, we could go this summer and then go back again next summer. It's impossible to see everything in one visit, as you know from before. We could go to certain places over there this year, and then when we return next summer we could visit other countries." She looked at Mandie and smiled.

Mandie felt bad because she just didn't want to go along with her grandmother's plans, and she said the first thing she could think of. "Grandmother, we've already taken part of our vacation this year to come up here. I think we ought to go visit the Pattons in Charleston after we go home."

"To Charleston?" Mrs. Taft repeated thoughtfully.

"Yes, all my friends here would like to do that," Mandie added. "We could go just as soon as we get back home."

Everyone watched and listened.

Mrs. Taft finally spoke again as she looked around the room. "What do all the rest of you think about that, going to Charleston, that is, instead of Europe?"

"I wouldn't be able to go anywhere any time soon, so don't count on my input," Dr. Plumbley said.

"I'm afraid that applies to me, too," Dr. Woodard added. "I don't think I could stay away from my patients that long after taking time to come up here."

"Yes, that includes me, too, of course," Mrs. Woodard added.

Elizabeth looked at Mrs. Taft, smiled, and then said, "Mother, that would suit us just fine. We've been wanting to visit the Pattons."

John Shaw nodded in agreement.

Jane Hamilton smiled at Celia and asked, "Yes or no?"

Celia nodded with a big grin. "Yes, Mother, let's do."

Jonathan had not said a word, and now he looked across the room at his father.

Lindall Guyer smiled at him and said, "Now, if you are planning to go right away, I might just be able to go with you to Charleston. I have a few days I can take off."

"Thanks," Jonathan said with a big grin.

Mandie knew Jonathan and his father had very little time together because of the work Mr. Guyer did for the government. She could tell Jonathan was thrilled with the prospect of traveling with him.

Dr. Woodard spoke to Joe, "Son, if you would like to go with them to Charleston, go right ahead. You need a little vacation before you return to college."

"I was thinking . . ." Joe slowly began. "I hate to go without you and Mother, especially since I don't have much time at home anyway."

"Now, Joe, don't let that bother you," Mrs. Woodard quickly told him. "A few days on the beach down there would be good for you."

"A few days? They may be staying longer than a few days," Joe said, looking across the room to John Shaw.

"You can always go home anytime you get ready, Joe, if you don't want to visit as long as we do, and right now I'm not sure how long we plan to stay," John Shaw said. He looked across the room at Mrs. Taft.

"If we are going to Charleston, I can only stay two weeks and then I need to get back home," Mrs. Taft said.

Mandie looked at her in surprise. Here she was trying to talk everyone into going to Europe, which would take a few weeks, and now she was saying she needed to get back home in two weeks. Could it be because Mr. Guyer had said he would like to go with them?

"Why don't we all go down together and return whenever anyone gets ready?" John Shaw said, looking around the room.

Everyone agreed to that. And now that their vacation was settled, Mandie was in a hurry to leave the parlor. She looked around the room. As far as she could tell, all the coffee had been finished.

Lindall Guyer looked at John Shaw and said, "Since Jonathan and I are going with you to Charleston, we might as well go back to North Carolina with you—that is, if you plan to leave immediately upon arriving at your home."

"Yes, no use in wasting any time," John Shaw replied. "What about leaving for North Carolina on Monday? Today is Thursday, and I believe the ladies would like to go shopping before we return home."

"That would be just right for me," Lindall Guyer said. "I'll check in with my office tomorrow and alert them I'll be away then."

Mandie looked across at her grandmother, who was talking to Elizabeth. Mrs. Taft had never promised a journey to Europe next year during all this discussion. Mandie hoped she had not decided not to give Mandie and her friends this for their graduation present.

"Come on," Jonathan suddenly said, looking at the young people. "I believe we can get out of here now. Let's go." He quickly stood up.

While the adults were engaged in various conversations, the young people hurried after Jonathan.

Mandie knew where he was headed. He also wanted to find out more about that long-ago romance.

# CHAPTER EIGHT

# OLD SECRETS

Mandie, Celia, Joe, and Jonathan returned to the old library to search for possible information on Mr. Guyer and Mrs. Taft. Most of the books were stacked double on the shelves, which meant there were twice as many books as shelves. Therefore, the young people had to take down two books at a time and try to keep them in order. There was a section on history, one on government, one on antiques, many, many fiction titles, and a large section of mixed subjects. It was a slow job.

"I would like to say we could move faster," Jonathan told them as he stood on the ladder to reach the top shelves. "However, if we don't keep the books in their original order, then someone might notice and wonder why these old books have been disturbed and then investigate."

Joe was on a ladder on the other side of the room, taking down books from the top shelves there. "I agree with you," he said. "We need to be sure to put the books back exactly where we found them."

"That's hard to do, because if you notice, a lot of them aren't in any special order, not alphabetically by author, or geographically," Mandie said as she and Celia worked on the lower shelves.

"Please be careful to look closely behind all the books to be sure nothing has slipped down behind them," Jonathan told them.

Mandie suddenly found a paper inside a large book. "Look!" she cried, opening the book. "There's a paper in here."

The other three came quickly to look as she pulled out the paper and handed it up to Jonathan, saying, "You read it. It is your property."

Jonathan quickly unfolded the single sheet of paper, scanned the page, and then laughed. "It's only a letter that came with the book from the publisher when my grandfather ordered it." He held it up for them to see.

"Oh, shucks!" Mandie exclaimed in disappointment.

"Oh well, we have lots more to go through," Joe said, turning back to the shelf he was working on.

Jonathan turned back to the top shelf where he had been examining the books.

After a while Mandie suddenly remembered that she hadn't been to the kitchen to get Snowball. "Oh, I forgot to get my cat!" she exclaimed, laying down the book she was holding. "I'd better go get him right now, if I can find the way."

Jonathan came down from the ladder as he said, "I'll go with you."

"So will I. I need a little break from all this hard work," Joe joked as he joined them.

"Then I'll go along, too. I'm not staying here in this strange room all by myself," Celia decided.

"All right, let's go," Jonathan said, opening the door and waiting for everyone to go out into the hallway. "Turn to your left here."

As they walked down the corridor, they discussed possibilities they might find in the old library. Jonathan had left the envelope with the clippings in its hiding place while they had searched the other shelves.

"Maybe we ought to get those clippings that you found back out, Jonathan, and look them over again," Mandie suggested. "Maybe we could get some clue about something or other from rereading them."

"I have looked at them several times, but I'll get them down for you all to see again," Jonathan promised.

"I wonder who put the clippings in there in the first place," Celia said thoughtfully as they continued down another hallway.

"I would imagine my father put them there when he was young

and in love with Mandie's grandmother," Jonathan said, grinning at Mandie.

Mandie frowned and said, "Maybe they weren't in love. Maybe they were just good friends."

"I can't imagine escorting a girl all over town to all these social events unless I was in love with her," Joe said, smiling at Mandie.

"Well, maybe Mr. Guyer was in love with my grandmother, but maybe my grandmother was not in love with him. Knowing her like I do, I would say it just might have been a social thing for her, you know, a dependable escort."

Everyone stopped in the corridor and laughed.

"Do you mean your grandmother might have been keeping my father on a string just for social reasons?" Jonathan said, laughing loudly.

"I've heard of such things," Celia spoke up.

"Yes, and I do know my grandmother seems to be a social climber," Mandie said.

They walked on down the corridor and came to the kitchen door. Jonathan pushed the door open for the others to enter. There was no one in the kitchen but Snowball, who had evidently been asleep. He jumped up and began howling.

Mandie quickly went to unfasten his leash from the cabinet handle and picked him up. "Sorry I plumb forgot about you, Snowball," she said, holding him close and smoothing his fur with one hand. Snowball began purring loudly.

"That is a spoiled cat," Joe said, grinning at Mandie.

"You know, my dog, Whitey, has started acting like that, too," Jonathan said. "As soon as he sees me, he starts whining to get loose or come in the house. Do you suppose he's learning that from Snowball?" He laughed.

"Snowball hasn't been around Whitey enough to give him his habits," Mandie quickly said.

"Don't y'all think we had better get back if we're going to finish searching that library tonight?" Celia asked.

"Oh yes, let's go," Jonathan said.

"Since we will probably have to go shopping again tomorrow, which is Friday, and then y'all are going home with us on Monday, we don't really have much time left to look for any more information," Mandie said, following the others out into the hallway as she carried the white cat.

"I do hope we can find some answers to some of our questions while we have Mrs. Taft and my father together," Jonathan said as he led the way. "We might uncover something we would like to mention to them." He grinned at the others.

"You mean tell my grandmother and your father that we know something about them?" Mandie quickly asked in surprise.

"Of course," Jonathan replied. "In a subtle way, of course. If they know that we know something, maybe they would voluntarily give us some explanation."

"I wouldn't want to poke into Mrs. Taft's private business and let her know it," Joe said.

"Neither would I," Celia added.

"I'm not sure whether I would tell my grandmother about anything we found out or not. It would depend on what it is," Mandie finally said.

They came to the door of the old library. Jonathan pushed it open and waited for everyone to enter.

"Now, let's see what else we can find, if anything," Jonathan said, starting back toward the shelves he had been searching.

"Jonathan, let's look at those old clippings again and see if we can notice anything new about them," Mandie said, setting Snowball down after the door was securely closed.

Jonathan shrugged and said, "All right, I'll get them down." He climbed the ladder. Looking back down at Mandie, he said, "But you know we have a lot of territory to search yet in this room, so we'd better hurry."

"I know," Mandie agreed. "I just thought maybe with a fresh look at the clippings you already have, my mind might figure out something else while I work." She grinned at him.

Jonathan moved the books that he had removed before and then put his hand behind the other books to feel for the envelope. The others watched as he suddenly began quickly running his hand around the back of the shelf and then bent to squint between the books. "Now, I know this is the right place," he said.

"Yes, those are the same books you took out when you showed us the clippings," Mandie agreed.

"Maybe they fell through to the next shelf," Joe suggested.

"I don't believe they could have, because the shelves are built tightly with no cracks between them," Jonathan replied, continuing to reach into the space between the books. Looking down at Joe, he finally said, "How about bringing your ladder over here next to mine and let's just take all these books out of the shelves. Maybe I put them back in the wrong place."

"I was watching, and I know you put them back in the same place," Mandie assured him.

Joe moved his ladder over next to Jonathan's, and together they began taking out books and handing them down to the girls. There was nothing behind them.

"They have plumb disappeared," Celia declared as she watched.

"That means someone else knew they were there," Mandie said.

Jonathan looked down at the girls and said, "But no one ever comes in here or reads any of these books, that I know of, so how would they have found the clippings?"

"Maybe someone heard you talking about them," Joe said.

Jonathan suddenly hurried down the ladder. "Let's look around on this floor and see if anyone else is around," he said, going to the door and opening it.

The others followed. He led them down the long corridor, opening every door they passed and looking into each room. There was no sign of anyone near.

"You know, Jonathan, someone could have gone in the library while we were in the kitchen getting Snowball," Mandie said.

"Yes, we were gone long enough for someone to go in the library and take them," Joe added.

Jonathan frowned thoughtfully and asked, "But who could it have been? I would say my father and your grandmother, Mandie, are in the parlor."

"Let's check and see," Mandie said.

Jonathan quickly led the way to the parlor, but when they came to the doorway, they stayed back and peeked in so no one would see them.

Mandie stepped back to whisper, "Everyone is in there." She saw her grandmother talking with Mrs. Woodard. Mr. Guyer seemed deep in conversation with the men. Elizabeth and Jane were talking together.

The young people backed off out of sight of anyone in the parlor and discussed the situation in low voices.

"Maybe it was a servant," Celia suggested.

Jonathan smiled at her and said, "I don't think any of the servants would even be interested in such a thing."

"I suppose all the servants are too young to have worked here when my grandmother and your father knew each other," Mandie said.

"Well now, let me see," Jonathan said, thoughtfully running his fingers through his dark curly hair. "I believe Mrs. Yodkin's mother worked here when Mrs. Yodkin was a child, and also, Hodson is pretty old and could have worked for my grandfather. I'm not sure."

"You don't remember any old stories about Mrs. Yodkin or Mr. Hodson, do you?" Celia asked. "What I mean is, have they ever told you old stories about your grandfather and way back then when your father was young?"

"No, as you know, Mrs. Yodkin never talks much except business, and Hodson says practically nothing at any time," Jonathan answered. "But why would either one of them take the clippings?"

"Maybe they plan on blackmailing your father or Mandie's grandmother," Joe teased with a big grin.

"But there's nothing to be blackmailed now. If they were going to do that, it would have been when my father married my mother, don't you think?" Jonathan replied. "Let's go back and keep on searching the shelves. Maybe someone just moved the clippings to another place."

"That could be," Mandie agreed.

They followed Jonathan down the maze of hallways back to the old library. As they came to the door, Mandie saw that it was standing open and she rushed inside calling her cat. "Snowball, where are you?"

Her friends helped her look, but there was no white cat in the room.

Mandie stomped her foot and said, "I know we closed the door when we left. Someone has let him out."

"And there's no telling who that someone was," Jonathan said. "It could have been whoever took the other clippings looking for more because they knew we were in the room searching."

"You're right," Joe agreed.

"But, Mandie, we'd better look for that cat right now," Celia told her.

"Yes, you're right," Mandie agreed.

Jonathan quickly said, "I'll help you look since I know my way around. Joe, you and Celia stay here in case someone comes back again."

"If someone does come back in here, what do we do or say?" Joe asked.

"Just continue working on the books and give them the impression that you are looking for a certain book," Jonathan said.

"And if y'all find any more clippings or anything, don't lay them down," Mandie said. "Keep them in your hands till we get back."

"Don't worry, I won't let anyone take anything else while I'm in here," Joe assured her.

"And I'll help guard it if we find anything else," Celia added.

Jonathan led Mandie down several hallways, looking for the white cat. He opened all the closed doors for a second, peeked inside, and called, "Snowball," without any results.

Finally, Mandie asked, "Do you suppose he could have gone back to the kitchen, where the food is?"

"If someone let him out, they might have been carrying him, and he would have to go wherever they went," Jonathan replied. "However, let's check the kitchen."

When he pushed open the door to the kitchen, Mrs. Cook was there, cleaning up after her cooking. She looked at him and said, "Now, Mr. Jonathan, don't come begging. You had a right large meal tonight."

Jonathan laughed as he and Mandie went on into the kitchen. "No, ma'am, I'm not begging for food. We've lost that white cat and thought he might have come back here to beg for more food."

"I haven't seen that white cat in the last hour I've been in here,"

Mrs. Cook said. "And if he does come back here, I'll be sure to tie him up and send you word. Now, off with you. I've work to do."

"Thank you, Mrs. Cook," Mandie said as they stepped back out into the hallway.

"Let's continue our search," Jonathan said with a deep sigh.

Mandie smiled at him as they started on down the hallway and said, "I'm sorry, Jonathan, that you have such a big house my cat got lost in it." She laughed.

"Now, now," Jonathan replied, grinning. "Maybe we didn't close the door when we left the old library."

"I'm positive I did," Mandie replied. "I thought he would be safe in there until we came back. After all, you said the room was never used, so I thought no one would go in there."

"Oh, but they did, remember," Jonathan reminded her as they walked on. "Someone took the clippings. Therefore, someone has been in the room since I showed you and your friends the clippings earlier."

"You're right," Mandie agreed. "I'm just so disgusted with Snowball running off all the time, I'm not thinking right."

"But you don't know that he ran off," Jonathan said. "If you did in fact close the door, then someone had to open that door and let him out."

Jonathan had continued around the corridors until they were at the door to the glass room with the plants, and that door was standing open.

"Aha!" Jonathan exclaimed when he saw the open door. "We may have found that white cat. Remember when you came to visit before, he seemed to love this room with all the plants and kept going there?" He led the way into the room.

"Yes, that's right," Mandie agreed. She quickly walked around the dozens and dozens of tall plants, calling, "Snowball, Snowball, where are you?"

She suddenly heard a scuffling noise and started running in that direction across the room. She didn't see anyone, but there was Snowball sitting beneath one of the tall plants in a large pot, washing his face. He looked at his mistress and meowed.

"Oh, Snowball, how did you get in here?" Mandie exclaimed.

"Someone ran away," Jonathan said. "Didn't you hear that noise like someone walking on the cement?" He walked around the room, looking.

"Yes, but I instantly saw Snowball and figured I'd better grab him while I could. Which way did they go?"

"I don't know," Jonathan said. "I had the same idea as you, that we'd better catch the cat first."

"Oh well. As long as I caught him I suppose we'd better go back and let Celia and Joe know we found him," Mandie said, disappointed that someone had run away.

Jonathan agreed and led the way back to the old library. When he opened the door for Mandie, they were greeted by Joe and Celia excitedly waving papers in the air.

"We found more," Celia told them.

"And some interesting facts," Joe added.

"What is it?" Mandie quickly asked, setting Snowball down and coming to look at the papers they held.

"Wait!" Jonathan called to Mandie. Mandie turned to look back at him and he said with a big grin, "You didn't close the door. We may have to go on another cat hunt."

"Oh no!" Mandie replied, stooping to look for Snowball. He was curled up in a chair pushed up to the table. "Here he is."

"Thank goodness!" Jonathan said, firmly closing the door to the room. "Now, what did you find while we were gone? More romance?" He grinned at Joe and Celia as the two handed the papers to him.

Mandie came to read over his shoulder.

"Let's sit down. Some of this is startling indeed," Jonathan said, blowing out his breath as he sat at the table and spread out the papers.

Mandie pulled up a chair next to him and bent closer to see what he had.

"Oh my!" Jonathan exclaimed as he read. "This reporter evidently didn't like my father."

"Or my grandmother," Mandie added.

Celia and Joe pulled chairs up near theirs.

"Don't you think it's time we discussed these things and tried to come to some explanation?" Joe asked.

"Definitely," Mandie agreed. "I feel like asking my grandmother for an explanation."

Mandie wondered what would happen if Mrs. Taft and Mr. Guyer were confronted with their latest find. It would really be interesting.

# CHAPTER NINE

# SEARCHING

While the four young people were still inspecting the papers that Celia and Joe had found, there was a light knock on the door. They looked at each other and silently stacked the papers and quickly pushed them back into the envelope.

The knock sounded again. Jonathan rose, walked over and opened the door, and asked, "Yes?"

Monet was in the hallway. "All of you are wanted in the parlor immediately, the ladies said," she told him and then moved to look beyond Jonathan into the library.

"We will be right there, thank you," Jonathan replied, glancing back at his friends.

Mandie stood up and stepped in front of the envelope on the table. At the same time Snowball suddenly jumped up from the other side and stepped on the envelope, causing it to slide off.

Monet continued standing there in the hallway. Jonathan repeated his reply to her. "We will be along shortly." And he closed the door in Monet's face.

"Now, what will we do with this?" Mandie whispered, stooping to pick up the envelope. She handed it to Jonathan.

"Yes, what should we do with this?" Jonathan asked, looking at the large envelope.

"Monet probably saw it," Celia whispered, looking at the door.

"How did she know we were in here?" Joe asked.

"She has probably been watching us all night and is probably still outside the door," Jonathan said.

"Maybe we could hide the papers somewhere and take the empty envelope with us. If she knows we have the envelope, maybe she will think whatever we found in it is still inside," Mandie suggested.

"That's a good idea, but where could we hide the papers in here?" Joe asked.

The four turned around and surveyed the room.

"Remember that someone took the other clippings. Therefore, whoever it was may come back looking for more," Celia reminded the others.

"But if we take the empty envelope and my father sees it, he might recognize it," Jonathan told them, turning the envelope over.

"But it's just a plain envelope without any print on it whatsoever," Joe said.

"And I know where we could hide the papers," Mandie suddenly decided. "We could put them under the carpet." She smiled at her friends.

The other three looked at her and also smiled.

"Now, that is a good idea," Jonathan said, quickly withdrawing the papers from the envelope and looking around at the carpet.

"We could move that chair there and put them under the corner of the carpet and then place the chair back where it was," Joe suggested.

"Yes," they all agreed.

Joe moved the chair, Jonathan slipped the papers under the carpet, and then Joe replaced the chair.

The four stood back and smiled. Jonathan picked up the envelope.

"I don't believe anyone will find them there, but as soon as we go to the parlor and can get away, I think we'd better come back and move them to another place somewhere," Jonathan said.

"Yes, but where?" Mandie asked as everyone started for the door.

"We'll have to figure that out. In the meantime, I don't like the idea of carrying this envelope to the parlor," Jonathan said, opening the door and quickly looking out into the hallway. "She is gone," he added.

"Couldn't you just stick the envelope in the hall tree outside the parlor door?" Mandie asked as they all stepped out into the hallway. She carried Snowball.

"We can sit where we would be able to see the hall tree from inside the parlor," Celia told them.

"And if we see anyone stop at the hall tree, one of us can just have an excuse to step out into the hallway," Joe added.

"Yes, I think we have it all planned out now," Mandie agreed. "However, we do need to do some thinking about the papers Celia and Joe found." They started down the hallway.

"We can discuss it as soon as we are able to leave the parlor," Jonathan promised.

When they reached the parlor, Mandie, Celia, and Joe paused in the doorway while Jonathan went behind them and slipped the envelope into the base of the hall tree, where the umbrellas stood. Then he joined them as they all entered the room.

Mandie's mother, Elizabeth Shaw, spoke from across the room. "Amanda, Dr. Plumbley is getting ready to leave, and I thought you'd want to say good-bye."

Dr. Plumbley stood up as Mandie hurried over to him. "But I'll catch up with you again before you leave New York, Miss Amanda," he said, and smiling, added, "the good Lord willing and the creek don't rise."

Mandie laughed and said, "I don't believe there is a creek between here and your house, Dr. Plumbley."

Dr. Woodard, John Shaw, and Lindall Guyer rose from their chairs.

"I'll just go out for a breath of fresh air with you, Dr. Plumbley," Dr. Woodard said.

"Yes," John Shaw said.

"My idea, too," Lindall Guyer added.

"Dr. Plumbley, we'll probably be gone shopping tomorrow," Mandie said, glancing at her mother. She held on to Snowball, who was trying to get down.

"Yes, Amanda. However, we won't be leaving for home until Monday," Elizabeth Shaw said.

"I'll see you sometime before then," Dr. Plumbley promised.

"Don't forget," Mandie said as the men left the parlor.

Then Jane Hamilton said, "Y'all sit down for a few minutes now. We've got to plan our day for tomorrow."

As the young people found seats near the ladies, Elizabeth Shaw added, "Yes, we need some kind of schedule so we don't all go running in different directions tomorrow."

"Elizabeth, don't count me in on your shopping expedition tomorrow. I have done all the shopping I plan to," Mrs. Taft said.

"But, Mother, if you don't go with us, you'll be left here alone for at least the morning, and I had thought we could dine out somewhere nice for the noonday meal tomorrow," Elizabeth replied.

"You just don't worry about me. I may have plans of my own," Mrs. Taft told her.

The young people quickly glanced at her and then at each other and smiled.

"That's fine then, Mother," Elizabeth said. Turning to Mandie, she said, "Now, Amanda, we have all agreed that we should leave as soon as we finish breakfast tomorrow, and by doing that we should have our shopping finished by noon and have the rest of the day free."

"And it's getting late, so, Celia, you should be getting to bed soon," Jane Hamilton told her daughter.

"You too, Amanda," Elizabeth added.

"Yes, ma'am," both girls answered.

"And, Joe, your father would like for you to go on an errand with him tomorrow morning while we shop," Mrs. Woodard said from across the room.

"Yes, ma'am," Joe replied. "I'm glad I don't have to go shopping again."

"But the little errand with your father may include a little shopping," Mrs. Woodard said. "Just be ready to leave with him immediately after breakfast."

"All right, yes, ma'am," Joe agreed with a frown.

Mandie looked at him with a smile. "You just can't get out of shopping here in this city," she said.

Jonathan cleared his throat loudly and grinned as he said, "Well now, I don't believe I was included in all that shopping tomorrow."

"Jonathan, your father will tell you, I know, but he said he would like for you to join Joe and Dr. Woodard tomorrow since he will be tied up with business appointments," Mrs. Woodard said.

"Yes, ma'am," Jonathan said, grinning at Joe. "I'll be glad to get out of that shopping spree with the ladies."

Mandie, curious about why Mrs. Taft was not going with them and about what she had planned, asked, "Grandmother, do you not want to go shopping with us? You always seem to be real good at finding what we want."

Mrs. Taft smiled at her and said, "No, Amanda, there is nothing else I need to buy."

Mandie smiled back and couldn't think of an answer.

"Amanda, I think you should begin getting ready to retire for the night," Elizabeth said.

"And you, too, Celia," Jane Hamilton added.

The girls stood up and said, "Yes, ma'am."

Joe also rose. "I think I'll retire, too, if you'll just tell Dad I'll see him at breakfast."

"All right, son," Mrs. Woodard agreed.

Then Jonathan finally stood up to join his friends. "Well, since everyone seems to be retiring for the night, I suppose I should, too. I will see everyone at breakfast."

Good-nights were said, and the four young people hurriedly left the parlor. Jonathan quickly snatched the envelope from the hall tree and led the way down the corridor. He glanced at the others, put his finger to his lips, and said, "Shhh! No talking in the halls. You know why."

Everyone nodded. Mandie understood why. There was a possibility someone might be nearby and hear their conversation. And she was thinking there must have been an eavesdropper who had heard them discussing the newspaper clippings Jonathan had found and which had mysteriously disappeared.

When they reached the door to the library, Jonathan quietly pushed it open and everyone went in. He closed the door behind them and clicked the inside latch so no one could open it from the outside.

Mandie quickly put Snowball down and said, "The papers," as she started toward the corner of the carpet.

Joe moved the chair and Jonathan turned back the corner of the carpet.

"Still there!" Mandie said with a big smile as Jonathan picked up the papers and kicked the carpet back in place.

"Yes, but we weren't really gone long enough to give the thief a chance to do much searching this time," Jonathan replied. He took the papers over to the table, and everyone gathered around as he spread them out.

"There is no date on this clipping, so we don't know whether this episode happened before or after the other one you found before we got here, Jonathan," Mandie told him.

Jonathan laughed and said, "I would think this one was written after the other one."

"I agree," Joe said. "Their behavior in this one was so bad out in the public like that, how could they ever be seen together again?"

"Too bad this reporter was not sitting near enough to hear what they were arguing about," Celia remarked.

"It must have been terribly embarrassing to your father, Jonathan, when my grandmother jumped up from the table and spilled coffee all over him," Mandie said with a deep frown as she reread the account of her grandmother's sudden departure from the table where she had been sitting with Mr. Guyer.

Jonathan grinned and said, "Well, I think he got even with her by grabbing the frill on her dress to keep her from leaving and then the lace ripping off." He laughed loudly.

"One of these days I think I'll tell my grandmother that I know about her public display of anger," Mandie said. "And all the time she has been telling me I should act like a young lady. I wonder what she would say if I created a scene like that."

"Mandie, you wouldn't!" Celia exclaimed.

Jonathan grinned and said, "Just wait until you and I are old enough to do the town. Then we can put on our own little show and be sure that your grandmother and my father know about it."

"And I will say I never heard of a girl named Mandie Shaw," Joe said sternly.

Mandie laughed and said, "By the time we are that old, we will probably have forgotten about this."

Celia looked at the other papers and said, "These other columns don't have any dates on them, either. I wonder if their friendship ended after that scene in the restaurant."

"Since they are not complete columns, we can't tell whether the same writer wrote these others or not," Jonathan said. "However, if it was the same man, I would say these others were written before that nasty one. He sounded like he was fed up with them for good."

"Jonathan, I was just thinking. Could it have been your father who took the other clippings you had found? Do you think he knows about all these and that they are hidden away in here?" Mandie asked.

"Yes, I would imagine he knows about all these clippings because he would be the most likely person to have hidden them here in the first place," Jonathan replied. "However, I wouldn't think he was the person who took the ones I found without taking these, too."

"Why don't we search a little bit more before we have to go to bed," Mandie suggested. "Tomorrow we will be out shopping and won't have a chance to do much."

"Maybe we could do one more section of the shelves if we all work together," Jonathan replied, pushing back his chair to stand up.

"What are you going to do with these?" Celia asked.

Jonathan reached back to gather up the papers. "Let's just put them back under the carpet for the time being." He stuffed them into the envelope.

"Here, I'll help you," Joe said, going to move the chair again and raising the corner of the carpet.

After Jonathan placed the envelope under the carpet, he turned back to the shelves. "Joe, you and I could do the top shelves and let the girls search the lower ones," he said.

"We had better work fast before someone finds out we didn't go straight to our rooms for the night," Celia reminded them as she and Mandie began on the bottom shelf.

The top shelves in that section were not stacked double like most of the others, so Jonathan and Joe quickly searched their way down and caught up with the girls.

"We only have one more shelf to go," Mandie remarked, indicating the shelf directly above the one she was searching.

Jonathan began on that shelf. Suddenly he stopped and held up an envelope he had found there. "This looks like the envelope I first found," he said, excitedly stepping down from the ladder to look inside the envelope. "It is."

The others gathered around to look as he held up the clippings from the envelope.

"That is odd, that someone would take the clippings and then bring them back and put them in a different place," Joe said, frowning.

"But we don't know that they ever took them out of here," Mandie reminded him. "Whoever it was might have just put them in a different place to confuse us."

"Anyhow, whoever it was must have read them," Jonathan said, turning the clippings over. "They are not in the same order I had put them in the envelope."

"Now that we have finished that section of shelves, I suggest that we quit for the night," Celia said.

Mandie looked at her and smiled. "You are right. We can't stay up all night searching this library."

"It is late," Jonathan agreed, hastily putting the clippings back into the envelope. "I suppose we should put this envelope with the other one under the carpet. What do you think?" He looked at the other three.

"Good idea," Joe agreed, going to move the chair one more time.

"Yes, that's the best place in here to hide something," Mandie said. "But, Jonathan, you could take all of it to your room."

"Oh no," Jonathan disagreed. "With maids running in and out of all the rooms all the time, the envelopes would be safer under the carpet." He stooped to place the envelope next to the other one. Then he pushed the carpet back into place.

Mandie reached for Snowball, who had curled up in a chair and gone to sleep. "As soon as we all get finished with errands tomorrow, do y'all want to come back in here and finish the other shelves?"

"Definitely," Jonathan agreed.

"We don't know who will get back to the house first," Joe said. "However, we could all check in here now and then to see if anyone else has come back."

"Yes, and you and Jonathan will probably be back first. I think my mother is planning for us to all eat somewhere downtown at noon tomorrow, so that will delay us," Mandie said.

"But we are supposed to have the afternoon free, according to your mother and my mother, Mandie," Celia reminded her.

Jonathan stepped over to the door and said, "Now, we need to be absolutely silent going down the hallway so if anyone is around they won't hear us."

The others agreed, and he silently opened the door. Jonathan motioned to the others to follow him as he showed them the way to their rooms. Once there, he went on down the hallway to his own room.

Once in their rooms, Mandie and Celia quickly got ready for bed. Snowball curled up at the foot of the bed and went back to sleep.

Mandie wanted to talk, but Celia wanted to go to sleep.

"I'm sorry, Mandie, but I am sleepy," Celia said with a loud yawn as she turned over on her side of the big bed. "Good night."

"Good night, Celia," Mandie replied.

Although it was late, Mandie was too excited to go to sleep right away. She had to rethink the whole story of the information they had found about her grandmother and Jonathan's father.

She wondered if her grandmother's parents were strict with her and whether they had ever known about the incident in the restaurant that the reporter had written about. Someday she was going to ask some questions in a roundabout way to see what she could find out. She didn't even know where her grandmother and her parents were living at the time the columns were written. However, if they lived in New York, the parents were bound to have known about the columns in the newspapers. What had they done about the incident in the café? Did they pack up and leave town in order to get her grandmother away from the gossip?

"Hmm," Mandie whispered to herself. Her grandmother had never mentioned living in New York.

There were lots of things she intended finding out.

# CHAPTER TEN

# *MORE INFORMATION*

The next morning the four young people gathered at the top of the main staircase to discuss plans before going down to breakfast. They sat on the chairs clustered around a small table there. Leila, the young maid, had already taken Snowball down to the kitchen for his breakfast.

"I wish somebody knew when we'll all get back today," Mandie complained.

"I have no idea where my father will be taking Jonathan and me," Joe said. "Therefore, I don't know when we'll return."

"And shopping with my mother could take all day," Celia added.

Mandie quickly looked at Celia and said, "I may know how to cut our shopping journey short. You and I can both keep telling our mothers we really don't want to buy anything else, or when they find something for us we could just say, 'That's fine.' Therefore, we won't have to spend time looking at everything in the stores."

"That might work," Celia agreed. "However, my mother may pick out something or other for me that I absolutely don't want, and if I say it's fine she'll buy it and I'll have to wear it."

"If you didn't like something, you could just take it on to school with you and hang it up and never wear it," Mandie told her.

"Oh, what a problem it is to be a girl," Jonathan teased.

A sudden rushing noise came from down the hallway. The four stood up to look. Angelina, Jens's ten-year-old daughter, came rushing toward them with Jonathan's dog, Whitey, on a leash. The dog was pulling her along as the cat chased the dog.

"Angelina!" Jonathan exclaimed, quickly stepping into her pathway and snatching the leash out of her hand. "Just what are you doing with Whitey up here?"

Mandie quickly stooped and picked up Snowball, whose fur was standing up as he growled at the dog. "Hush, Snowball, hush," she told him.

Angelina, pushing back her long dark curly hair, stood with her feet spread as she confronted Jonathan. "I am allowed to play with Whitey," she said in an angry voice.

"Not up here on this floor," Jonathan told her firmly, holding on to the white dog as he tried to get loose.

"I was going downstairs with him, and that white cat chased us," Angelina replied with a deep frown as she looked at Snowball.

"It doesn't matter about the cat. You are not supposed to be up here on this floor at any time, and neither is Whitey," Jonathan replied. "It was agreed when my father gave your father the apartment in the building next door that you were not to roam around in this house, and you know that."

Angelina pouted and wouldn't look at him.

"Where did you find Whitey?" Mandie asked her, trying to calm her cat. "And where did you find Snowball?"

Instead of replying to any more questions, Angelina suddenly turned and ran down the staircase without even looking back.

"I have to take Whitey back outside to the garden, and I'll have to hurry," Jonathan told his friends as he started for the stairs.

"And I have to take Snowball back to the kitchen," Mandie said, following.

As Joe and Celia came behind them, they met up with Leila, who was rushing up the staircase.

"Oh, Master Jonathan, I've been chasing that girl trying to get that dog. Let me have him. I'll put him outside," Leila told Jonathan, reaching for the leash.

"Thank you, Leila," Jonathan replied, handing over the end

of the leash. "That girl is not supposed to be in this house without permission."

"She was not seen, Master Jonathan," Leila told him as she went ahead down the stairs with the dog. "We watch to keep her out, but this time no one saw her."

"Leila, Snowball was running loose, too, chasing after Angelina and the dog. She must have let him out of the kitchen, where he was supposed to be eating breakfast," Mandie said as they all continued down the huge staircase.

"Yes, must have. I take cat, too," Leila offered as she stopped and turned back.

"Thank you, but I'd better take him myself. He's in a scratching mood right now," Mandie replied. "As soon as you get that dog out of his sight, he will calm down."

"Yes, miss, I hurry," Leila replied and rushed on down and disappeared in the corridor to the right.

"Let's go left here to the kitchen in order to avoid Whitey," Jonathan told Mandie, leading the way.

When they got to the kitchen with the cat, Mrs. Cook was surprised to see them. "Well, I never saw you take that cat. Last thing I knew he was eating breakfast over there," she said.

Jonathan explained about Angelina. "So she probably slipped in here and untied Snowball's leash," he said.

Mrs. Cook stepped over to the back door and flipped the latch. "I lock the door to outside this time," she said.

Mandie put the cat down at his plate, and he began eating. She firmly tied his leash to the handle of the cabinet door. "I tied him up, Mrs. Cook," she said.

"Yes, now he will stay and eat," Mrs. Cook agreed.

"We'd better hurry or we'll be late for breakfast," Jonathan said, turning to leave the kitchen.

"Yes, time to go to the dining room and eat," Mrs. Cook told him.

As he led the way out into the hall, Mandie saw the adults coming from the other direction toward the dining room door. "Oh, thank goodness we are not late," she whispered to her friends.

"Yes, we could have delayed everyone's plans for the day," Joe said, grinning at her.

"And my grandmother is not going with us, so it would be my mother who would scold us for being late," Mandie whispered as the young people fell in behind the adults and entered the dining room.

Everyone seemed to be in a hurry, and the meal was quickly consumed.

"Jens will drive me in the motorcar to my office, and I believe the rest of you will fit into the carriage," Lindall Guyer said, laying his napkin by his plate.

"Yes, that would be fine if Hodson would just drop me and the boys off at Dr. Plumbley's office and bring us back when we are finished with our errands," Dr. Woodard said.

Everyone rose from the table as John Shaw said, "Don't forget I'm going with you, Dr. Woodard."

"Oh yes, of course," Dr. Woodard replied.

Elizabeth turned to her mother and asked, "Are you sure you don't want to go with us, Mother?"

"No, Elizabeth, I told you I do not need to do any shopping. I'll be fine right here while y'all are out," Mrs. Taft replied.

As they all went their way and Hodson ended up taking them to the shopping district, Mandie noticed they were going into the same store they had been in with her grandmother. As she and Celia followed the ladies out of the carriage, she said under her breath, "We've already been through this store."

"I know," Celia whispered back.

This time, however, the girls found the ladies leading them into a different part of the huge store. They went to the ladies' clothing department.

Mandie daydreamed about searching for the clippings as she and Celia followed their mothers and Mrs. Woodard through every section of the place. She was also wondering what exactly her grandmother was doing. She didn't believe she would just sit around the house while they were gone. Suddenly she leaned over to Celia to whisper, "I hope Angelina doesn't bring that dog back into the house while we are gone. My grandmother will be awfully upset if he gets near her."

"Maybe Leila or one of the other servants will be sure he stays outside," Celia replied.

After looking at merchandise in every department and buying

a few things, the ladies finally announced it was time for the noon-day meal and that immediately after that they would return to the Guyers' home.

"So now we have to decide where to dine," Elizabeth told the girls after they'd given the clerk at the desk their orders for the merchandise, which would be shipped to their homes.

Elizabeth and Jane discussed places to eat. They were familiar with New York and its restaurants and stores. Mrs. Woodard remarked that it was up to them to decide, because she wouldn't know where to go.

Mandie wished they would just go on somewhere, anywhere, and eat. They were wasting time, and she was in a hurry to get back to Jonathan's house.

When the decision was finally made, they had to get Hodson and go in the carriage because it was not near enough to walk. That took time in the traffic, and when they got there Mandie decided it must be an awfully expensive restaurant. Her mother ordered for her after the waiter recited the day's menu in French. And when the food came, she couldn't tell exactly what she was eating.

About an hour later they were finally on their way back to the Guyers' house.

As they traveled through the heavy traffic, Mandie told Celia, "I hope Jonathan and Joe are back by the time we get there."

"I imagine they will try to hurry back, because they are interested in helping us look for more," Celia whispered.

Mandie glanced at her mother, Mrs. Woodard, and Jane and decided they were not listening to the girls' conversation. "I hope we find more," she whispered back.

As soon as they arrived at the Guyers' house, all three ladies decided they would go directly to their rooms and rest for a while since none of the men were back. As they started toward the staircase, Elizabeth looked back at Mandie and Celia, who had sat down in the parlor. "Amanda, you should go relax a spell before teatime."

"But I'm not tired, Mother," Mandie objected.

"You too, Celia," Jane Hamilton said.

"I'll just relax here in the parlor for a while," Celia answered.

Mandie waited for a few minutes to give the ladies time to get out of the hallway and to their rooms, and then she said, "I'll go get Snowball from my room, and then let's go to the old library." She quickly stood up.

"I'll go with you," Celia replied as she rose.

Mandie found Snowball sitting up in the middle of Mandie's bed, washing his face. She scooped him up in her arms, and he stuck his tongue out to lick her face.

"Snowball, stop that," Mandie protested.

"He probably smells the food that you ate in the restaurant on your mouth," Celia told her.

"And I imagine he has been asleep all the time we've been gone and has not had anything to eat. I suppose I'd better take him by the kitchen and find out," Mandie replied.

"Yes, I would do that," Celia agreed.

When Mandie pushed open the kitchen door, there was no one there, but she immediately saw a bowl of food for Snowball by the cabinet. She set him down, and he raced for the food as she tied his leash to the cabinet door handle.

"I'll leave him here so he can eat and come back after him in a little while," Mandie said as she stood up.

"Do you think you can find the way to that library?" Celia asked as they left the kitchen and stepped into the long corridor.

"Let's see, now. I believe we go left here and then go right at the first cross hall," Mandie said as they walked down the hallway.

"If we had gone straight to the library from the parlor, I could have found it, but I'm not sure which way from here," Celia said.

The girls wandered up and down the hallways, but since all the doors along the way looked alike, they couldn't decide which one to try.

Mandie suddenly paused and said, "Here, this looks like the right door." She turned the doorknob and pushed the door open slightly. Glancing inside, she saw it was a sitting room and was about to close the door when she faintly heard voices from a connecting room behind it. Putting her finger to her lips, she looked at Celia and said, "Shhh!"

They stood there looking at each other as Mandie tried to figure out what the conversation inside was about and who was in there.

Then her eyes popped wide open at Celia as she heard her grand-mother saying, "I forgave you a long time ago, because after a while it didn't matter anymore."

Both girls held their breath as Mandie waited and listened for a reply.

"But it did matter a lot to me and still does," Lindall Guyer replied.

Mandie was afraid they would hear her heart beating, she was so excited.

"You know Sarabeth died about eight years ago, I suppose," Mrs. Taft said.

"No, I did not hear about that. What happened?" Mr. Guyer asked.

"She was thrown from a horse and died instantly," Mrs. Taft replied.

"How horrible!" Mr. Guyer exclaimed.

"I think I'd better get up to my room now and freshen up. The others should return soon, and it'll be time for tea," Mrs. Taft said.

"Yes," Mr. Guyer replied.

The two girls quickly darted down the hallway and tried several doors before they found one that was unlocked. They jumped inside the room and closed the door, leaving a slight crack so they could hear.

They were about to decide the adults had gone the other way when Mandie finally heard her grandmother talking as she passed the door behind which they were hiding. But the conversation was too low for Mandie to understand what was being said. She listened until there was no more sound and then quietly opened the door and looked up and down the hallway. There was no one in sight.

"We can go now," Mandie whispered to Celia, stepping outside.

"Now what do we do?" Celia asked.

"I don't want to go to the parlor, because we can't talk in there," Mandie replied. "Or the old library, either."

"Why don't we sit at the top of the staircase and wait for Joe and Jonathan to come back?" Celia asked.

"That's a good idea," Mandie agreed. "Now, if we can find the right staircase."

They found the way up without any trouble and sat down in the chairs they had occupied that morning.

"Could you hear everything they were saying?" Mandie asked.

"Yes, I think so," Celia replied. "Your grandmother has long ago forgiven Mr. Guyer for something."

"Yes, something," Mandie agreed. "I wonder what that something was."

"It could be that incident in the restaurant, don't you think?" Celia asked.

"Yes, it could be," Mandie agreed. "But we still don't know what they were arguing about in that restaurant."

"They probably had lots of ups and downs if they saw each other over a long period of time," Celia said.

"You're right about that. My grandmother is not the easiest person in the world to get along with," Mandie said. "But who was Sarabeth, the person who was thrown from a horse?"

There was the sound of someone walking below. Mandie stood up to look down the staircase. She turned back to Celia. "It's Joe and Jonathan. They're back."

When the boys got to the top of the stairs, Mandie excitedly told them, "You will never guess what we happened on to."

Joe looked at her and grinned as he said, "I have to go to my room first and put these packages away."

"So do I," Jonathan added. "But I'll be right back. Wait for me."

Both boys were carrying an armful of packages.

"So y'all did go shopping, too," Mandie remarked as the two went on down the hallway.

"Yes," they both replied.

They were back so fast Mandie knew they must have just dumped their packages into their rooms and hurried back to find out the news. They sat down on chairs nearby and waited.

"You didn't find more clippings, did you?" Jonathan asked.

"No, we haven't been in the library yet," Mandie replied with a big smile. "We've been eavesdropping."

"Eavesdropping?" both boys exclaimed.

"Yes, and here is what we heard," Mandie said, and she related the conversation they had overheard between Mr. Guyer and Mrs. Taft.

Both boys listened in surprise.

"Are you sure you didn't make this up?" Jonathan asked teasingly.

"It sounds about like that, sure enough," Joe added.

"Oh, stop teasing," Mandie told them. "Of course I didn't make it up. I heard it with my own two ears."

"Yes, we really heard it," Celia confirmed.

"Well then, if we could only find out who Sarabeth was, we might have a clue about what they were discussing," Jonathan said.

"She must have been someone your grandmother had kept in touch with for her to know what happened to her," Joe decided.

"And it was someone my father had not stayed in touch with," Jonathan added.

"I've been wondering if Sarabeth might have been the cause of that argument in the restaurant," Celia said.

"Do you mean you think that argument was over another woman?" Jonathan asked.

"Another woman would have been a good excuse for an argument," Celia replied.

"I see what you mean," Mandie said thoughtfully.

"Where is my father? I didn't see him when we came in," Jonathan asked.

"My grandmother was going to her room, so maybe your father went to his," Mandie told him. Then, looking at Celia, she added, "Maybe we had better go to ours and freshen up. It's about time for tea."

Celia stood up and said, "Yes, we should."

Mandie started to follow her but stopped and said, "I almost forgot. I need to go get Snowball from the kitchen and put him in our room."

"I'll go with you," Jonathan said, rising from the chair.

"And I will, too," Joe told her.

"Since I don't know exactly where we are in relation to our rooms, I'll have to go with y'all," Celia told them.

Mrs. Cook was in the kitchen, and she told them, "Almost time for tea."

"Thank you, Mrs. Cook. We'll just take that white cat out of your way," Jonathan replied.

Mandie looked at the bowl, which was now empty. "Snowball must have been awfully hungry," she said, untying his leash from the door handle.

"Yes, he eats good," Mrs. Cook agreed.

As they walked toward their rooms they discussed the conversation, but no one could decide exactly how it would fit in to what they knew already about Mrs. Taft and Mr. Guyer.

"As soon as tea is finished, are we going back to the old library to search some more?" Mandie asked Jonathan.

"Of course," Jonathan agreed. "The minute we can escape from the adults."

They all laughed as they went on down the hallway.

# CHAPTER ELEVEN

# *MORE MYSTERY*

When everyone gathered in the parlor for tea that afternoon, Mandie and her friends held whispered conversations now and then as they watched Mrs. Taft and Mr. Guyer.

"They are ignoring each other," Mandie whispered behind her hand.

"With her sitting on one side of the room and him on the other, they act as though they don't even know each other," Jonathan said.

"At least they aren't arguing like they were in that newspaper clipping," Celia added.

"They're too old for that now," Joe said.

When they had almost finished their tea and sweet rolls, Lindall Guyer stood up and said, "Please excuse me for a few minutes. I'll be right back." He looked across the room and smiled at Mrs. Taft.

Dr. Woodard also rose and said, "If you're going outside for a breath of fresh air, I'll join you."

Mr. Guyer seemed flustered as he replied, "Ah, no, not outside. Just a little errand I have to do. I'll return shortly. Then we can go outside for that air."

Dr. Woodard sat back down as he said, "Fine."

Mr. Guyer quickly left the room. To Mandie's surprise, Jonathan hurried after him.

"Jonathan," she whispered.

Jonathan turned to look back, shook his head, and said, "Right back." Then he disappeared into the hallway.

Mandie glanced around the room. The adults seemed deep in their own conversation. She whispered to Joe and Celia, "I wonder why Jonathan followed his father in such a big hurry."

"Maybe it was prearranged for them to meet and talk about something they didn't want to discuss in front of the rest of us," Joe suggested.

"Both of them said they would be right back," Celia added.

Mandie grew impatient for Jonathan to return after a few minutes. She debated going out into the hallway herself. Jonathan must know something he had not discussed with her and her friends.

"I could go get Snowball and look around on the way," Mandie told Joe and Celia.

"No, Mandie," Joe quickly replied. "That would be snooping into other people's business."

"Oh shucks!" she replied.

Before Mandie could think up an excuse to go out into the hallway, Jonathan returned, grinning as he came to sit by her and her friends.

"Guess what?" he said, still grinning. "My father went into the old library and locked the door."

"He did?" Joe said.

"But why?" Mandie asked, frowning at Jonathan.

"Why? What do you mean, why?" Jonathan asked her. "Evidently he didn't want anyone following him into the library. And you all should know, as well as I do, the reason he went in there. He's going after the clippings."

"Of course!" Mandie exclaimed. "You had said you thought he was the one who put the clippings in there in the first place."

"Yes, and he will know they have been moved if he remembers where he put them, which must have been years ago," Jonathan replied.

"Do you think he'll find any of them?" Joe asked.

"Probably not, because we hid them under the carpet," Jonathan replied.

As the four stayed huddled in their own group, they continued talking in whispers and occasionally glanced at the adults. The adults did not seem to notice.

"What do you suppose he wanted to do with them?" Mandie asked.

"Perhaps he intended showing them to your grandmother," Jonathan said with a grin.

"I wonder what my grandmother would have said to him," Mandie said, also grinning.

To the surprise of the young people, Lindall Guyer returned to the parlor after a few minutes, carrying a large envelope, which he placed on a table by his chair. Then he picked up on the conversation going on between the other men.

"Well!" Mandie exclaimed.

"Looks like he might have found at least some of the clippings," Jonathan whispered to the young people.

"I wonder what he is going to do with them," Mandie leaned forward to whisper to her friends.

"We'll have to watch and find out," Jonathan said.

Dr. Woodard stood up and, looking around at the men, said, "I believe it's time for some fresh air now." He looked directly at Mr. Guyer.

"Yes," John Shaw agreed.

Mr. Guyer rose and led the way through the vestibule out the front door. The women didn't seem to notice that the men were leaving but continued with their conversation.

"Look!" Mandie quickly whispered to her friends.

Mrs. Taft had risen and went over to sit in the chair vacated by Mr. Guyer. She stared at the envelope on the table for a minute.

The group held their breath, waiting to see Mrs. Taft pick up the envelope and perhaps open it. However, they were disappointed when Mrs. Taft rose and went back to her chair.

"Nosy," Jonathan said.

"Jonathan, can you tell if that is one of the envelopes we found?" Mandie asked.

"It looks like the others. However, they are all just plain envelopes, nothing unusual about them, and if you remember, the envelopes we found were alike," he replied.

The men came back into the parlor then and sat down. Mr. Guyer looked around the room at the adults and asked, "What do you say we all go out on the town tonight?" And then turning to Jonathan he asked, "Son, do you think you could entertain your guests while we are gone? You are all too young to go with us."

The four young people looked at each other and grinned. Jonathan smiled at his father and replied, "Yes, sir, we can find things to do here, that is, provided we have a big dinner of our own."

"All you have to do is tell Mrs. Cook what you'd like," Mr. Guyer replied.

"And where are you planning on taking us?" Jane Hamilton asked.

"Well now, I thought we'd start with the New York Dinner House and then move on to the Broadway Club for coffee." He looked directly at Mrs. Taft.

Mrs. Taft seemed shocked but didn't say a word. She glanced at the other adults, who were all nodding in agreement.

"Broadway Club? That's the place in the clipping!" Mandie excitedly whispered to her friends.

Jonathan nodded and grinned.

"Oh, I do believe they've kissed and made up," Celia whispered.

"I'm not sure about that," Joe said. "Mrs. Taft hasn't said a word about their plans for tonight."

"Oh, that would be a wonderful night," Jane Hamilton said.

"Yes, I would enjoy that," Elizabeth Shaw added. Then, looking at her mother, she asked, "What do you think, Mother? Sounds like an entertaining evening, doesn't it?"

Mrs. Taft seemed flustered and glanced at the others as she said, "Whatever y'all decide will be fine with me." She did not look at Mr. Guyer, who was watching her closely and then grinned at her reply.

"I wish we could go," Mandie quickly whispered to her friends.

"Sorry, you are underage," Jonathan teased.

"At least we'll have an opportunity to continue searching the old library," Celia reminded them.

"I suppose I should go to our room and decide what I will wear tonight so I'll be ready on time," Mrs. Woodard said, rising.

Elizabeth and Jane both agreed as they joined her. Mrs. Taft finally stood up and asked, without looking at anyone in particular, "And what time are we expected back here in the parlor to leave?"

Everyone stopped talking and looked at Mr. Guyer, who said, "How about six, if that's not too early?" He looked at the ladies.

They all agreed they would be ready and waiting in the parlor at six o'clock, then left the room. The young people watched Mr. Guyer, hoping he would leave the envelope on the table. He got to the door to the hallway and then hurried back to pick it up.

"Oh shucks!" Mandie exclaimed as soon as he was out of hearing.

"Yes, I was hoping to get my hands on that envelope to see what's inside," Jonathan said. "But I suppose we should go to see Mrs. Cook now and order our menu for dinner."

"And then continue the search?" Mandie quickly asked as the four started out of the parlor.

"Of course," Jonathan replied. "We'll have enough time alone, with them all gone, that maybe we can finish and find something somewhere."

Jonathan led the way down corridors to the kitchen, where they found Mrs. Cook tying on a clean apron.

"And now, Master Jonathan, it's too early to come begging," she told him with a smile. "Nothing is finished yet."

"That's what we wanted to talk to you about. You see, my father is taking all the old people out, and it's just us kids left here for supper tonight," Jonathan began with a serious face. "And we'd like to save you the trouble of cooking a great big dinner tonight, because all we want is chocolate cake." He looked at his friends and grinned.

"Jonathan!" Mandie said, with Joe and Celia echoing her.

"You shall not have chocolate cake, Master Jonathan, unless you eat decent food first," Mrs. Cook told him, frowning.

"Like what?" Jonathan asked. "What would you suggest?" Turning to his friends, he asked, "Anyone got any ideas other than chocolate cake?"

"How about a nice big baked potato with lots of butter?" Celia asked.

"And some green peas with lots of salt and pepper," Joe added.

"And a piece of meat of some kind, ham or whatever," Mandie said.

"That makes a right nice order, it does," Mrs. Cook agreed. "So we will be having baked potatoes, green peas, and a nice juicy ham. Will that be satisfactory?" She looked at Jonathan.

"Yes, ma'am, that sounds just right, provided we have chocolate cake, too," Jonathan replied, grinning.

"It will be done, then," Mrs. Cook said. "Now skiddoo. Mrs. Yodkin will announce dinner when it is ready." She fanned her large white apron at them.

Jonathan bowed slightly and with a serious expression said, "And we do thank you, Mrs. Cook."

Everyone burst into laughter, including Mrs. Cook, who immediately pushed the door closed in their faces.

"Jonathan, I didn't realize you were such an actor," Mandie told him.

"I like to tease Mrs. Cook. She took care of me when I was a baby," Jonathan explained as they started down the hallway. "You see, my mother died when I was a baby, and my father just turned me over to Mrs. Cook to raise. Then when I got too big for her to handle, she took over the cooking."

"That is very interesting," Celia said.

"I can tell she loves you, Jonathan," Mandie told him as they walked on. "She is not old enough to have been working here when your father was young and taking my grandmother out, is she?"

"No, she came with my mother when my father married her. Mrs. Cook had worked for my mother's family a long time," Jonathan explained.

"Oh, I wish I could see my grandmother when they go in that restaurant," Mandie said.

"I'd like to know what their argument there was about," Celia said.

When they got to the door of the old library, Jonathan stepped forward to open the door. It wouldn't budge. "It's locked," he said in surprise.

"Your father must have locked it," Joe said to Jonathan.

"Now what do we do?" Mandie asked in disappointment.

"I know another way to get into this old library," Jonathan said. "Come on." He quickly led the way down the corridor and then opened a door on the left and went inside. The others followed.

"This must be a storage room," Mandie remarked, looking around at stacks of boxes.

"Yes, it is," Jonathan agreed, walking across the room and opening a door on the other side. "This way."

He led them through several other rooms that seemed to be all connected. Finally, he opened a door, pushed a sliding panel aside, and there was the old library.

"Here we are," he announced, leading the way into the library. Then he stopped in surprise. The others gathered around him to look. There was Angelina sitting on the floor with clippings scattered all over the rug. "Angelina! What are you doing in here?"

The girl slowly got to her feet and didn't take her eyes off Jonathan.

"I asked you a question, Angelina," Jonathan said. "What are you doing in here, and where did you get all those papers?"

"You got them out of the shelves, and I wanted to see what you had found," Angelina told him, never taking her eyes off his face.

"How do you know we got them out of the shelves?" Jonathan demanded.

"I look through that door and see you all the time," Angelina said. "You look and look and find papers, so I look for papers and find papers, too."

"So you have been watching us all the time," Jonathan said.

"I didn't hurt anything. I just looked," Angelina replied.

"What are you hiding behind you?" Jonathan asked as she continued holding her hands behind her.

Angelina spread out her hands and said, "Nothing. Everything is right there on the floor."

"You are not supposed to be in here. Now get home immediately and don't let me catch you in this house again or I'll tell your father."

Angelina didn't say another word. She turned and ran through the door by which they had entered. Jonathan quickly closed the door behind her and slid the bolt on it.

As everyone started to stoop and get the clippings off the floor, Mandie suddenly noticed something hanging on the wall between two sections of bookshelves. She rushed over to inspect it. "Look!" she told the others.

"I wonder where that came from. It wasn't in here before," Jonathan said, going over to where Mandie stood.

What looked like a large painting or photograph was entirely covered with a thick, rough cloth cover. The young people quickly tried to find an opening in the cover, but it was stitched tightly around the edges. There was no way to open it without tearing the cover off.

"I don't know what this is, but my father must have put it in here. I don't dare rip the cover," Jonathan said, finally standing back to look.

"Do you have any ideas as to what it is?" Mandie asked.

"I believe it is a picture, but of what I have no idea," Jonathan replied, frowning as he stood there looking.

"Your father probably put it in here for safekeeping and locked the door to keep everyone out," Joe said.

"I can't imagine why he would have a picture covered like that and locked up in this room," Jonathan said, frowning as he walked around the room.

"I have an idea," Mandie said. "Isn't your father still doing secret work for the United States government? Maybe it is connected with something that's secret."

Jonathan looked at her, thought for a moment, and said, "Yes, he's still doing secret work, but I've never known any secret work to be connected with something like a picture."

"While we think about that, why don't we go through these clippings that Angelina had and see if there are any that we haven't seen?" Celia asked, stooping to look at the papers on the floor.

"Let's do," Joe agreed. "We'll have to let someone know where we are when it gets to be time for supper, won't we, Jonathan?"

"We can keep up with the time and go back to the parlor when it gets close to suppertime," Jonathan replied. He sat on the floor.

The girls and Joe joined him, and they began reading and sorting the clippings.

Jonathan picked up some of them and said, "These are the original ones I found before you all came." He stood up and put them on the table.

The clipping about the restaurant incident was also on the floor, plus some new clippings they had not seen but which held no important information. They were just general gossip columns, and nothing seemed to have a date on it.

Jonathan stood up and said, "I just thought of something," he said. "If Angelina saw us put the clippings under the carpet, which she evidently did because they are all here, then maybe there are others under there, too."

Joe hurried to move the chair at the corner, and Jonathan lifted the carpet. There was nothing under it. They tried every corner in the room, but there was nothing else to be found.

"We haven't quite finished searching the shelves, so we probably ought to do that," Jonathan said, standing up to look around the room.

"I just thought of something, too, Jonathan," Mandie said. "Angelina could have put things in shelves that we have already searched."

Jonathan thought about that. "She said she had been watching us," he said. "So she would know which shelves we searched. Do you think she would go behind us and put papers in those?"

"Maybe," Mandie said. "Also, she may know who hung that thing on the wall there if she has been spying in this room."

"You're right. Now, why didn't I ask her?" Jonathan said.

"Because we didn't see it until she had left," Joe told him.

"Too late now. I'm sure she has left the house," Jonathan said.

They placed the clippings on the table and decided after a while that there were no more to be found.

"I think we'd better all go get washed up and meet in the parlor," Jonathan said, looking at his pocket watch. "Let's go back out the way we came in so the door will stay locked."

Mandie and Celia went to their rooms to wash up. Snowball was asleep on Mandie's bed, and when they came into the room he stood up and stretched.

"I need to take Snowball to the kitchen so he can eat, too," Mandie said.

"Let's hurry then and do that," Celia said.

They quickly freshened up. Mandie picked up Snowball, and they hurried toward the kitchen.

As they went down a cross hall and then downstairs, Mandie saw Angelina ahead of them. "Look, there's that girl," she told Celia and hurried on.

Angelina had looked back and seen them. She turned a corner and disappeared. Although Mandie and Celia tried going up and down each cross hall, they could find no sign of her.

"We might as well leave Snowball in the kitchen and go on to the parlor," Mandie finally decided. "That girl is too hard to find."

When they got to the parlor after leaving Snowball, Jonathan and Joe were already there.

"Where have y'all been?" Joe asked.

"I had to take Snowball to the kitchen so he could have his supper," Mandie explained. "However, we just saw Angelina in a hallway before we got to the kitchen, but she got away from us."

"Let's take another look," Jonathan quickly decided and led the way back out into the hallway.

He knew his way around the house, and it didn't take long to search all the hallways, but Angelina was not to be found.

Later, after the evening meal was over, they looked for the girl again but without any results.

They went back to the old library and read the clippings until everyone got sleepy. They decided it was time to retire for the night when the huge clock in the hall struck midnight. Mandie got Snowball from the kitchen.

Mandie was too tired to stay awake and do much thinking that night. She soon went to sleep. She dreamed of the picture hanging in the old library. In her dream she was unable to uncover it.

## CHAPTER TWELVE

# *FROM THE PAST*

"Mandie, Mandie, Mandie, wake up. We're going to be late for breakfast," Celia was telling her as she shook Mandie's shoulder.

Snowball sat up beside Mandie, stretched, and then reached over to lick Mandie's face.

Mandie quickly pushed him away. "Snowball, stop that," she said, sleepily opening her eyes and then seeing Celia standing by the bed. She sat up and asked, "What time is it?" She yawned a loud groan.

Celia was already dressed. "Mandie, if you don't get out of that bed instantly, you won't have any breakfast. We have about ten minutes to get downstairs," Celia told her.

Mandie swung her legs over the side of the high bed and slid down to stand up. "Why didn't you wake me up in time?" Mandie groggily asked as she hunted for something to put on. She pulled down a blue cotton dress from the rack in the huge wardrobe.

"You were actually snoring, Mandie," Celia said. "You must have been awfully tired when you went to bed. I'll help you." She rushed over to the bureau drawer and took out a pair of stockings. "Here, put these on." She stooped to look under the bed. "Where are your shoes?" She found them and pulled them out.

Mandie didn't understand why she was so sleepy. She stretched and yawned and bent every which way and finally reached down to put on her stockings and shoes.

"We haven't had much sleep since we've been here," Celia told her. "We are used to ten o'clock curfew at school, and even when we're home that sleeping habit stays with us. It was after midnight last night when we finally got in bed." She ran over to the bureau and brought Mandie her hairbrush.

Mandie quickly brushed her long blond hair and tied it back with a blue ribbon Celia found in a drawer.

"I should take Snowball to the kitchen so he can eat before I go in to breakfast," Mandie said, looking at the cat, who was sitting at her feet busily washing himself all over.

"We don't have time for that. Come on. You can take him down later," Celia insisted, going to open the door.

Mandie was hoping Joe and Jonathan would be waiting for them near the landing, but there was no one in sight. When she and Celia got to the parlor, no one was there.

"Where is everybody?" Mandie asked as they looked around the empty room. She finally felt like she was awake.

"Maybe they're already in the dining room," Celia said, leading the way back out into the hallway and starting toward the dining room.

Celia reached ahead of her to open the dining room door. As the door swung open, Mandie was greeted by all her friends and family gathered around the table. "Happy birthday, Amanda!" they were yelling at the top of their voices.

"Birthday?" Mandie asked in surprise. "Is it my birthday? Why, yes, it must be, because today is June the sixth." She laughed as Celia guided her to a seat at the table.

"Happy birthday, darling," Elizabeth Shaw told her, coming around to hug and kiss her.

"Thank you, Mother," Mandie replied, squeezing her mother tight.

Lindall Guyer, at the head of the table, tapped on a glass and said, "Let's eat now, and we'll have the presents in the parlor."

"That sounds like a good idea to me," Jonathan said.

Mandie finally looked around the table at all the people. She almost turned her chair over as she saw Uncle Ned, her father's old Cherokee friend, on the other side and scrambled to go over to him.

"Uncle Ned! I'm so glad to see you," Mandie said as the old man stood up and hugged her.

"Happy birthday, Papoose," Uncle Ned said. "Number of years now fifteen. Must be young lady." He smiled down at her.

"Fifteen? Oh goodness, am I fifteen? I must be, I suppose, but that sounds so old," Mandie replied, laughing.

As she started back to her chair, she saw another familiar face. Dr. Plumbley was sitting near Dr. Woodard at the other end. She rushed down to greet him. "Oh, Dr. Plumbley, I'm so glad you could come back today," she said.

"I promised I'd see you again before you left New York," Dr. Plumbley replied. "Happy birthday. You're getting to be a young lady now."

Joe spoke from the other side, where he was sitting with her friends. "Amanda Elizabeth Shaw, if you don't sit down and eat, we'll never get to that birthday cake, and I understand it is chocolate."

"Oh, I'll have to hurry for that," Mandie said, going back to her chair.

No one seemed to be in a hurry to finish the meal. Everyone was laughing and talking.

Jonathan leaned toward Mandie as he sat between her and Celia and asked, "Do we have to eat chocolate cake for breakfast?"

"Oh, I hadn't thought about that," Mandie said. "Why don't we save the cake for noon? Who planned this for breakfast?"

"It seems my father and your uncle John did, because this is the only time Dr. Plumbley could come," Jonathan replied.

"I'm glad he could come," Mandie said. "In that case, I suppose we had better go ahead and have the cake."

"I thought perhaps you could just blow out the candles and give Dr. Plumbley a slice to take home with him," Jonathan suggested. "I'm sure no one would want to eat chocolate cake for breakfast. We could have the rest of the celebration at noon. What do you say?"

"That's a good idea. Let's do it that way," Mandie agreed.

Jonathan got up and went around the table to speak to his father. Then Mr. Guyer stood up and said, "We will now proceed to the parlor for the cake-lighting ceremony. However, if you don't want cake this early please don't feel obliged to partake. We'll have cake at noontime."

There were sounds of relief around the table.

When everyone entered the parlor Mandie saw the huge chocolate cake standing in the middle of the mahogany drop-leaf table. The table's leaves had been extended to take care of all the presents around the cake. She wondered who had done this while they were having breakfast. These things were certainly not there when she and Celia had come into the parlor earlier. Then she saw Mrs. Yodkin, Monet, Leila, and Jens standing at the side of the room smiling.

The candles on the cake were lit as everyone gathered around the table. Mandie blew them all out in one puff.

"I know that Dr. Plumbley has to leave, so he gets the first piece of cake," Mandie said, reaching for the cake knife. Her mother stepped up to help her as she dislodged the piece from the huge cake and put it on a plate without spilling a single crumb. She blew out her breath in relief. The first piece was always the hardest to get out in one whole piece.

"Thank you for coming, Dr. Plumbley," Mandie told him. "And I do wish you could come back to Franklin to see us and all the other friends you have there."

Dr. Plumbley accepted the cake with a big smile and said, "I will do that one of these days. Soon, I think, because we are all getting older. If I wait too long, you will be a grown young lady and away from home. And my old friends there are also getting older. I hope you have a joyous day today for your birthday and that the Lord will bless you in many ways, Miss Amanda."

Mandie reached to hug him. Her mother quickly took the plate from Dr. Plumbley to prevent the cake from being smashed.

Mrs. Yodkin, standing by, spoke. "I can put that cake on a plate for the doctor to take home with him if he is not staying, ma'am." She looked at Elizabeth.

"Yes, please do," Elizabeth told her, handing over the cake plate. "And, Amanda, since Dr. Plumbley has to leave, maybe you should open his present to you first."

"Oh yes, ma'am," Mandie replied, looking at the pile of beautifully wrapped gifts. Turning to the doctor, she asked, "Please tell me which one is from you."

"The small one there in white paper with the blue ribbon," he replied.

Mandie picked up the one he indicated and removed the ribbon and paper. Inside was a small book titled *Memories of Franklin,* by Samuel Hezekiah Plumbley. She quickly flipped it open and then looked up at the tall man and said, "Oh, Dr. Plumbley, this is such a wonderful present. I can't wait to read it. And I know everybody back home in Franklin will be wanting to read it, too. Thank you from the bottom of my heart."

Dr. Plumbley smiled and said, "Now, if you hear tell of anyone else back there in Franklin who would like one of those books, just let me know and I'll send them one."

"I can tell you right now you will be getting at least a dozen requests that I can think of," Mandie replied.

After Dr. Plumbley left, Mandie opened the other presents. There was something from everyone except her grandmother, and she couldn't understand that. Mrs. Taft had been unusually quiet all morning. Then the mystery was solved in more ways than one.

"Now that you have finished with those presents, Miss Amanda," Mr. Guyer told her, "let's go down the hall and get the one from your grandmother and me."

Mandie wondered why he was jointly giving her a present with her grandmother, but she smiled and said, "Yes, sir."

Mr. Guyer led the way, and Mrs. Taft walked by Mandie's side down the long corridor outside the parlor. He made a turn or two, and to Mandie's amazement he stopped in front of the old library door. Looking back at her, he said, "It's in here." He opened the door and waited for her and her grandmother to enter the room, with the others following.

Then, to the amazement of all the young people, Lindall Guyer reached up and pulled the cover off the picture that had been hung on the wall.

Mandie quickly looked to see what it was. It was a landscape of Niagara Falls. She stepped forward to read the artist's signature. "Sarabeth," she said, gasping, as she looked at her friends.

"Yes, Sarabeth painted this," Mr. Guyer told her as he glanced at Mrs. Taft, evidently waiting for her to explain.

"Sarabeth was my dearest lifetime friend, Amanda. We grew up together, went to school together, and moved in the same circles," Mrs. Taft said. "She was a very promising artist until her hands became crippled with arthritis and she could no longer paint." Her voice quivered, and she swallowed hard. Looking at Mr. Guyer, she said, "Lindall here was also in our circle until he and I had a terrible disagreement." She stopped and looked at Mr. Guyer.

Mandie could hear her friends take deep breaths behind her.

"This painting broke up the friendship between your grandmother and me because I did a very foolish thing," Mr. Guyer explained. "Sarabeth had her paintings on display at the museum, and this one was in the group. Most of the others were for sale, but Sarabeth refused to sell this one because it was her favorite and she was unable to paint anymore." He paused.

The room was so quiet, they could have heard a pin drop.

"Lindall and I both wanted this painting very badly, but I knew it meant too much to Sarabeth and would not even mention buying it," Mrs. Taft said.

"But me, I was a brazen young thing," Mr. Guyer continued. "I went back and talked Sarabeth into selling it to me for a fabulous sum. When I told your grandmother what I had done, she was so furious she never got over it. Our friendship was lost. And I was so upset by what I had done that I wouldn't even hang the picture in my house. It has been in the attic all these years. When your grandmother and I settled our old dispute, we decided to give it to you for your birthday. It's too wonderful a painting to keep hidden away."

Mandie grinned as she looked from her grandmother to Mr. Guyer and said with a laugh, "So that's what the argument was about at the Broadway Club." Then she glanced at her friends, who were all smiling.

Mr. Guyer quickly understood. "You've been reading the newspaper clippings," he said. Turning to her grandmother he said, "You didn't know I kept all those columns. I thought they were well hidden, but it seems these young people were smart enough to find them."

"Amanda, I hope you never follow in my footsteps," Mrs. Taft said, smiling at her.

Before Mandie could reply, her mother spoke. "Mother, I always knew there was something wrong between you and Lindall, but I never dreamed it was such a thing as this." Looking at Mr. Guyer, she said, "I must read those clippings sometime."

"Of course," he agreed.

Mandie suddenly embraced her grandmother and then turned to Mr. Guyer and hugged him. "I don't know how to thank you both for such a present. I'll always treasure the painting."

Everyone in the room suddenly clapped and said, "Happy birthday, Amanda Shaw."

Mandie turned to look across the room at all the people. "I love you all," she said. Everyone returned to the parlor.

Suddenly out of the crowd Angelina pushed her way through, looked up at Mandie, and said, "I love you, too, Mandie. Do you love me?"

The word caused tears to come into Mandie's blue eyes. She stooped to hug the little girl as she said, "Of course I love you, Angelina, a whole bunch."

Jens, the girl's father, suddenly stepped through the crowd and said to Angelina, "You are not supposed to be in here," he said. "You must go home at once."

Before the little girl could reply, Mandie spoke up. "It's all right. We are having a party, and I want to give Angelina a big slice of cake to take home with her." She turned back to the cake. Her mother helped her slice a chunk of it, place it on a plate, and cover it with a napkin. Mandie held it out to Jens and asked, "Would you please carry it home for her so she won't drop it?"

Jens hesitated only a second and stepped forward to take the plate, saying, "Of course, miss. Thank you. Come along, Angelina."

"Thank you," Angelina called back with a big smile as they left the room.

Mandie thanked everyone for her presents again. Each gift was something she wanted.

As everyone finally settled down and found seats around the parlor, Mandie and her friends discussed the solution to their mystery.

"Imagine, breaking up a love affair for such a stupid thing," Jonathan said.

"It's good they did, Jonathan, or you and I might have been related somehow," Mandie teased him.

"This turned out to be a simple mystery, didn't it? No escapades to get us into trouble and all that," Joe said to Mandie.

"But think of all the years Mrs. Taft has lived through, detesting Mr. Guyer," Celia said. "Jonathan, do you think your father also hated Mrs. Taft all this time?"

"I don't believe they actually hated each other," Jonathan replied. "I think it was mostly regret for their behavior that broke everything up between them."

All of a sudden Mandie exclaimed, "Jonathan, you don't think they are still in love, do you?"

Jonathan grinned at her and said, "Could be, could be. We'll just have to wait and see what happens in the future."

"And thinking of the future, maybe we can find another mystery when we all get to Tommy Patton's house," Mandie said.

"You are forgetting Senator Morton," Joe reminded her. "I would think your grandmother and Senator Morton are attracted to each other."

"Grandmother and Senator Morton?" Mandie replied and then said, "Oh well, we have thought that for a while anyway. And that reminds me. Senator Morton is going to Charleston to see the Pattons with us. So is your father, Jonathan."

Jonathan grinned at her and said, "May the best man win."

"It will certainly be an interesting vacation," Mandie decided. She didn't know then how interesting the vacation would be.

# MANDIE

## AND THE
## NIGHT THIEF

This book is especially for
all those readers whose replies
to the questionnaire in
Book #35, *Mandie and the Quilt Mystery,*
were too late to win.

# CONTENTS

**MANDIE AND THE NIGHT THIEF**

"And forgive us our debts,
as we forgive our debtors"

(Matthew 6:12).

# CHAPTER ONE

# AN UNEXPECTED LETTER

Rain traveled with the train all the way home to Franklin, North Carolina, from New York. The windows had to be kept closed, and the air was warm and stale. Mandie and her friends kept wiping moisture off the glass, trying to see outside. A heavy downpour had started before they had boarded the train in New York.

"Oh, shucks!" Mandie said, giving a quick swipe to the window glass. "I can't see a thing. I'll never know what we've been through."

"But we've been to New York before," Celia reminded her.

"But most of our journey that time was in the dark," Mandie replied.

"I'm just thankful Jonathan's father was able to get this private car for us," Joe said.

Mandie glanced toward the adults sitting at the other end of the car. "That was an interesting argument between my grandmother and your father, Jonathan," she said.

Jonathan grinned at her and replied, "Your grandmother may own that ship line, but when it comes to trains my father is the winner. He never travels in an ordinary train car. He always has a private one."

"I'm glad we found out their secret while we were all at your house," Mandie told Jonathan.

"Yes," Jonathan agreed. "Otherwise we would never be making this trip together."

"We are only going to spend one night at your house, aren't we, Mandie, before we go on to Charleston?" Celia asked.

"That's what everyone agreed to," Mandie replied, sitting down in the seat by the window she had been wiping. "However, if Senator Morton is not at our house when we get there, we'll have to wait for him." She looked at Celia, who sat down next to her.

Joe and Jonathan flipped the back of the next seat so it was facing the girls and then sat down.

"Mandie, I just thought of something else," Celia said, turning to look at her. "Since Polly's mother didn't allow Polly to go to New York with our mothers, she is probably home and will be right over as soon as we walk in your door."

"Polly Cornwallis is not going with us to Charleston. I'll see to that," Mandie said firmly.

"Too bad she lives right next door to you," Jonathan remarked, "where she can keep up with your goings and comings."

The train went around a sharp curve. Everyone slid around in their seats.

"We certainly went around that curve in a hurry," Joe remarked.

"We feel it more than the other cars because we are on the end," Jonathan said.

Mandie glanced at her grandmother, sitting at the far end. "It didn't seem to bother Grandmother," she said. Mandie's white cat came from under her seat and jumped up into her lap. "Snowball, that must have shaken you awake." She rubbed the cat's head, and he meowed his thanks as he curled up.

"I suppose you are taking that cat with you to Charleston," Joe said.

"Of course," Mandie replied. "Snowball goes wherever I go. You know that." She grinned at Joe.

"Yes, I know that very well. All the escapades he has been involved in would make a book." He grinned back at Mandie.

"A book?" Mandie said, frowning as she thought about it. "Maybe I will write a book about Snowball."

"Mandie, it would never end because it just goes on and on, with Snowball into everything and anything," Celia remarked.

"All right, then. I could just call it *The Endless Book of Snowball's Adventures*. And that way I could keep adding on," Mandie replied with a laugh.

"I'm afraid no one would want to read it if it never ended, because every book has an ending," Jonathan said.

"And I hope this train ride has an ending soon," Joe remarked.

"You are in a hurry to get on down to Charleston, aren't you?" Mandie asked.

"Yes, and then on back home so I can have some time to spend with my parents before I have to go back to school," Joe told her.

"This is the first time my father has ever taken time off from work to go anywhere with me, and I am so grateful to be with him after all those boarding schools I have been sent off to," Jonathan said.

"And I've often thought it would be wonderful to be able to go to school near my home and not have to go off to Asheville to the Heathwoods' School," Celia said.

"I have, too," Mandie said. "But my mother wanted me to go to the Heathwoods' School because she went there, and she considers it the best education anywhere in the south." Looking at Celia sitting next to her, she added, "And now when we finish there next spring we'll have to go on to college."

"You girls should come on down to my college in New Orleans and study there," Joe said.

"No, you should come to New York for college. We've got lots of good schools," Jonathan said. "And I don't intend leaving New York to go to college, either."

"But you have all those colleges to choose from. Down in North Carolina where we live there aren't any schools where I can meet the entrance requirements to study law," Joe said. "Therefore, I have to go away to New Orleans where they allow me to catch up, but I shall return," he finished with a big grin as he raised his fist and shook it.

"I would like to go to college in Richmond so I could stay home. We are only a few miles out of town," Celia said.

Mandie quickly looked at her friend and said, "But, Celia, you said if we decided to go to college in Richmond we could live in the school even though your home is near there."

Celia looked at Mandie, smiled, and replied, "If you decide to go to college in Richmond, we could both live at my home, instead of in the school."

Mandie thought about that for a moment and replied, "I don't know about that, Celia. Your mother might not want to put up with me."

"I'm sure she would be delighted to have you. You could always bring Snowball with you, whereas in a college I'm pretty sure they won't allow the cat," Celia said.

The four young people finally became quiet and dozed in their seats. The journey from New York had been long and tiresome with rain beating against the windows of the train.

Mandie woke as the train gave a sudden lurch and came to a screeching halt. She grabbed the armrest and sat up to look out the window. She could see the sign "Franklin, North Carolina" hanging over the platform. Excitedly she told her friends, "Wake up, everybody. We're home!"

Her friends quickly straightened up, rubbed their eyes, and gazed out the window. Mrs. Taft had risen from her seat and was saying, "Gather up your belongings, you young people, and, Amanda, please don't let that cat get loose."

Mandie and her friends looked at each other as they stood up and smiled. Mrs. Taft always had to be in charge.

"Yes, ma'am," the four chorused as they picked up their bags and Mandie held tightly to Snowball.

As the young people followed the adults down the aisle toward the door, Mandie bent to look out the window. "I see Mr. Jason and Abraham out there," she told her friends.

"And I don't believe it's raining here," Joe said with a big grin.

Mrs. Taft led the way with Celia's mother, Jane Hamilton, right behind her and Jonathan's father, Lindall Guyer, carrying handbags. Mandie's mother, Elizabeth Shaw, and Mandie's uncle, John Shaw, who was married to Elizabeth, paused as they came up to the young people in the aisle.

"Be sure you have everything, Amanda," Elizabeth said.

"Yes, because this train is running late and it will be turning around and getting out of Franklin before you can say 'scat,'" John Shaw added with a big grin.

"Scat!" all four young people shouted.

"Now look at what y'all have done," John Shaw said, pretending to frown. "You've proved me wrong."

Mandie and her friends laughed as they followed the adults out of the train.

Jason Bond, who was John Shaw's caretaker, was waiting with the rig. He came forward to meet them. "Y'all brought the sunshine," he was telling John Shaw as he began taking their bags.

"Oh, Mr. Jason, it rained all the way from New York," Mandie said with a frown.

"Has Senator Morton arrived yet?" John Shaw asked Jason Bond as they walked on toward the rig.

"Yes, sir, Mr. John. He got here last night," the caretaker said, placing bags in the rig.

"I'm glad he did, because that means we can go on to Charleston tomorrow," John Shaw said.

Mr. Bond looked back at Mandie and said, "And that Miss Polly next door has been asking me every day if y'all were coming home." He grinned.

"Oh, goodness, Mr. Jason, she will probably be at the house when we get there," Mandie said with a loud moan as she looked back at her friends.

"Oh no!" Joe replied.

"We're in for some fun," Jonathan said, grinning at Mandie.

The adults had stepped into the rig, and John Shaw turned back to say, "Come on, get in. I see Abraham over there with the wagon. He'll get the trunks."

When they got to the Shaws' three-story house, Senator Morton was waiting in the parlor. The adults went in to greet him.

Mandie set Snowball down and said to her friends, "Come on, let's go see Aunt Lou." She led the way to the kitchen.

Mandie pushed open the kitchen door and found Aunt Lou, John Shaw's housekeeper, standing by the big iron cookstove, where she was stirring food in a large pot. When she saw Mandie, she put down the spoon, wiped her hands on her big white apron, and came to embrace the girl.

"My chile done got home," Aunt Lou was saying as she hugged Mandie. And then, looking at the others, she added, "And she done brought them special friends with huh, too." She walked over to give Celia, Jonathan, and Joe a little squeeze. "Happy to see y'all," she told them.

At that moment the back door opened and Liza, the young maid, danced into the room, grinning as she looked at Mandie. "Dat Miss Purty Thang next do', she done been over heah ev'ry day askin' when y'all comin' home, and I tells huh maybe y'all ain't gwine come home right now but she didn't believe a word I said."

Everyone laughed so much it was hard for Mandie to get her breath to greet Jenny, the cook, who came in behind Liza. "I hope you've got a chocolate cake baked," Mandie said.

"Why, in fact, we's got two chocolate cakes baked," Jenny replied, going to throw open the doors in the safe, showing the two cakes sitting inside.

Joe rushed to her side and asked, "Can we begin eating them now?"

"Yes, we're really starving," Jonathan added as he joined Joe.

Jenny looked at Aunt Lou, who told the young people, "Why, sho' nuff, y'all can eat cake right now, and we's got a pot o' coffee ready. Just sit down there at the table." She turned to the young maid and said, "Liza, git de cups and plates down."

As soon as Jenny had served the cake and Aunt Lou had poured the coffee, Elizabeth Shaw stuck her head inside the door. "Amanda, remember you will have to eat supper in about two hours." Then, turning to the servants, she told them, "I'm so glad to be home and get y'alls wonderful cooking. And, Aunt Lou, we will be leaving early tomorrow morning for Charleston."

"Tomorrow mawnin', Miz 'Lizbeth?" Aunt Lou replied. "Why, I was hopin' y'all would stay awhile befo' you gwine down to dat Charleston town. Y'all won't have time to git yo' breath by tomorrow mawnin'."

"We have to go on tomorrow because Jonathan's father is with us and he has to get back to New York and back to work in a few days," Elizabeth explained. "Then we'll be home for the rest of the summer."

"Rest of de summer ain't much left by den," Aunt Lou fussed as she poured another cup of coffee. "Miz Lizbeth, you be wantin' we should take coffee to de parlor now?"

"Yes, please do, Aunt Lou, and just a little sweetbread or something, not the chocolate cake. That's too rich for this time of day," Elizabeth replied as she left the room.

"Liza, set up a tray for the parlor," Aunt Lou said.

Liza danced around the room and replied, "Dat senit man, he been waitin' all afternoon fo' his coffee, want to drink it wid Miz Grandma, he say. So now Miz Grandma done got heah and he'll be wantin' coffee." She talked as she got the tray ready.

Mandie and her friends smiled and listened.

"I wonder what happened when your father walked in with my grandmother and the senator was waiting for her in the parlor," Mandie said, then started giggling and almost choked on her coffee.

"We should have stayed to watch," Jonathan said with a big grin.

"I wonder if your father and Senator Morton know each other," Joe said, taking a bite of his piece of chocolate cake.

"Or if Senator Morton knows about all that went on when they were young," Celia added.

"I'm not sure," Jonathan said, sipping his coffee. Then, turning to Mandie, he asked, "How long has your grandmother known Senator Morton?"

"Oh, goodness, for ages and ages," Mandie replied, wiping tears of laughter from her blue eyes. "In fact, Senator Morton was a friend of my Grandfather Taft, and you know he died years before I was ever born, as far as I know."

"Then they probably know each other, because my father also knew your grandfather," he told Mandie.

"I've been wondering if Grandmother would eventually marry Senator Morton, but now that she and your father have become friends again, I'm not sure what will happen," Mandie said.

"I'm sure there will be some interesting moments on this journey to Charleston," Jonathan said, grinning.

Aunt Lou had been listening to the conversation and asked, "My chile, did you git dat mail off de front table dat came fo' you whilst y'all been gone?"

Mandie looked up from her coffee and asked, "I got a letter?"

"You sho' did," Aunt Lou said as Mandie quickly rose from the table.

"I never get any mail. I'll be right back," Mandie told her friends.

Mandie rushed down the long hallway to the table near the front door where her uncle's mail was always put. She looked in the silver basket sitting on it, and sure enough, she spotted an envelope addressed to Amanda Shaw. Snatching it up, she started back toward the kitchen as she examined it.

"From Lily Masterson!" she said in surprise as she read the return address. "And she's back in South Carolina."

She tore open the envelope and exclaimed as she entered the kitchen, "A letter from Lily Masterson!" She pulled a single sheet of paper out of the envelope and unfolded it as she sat down.

"Lily Masterson, the girl who was on the ship with us when we went to Europe?" Celia asked.

"The older girl with the little sister named Violet?" Jonathan asked.

"Yes, yes," Mandie said as she quickly scanned the note. Then, looking at her friends, she said, "She has come back home to Fountain Inn, South Carolina."

"Is Fountain Inn anywhere near Charleston?" Celia asked.

"Why, I don't really know. Seems like it's on the way to Charleston," Mandie replied.

"Yes," Joe said. "It's not very far over the border into South Carolina from here. I've never been there, but I'm sure that's where it is."

Mandie was excited as she said, "I wonder if Mother would stop there on our way so we could visit Lily?"

"Mandie, we are going on the train," Jonathan reminded her. "You can't just stop the train and get off wherever you happen to want to go."

"But maybe the train goes through Fountain Inn," Joe suggested. "And if it does you could get off there."

"I've wondered whatever happened to Lily and her little sister,"

Celia said. "Remember her mother had died and her father was sending them to England to live with their aunt?"

"Yes," Mandie agreed. "I should have stayed in touch with her. But now that she has let me know they are back, maybe we could visit them. As soon as I get a chance I'll discuss this with my mother or Uncle John."

"Well, what did she have to say in the letter?" Celia asked.

Mandie held up the single sheet of paper and said, "Nothing much, just, 'We're back in Fountain Inn and if you and your friends are ever down this way please come to visit.' That's all she said."

"Then let's go visit," Jonathan said with a big grin.

"Would all of you want to visit her?" Mandie asked.

"Well, since I have never met her, I don't believe I do, especially since I will only be able to spend a day or two in Charleston and then must get back home," Joe said.

"I would like to if we can arrange it," Celia said.

"And so would I," Jonathan agreed.

"Then I'll talk to my mother," Mandie said. Then she quickly looked at her friends and added, "You know, Grandmother knows Lily, too. Remember how nice Grandmother was to Lily when her little sister got sick on the ship?"

"Maybe your grandmother could arrange all this for us?" Jonathan suggested.

"Yes," Mandie said with a big grin. "We definitely need Grandmother on our side for this."

She quickly tried to figure out how she could speak to Mrs. Taft without the other adults around. That was going to be hard to do since her grandmother had two interesting men following her around for this journey to Charleston. There must be a way. And she would find that way.

# CHAPTER TWO

# *SPYING*

As soon as everyone had finished their coffee and cake in the kitchen, Mandie told her friends, "Let's go to the parlor and see what's happening in there." Looking at Jonathan she added, "You know, between my grandmother and your father and Senator Morton."

Jonathan grinned at her as he rose and said, "Yes, let's do go to the parlor."

When the four young people entered the parlor, Mrs. Taft was not there. Mandie glanced at her mother as they sat down across the room from the adults.

"Where is Grandmother?" she asked.

"Mother has gone to her room to rest until time for supper," Elizabeth replied.

"Oh, shucks!" Mandie said to her friends.

"Amanda, you need to repack your trunk tonight with clothes for Charleston because we will be departing early tomorrow morning," Elizabeth told her.

"You too, Celia," Jane Hamilton said to her daughter.

"I suppose that includes us, too," Jonathan said, looking at Joe.

Joe stood up and said, "And I think I'll go do that right now,"

Mandie glanced at Celia and said, "We might as well do ours, too."

"Yes," Celia agreed.

"Be sure y'all are back down here on time for supper," Elizabeth reminded them as they left the room. "Six o'clock sharp."

"Yes, ma'am," the group chorused.

Celia always shared Mandie's room when she came to visit. Her trunk was sitting beside Mandie's on the far side of the huge room. Snowball was curled up asleep in the middle of the big bed.

Mandie bent over her trunk and began removing the contents and hanging up her clothes. "I'm not taking as much to Charleston as I did to New York," she said. "I didn't even wear all the things I took to Jonathan's house." She went to the wardrobe with an armful of dresses.

"I'm not, either, but remember, Mandie, when you visited the Pattons before, you said they dressed for dinner every night," Celia reminded her. "Therefore, we will need some dresses for that."

Mandie paused to look at the clothes in her arms. "I think I could mix some blouses and skirts and cut down on some clothes that way. Like this white lacy blouse here." She pulled out a hanger from the stack. "I could wear this several times with different skirts, or I could wear this black skirt several times with different blouses." She looked at Celia and asked, "What do you think?"

"Yes, that would be a very good idea," Celia agreed. "And I'll do the same thing. And be sure to take lots of ribbons. Those will help change the looks of anything we wear twice." She lifted a pile of clothes from her trunk and laid them on the big bed to sort them.

Snowball woke up, stretched, and began washing his face.

There was a slight tap on the door and Liza stuck her head inside. "Dat Miz Purty Thang next do' be down in de parlor."

"Polly Cornwallis is in the parlor?" Mandie quickly asked.

"She sho' is," Liza replied. "And huh mother, she be wid huh."

Mandie blew out her breath and said, "Well, maybe she'll go back home with her mother. I hope she doesn't stay for supper."

"Nope, she ain't stayin' 'cuz dey got comp'ny comin', huh mother said," Liza explained.

"I'm glad to hear that," Mandie said as she continued hanging clothes in the wardrobe.

"Huh mother tol' yo' mother maybe dey come back later and yo' mother say y'all gwine bed early tonight 'cuz y'all be leavin' early tomorrow," Liza explained, grinning as she looked at the two girls.

"Maybe we won't have to see them, then," Mandie said to Celia. Then, turning to Liza, she said, "Would you please come back and let us know when they go home? We could just stay up here until time for supper."

"I sho' will," Liza said and went on down the hall.

The girls repacked their trunks and then cleaned up and changed clothes for supper. And Liza still had not come back to let them know Polly had gone home.

As Mandie finished brushing her long blond hair and tying it back with a red ribbon to match her calico dress, she said, "We will have to go down in a few minutes. Mother said six o'clock sharp for supper and it's five minutes till." She looked at the clock on the mantelpiece.

"Yes, and I'd rather not be late," Celia said, shaking out the folds of her long skirt before the full-length mirror in the corner.

There was a knock on the door, and Mandie opened it to find Joe and Jonathan outside.

"Y'all ready to go downstairs?" Joe asked.

Mandie looked back at Celia and said, "I suppose we'd better go now." Then, turning to the boys, she said, "Liza let us know Polly is in the parlor with her mother."

Mandie and Celia followed the boys down the hallway as they talked. "But she said they are going home when we have supper," Celia said.

"We don't have much time here at your house anyway," Joe reminded her. "Did you girls get everything repacked?" They went down the staircase.

"Yes, we did," Mandie replied. "And I believe we'll be leaving about daylight in the morning."

As they came to the parlor door, Mandie was relieved to see that Polly and her mother were not there. Liza came hurrying up behind them, stuck her head in the doorway, looked directly at Mandie's mother, and announced, "De food on de table, Miz 'Lizbeth."

"Thank you," Elizabeth replied and the adults all rose.

Turning to Mandie, Liza whispered, "Dat Miz Purty Thang, she dun went home jes' now wid her mother." She danced on down the hallway toward the kitchen.

The young people followed the adults into the dining room. Mrs. Taft had been in the parlor, and Mandie tried to catch up with her as they walked along. However, Elizabeth kept up a steady stream of talk until they were all seated at the long table. The young people were placed together on one side of the huge dining table, so Mandie could not speak to her grandmother, who sat at the end of the other side. And Senator Morton sat directly across from Mrs. Taft. Mr. Guyer was placed next to Jane Hamilton.

Mandie whispered behind her hand to her friends, "I wonder who decided to put Mr. Guyer next to Celia's mother. Do y'all think they are interested in each other?"

Her friends all laughed, causing the adults to glance in their direction.

"Oh no, Mr. Guyer is too old for my mother," Celia quickly told them.

The young people laughed again. And Jonathan said, "My father and Celia's mother have been friends a long time, I believe."

"Senator Morton is certainly keeping his eyes on my grandmother," Mandie whispered. "And my grandmother is not exactly looking at anyone."

"Would you like for your grandmother to marry the senator or my father?" Jonathan asked Mandie, grinning at her.

Mandie blew out her breath and replied, "Neither one."

"Neither one?" Celia asked. "I thought you wanted your grandmother to marry Senator Morton and go to live with him down in Florida so she wouldn't be around watching us."

"Well, that was before I found out about Mr. Guyer and my grandmother," Mandie said, smiling at Jonathan. "I just couldn't decide which one I like better."

"I don't believe your grandmother is interested in my father anymore," Jonathan said. "After all, that was many years ago when they knew each other."

"You just don't want my grandmother for your stepmother," Mandie said with a giggle. "And I would agree with you."

Joe finally joined the conversation. "Mandie, I would say that none of us would have any say-so about it. After all, I know your grandmother very well and she is usually the boss," he said, grinning.

Mandie straightened up in her chair, blew out her breath, and said, "You are absolutely right, Joe. So I'm going to mind my own business while we are in Charleston." She tried to look serious.

"I don't believe that," Joe said, laughing.

"And neither do I," Celia added with a big smile.

"I'll volunteer to help you with your snooping in Charleston," Jonathan said, grinning at Mandie.

"Just remember you said that, Jonathan Guyer," Mandie replied.

No one seemed to be in a hurry to finish the evening meal. Mandie kept hoping she would be able to speak to her grandmother about Lily's letter, but when the meal was finally finished everyone went back to the parlor for coffee.

"Do we have to go to the parlor, too?" Jonathan whispered to Mandie as they rose from the table.

"I suppose so. My mother didn't say," Mandie whispered back. "However, maybe we can find an excuse to get out of there before too long."

"The chocolate cake will probably be served in the parlor," Joe reminded the others as they followed the adults.

"As soon as we can eat the cake, then, let's try to slip out and go sit somewhere where we can talk without the grown-ups overhearing everything," Jonathan said.

They followed the adults back to the parlor and sat down at the end of the room. Cake and coffee were served and the young people hastily ate theirs.

Mandie looked at her friends and whispered, "Maybe we could leave now."

Before anyone could reply, Elizabeth spoke from across the room, "Amanda, you should prepare to retire for the night now. We will be up before daylight in the morning."

Mandie glanced at her friends and then said, "Yes, ma'am." She stood up and whispered to the others, "Let's go." Turning to look across the room, she said, "Good night, everyone."

As she left the parlor the others followed. She led the way down the main hallway to the back parlor, where one lamp was burning, and as soon as everyone had come into the room she softly closed the door.

"I would like to talk to my grandmother, but I haven't had a chance," Mandie said as she sat down on the settee and her friends found seats nearby.

"Couldn't you just tell her you want to talk to her?" Joe asked.

"And then everyone who heard me would wonder why I want to talk to her," Mandie said. "Or, knowing my grandmother, she might just ask out loud what it was about."

"You want to talk to her about Lily's letter, don't you?" Celia asked.

"Yes, I'm hoping she can figure out how we could visit Lily," Mandie replied.

"Maybe you could go to her room later tonight after everyone has retired," Jonathan suggested.

"If I can catch up with her," Mandie agreed. "But since she evidently had a nap in her room before supper tonight, she may stay up late."

"We can keep watch for her to leave the parlor and you could catch her on the way to her room," Celia said.

Mandie went over to the door and quietly opened it a little. "I think we will be able to hear her whenever she leaves the parlor because she has to come down this way to go up the stairs." She went back to sit on the settee.

"What if she sees us in the parlor here? Won't she wonder what we're doing since we were supposed to go to our rooms?" Joe asked.

"She won't be able to see us if we stay away from the doorway," Mandie replied.

The four young people sat quietly while they listened for the others to leave the front parlor. Time passed slowly and Mandie became impatient.

"I thought they would be going to bed early," Mandie whispered to her friends. "Shh!"

At that moment they heard voices in the hallway.

"That's my mother, Celia's mother, Uncle John, and Mr. Guyer," Mandie said to her friends. "But I don't hear Grandmother." She quickly went to peep through the small opening in the doorway. "And they're going up the steps."

As soon as the voices died away up the stairs, Jonathan said, "Your grandmother and Senator Morton must be still in the parlor."

"Yes, maybe they'll come out soon," Mandie replied.

The four young people waited and waited, and nothing else happened. They were all beginning to get sleepy.

"Why don't we all go to our rooms, Mandie, and you could try catching your grandmother tomorrow morning," Joe suggested.

"I know we can't just sit here all night, but what in the world is my grandmother talking about all this time with Senator Morton?" Mandie said. She stood up and added, "I think I'll slip down the hallway and try to look into the parlor."

"Do you want me to come with you?" Celia asked.

Mandie paused at the door, looked back, and said, "If I'm caught I may be in trouble, Celia, and I wouldn't want you to get involved, too."

Jonathan quickly stood up and said, "I'll go with you. I won't be in trouble for staying up late if I'm caught, because we stay up all hours at home anyway."

Mandie shrugged her shoulders and said, "You can come if you want to, but don't blame me if anything goes wrong and we get in trouble." She pushed the door open enough to slip through into the hallway.

Jonathan came right behind her and together they quietly walked down the hall toward the parlor door. Just as they got there Mrs. Taft and Senator Morton came out.

"Amanda, I thought you went to your room," Mrs. Taft said, glancing at her and then at Jonathan.

Senator Morton stood by Mrs. Taft's side, listening to the conversation.

Mandie looked at the senator and then at her grandmother. "I had something I wanted to do before I went to bed."

"And so did we, dear. So much has happened since we last saw Senator Morton," Mrs. Taft replied, looking up at the tall man.

"Indeed it has," Senator Morton agreed. He laughed and added, "And we still haven't caught up with the latest."

"Now, Amanda, you should run along and do whatever it is that you wanted to do and then get some sleep. Otherwise you are going to be awfully sleepy tomorrow for our journey." She walked on down the hallway toward the staircase with Senator Morton following.

Mandie stood there with her mouth open and then said to Jonathan, "Now, why didn't I just ask her to talk with me a few minutes?"

Mandie and Jonathan watched as Mrs. Taft and Senator Morton went up the stairs.

"There's nothing left to do but what Joe suggested: Get up early tomorrow and catch her before breakfast," Jonathan told her.

"I suppose that's what I'll have to do," Mandie replied, blowing out her breath and walking back toward her friends.

Celia and Joe waited for them in the doorway.

"Grandmother and Senator Morton are catching up on news, or whatever," Mandie told her friends. "And I didn't say anything about talking to her." She went back into the back parlor and flopped on the settee. Her friends followed.

"I say we all go to our rooms and get some sleep," Joe said, walking about the room.

"Yes," Celia agreed.

"I suppose we had better," Mandie replied with a loud moan. She stood up.

"Shh!" Jonathan warned. "Someone's coming down the staircase." He stood in the doorway and looked down the hall.

The others crowded behind him.

"Why, it's Liza," Mandie said as the girl came down the steps and into the hallway toward them.

When Liza saw them, she stopped and said, "Lawsy mercy, y'all s'posed to be in yo' beds sleeping. Now whut y'all a-doin' back heah?" She came to the doorway.

"We're going right now, Liza, but what are you doing yourself? Aren't you supposed to be in bed now?" Mandie asked.

"Aunt Lou, she say I should go and be sho' dem men didn't leave no pipe burnin' in de parlor," Liza explained. "And de doors all locked up."

"But that's Mr. Jason's job, isn't it, Liza?" Mandie asked.

"Dat Mistuh Jason ain't heah right now," Liza replied as she danced around the hallway. "He be gone to Asheville."

"To Asheville? What for, Liza?" Mandie asked.

"Mistuh John, he send a paper to his lawyer man in Asheville, I heard him say," Liza replied. "And Mistuh Jason, he won't be back till 'morrow." She came to a halt in front of Mandie and asked, "And whut y'all be doin' down heah at dis heah hour?"

"We were starting upstairs when we heard you, and we waited to see who it was," Mandie explained.

"I'se s'posed to come and wake y'all up at five o'clock in de mawnin'. Y'all ain't got long to sleep tonight," Liza said.

"All right, all right," Mandie said. "We're going now." She started toward the staircase and her friends followed. She stopped and looked back. "Liza, where is Snowball? Have you seen him tonight?"

"I sho' has," Liza said with a big grin. "He's a smart cat. He done gone to bed on yo' bed. Now dat Miz Grandma, she ain't dat smart. She sittin' on de settee down de hall jes' a-talkin' up a blue streak to dat senit man."

The young people looked at each other. Mandie blew out her breath and said, "All right, she can just sit there all night. We're going to bed. Good night, Liza." She continued down the hallway and her friends followed.

Mandie muttered to her friends, "I wonder what she has found to talk so much about."

"She's probably making plans for everyone when we get to Charleston," Jonathan said as they continued up the staircase.

Mandie looked back and said, "If they're sitting on the settee at the other end of the hall, we won't be passing them, so we can't hear what they are saying."

"We shouldn't eavesdrop anyway, Mandie," Celia said close behind her.

"Yes, I know," Mandie agreed. "Well, anyhow, good night, Joe and Jonathan. We'll see you early in the morning." She stopped to open the door to her room as she glanced at Mrs. Taft and Senator Morton sitting at the far end of the hall.

Joe and Jonathan were sharing a room across the hall. Jonathan opened the door to their room and the boys went inside after saying good-night.

Mandie opened the door to her room and she and Celia hurried inside to get ready for bed.

"I'll try to catch Grandmother before breakfast," Mandie said as she began turning the covers on the bed down, causing Snowball to scramble up to the pillows. "And, Snowball, you are not sleeping on my pillow." She pushed him down to the foot of the bed.

Mandie stayed awake a long time after she and Celia went to bed, trying to figure out how she could catch Mrs. Taft alone. Maybe tomorrow morning she would go to Mrs. Taft's room before they went down to breakfast. That is, if she woke up in time.

# CHAPTER THREE

# IS THERE A MYSTERY?

Mandie felt as though she had just gone to bed when Liza came into her room, talking loudly as she drew back the draperies.

"Time to git up now," Liza was saying as Mandie tried to pull the covers over her head.

Celia sat up in the bed and yawned. Snowball opened one eye to look at her.

"Gotta git up now, right now," Liza told Mandie as she yanked the covers off her.

Mandie rubbed her eyes and slid out of bed. Celia followed.

"We just now went to bed," Mandie fussed as she stretched.

"I done tole y'all you have to git up at five o'clock," Liza said, pulling back the last curtain. "Now git yo' clothes on and git down to de dinin' room. Breakfast is already on the table."

Mandie looked at Liza and asked, "Is Grandmother already downstairs?"

"Ev'ybody done downstairs 'ceptin' y'all," Liza replied. "Now git a move on, 'cuz I has to stay heah and be sho' y'all git dressed. If you want any breakfast you bettuh hurry."

The girls quickly scrambled into their clothes, which they had hung out the night before and which they would be wearing on the train trip.

"I'm ready," Mandie said as she brushed her hair and tied it back with a ribbon.

"So am I," Celia said, tying the bow at the neck of her blouse.

"Den let's git movin'," Liza said as she opened the door. Snowball jumped off the bed and stretched on the floor.

When the girls got to the dining room, Liza gave them plates and they went to the buffet to get their food. Everyone else was already there and everyone seemed to be talking at one time.

"Grandmother is still talking," Mandie said to Celia as she glanced at Mrs. Taft sitting between Mr. Guyer and Senator Morton at the table.

"I'd say she is enjoying having the attention of two men at one time," Celia replied with a big grin.

"I agree," Mandie replied.

The girls filled their plates and went to sit with Joe and Jonathan at the table.

"Glad to see you girls finally made it," Jonathan teased as he took the last bite of food on his plate.

"We were afraid we would have to go without you all," Joe said with a big grin.

"We got up at five o'clock. Y'all must have stayed up all night to get down here so early," Mandie teased back, quickly drinking her coffee.

"We didn't stay up all night, but your grandmother might have. She's still talking," Jonathan said, rolling his eyes in the direction of Mrs. Taft. "You will probably never get a chance to talk to her."

"I'll figure out a way to talk to her sometime before we start back home from Charleston," Mandie said firmly.

Everyone finally got ready and got down to the depot and into Mr. Guyer's special train car, which had been pulled over on a side rail waiting for them. The train came into the depot, coupled it up at the end, and they were on their way to Charleston.

The young people slept most of the way after not getting much rest the night before. Snowball had his own seat and only woke up to use his sandbox and nibble on food in his dish. The adults talked now and then and dozed in between.

Mandie was jerked awake by the train rounding a curve sharply. She looked out the window and became excited.

"Look!" she told her friends, who were also straightening up in their seats after the jolt. "There's the Spanish moss! We are getting close to Charleston now. See the swampland? We'll be in the city soon."

"I'm so glad we are almost there. This seat has not been comfortable to sleep in," Celia said with a frown.

As the buildings of the city came into view, Mrs. Taft rose and straightened her hat. Elizabeth sat up in her seat and looked out the window and then spoke to Mandie down the length of the car. "Amanda, get your things together now. And please hold on to that cat."

Jane Hamilton added, "And, Celia, please don't leave anything on here."

Lindall Guyer rose from his seat and said, "This car will be put on a sidetrack here and will be locked up until we are ready to go home, so if anyone does leave anything in here it will be safe."

"Thank you, Mr. Guyer, for bringing us in your special car," Mandie said as he came toward them and the door.

"Yes, sir, thank you," Joe added.

"And I thank you," Celia said.

"Not to be outdone by my friends, Dad, I am most grateful for this journey with you," Jonathan told his father.

Mr. Guyer stopped and looked at the young people. "After all these thanks, I hardly know what to say. Could it be that the group is hinting for something else special?" He grinned at them as he reached the door.

Two redcaps came into the car to take the luggage, and soon everyone was out on the platform, where Tommy Patton and his father waited for them.

After exchanging greetings, Mr. Patton told them, "We have the carriage here for the adults, and Tommy will take the young ones in the rig. Don't bother with luggage checked. My driver is waiting over there for the train to be unloaded, and he will bring it to the house."

Mandie and her friends quickly went over to the rig in the yard with Tommy. She held tightly to her white cat. "Do you really know how to drive this rig?" she asked teasingly.

Tommy grinned back at her and said, "Of course. Been driving it since I learned to ride a horse, and that was ages ago."

Mandie looked up into the rig as she started to step aboard. She paused, reached for Celia's hand behind her, and exclaimed, "Celia! Look who's here."

Robert, Celia's friend at Mr. Chadwick's School for Boys in Asheville, rose from a seat in the rig and jumped down and came to stand by Celia.

"Robert!" Celia exclaimed. "When did you get here?"

"I came home from school with Tommy," Robert explained, smiling down at Celia, "after I heard y'all were going to be here."

Celia looked up at the shy young man as he ran his fingers through his unruly brown curls and smiled shyly at her. "I'm so glad you did," she said.

Mandie looked at her friends and smiled. She knew Celia liked Robert a whole lot. And the feeling seemed to be mutual.

Tommy followed in the rig behind the carriage, and as they all pulled up through the gate before the Pattons' huge three-story mansion, Mandie felt as excited as she had been the other time she had been there to visit.

Mrs. Patton was waiting for them in the parlor and greetings were exchanged. All the adults had been friends for years and years.

Mandie looked around for Tommy's sister, Josephine, but did not see her anywhere. Turning to him she asked, "Where is Josephine?"

"Josephine is visiting some friends out at the beach this week. I'm not sure when she will be back," Tommy explained.

"I hope she didn't go away because we were coming," Mandie replied with a frown.

She and Josephine were certainly not friends. The girl was forever trying to stir up trouble when Mandie had visited before. Mandie was glad she was not home this time.

"I'm not sure she even knew y'all were coming," Tommy said. "This visit to her friends had been planned for a long time."

Mandie looked around the parlor. Everything was expensive and beautiful. She noticed Joe also gazing around the room. She leaned close to him and said, "It looks like a room out of a castle."

Joe muttered back, "Yes, even though I saw it before when you left from here to go to Europe, I have to gaze around."

Mandie leaned closer again as she sat next to him on the settee. "I'll take Charley Gap any day," she whispered.

Joe grinned at her and said, "So would I."

One of the servants came to let Mrs. Patton know the guests' luggage had been put in their rooms. Looking around the parlor Mrs. Patton said, "Now, if any of you would like to go to your rooms and freshen up, your things are already there. Let's meet in the drawing room at six o'clock before we go to supper."

The Pattons seemed to have an endless number of servants hovering around the hallway to take the guests to their rooms.

Mandie was delighted to find that she was being put in the same room she had used during her other visit. And Celia was sharing it with her.

"This is such a beautiful room," Mandie exclaimed as she and Celia were left alone in the room. "Everything in it is blue. Blue, blue, everywhere. And I like blue." She twirled around in the middle of the huge bedroom.

"Yes, it is a beautiful room, in case you like blue," Celia replied teasingly.

Mandie stopped to look at her friend. "You are excited because Robert is here, aren't you?"

Celia grinned as she plopped down into a chair and said, "Well, I suppose so, a little, anyhow." She jumped up and went to the wardrobe. "Now I have to find something to put on." The servants had already hung up their clothes.

"Yes, me too, and get rid of this traveling suit," Mandie said, beginning to shed her clothes as she followed Celia.

Snowball sat in the middle of the huge bed, washing his face and watching his mistress. Mandie glanced at her cat and said, "You know, Celia, I just remembered something. Mrs. Patton is allergic to cats, I believe."

"Oh dear!" Celia stopped to look at her as she replied, "What are you going to do with Snowball?"

"When we were here before I tried to keep him away from her, and Mr. Patton said it was all right if Snowball came with us to visit that time, so I suppose it is all right this time. I'll just have to watch Snowball and try to keep him away from her this time."

"I'll help you watch out for him," Celia promised.

"Will you also help me watch Grandmother? I hope she has a room near us on this floor," Mandie said, putting on a blue dress with white lace and ribbons on it. "I'd like to talk to her about Lily and get that settled."

"Yes, I will let you know if I find out where her room is," Celia replied. She smoothed down the skirt of the green dress she had put on. She turned in front of the full-length mirror and then asked, "Do I look all right?"

Mandie grinned and said, "You look fine, Celia, and I know Robert will think so, too."

"That was a big surprise, finding him here," Celia said, continuing to turn in front of the mirror.

"You know Tommy invited him here because of you," Mandie said, adjusting the sash on her dress.

Celia stood still and looked at her. "But suppose I had not wanted him to come here?" she asked.

"Oh, Celia, anyone who has seen you and Robert in the same company could tell that y'all are attracted to each other," Mandie said. "Now come on. Let's go down to the drawing room a little early and see who's there." She started for the door. Looking back at Snowball asleep on her bed, she said, "I'm leaving him here for the time being."

Celia followed Mandie out into the hallway. "Don't walk so fast, Mandie. People will think we are in a big hurry to get back with the boys," she said.

Mandie slowed down a little and continued on her way to the huge staircase. Celia followed, looking all about as she went.

The boys were in the drawing room, but Mandie gazed about her as she entered. She had never seen such a luxurious room before. She remembered when she saw it for the first time on her previous visit to the Pattons. The furniture was upholstered in peach and gray silk brocade. The draperies were a darker shade of gray with gold tassels. The carpet, which covered most of the parqueted floor, was so thick she sank into it as she walked. And there was Melissa Patton's portrait hanging over the gray stone fireplace that covered almost an entire wall.

Tommy stood up and stepped forward as the girls looked at the portrait and said, "This is one of my father's grandmothers, remember, Mandie?"

"Oh yes, I remember, and I think she is so real-looking, as though she's about to speak," Mandie replied.

"She is so beautiful," Celia commented.

Robert joined them standing there in front of the fireplace. "We came down early, hoping you girls would, also," he said.

Joe came to join them and said, "Well, I came down early hoping to find a little food somewhere." He grinned.

"We'll be going into the dining room in about a half hour, after all the others have joined us," Tommy told him.

Turning to Celia, Mandie said, "I hope my grandmother comes down before the others and that she is alone."

Jonathan overheard the remark and said, "I doubt that you will be able to get your grandmother alone for a single minute, with two admirers following her around." He grinned at Mandie.

"Admirers?" Tommy asked.

Mandie explained what had been going on, that Jonathan's father and Senator Morton both seemed interested in her grandmother. "And I've been trying to catch her alone to talk to her about Lily. Remember Lily that I met when we went to Europe? She is back home in Fountain Inn and I want to go visit her. Therefore I need my grandmother on my side when I approach my mother with this request."

"Is there anything I can do to help?" Tommy asked.

"No, not that I know of. Thanks anyway," Mandie replied.

"Let's sit down," Jonathan said.

The group moved across the room to two settees facing each other.

Soon thereafter the adults began coming into the drawing room. Mr. and Mrs. Patton were the first ones, and as soon as they sat down, Mandie's mother, Elizabeth, and Uncle John followed; then Jane

Hamilton came in with Lindall Guyer, and finally Mrs. Taft joined them with Senator Morton.

"I'd say your grandmother is awfully interested in the senator and is ignoring my father," Jonathan whispered to Mandie.

"Grandmother can be very misleading sometimes," Mandie whispered back. She watched as Mrs. Taft sat down near the fireplace and Senator Morton took a chair opposite her.

"Celia, it looks like my father and your mother are getting around together," Jonathan whispered to Celia.

Celia looked at her mother. She had sat down near Elizabeth, but Lindall Guyer had taken the chair next to her. Turning back to Jonathan, Celia said, "I don't want my mother to get interested in your father, Jonathan, because I certainly am not going to move to New York." She smiled.

"Oh, but your mother loves New York," Jonathan reminded her.

"This is all silly talk," Celia said. "Just because my mother sits next to your father or enters the room with him is not saying that they are anything but friends, and they have been friends for many years, remember." The smile faded off her face as she added, "Besides, my mother is still in love with my father even though he died a long time ago now."

The other young people were silent. Then Joe said, "I wonder if we'll have chocolate cake for dessert." He smiled at his friends.

"Joe Woodard, one of these days you are going to get fat, always eating chocolate cake," Mandie teased.

"We may be having coconut cake tonight," Tommy Patton told them. "That is my mother's favorite, and our cook can make the best I've ever had."

"Oh, let's talk about something other than food," Mandie said with a deep sigh. Looking at Tommy she asked, "Have you had any mysteries around this big house lately?"

"I knew it would be about mysteries," Joe said, pretending to be bored.

"I'm not sure it would be called a mystery, but we have heard on the third floor a couple of times what we thought might be squirrels, but no one has investigated," Tommy said.

Mandie immediately perked up. "Exactly what kind of noise was it? Was it inside the walls or closets, or what?"

"I'm sorry, but I don't know," Tommy said. "I just overheard Rouster telling the other servants about hearing something. So now the other servants won't go up on that floor alone. You know they're all suspicious of ghosts and things." He laughed.

"Maybe we could find out what it is," Mandie said, smiling at Tommy. "Why don't we go up there and look around?"

"Mandie!" Joe said.

"Well, we could go up there, but we probably wouldn't hear anything," Tommy said. "Rouster has been listening for it whenever he goes up on the third floor. But after those two times that he did hear it there hasn't been any more noise up there," Tommy explained.

Mandie leaned forward and said, "Couldn't we just go up and look around?"

"Now, why didn't I keep my mouth shut?" Tommy said with a grin. "I should have known you'd build it into a mystery."

"But couldn't we just go up there?" Mandie insisted.

"Yes, but I don't know when we'll have the opportunity," Tommy replied. "I think my mother has lots of things planned to do while you all are here."

"All right, in between whatever she planned, then," Mandie said. "She can't have every minute filled up."

"All right," Tommy agreed. "We'll pick the right opportunity and go look."

"I knew you would agree," Mandie said. "Thank you, Tommy." She smiled at him.

"I hope we don't have to spend all our time listening for sounds in the walls," Joe said, blowing out his breath.

"We won't be doing that, because I believe my mother is planning on going out to Mossy Manor to stay part of the time y'all are here," Tommy said.

Mossy Manor was the Pattons' old plantation house that Mandie and the others had visited while they were in Charleston on another visit.

"Maybe we would be able to find out what the noise is before we go out there," Mandie said.

"Yes, let's work real fast and solve the mystery so we can do other things," Joe said with a big grin.

"Yes, we can do that," Mandie agreed. She was secretly wondering how she could get up to the third floor and look around. Surely she would have an opportunity to do so.

# CHAPTER FOUR

# SECRETS ABOUT CHARLESTON

All during the evening meal Mandie tried to listen to the adults' conversation and carry on a conversation with her friends. She was anxious to know what everyone's plans were for the evening because she intended slipping away from her friends and going to investigate the third floor if she had an opportunity at all.

Also, she was trying to figure out exactly what her grandmother would be doing for the rest of the night, whether she would retire early or sit and talk with Mr. Guyer or Senator Morton. Mandie was hoping Mrs. Taft would be tired from their journey that day and would go to her room after supper.

Then she became aware of the conversation among her friends.

"What is on the third floor of this house? I mean, do y'all use that floor, too, just you and your mother and father?" Celia was asking.

"It is furnished, like the rest of the house, but we very seldom open it up. Sometimes we may have lots of guests overnight and we put them up there," Tommy replied.

Mandie smiled at him and asked, "You put your guests up there with this noise you told us about?"

"None of our guests have heard it that I know of. It was some of the servants, or I believe Rouster, who started this tale about the noise," Tommy replied.

"What did your parents say about it when Rouster told them?" Celia asked.

"Oh, they just laughed and said it was probably squirrels, and we do have lots of squirrels around here," Tommy said.

"So they didn't think it was important enough to investigate?" Joe asked.

"I don't suppose so. They haven't done anything about it that I know of," Tommy said.

"Well, then, there seems to be no problem," Robert added.

"But don't y'all want to know what made the noises right here in your own house?" Mandie asked Tommy.

"It doesn't bother me. It's the servants who are making such a big to-do about it," Tommy said as he drank his coffee.

"Well," was all Mandie could think of to say to that. However, she was secretly thinking she would investigate on her own if no one cared to go up there with her.

"Are y'all interested in going out to our beach house for a day or two?" Tommy asked.

"Oh yes, I'd like that," Joe said. "You know we aren't close to the ocean back home in North Carolina."

"Yes, that would be nice if I don't have to stay out in the sun there, because you know with my red hair I freckle awful in the sunshine," Celia said, pushing back her long curly hair.

"You could just come out on the beach after the sun goes down," Robert teased her.

"And what would I be doing during the day when y'all are out there in the sand having fun?" Celia asked.

"There is always shade made by the house, at different angles during the day, depending on the movement of the sun," Tommy explained.

Mandie realized everyone was finished with the meal and Mrs. Patton has risen. "Coffee in the drawing room," she was saying to the maid.

Everyone else stood up, and Mrs. Patton led the way into the drawing room.

Mandie reluctantly went with the group. She wanted to get away and slip upstairs. Then, as she was walking along with her friends down the hallway, she suddenly remembered her cat. "Oh, Tommy, Snowball is in my room, and he needs something to eat."

All the young people stopped.

"I would imagine that one of the maids has seen to that," Tommy said.

"I think I'd better go see," Mandie replied. Before anyone could object she started in the other direction down the hall and called back, "I'll only be a few minutes."

"Please hurry," Tommy said.

Mandie ran up the huge staircase and down the long hallway to the room she and Celia were occupying. Pushing open the door, she looked around for her white cat. He was not in the room.

Just as Mandie was leaving the room, she ran into Cheechee, the young maid.

"Dat white cat be in de kitchen eatin' his supper," the girl said and then turned and ran down the hallway.

"Thank you," Mandie called after her, but the maid didn't look back.

"Well," Mandie said to herself and started down the hallway in the opposite direction to return downstairs and join the others. She wondered why the young girl seemed to be afraid of her.

When she joined her friends in the drawing room, she said to them, "Cheechee ran away from me like she was terrified of something."

Tommy laughed and said, "Don't you remember? When y'all came to visit us at the beach house it was Cheechee who was trying to scare you."

"I remember that but I'd think she would have forgotten about that by now," Mandie replied as she sat down on the settee next to Celia.

When Joe looked at her, Mandie added, "It was something silly that Josephine had put her up to. Anyhow, she said Snowball is in the kitchen eating his supper, so I suppose he's all right."

Tizzy came in with a cart holding the coffee and dessert. As she went past the settee where the group of young people were sitting, Mandie asked, "Do you know if my cat is eating in the kitchen?"

"He sho' is, eatin' ev'rything in sight. He gwine be a fat cat one of dese days," Tizzy replied as she went on toward Mrs. Patton.

Mandie smiled and said to her friends, "Every place I take Snowball to visit with me, people feed him like he had never had a bite to eat."

"That's because he is always meowing for something to eat," Jonathan said, grinning. "And he sure likes New York food."

"That's because you New York people eat so much meat," Mandie said. "At home he'll eat whatever we have, even beans and corn bread."

"But the corn bread has cracklings in it, doesn't it?" Jonathan asked. "And even I know cracklings is some kind of meat."

Tizzy came back across the room with coffee and slices of cake on a tray for the young people.

"I told you we would have coconut cake," Tommy reminded everyone.

"Oh, it's delicious," Mandie said, taking a bite of her slice.

The others agreed.

"Almost as good as chocolate cake," Joe said with a big grin.

"Maybe we'll have chocolate tomorrow," Tommy said.

While her friends were carrying on a conversion, Mandie was trying to figure out how she could get up to the third floor. At night it was probably dark up there. And she certainly didn't know her way around the third floor. Maybe she could slip off up there early tomorrow morning, that is, if she woke before Celia did.

"You must be having some serious thoughts," Joe teased her.

Mandie quickly straightened up and smiled. "Not really," she said. "It has been a long day."

"Yes, I imagine you all are tired after that long train ride," Tommy said. "If y'all would like to retire, we could always just tell my mother good-night."

"Oh no, no, Tommy, I'm not that tired," Mandie quickly told him. She looked across the room and saw her grandmother talking to Senator Morton, and Mr. Guyer was seated next to Celia's mother. She laughed and said, "I think we need to stay up and watch what goes on with our elders."

Her friends looked at the others and laughed.

"Somehow or other I'll catch up with Grandmother and get a chance to talk," Mandie sighed.

"All we need to do is get her away from Senator Morton so she wouldn't have anyone to talk to," Joe teased.

"Oh, but then she would probably be talking to my father," Jonathan reminded him.

"Do you think they are really friends now after having not spoken for all those years?" Celia asked.

"My grandmother and Jonathan's father? Maybe. Grandmother does not always act out what she is actually thinking," Mandie said.

"Neither does my father," Jonathan said. "His actions can be very deceiving sometimes."

Mandie looked across the room and noticed that all the adults seemed to be rising.

Then her mother spoke to her. "Amanda, we are all going outside for a walk, if you young people care to join us."

Mandie quickly looked at her friends and asked, "Do y'all want to go walk?"

"Not really, but I suppose we should," Joe said, rising from his chair.

"I need some exercise," Celia agreed as she, too, stood up.

"Guess we might as well all go," Jonathan added.

The young people followed the adults out the front door, but when the adults turned to the left to walk in that direction, Tommy quickly said, "Why don't we walk this way? They are heading for the water. This way goes toward the city." He turned right and the group followed.

Tommy gave a description of the people who lived in the mansions they passed, some of it good and some of it bad.

"Now, the people in this house, the Yertzens, are newcomers, and they are not very friendly with the local people. It seems they came here from out West somewhere and are very wealthy, but no one knows where they got it," Tommy was saying as they slowed down past a huge two-story mansion.

"They must have lived in New York at some time or other, because that's the way New Yorkers live," Jonathan said as they walked on.

"And the family who lives here," Tommy said of the next house, which was quite a distance from the other one, "these people are a local family from way back, and everyone knows where they got their money."

"They do?" Mandie asked.

Tommy looked down at her and said, "Sure. All the families with inherited wealth like to brag about it. Therefore, everyone knows they are honest because they inherited their money. They didn't make it with dishonest businesses."

"Do you mean some of these people with lots of money didn't make it honestly?" Celia asked.

"Let's say a little dishonesty," Tommy replied. "They didn't go by social standards to make their wealth."

"My goodness, I didn't know you had such people living here in Charleston," Mandie said in surprise.

"Oh, Mandie, there are honest and dishonest people in every city. It just happens that the old-timers are nosy and learn all these things about any newcomers who move here," Tommy explained with a laugh.

Mandie looked up at Joe and asked, "I don't know of any dishonest people living in Franklin, North Carolina, do you, Joe?"

"No, but I imagine everyone there has lived there forever," Joe replied. "And Franklin is not a large city like Charleston here."

"Now, this house here," Tommy continued, "the people who own it are not living in it at the present but have leased it out to some strangers who will have nothing to do with anyone else. Therefore, no one knows anything about them, except my sister, Josephine."

"Josephine?" Celia asked.

"Yes, for some reason or other she has become friends with them, and my mother does not like that one bit. They have a daughter about her age, and she slips off now and then and comes down here," Tommy continued.

"How do you know she does that if you all are not friendly with these people?" Jonathan asked.

"My mother has Tizzy spying on Josephine sometimes in order to keep up with her, and Tizzy has seen her go in this house," Tommy explained. "But of course when my mother asks Josephine about it she just says she was walking past the house when the girl living there came out and talked to her. However, my mother does know that Josephine goes into the house and plans to catch her one of these days."

"From what you've been telling us I'd hate to be in Josephine's shoes," Robert said.

"Rest assured my mother will put a stop to it somehow," Tommy said.

"But why can't Josephine be friends with the girl?" Mandie asked.

Tommy looked down at her and said, "Because my mother knows nothing about what kind of people they are."

Now this mystery had Mandie interested. Where she came from, people were not judged by their social status.

"Just because someone doesn't want to tell everyone all about their private affairs doesn't mean they are bad people," Mandie argued.

"Why else would they want to keep their business private?" Tommy asked.

"Where I come from people are not judged by how much wealth they have or where they got it," Joe said. "And of course since my father is the doctor in our part of North Carolina, he eventually knows everyone's business. And it doesn't matter to anyone else who is wealthy and who is not."

Jonathan grinned and spoke up. "This city sounds like a bunch of snobs." He laughed.

"I agree," Tommy replied. "But it's not me doing that. It's the old-timers who are judging the other people."

"What is this family's name where Josephine goes to visit?" Mandie asked.

"Mr. and Mrs. Warren Bedford," Tommy replied. "And the daughter is called Ernestine, and don't ask me what she looks like because I have never seen her, even though they've been living here for several years."

"You mean she never goes out?" Celia asked.

"I don't know. I've never seen her," Tommy replied.

The group had walked way past that particular house. Mandie stopped and said, "Let's walk back so I can look at that house again."

"You want to look at that house again? I can assure you, you won't see anyone there. No one ever does," Tommy replied. "All right, we should return anyway or the others will be wondering where we went at this time of the night."

He led the way back down the street. Mandie tried to see the house in the darkness, but lots of shrubbery hid most of it from view. And there was no sign of any light.

Looking up at Tommy, Mandie said, "You know what? I think we ought to find out who these people are. I could go up to the door and knock. They wouldn't know me because I don't live here."

"Oh no you don't!" Tommy quickly responded. "My mother would not like that at all and we'd be in trouble." He hurried on down the street.

Mandie caught up with him and said, "I didn't mean I'd do that tonight. Maybe tomorrow in the daylight."

"No, no, no!" Tommy adamantly told her.

"Mandie, we can't go poking into other people's business," Joe told her. "Especially when it's in another town and no connection to us."

Mandie stomped her feet and said, "All right, all right."

No one had anything else to say, and the group returned in silence to Tommy's house, where the adults were just entering the parlor.

"I think I'd like to retire now," Celia said. "It has been a long, tiresome day with all that traveling we did."

"Yes, we should all get some rest, because my mother will probably keep us going all day tomorrow doing something," Tommy agreed.

Mandie and Celia stopped by the parlor long enough to say good-night and then went to their rooms. The boys weren't far behind them.

When Mandie opened the door to their room, she found Snowball curled up asleep in the middle of the bed.

"Thank goodness he is here and I don't have to go get him," Mandie said as she began to get ready for bed.

"And thank goodness we can finally relax," Celia said, yawning.

"I am awfully tired." She turned to look at Mandie. "We forgot to ask what time we're supposed to get up for breakfast."

"Maybe we'll just sleep right through it," Mandie said, laughing. "However, I imagine someone will come to wake us." As she changed into her nightclothes, she said, "This town is full of strange people, isn't it?"

"I was thinking the same thing, but I didn't want to say that because, after all, this is Tommy's home," Celia said, brushing out her long hair.

"In a way I wish Josephine would come home, because she gets involved in everything and we might find out things from her," Mandie said, reaching to pull down the counterpane on the bed and displacing Snowball, who protested.

"Maybe Josephine will come home while we are here," Celia said. "Tommy doesn't know when she's due back."

Mandie lay awake a long time, even though she was tired. She would like to sneak up to the third floor, but not in the dark in the middle of the night. Maybe she would wake up early enough before breakfast.

Then, too, she kept wondering about those people named Bedford. They were probably just common people and didn't want to mix with the wealthy crowd that Tommy's family belonged to. And she decided that wealthy circles must be a bunch of snobs. And she didn't think she would want to live in Charleston among such people.

Right now she was tired. Maybe tomorrow things would look better.

# CHAPTER FIVE

# A DISCOVERY

Mandie was angry with herself the next morning. She overslept and would not have time to go up to the third floor. When she opened her eyes Celia was sliding out of bed to get dressed. And at the same time the door to the hall opened.

"Breakfast in fifteen minutes," Cheechee announced as she stuck her head in the doorway.

"Fifteen minutes?" Mandie exclaimed, jumping out of bed.

"Dat's right," the young maid said and closed the door as she stepped back into the hallway.

Mandie hurried to the wardrobe to find something to put on as Celia pulled down a dress.

"Oh, I should have already been up," Mandie mumbled to herself as she found a blue cotton dress and snatched it from the hanger.

"Yes, me too," Celia said, quickly pulling on her dress.

"They sure don't give us much time to dress," Mandie continued mumbling as she shed her nightclothes and put on the blue dress.

"Maybe Cheechee forgot to let us know in time," Celia said, buttoning the bodice of her dress.

"She probably put us off till last because I believe she is still afraid of me," Mandie said, hurrying to the bureau to brush her hair.

"She probably thinks I'm angry with her for that trick she played on me when I was here before."

"I wonder if the boys have already gone downstairs," Celia said, tying back her hair with a ribbon.

"Come on. We'll find out," Mandie said, leading the way to the door. She glanced back at Snowball, who was still sitting on the bed. "I'll have to remember to ask for some breakfast for Snowball." She opened the door and went out into the hallway.

Celia followed as Mandie stepped across the hall and knocked on the door to the room Joe was sharing with Jonathan. There was no answer.

Going to the door to the next room, Celia knocked on it and did not receive any response. "I suppose Robert and Tommy have already gone down, too."

"Well, we sure are the cow's tail," Mandie muttered. "Come on, let's go." She hurried toward the staircase.

When they got down to the main hallway, they met up with Tizzy.

"Ev'rybody dun in de breakfast room," she told the girls. She pointed as she said, "Dat way."

"Thank you, Tizzy," Mandie replied as she and Celia continued on their way.

The girls caught up with Joe, Tommy, Robert, and Jonathan just as they were entering the breakfast room.

"Well, y'all finally got here," Joe teased.

"We thought perhaps you weren't coming down today," Jonathan added.

"Y'all almost didn't make it yourselves," Mandie replied with a big smile.

"We were right behind y'all," Celia said as she stopped next to Robert.

As the group entered the breakfast room, Mandie quickly looked to see if her grandmother was there. She was seated beside Jane Hamilton on the other side of the table and they were both eating. The other adults were helping their plates at the long buffet of food.

"My grandmother and your mother must have been the first ones here," Mandie told Celia.

"Yes, they must have been hungry," Celia agreed with a big smile.

"What are we doing today?" Joe asked Tommy as they stood in line.

Mandie quickly turned to listen.

"I believe my mother decided you all should just have a day of rest before we do anything else," Tommy replied.

"You mean we can just eat and sleep today?" Jonathan asked, grinning.

"Whatever you wish," Tommy replied, laughing at Jonathan's remark.

"So we can do just anything we want to, then?" Mandie asked.

"Yes," Tommy told her.

"Like inspect the third floor and walk by that house again where the Bedfords live?" Mandie asked as the group moved closer to the buffet.

Tommy looked at her, smiled, and said, "Well, depends on how you want to go about that."

Celia and Robert moved up to the buffet and Mandie quickly followed them. The adults had filled their plates and were taking places at the table. She picked up a plate and began putting food on it as she talked.

"We just go up to the third floor, look around, and listen for any noise there may be up there," Mandie said, frowning as she almost dropped the bacon she was placing on her plate. "And we could take a walk down the street like we did last night and go past the Bedfords' house."

"That sounds all right if you don't plan on stopping at the Bedfords' house," Tommy replied. "However, I would never agree to stopping in front of their house, especially not in the daytime when they could see us. That is definite because my mother would be really angry if we did."

Mandie quickly filled her plate and turned to find a place at the table. She noticed that Senator Morton had sat down beside her grandmother, and Mr. Guyer had taken the seat next to Mrs. Hamilton. The other adults were at the far end of the table.

"Let's sit here," Mandie told her friends as she set her plate down at the end away from the adults. The others followed.

Tizzy quickly came to fill their cups with coffee. And Mandie remembered Snowball. "Tizzy, I left my cat in my room," she said. "Would you please see that he gets something to eat?"

"I sho' will, missy," Tizzy said, smiling at her as she poured the hot, rich coffee into her coffee cup. "Don't you worry none 'bout dat cat. I take care o' him."

"Thank you," Mandie replied.

The young people talked about various topics as they ate. Mandie kept watching her grandmother now and then to see what she was doing. Then she saw Mrs. Taft and Mrs. Hamilton leave the table after finishing their meal, and Senator Morton and Mr. Guyer followed them out of the room.

"I wish somebody would get Senator Morton away from my grandmother for a little while so I could talk to her," Mandie said, blowing out her breath.

Her friends turned to watch the four adults leave the room.

"We'll have to think up some way to do that," Jonathan said.

"I think that would be hard to do," Joe said.

"Mandie, maybe I could ask my mother to help somehow," Celia suggested.

"What if I ask Senator Morton to tell us about the latest doings in Washington? Do you think he would?" Tommy asked.

"He might agree to that, but Mandie's grandmother might want to listen, also," Robert said.

"Probably, because my grandfather was also a senator and I suppose my grandmother is still interested in politics," Mandie told them.

"Mandie, I would just walk right up to her and say, 'Grandmother, may I have a private word with you?' Don't you think that would work?" Joe suggested.

"You don't think I would be rude to say that in front of Senator Morton?" Mandie questioned.

"No," her friends chorused.

The other adults, Elizabeth and John Shaw and Mr. and Mrs. Patton, rose from the table and walked by the young people on their way out the door.

"Amanda, today is a free day to do whatever you please, rest or whatever, but please don't get into any trouble," Elizabeth Shaw told Mandie as she stopped by their end of the table.

"Yes, ma'am," Mandie replied. "I won't." Her mother and the others left the room. She looked at her friends. Everyone had finished their breakfast. "If everyone's finished, let's go."

"Third floor?" Tommy questioned her as everyone rose from the table.

"Yes," Mandie said with a big smile.

As they followed Tommy out of the room, Mandie said, "Let's look in the parlor and see if my grandmother is in there before we go upstairs."

"If she is I don't imagine she is alone," Celia remarked as they started down the hallway.

Celia was right. Mrs. Taft was sitting in the parlor, but so were all the other adults.

"Oh well," Mandie said. "Let's go upstairs."

"Come on, this way. We'll go up the back stairs," Tommy told them, leading the way to the rear hallway.

Sliding double doors closed off the end of the hallway. Tommy pushed them open, revealing an ornately paneled corridor at the center and a winding carved staircase going up.

"This is the servants' stairway," Tommy explained as he led the way up the steps.

"Won't they resent our intrusion into their territory?" Jonathan asked.

"I don't think so," Tommy said. "Not at this time of day, anyway. They are all probably in different parts of the house working right now."

"What would they say if we met up with any of them back here?" Mandie asked, closely following Tommy.

"More than likely nothing," Tommy replied. He came to the landing for the second floor. Looking back at his guests, he added, "One more flight," and continued up.

From there up all the shutters were closed on the windows along the stairs, making it dark inside. However, Tommy knew where all the electric switches were and he kept turning them on as they went.

"I'm glad you have electricity in this house," Mandie commented. "Otherwise we would have to carry lamps all the way up."

"So am I," Tommy looked back to say. "But my mother and father were some of the first in Charleston to hook on to the electricity when it became available."

"We got it at our school in Asheville, you know, before your school got it," Celia said. "All those funny-looking wires hanging down from the ceiling with a light bulb on the end."

"We still don't have electricity at Mr. Chadwick's School," Robert said. "He has said he saw no reason to rush into anything that new."

"Here we are," Tommy said, pushing open a door at the top of the stairs. He reached inside, found a switch, and turned on the electric lights.

Mandie looked around the third-floor hallway as they entered it. The group stopped behind her.

"It looks almost like the hallway on the second floor, doesn't it?" Mandie said, gazing down the length of it where small tables, chairs, and settees were placed.

"Yes, if you walked in your sleep and woke up up here you'd probably think you were on the second floor," Joe teased.

"Now, Mandie, you've been up on the widow's walk, remember?" Tommy said, stepping over to a small door and opening it, revealing a spiral staircase inside. "You see? This is the entrance. Remember?"

"Oh yes, I remember very well," Mandie replied with a smile. "I thought I'd never get up to it that time with you." She turned away from the entrance to the widow's walk. "But whereabouts did the servants hear that noise?" She looked down the hallway.

"Oh, it was up near the front of the house," Tommy said, closing the door to the spiral staircase. "Come on, I'll show you."

Tommy walked across the back hallway and opened a door going into the main third-floor corridor. "This way," he told the others.

Mandie and her friends followed Tommy down a long hallway to the intersection of a cross hall. Here, Tommy turned left. All the doors to the many rooms they passed were closed. This reminded Mandie of the confusing network of corridors in Jonathan Guyer's home in New York.

Mandie glanced back at Jonathan behind her and said, "They keep all their doors closed like y'all do in your house."

"Doesn't everybody keep doors closed to rooms they are not using?" Jonathan asked.

"We don't at my house," Mandie said. "My mother says all the doors should be left open just a tiny bit so the rooms won't smell stale."

Tommy stopped and looked at her. "So you think our rooms must smell stale?" he asked, grinning at her. Then he stepped over to a closed door and opened it, revealing a large bedroom. "Smell."

"Oh, Tommy, I didn't mean that," Mandie said, looking beyond him into the room. Her friends also stopped to look.

"My mother keeps the doors slightly open all the time in our house, too," Celia added.

"Well, we don't have a large house, so all the doors are open or closed according to what is going on, I suppose," Joe said.

"I had not even thought about that, but I don't remember whether our doors stay open or closed," Robert said. "I promise to let you know when I go home and look." He smiled at Celia.

"I suppose the noise your servants heard up here was in a room with the door closed," Mandie told Tommy.

He closed the door to the room he had opened and continued on down the hallway. "Yes, since we close the doors to all the rooms," he replied, grinning down at Mandie. "This way."

Tommy stopped at the far end of the corridor and opened a door. "The noise seemed to be coming from inside this room, Rouster said, but of course the servants didn't wait to investigate—they fled in fright," he explained. He stood back so the others could look inside.

Mandie walked on into the room. It was a nicely furnished bedroom, and she went over to look out the window, which she noticed was not shuttered.

"This is over the side of the front of the house, isn't it?" she asked Tommy as the others followed her.

"Yes. In fact, this room is connected with the outside staircase," Tommy said. He went over to what Mandie had thought was a door to an adjoining room and opened it, revealing steps going down outside.

Mandie frowned as she thought about the doors. "You close all the doors but you don't bother to lock the door to the outside like this one," she said, looking at Tommy.

"Yes, I suppose you are right. No one has ever thought about locking this door," he replied.

"Someone could come up those stairs and get into the house," Celia remarked.

"But why would anyone want to come up such steep narrow steps to get inside the house?" Tommy asked.

"For no good reason," Jonathan said. "At least in New York we do keep all the outside doors locked."

Mandie walked around the room, looking at the spotless furniture. Then she stopped, gazed up at Tommy, and asked, "What did the noise sound like?"

"What do you mean, what did it sound like? It was a noise, that's all Rouster said," Tommy replied.

"What I mean is, was it a metal-like sound or a paper-rattling sound or a glass sound or what?" Mandie asked.

"I have no idea," Tommy said. "Rouster just said the servants heard a noise somewhere around this area of the house."

"Oh, shucks!" Mandie exclaimed as she stomped her foot. "Tommy Patton, you would never make a detective!"

"Why, I had just recently decided that when I finish school I might set up a private detective agency," Tommy teased. "I suppose I'd have to get you to come and run it for me."

"No, thank you, if I am going to run such a business it will be my own," Mandie replied, also grinning.

"Mandie, please don't go getting ideas of becoming a detective when you finish school," Celia said. "It would be an unsafe job for a woman."

"Unsafe?" Jonathan spoke up. "She is already running into all these unsafe mysteries everywhere she goes."

"She will outgrow that idea," Joe said, grinning at her.

Mandie ignored the conversation, walked over to the huge bureau, and opened the top drawer. She looked inside, surprised at what it held. "Tommy, this drawer is full of books," she said.

Tommy and the others came to look. He shuffled through the books and said, "These are all very old books. I have no idea as to what they are doing in a bureau drawer." He looked puzzled.

"That sure is a strange place to store books," Joe remarked.

Tommy began opening the other drawers. They were all empty.

"Have you ever seen these books before in another place, like on a bookshelf?" Jonathan asked.

"I'm not sure," Tommy said. "We have quite a few books in different shelves and cabinets throughout the house. I suppose these must belong to us. But why would they be in one of our bureaus like this?"

"Maybe all the bookshelves are full everywhere and there was no other place to put them," Celia suggested.

Mandie suddenly had an idea. "Maybe there are things stored in other rooms in bureaus and things," she said.

Tommy straightened up to look at her and said, "Now, that kind of investigation would take time to accomplish."

"Not if we scattered out and each one of us searched so many rooms each," Mandie said with a big grin.

"Mandie, please don't go getting that kind of idea," Joe moaned. "That sounds like work to me."

"Yes, it does," Jonathan agreed. "Besides, I thought we were going to walk past that house where the people called Bedford live."

"But we have the whole day free," Mandie replied. "We could do this up here, and after the noontime meal we could go walking."

"No, no, no, not unless you want to bake in the afternoon sun," Tommy protested. "The weather is hot in the afternoon, too hot to go strolling around town."

"Well, then," Mandie said thoughtfully, "why don't we go for the walk now and then this afternoon we come back up here and search." She looked up at Tommy.

"Well, I suppose we could do that," Tommy reluctantly agreed and then asked, "but what are we looking for in the other bureau drawers and things?"

"More books," Mandie replied and then added, "or whatever."

"Come on," Tommy said. "Let's go for a stroll and we can discuss this while we walk."

"We need to get our hats, Mandie," Celia reminded her. "I freckle in the sunshine."

"All right," Mandie agreed. "We'll get them. Tommy, will you please explain how we can get to our room without going through all those hallways again?"

"That's easy. Your room is almost directly beneath this one," Tommy explained. "I'll show you and then I'll wait in the front hall for y'all."

The boys went on with Tommy after he showed the girls their room.

Mandie opened the door and found Snowball curled up asleep on the bed. "Oh, I need to take Snowball out for some air," she said, quickly picking up his red leash from the bureau and fastening it to his collar as he stood and stretched.

"I'll help you with him," Celia said, quickly putting on her straw hat.

Mandie found her hat and stood before the mirror to fasten it on with a large hatpin. "Celia, do you think we might see that Bedford girl when we walk past that house?" she asked.

"I don't know, Mandie," Celia replied, straightening her hat before the mirror. "Anyhow, please remember that Tommy said we could not stop or speak to anyone there."

"Yes, I know," Mandie said, opening the door as she led Snowball out into the hall on his leash. "But what are we supposed to do if that girl sees us and speaks?"

Celia frowned and said, "I still wouldn't speak to her."

They hurried down the hallway to the main staircase.

"Well, at least we can look at her if she appears," Mandie said. And she would really like to know what the girl looked like, since she had become friends with Josephine. She didn't see how anyone could be Josephine's friend because of the girl's attitude and manners.

They hurried on to meet the boys in the front hallway.

CHAPTER SIX

# THE GIRL

Mandie and her friends walked toward the section of huge mansions where the Bedfords lived. The sunshine was already becoming hot and there were few people on the streets. But Mandie was not conscious of the heat. She was hoping the Bedford girl would be outside her house and she could get a good look at her.

"Snowball, slow down," Mandie told the white cat as she tightened her grip on the red leash when he tried to run ahead.

Snowball looked back at her and growled.

"What did Snowball say?" Tommy teased as he walked along beside Mandie.

Mandie grinned up at him and said, "I believe he said, 'I won't do it.'"

Joe, walking on the other side of Mandie, said, "He is a very independent cat. And you should see him chase dogs."

Jonathan stepped forward from behind and said, "Isn't that the Bedfords' house on the next block? The one with all those bushes in the yard?"

"Yes, it is," Tommy replied.

Mandie was overwhelmed with the many, many huge mansions in Charleston. "Why does everyone in this town build such huge houses?" she asked as they walked on.

"Some areas have huge houses like these, but other parts of town have much smaller, cheaper houses, even shacks now and then," Tommy explained. "And not all the people living in these big houses are wealthy. Some of them are living more or less on the credit."

"On the credit?" Mandie questioned. "Why would anyone want to live in such a house they can't really afford?"

"It probably makes them feel rich," Tommy said with a big grin.

They crossed a side street, and the Bedford house was in that block.

"Let's don't walk too fast so I can look at the house," Mandie said to her friends as she slowed down.

It was built of stone and rose three stories in the air, but there were very few windows in it. A flower-covered wall closed off any view of the front door and porch. As they came to the lacy black iron gate, Mandie tried to see through tiny open places in the pattern, but she remembered that Tommy had said very emphatically that they were not to stop in front of the house.

"Keep walking," Tommy reminded her in a loud whisper as he came up behind her, and the others moved on.

Mandie reluctantly followed her friends. She looked up at Tommy and said, "You said we couldn't stop in front of the house. However, you didn't say how many times we could walk past it." She smiled at him.

"Twice," Tommy replied. "We just passed it and we will pass it again on our way back. Twice."

The young people walked one more block, which was a long one, and then turned around to go back toward Tommy's house. Mandie slowed down and let them all get ahead of her so she could have a clear view of the Bedford house when she passed it. Snowball pulled at the leash and tried to walk faster.

Joe dropped back to walk beside Mandie. "I suppose we'll have the noon meal before we begin that search on the third floor, don't you think?" he asked.

"Yes, I would imagine so," Mandie agreed. She looked ahead as they approached the front of the Bedford house again.

Tommy, Celia, Jonathan, and Robert all paused to look back.

And at that moment Snowball gave a strong jerk to his leash and it snapped open, giving him freedom to run.

Mandie, holding the leash in her hand, started after the white cat. "Snowball, come back here," she yelled at him.

Snowball leaped into the air and landed on top of the rock wall in front of the Bedfords' house. He paused to look back at his mistress and then dived off the other side into the yard.

Mandie ran to the gate to peep through, trying to see where he had gone. "Snowball, come here!" she called to him but couldn't see him.

All her friends had rushed to her side and were trying to look into the yard.

Mandie pushed at the gate, but it wouldn't budge. She raised her foot to kick it and it still wouldn't move. "Snowball!" she kept yelling.

Joe joined in. "Snowball, you cat, get back here," he called, also trying to see inside the yard.

Then the whole group added their calls.

Mandie looked at the high wall and the locked gate, raised her long skirts, and tried to climb the gate. Tommy rushed up behind and pulled her down. "Mandie! You can't do that!" he told her.

Before Mandie could reply as she straightened her clothes, she saw a girl behind the shrubbery bushes inside the yard, and the girl was holding Snowball.

"Give me my cat!" she yelled at the girl.

"He's mine now. He came into my yard," the girl yelled back, staying behind the bushes.

Tommy moved closer to Mandie and called to the girl, "Bring us that cat. He doesn't belong to you."

"Let's all go over the wall and get him," Jonathan told the others as he prepared to climb up the post and get on top of the wall.

"No, no, Jonathan," Tommy said, coming to Jonathan's side.

"Why not? That's the only way we're going to get that cat back," Jonathan replied, still standing by the post.

"Let's stand still here and think this situation out," Tommy told the group.

"There's nothing to think out," Jonathan said.

"Well, while we are standing here thinking, that girl has disappeared with Snowball," Mandie protested.

Joe looked down at Mandie and asked, "Do you want me to go over the wall and get him? It wouldn't be any problem for me to cross that wall."

"Yes, yes, please, Joe, go get Snowball," Mandie immediately replied, tears brimming in her blue eyes.

"And I will go with you," Jonathan added.

Tommy stepped forward and confronted Joe and Jonathan. "You all will be causing a lot of trouble if you trespass into that yard," he told them.

"I'll worry about the consequences. In the meantime, I intend going after that cat," Joe said, turning to look up at the wall.

"And I'm with you," Jonathan added.

Celia and Robert stood by watching and did not participate in the conversation. Tommy silently stepped back beside them.

"I go first," Joe told Jonathan as he pulled himself up the post and managed to get on top of the wall.

"I'm right behind you," Jonathan said. He quickly joined Joe on the wall. They looked down into the yard.

Mandie watched and asked, "Can you see Snowball? Has that girl still got him?" She tried to peek through the openwork of the gate.

"I don't see him or the girl, but I'm going to jump down inside," Joe said, giving a leap down into the yard.

Jonathan quickly followed.

Mandie waited but there was nothing but silence in the yard. She listened but couldn't hear Joe or Jonathan moving about behind the wall. And there was no sound of Snowball. She figured the boys might be trying to slip up on the girl and catch her unawares and then grab Snowball. So she didn't call to them.

Celia stepped up to Mandie and reached for her hand. "I hope they get Snowball," she whispered.

"Thank you," Mandie whispered back, squeezing Celia's hand.

Mandie looked back and saw that Tommy and Robert had moved away a few feet and were talking in low tones. She knew Tommy was upset with what they were doing and that he would probably be in trouble with his mother about it. But Snowball had caused all this, and Mandie thought to herself that she should have left him at home in North Carolina. If she ever came to visit the Pattons again, Snowball would definitely stay at home.

Suddenly Joe appeared on the other side of the iron gate. And he was whispering, "He's not here. She must have taken him into the house."

"Knock on the door, and whoever answers it, tell them to give you my cat," Mandie replied in a whisper.

"All right," Joe agreed and quickly vanished among the thick bushes in the yard.

Mandie stood there, practically holding her breath. She heard the knock on the door and then in a few moments there were voices, but she could not hear them well enough to know what was being said. And then there was complete silence.

She turned to Celia, who was standing by her, and whispered, "Can you hear anything? What happened to everyone in there?"

"I believe someone did come to the door when Joe knocked," Celia said.

"Yes, but what happened? I don't hear a thing now," Mandie said. "Do you think it could have been that Bedford girl?"

"It could have been," Celia agreed. "But Joe must have gone inside the house, because the voices stopped."

"Jonathan seems to have completely disappeared," Mandie said to Celia as they both tried to see through the gate.

Suddenly Jonathan popped up in front of them on the other side of the gate. "Shh! Joe went inside the house," he whispered.

"Why didn't you go with him?" Mandie asked.

"We decided not to let them know there are two of us, so one of us can stay outside and watch," Jonathan explained.

"Who came to the door? Was it the girl?" Mandie asked.

"No, it was a man, a real old man," Jonathan explained. "The girl must have gone inside the house with Snowball before we jumped the wall. We haven't seen her at all."

"Can you see the door from here if Joe comes back out?" Mandie asked.

"Not too clearly. There are so many bushes in this yard," Jonathan replied.

"I wonder why Joe went inside that house anyway. Why didn't he just tell the man we wanted my cat?" Mandie said.

"I don't know. As far as I could hear, the man just opened the door and started saying, 'Come in the house, come in the house,' and didn't give Joe a chance to say anything," Jonathan whispered through the gate. Then he asked, "What are Tommy and Robert doing? I can't see them from here."

Mandie glanced back at the two boys, who were still standing at the edge of the road talking. "Still talking," she told Jonathan.

All of a sudden Joe came up behind Jonathan with Snowball in his arms. "Now we have to figure out how to get back over that wall with this cat," he told Jonathan.

"Oh, you got him, Joe! Thank you, thank you," Mandie cried excitedly as she got a glimpse of white fur through an opening in the gate.

"Why didn't they unlock the gate to let you out?" Jonathan asked.

"The old man was not very bright," Joe replied. "I couldn't make him understand very much. We were standing in the parlor and Snowball came running into the room. I snatched him up and headed for the front door."

"Did you see that Bedford girl?" Mandie asked.

"Yes, I only got a glimpse of her and also another girl in a room down the hallway. Soon as they saw me they disappeared," Joe replied. "Now, let's get this cat across the wall, Jonathan."

"I'll climb up on top of the wall and you hand him up to me," Jonathan said. "And then I'll just drop him down the other side and Mandie can catch him." He quickly made his way to the top of the wall.

Mandie stepped back to watch.

"Here he is," Joe called from the other side as he tossed Snowball up to Jonathan.

Snowball growled and huffed up his fur as he landed on the wall. And before Jonathan could catch him he jumped down and landed at Mandie's feet. She quickly snatched him up.

"Oh, Snowball, you are such a troublemaker," Mandie told him as she held him tightly in her arms.

Jonathan jumped down and Joe followed.

Tommy and Robert walked over to them. "I'm glad you were able to get Snowball," Tommy said to Joe and Jonathan. "I think we'd better get on back to the house."

Joe stepped in front of Tommy and said, "Hold on a minute. I saw the girl who was in the yard. She was in another room in the house with another girl." He paused and looked directly at Tommy. "And that other girl looked very much like your sister, Josephine."

"What!" Tommy exclaimed as the others gathered around in excitement. He took a deep breath and said, "I'm sure you are mistaken. Josephine is at the beach with friends. Now, let's get back." He started walking toward his house.

"I think you should ask your mother to check on Josephine," Joe insisted as he kept up with Tommy.

Mandie thought about things for a moment and then said, "Maybe this Bedford girl was visiting at the same place as Josephine was and they came back to the Bedfords' house together."

"I don't think so," Tommy insisted as he hurried on.

"Tommy, I'm sorry Snowball caused so much trouble. I'll see that he doesn't get outside again unless I am holding him and he can't get away," Mandie said, trying to keep up with the boys, who seemed to be in such a hurry.

Tommy didn't answer.

"I'll help you with him, Mandie," Celia told her.

"He's no trouble. That was a lot of fun," Jonathan said, grinning at the girls.

"Fun? Oh, Jonathan, I was worried sick about him," Mandie said, holding the cat tightly in her arms.

Jonathan stepped up close to Mandie and Celia and whispered, "Just think. Snowball was the cause of us finding out a secret."

Mandie looked at him and repeated, "A secret?"

"Yes, that Josephine is not where she's supposed to be. I imagine some fur will fly about that," Jonathan continued whispering.

"But it might not have been her," Celia said.

"What do you think Mrs. Patton will do if someone tells her that Josephine is probably at the Bedfords' house?" Mandie asked as she watched the boys moving on ahead of them.

"First of all, someone will have to prove that was Josephine in that house," Jonathan said.

"And how are they going to do that?" Celia asked.

"Well, now, if they would like, I'll be glad to go back and knock on that front door and inquire," Jonathan said with a big grin.

"That's no sign you will be able to get inside the house," Mandie reminded him.

"I can guarantee you if I knock on that door and someone opens it I will get inside that house," Jonathan said.

Joe came up to Mandie as they walked. "What are you going to do with Snowball for the rest of our visit?" he asked.

"I'll keep him shut up in our room," Mandie said, glancing at the red leash in her hand. "And I'll need to be sure the catch on this leash is working."

Joe reached for the leash, looked at it, and said, "I'll fix it for you. The little hook that clasps onto his collar is bent. It'll be all right."

They finally came to the front of the Pattons' house. Mandie took a deep breath and braced herself to face the storm that Tommy seemed to expect from his mother when she was told they had been at the Bedfords' house.

All the young people fell silent as Tommy led the way and held the front door open for everyone. "I believe everyone is already in the parlor waiting for us to return for the noon meal," he said, waving them on toward the parlor.

Mandie stopped in the hallway and said, "Tommy, I need to go up to my room and leave Snowball. I'll be right back."

"I'll go with you," Celia quickly told her, and the two girls hurried down the wide hallway toward the main staircase.

"If you could loan me a hammer and screwdriver, Tommy, I could repair this leash in half a minute," Joe said.

"All right, come on back to the workroom," Tommy said, and the boys followed him toward the back.

In Mandie and Celia's room the girls quickly freshened up while Snowball curled up on the bed to take a nap.

"I dread facing my mother when she finds out what we've been doing," Mandie said, brushing her long blond hair.

"It was an accident that Snowball got loose, so I don't think anyone can blame you too much," Celia said, retying the sash on her pale green dress.

Mandie grinned at Celia and said, "I just hope that *is* Josephine at the Bedfords' house. That will take part of the trouble off me, because if it is, we did find her and Mrs. Patton ought to appreciate that."

"Yes, Mrs. Patton will probably be more upset about that than what happened to Snowball," Celia agreed.

"I'm just sorry that Tommy seemed to get upset with us. I don't know what else we could have done. We had to get Snowball back," Mandie said.

"And our mothers, Mandie," Celia reminded her. "What do you think they will do when they hear our story?"

Mandie thought for a moment and said, "I'm not sure what my mother will do, but I'm hoping my grandmother will be around to take my side of it."

"I do, too," Celia agreed.

"In fact, maybe I will have a chance to talk with my grandmother about that letter I received from Lily," Mandie said.

"If your grandmother is not too engrossed in conversation with Senator Morton or Mr. Guyer." She grinned at Mandie.

"We might as well go find out," Mandie said, laying down her hairbrush and going to the door. "And I want to be sure Snowball is shut up in here." She allowed Celia to step out into the hallway and then firmly closed the door and checked it to be sure it was closed.

When they came to the door of the parlor, Mandie instantly spotted her grandmother sitting alone on the far side of the room. The senator and Mr. Guyer were not in the room. She quickly walked over to Mrs. Taft.

"Grandmother, I need to talk to you about something," Mandie said, sitting down on the stool by Mrs. Taft. Celia went to the other side of the room where her mother, Mandie's mother, John Shaw, and Mrs. Patton were all talking.

"What is it, dear?" Mrs. Taft asked, smiling at Mandie.

"Guess what? I received a letter from Lily Masterson. Remember her on the ship when we went to Europe?" Mandie asked, trying to hurry.

"Of course, I certainly do remember that girl and her little sister. And I have wondered whatever became of them," Mrs. Taft replied.

"They are back home in Fountain Inn, South Carolina," Mandie explained. "And Lily wrote in her letter that if we are ever that way we should come visit." Mandie paused to look up at her grandmother. "Do you think we could really go visit them, Grandmother? Do you think it's possible?"

"Yes, I believe it would be possible to go visit them someday," Mrs. Taft replied with a smile.

"But, Grandmother, I thought maybe we could stop there on our way back home if the train goes through there," Mandie excitedly suggested.

"We'll see, dear, we'll see. Now here comes Senator Morton," Mrs. Taft said, looking across the room.

Mandie took a deep breath and stood up to join Celia. At least her grandmother was now aware of the letter and would have time to think about it while they were here at the Pattons' house. Maybe she would be able to figure how they could go visit.

# CHAPTER SEVEN

# WHERE DID THAT COME FROM?

When everyone went in to the noon meal, the young people were grouped together near the end of the long table. They could carry on their own conversations without being heard by the adults at the head of the table. On the other hand, Mandie could not listen to what her grandmother and the others were talking about.

Her friends were mostly silent at the table, and she felt it was because of the escapade with Snowball. Sitting directly across from Tommy, she asked him, "Aren't you going to tell your mother about that other girl in the Bedfords' house?"

"I haven't decided yet," Tommy replied, glancing at his mother, who seemed to be carrying on a conversation with all her guests.

"If that was Josephine I saw, I'm sure your mother would want to get her home," Joe said, sipping his coffee.

"I'm not sure I want to explain to her exactly what we were doing at the Bedfords' house," Tommy said, laying down his fork and straightening up to look across the table at Mandie.

"But you didn't do anything wrong, Tommy," Mandie said. "And I don't mind if you explain to her what happened because I don't believe I did anything wrong. I think my mother would agree with me."

"I'm sure your mother would want to know if that is your sister at the Bedfords' house so she could get her home, as Joe said," Jonathan told him.

Tommy sipped his coffee and looked at his friends. "If Josephine is out there, it's not the first time this has happened. I suppose she's all right there. It's just that my mother does not want to associate with those people because no one knows what kind of reputation they have. And also my mother wants Josephine to learn to obey. So if I tell my mother anything about what happened, she would have someone investigate and bring Josephine home if she is there." He paused, blew out his breath, and added, "And Josephine can be awfully mean sometimes. So she would probably vent her anger on all of us."

Mandie smiled at Tommy and said, "That's all right with me. I've seen her angry before when she made up all those ghost tales about this house, remember?"

"Tommy, if Josephine is all right with the Bedfords, I would leave things alone for now," Celia told him. "If we do move on to your beach house, then we should tell your mother that she may be at the Bedfords. But as long as we are here in this house and you think she is all right, then I would leave things alone."

"I've been thinking the same thing," Tommy agreed. "I'd just hate to stir up a hornet's nest and ruin y'all's vacation with us."

Mandie smiled at Tommy and said, "Then let's forget about all that for the time being and go up to the third floor and search all those drawers that we had planned on looking into."

Tommy smiled back at her and said, "That sounds like a good idea." He looked around the table at the young people and asked, "Are y'all in agreement?"

"Yes," went around the group.

As soon as the meal was finished, Tommy got them all excused from cake and coffee in the parlor and they headed for the third floor.

He led the way into the first room at the top of the stairs and told the group, "I don't know exactly what y'all are looking for, but if you find anything at all in any of the drawers, please let me know and we'll decide whether it's important or not. And let's do one room at a time."

Mandie decided just about every piece of furniture up there had some kind of drawer in it, and they all seemed to be empty.

After searching the fourth room and not finding anything at all, Joe straightened up from the drawer he had pulled out and said, "This is a hopeless cause. We should have taken time to eat some of that delicious-looking chocolate cake I saw on the sideboard."

Tommy looked at him and grinned. "I can fix that," he said. "I'll run down to the kitchen and ask Tizzy to send us some up on the dumbwaiter." He started for the door. "I'll be right back." And he went out into the hall.

Mandie glanced around the bedroom they were in and said, "Where shall we eat the cake? Let's find a table somewhere."

The group moved out into the hall and began looking in rooms for a table. Finally they opened the door to what seemed to be a very small library. One wall was lined with shelves loaded with books, and a carved mahogany library table stood in the center of the floor with chairs clustered around it.

"Oh, this is perfect," Mandie said, walking around the room. "There are six of us and there happens to be six chairs. Perfect."

"I wonder where the dumbwaiter is," Celia said. "I hope we're near it."

"Wherever it is I won't mind walking to it to pick up the cake," Joe said with a big grin.

Mandie went over to inspect the books. "A lot of these books are on the history of Charleston," she said. "This one is the British Occupation of Charleston during the Revolutionary War and here is one about Fort Sumter. And a book about the earthquake in 1886."

Joe came to look over her shoulder as she took down each book. "Charleston is full of history," he said, and looking down at Mandie, he added, "This would be a wonderful place to live when I finish my schooling."

Mandie quickly looked up at him and said, "You'd live here in Charleston? This is an awfully long way from home in North Carolina, Joe."

"Not as far as New Orleans, where I go to college," Joe said.

"And you know if I am to practice law I will have to live somewhere that I can make a living."

"Oh, Joe, you could set up practice at Charley Gap or at least in Bryson City. Everyone there knows you and would give you their business, I'm sure," Mandie quickly told him, frowning as she looked up into his brown eyes.

"I could, but I wouldn't make much of a living," Joe replied. "You know if my father had not inherited all his money, he would never have set up a medical practice at Charley Gap and made a living. The poor people there don't have much and want to trade chickens, corn, or whatever they have for medical help."

"Then if your father inherited a lot of money, you will inherit it from him someday since you are an only child. I'm sure Dr. Woodard would be glad to help you get started in law practice," Mandie replied, frowning as she thought about her future.

"Of course he would do anything to help me and to get me to stay close to home, but I want to do things on my own, Mandie," Joe replied. "I want to prove to myself that I can do it."

"Well, so do I," Mandie quickly told him. "I don't want all that wealth my mother and Uncle John and my grandmother have. I want to be independent."

Joe grinned at her and asked, "Independent like what?"

Mandie stuttered for a moment and then said, "Well, like having my own business. Maybe I'll set up practice as a lady detective."

"Lady detective?" Joe asked in surprise. "Mandie, you don't want to be a lady detective. Why, that could be dangerous work. You won't ever have to work. You can marry me and I'll see that you get anything you ever want."

Mandie felt her face flush, and she wouldn't look into Joe's eyes as she replied, "Joe Woodard, marriage is a long way in the future, and who knows what may transpire between now and then." She quickly turned away to look at Celia, who was opening the drawer in the table.

"I found something!" Celia exclaimed as she stood there looking into the drawer.

"What is it?" Mandie asked, quickly rushing to her side. She gasped when she saw what Celia had found.

Her friends were also curious and came to see for themselves just what was in the drawer.

"I thought maybe it was a snake," Jonathan joked.

At that moment Tommy opened the door and came into the library. "I'm glad y'all found this room," he said, walking over to a panel in the wainscoting. "I meant to tell you the dumbwaiter opens in here." He quickly slid the panel open, revealing a tray on a shelf hanging from ropes. The aroma of coffee filled the room.

"Coffee!" Jonathan said, going to inspect the contents of the tray.

"And chocolate cake," Joe added as he stepped back to look.

Tommy turned to look at the girls and Robert, who were standing in front of the library table. "Is something wrong?" he asked.

"We don't know," Mandie replied, not budging from in front of the open drawer.

"Look," Celia told Tommy, pointing to the drawer.

"What is it?" Tommy asked, coming to join them. He looked down into the drawer and picked up what Celia had found. "I can't imagine what this is doing in the library table."

"It's someone's hair," Mandie said, frowning as she stared at the piece of blond hair tied together with a blue ribbon, forming a curl.

"Yes, and I have no idea where it came from or how it got in that drawer. Was anything else in there?" Tommy asked as he bent to run his hand around the entire inside of the drawer. Not finding anything else, he straightened up and said, "Let's leave it in there until we at least eat our cake and coffee." He dropped the piece of hair back in the drawer and closed it.

Going back over to the dumbwaiter, he took a tray of coffee cups and a percolator of hot coffee from it, put them on the library table, and then took out the slices of chocolate cake.

"Ummm," said Robert. "Smells good."

"Help yourselves," Tommy told them.

Everyone settled down at the table with cake and coffee.

"Mandie, your cat was in the kitchen being well fed by Tizzy," Tommy said. "She said she would take him back up to your room when he finishes his food."

"Thanks, Tommy," Mandie said. "I meant to ask Tizzy to feed him."

"You won't have to worry about him. Tizzy will take care of him," Tommy said.

"Where is everyone? Are they all in the parlor?" Mandie asked as she sipped the hot coffee.

"I believe so. I passed the parlor door and didn't stop to look in," Tommy said. Looking around the group, he asked, "Now, what else have y'all found while I was gone?"

"Nothing," everyone chimed in.

"Do you have any idea as to whose hair that is that Celia found?" Mandie asked.

"Not offhand," Tommy replied. "My mother would probably know, but then we'd have to tell her where we found it and I imagine that is not the place where it is supposed to be. We have a whole collection of baby stuff, bibs, clothes, shoes, photos, and everything from probably a hundred years ago, but it is all supposed to be in a section of the attic that is allocated for that purpose."

"In the attic? You have an attic up above here? I thought this was absolutely the top floor," Mandie said.

"Oh no, we have a full-sized attic that goes over most of the house," Tommy explained. "The house is so tall you can't really tell it's there from the outside."

Mandie grinned at him and asked, "Are you going to show it to us?"

"I knew that question was coming," Joe teased.

"Of course," Jonathan said. "We have to see everything."

"Let's finish searching the drawers on this floor real fast and then go up there," Mandie suggested.

"I almost forgot to tell y'all," Tommy said, looking at the group. "My parents are taking all the adults out for dinner tonight, so we are on our own. Tizzy will give us supper whenever we are ready."

"So we are free without adult supervision tonight," Celia remarked, drinking her coffee and hurrying to eat her cake.

"That gives me a nice feeling, that we can do whatever we please," Jonathan said with a grin.

As everyone finished their cake and coffee and piled the dirty dishes back on the dumbwaiter, they discussed their plans for the evening.

"Why don't we split up into two groups to finish searching the drawers on this floor? That would cut that into half the time necessary," Mandie suggested.

"That's a good idea. We'll do that," Tommy said, giving the dumbwaiter a pull to send it down to the kitchen and then closing the panel over it.

With something else to look forward to, the group quickly finished searching the drawers on the third floor. They did not find a thing. Everyone met in the hall at the front of the house on the third floor.

"Now can we go to the attic?" Mandie asked, smiling up at Tommy.

Tommy looked around the group and asked, "Does everyone want to visit that smelly old attic?" He grinned at Mandie.

Everyone did, so he led the way through a narrow door at the end of the hallway and up steep steps to the room full of old treasures above. Pushing open the door, he reached inside and turned on the electric lights.

"Now, these lights are like what we have in our school," Celia said, looking at the wires suspended from the ceiling with a light bulb attached to the end hanging down.

Joe stooped to walk under one. "I wonder why they hung them so low you could bang your head on them," he said.

"They haven't really finished with these lights," Tommy said. "They are supposed to come back and put fixtures on the wall and do away with all this wire hanging down. In the meantime watch your head."

"Now, where is the collection you mentioned, Tommy?" Mandie asked, looking around the room. Everything was clean and neatly stacked and placed in position to be accessible.

"Over here," Tommy said, leading the way across the huge room. He stopped at the far corner where there were all shapes and sizes of glass-doored cabinets filled with items from years long ago.

"Oh, how nice. I'm going to ask my mother to fix up our attic this way," Mandie said, moving along to look through the glass doors.

"The doors are all locked," Tommy told her. "That's to keep people from jumbling everything up or taking things out. You can see the various cards labeling the items. This collection was organized before I was ever born."

Mandie looked up at Tommy and asked, "Now, if that piece of hair in the library drawer came from here, how did anyone get it out?"

"Which cabinet did it come out of?" Celia asked.

Tommy quickly went down the rows and rows of cabinets and finally said, "I don't see a single vacant space where it could have been."

"Then maybe it didn't come out of any of these," Mandie said.

"Maybe it didn't," Tommy agreed. "But it looked similar to the other hairpieces in these." He waved his hand down the row.

Mandie had noticed that there were quite a few hairpieces in the cabinets. "Who would have access to the keys for the cabinets?" she asked.

"I suppose anyone who was able to get in my mother's private safe in my parents' room, and that person would have to know the combination, which even I don't know," Tommy explained.

"Are you going to mention this to your mother?" Celia asked.

"I don't think so, not right away," Tommy replied. "There are so many things happening that could be upsetting."

"How about if we go downstairs and be lazy for a while in the parlor before supper?" Jonathan asked.

"Yes, we've had an awfully busy day," Robert quickly added.

"And I might possibly catch my grandmother alone to ask if she has decided what we can do about visiting Lily," Mandie told her friends.

"Let's go," Tommy said. He led the way down to the main floor and into the parlor.

"Oh, shucks!" Mandie exclaimed, looking around the room. "No one is in here."

"They are probably all in their rooms right now getting dressed to go out," Tommy told her.

"Yes, I suppose so," Mandie agreed as she sat down on a small settee.

"What are your plans for us tonight?" Jonathan asked Tommy as he sat beside him on another small settee.

"If everyone is not too tired, I thought we could go for a walk after supper when the air has cooled off," Tommy replied.

Everyone quickly agreed.

Mandie looked at Celia and secretly smiled at her. She knew Celia could read her mind and that she planned to walk past the Bedfords' house when they went out. She was determined to find out if the other girl in that house was actually Josephine. She had no idea as to how to find out, but she would think of some way to do it.

When the adults finally came into the parlor, they didn't even sit down but said good-night to the young people and left for their dinner out in town. Mrs. Taft was not alone, so Mandie could not approach her with any questions about anything, but she planned to accomplish that soon.

# CHAPTER EIGHT

# WHERE DID IT GO?

Mandie and Celia were both sleepy and tired that night and didn't waste time getting ready for bed. Mandie pulled the counterpane down and upset Snowball, who was sleeping in the middle of it. He growled his displeasure and curled back up at the foot.

"I thought it was strange that there weren't any lights on in the Bedfords' house when we passed by tonight," Mandie said, crawling under the sheet.

"We were by early enough that someone should have been up," Celia said. She plumped up her pillow and relaxed.

"Maybe they were all out somewhere, but you'd think they'd at least leave a light burning," Mandie said. "We didn't solve anything today. All that searching of drawers and we didn't find anything. And we never even found out where those books came from in the bureau drawer because Tommy had never even seen them before."

"I wonder what we will do tomorrow," Celia mumbled, half asleep. "I forgot to ask Tommy if anything is planned."

"M-m-m," Mandie muttered. "Good night."

"Night," Celia answered.

And the next thing the two girls knew it was morning. The sun was shining brightly through the thin curtains. Snowball was sitting up in the middle of the bed washing his face and purring as he did it.

Mandie raised up on her elbow and said, "It must be time to get up." She rubbed her eyes.

"Yes," Celia agreed and tumbled out on her side of the bed.

Mandie threw back the thin sheet and slid to her feet, yawning and stretching as she looked around the room. "I wonder why no one came to wake us."

"I don't know, but I suppose we'd better hurry and go downstairs so we won't be late for breakfast," Celia said, rushing over to the wardrobe to pull down a dress.

"I don't think I even know what time breakfast is supposed to be," Mandie said, joining Celia at the wardrobe to get a dress.

Celia stopped by the mantelpiece to look at the clock. "Mandie, it's only five minutes to seven," she said.

"Five minutes to seven, but the sun looks like it is already high in the sky," Mandie said, glancing out the window. "I suppose that's because we are here near the ocean and not down between the mountains like we are at home." She quickly dressed.

"The boys are probably already downstairs," Celia said, fastening the buttons of her dress.

Mandie went over to the bureau to get her locket. She looked all over for it. It wasn't there. She became worried. "Celia, I can't find my locket," she said. "I know I put it here on the bureau last night when I took it off." She began moving everything around on the bureau. "Oh, where is it?" She was becoming frantic. Her locket contained the only picture she had of her father. It was made right before he died.

The bureau stood next to an open window. Celia hastily scanned the surface for the locket and then said, "Mandie, do you think it could have blown out the window?"

Mandie frowned and then laughed. "Oh, Celia, I don't think my locket could blow away. It's too heavy."

"But the winds are awfully strong here sometimes," Celia reminded her.

"I was awfully sleepy when I went to bed last night. Maybe I dropped it," Mandie said, getting down on her knees to look around the floor.

"Do you think Snowball could have jumped up on the bureau

and played with it, maybe knocking it down on the floor?" Celia asked, also stooping to look around the carpet.

Mandie went back to the bed, pushed Snowball off, and shook the sheets and counterpane to see if the locket could have fallen there. She went to the wardrobe and examined the pockets of the skirt she had had on the day before, but they were empty.

"It just isn't anywhere," Mandie said, standing in the middle of the room and looking around.

"Are you sure you had it on when we came to our room last night?" Celia asked.

"Well, yes, pretty positive," Mandie replied. "I always take it off and put it on the bureau at night wherever I'm staying."

"But you don't wear it every day, do you?" Celia asked, standing up and straightening her long skirts.

"Almost every day," Mandie said. She looked around the room as she walked and said, "I've got to find my locket." She stood still to stomp her foot.

"Mandie, let's go downstairs and talk to the boys and see if they can offer us any advice," Celia suggested.

"All right, but I don't know how I can eat any breakfast until I find my locket," Mandie replied, going across the room to open the door. She looked back at Snowball, who had jumped back up onto the bed. "And I don't want to lose you, Snowball, so you just stay here, you hear?"

Snowball answered with a loud meow.

Mandie allowed Celia to go out first so she could be sure the door to their room was firmly closed. Then they walked down the long hallway to the main staircase.

All four boys were in the parlor, but no adults were in sight.

"Well, well, y'all are up bright and early," Tommy greeted them as he rose from the chair he was sitting in.

"It gets daylight here so early," Celia said, going to sit by Robert.

Mandie looked around the room and said, "If anyone finds a locket, I've lost mine,"

Joe came to her side and asked, "Do you mean the locket with your father's picture in it?"

"Yes, that's the only one I ever wear," Mandie replied, sinking down on a small settee, and Joe sat beside her.

Joe looked at the other boys and explained, "That locket contains the only picture Mandie has of her father, who died three years ago, as y'all probably know."

Jonathan came to kneel in front of Mandie and held her hand. "I'm sorry," he said. "We'll do our best to find it. It has to be somewhere."

"Thank you, Jonathan," Mandie replied. "It has to be in our room, but I can't find it."

Tommy came to sit in a nearby chair. "Mandie, do you think you could have lost it yesterday while we were at the Bedfords' house?" he asked. "Could it have fallen off? Remember Snowball's leash came unhooked. Maybe your locket also came unhooked."

"I don't think so, Tommy," Mandie replied. "I'm sure I had it on when we went to our room last night. Celia and I looked everywhere in the room and couldn't find it."

"Would you like for us to come and help you look?" Tommy asked, indicating himself, Joe, Jonathan, and Robert.

Mandie shrugged her shoulders and said, "I suppose it would be all right for you fellas to come and look if we leave the door open."

"Then let's do it," Joe told her as he stood up.

"Yes, right now, before we have to go in to breakfast," Tommy said.

They hurried to Mandie and Celia's room, and the first thing the boys did was jerk all the covers off the bed to be sure the locket was not between the sheets. Snowball protested and went racing about the room looking for another place to sit. It took only a few minutes for the four to search every inch of the room. The locket was nowhere to be found.

"It's definitely not in this room," Joe decided as they stood and looked about.

Cheechee had been attracted by the noise when she was going down the hallway, and she had stopped to watch and listen. Mandie saw her standing in the doorway and stepped over to explain. "We are looking for my locket, Cheechee," she explained. "Have you seen it?"

Cheechee shuffled her feet around and wouldn't look directly at Mandie. "De spirit in de night dun come and tuck it," she muttered.

"Now, Cheechee, you know I don't believe in ghosts and things like that, so please don't tell me some spirit came and got my locket," Mandie replied. "Did you see someone take it?"

"No, no, no," Cheechee quickly replied, violently shaking her head. "De spirit tuck it."

Mandie blew out her breath and looked at Tommy across the room. "Tommy, do you have spirits in this house?" she asked as she turned her back to Cheechee so the girl wouldn't see the grin on her face. "Cheechee says a spirit took my locket."

Tommy came across the room and looked at the young maid. "Cheechee, now what are you talking about? Do you know where her locket is? Tell us if you do." He smiled at her and added, "Please."

Cheechee looked down at the floor, shuffled her feet, and said, "I ain't seen no locket." She turned and rushed down the hallway.

Tommy turned back to Mandie and said, "I don't believe she knows anything about your locket, or she would have been bragging about it."

"I was hoping she did," Mandie said.

"I'm sorry, but I think we'd better get back downstairs. Everyone is probably ready for breakfast," Tommy replied.

Mandie shut Snowball up in her room, and all the young people went down to the parlor to join the adults for breakfast. All the time Mandie was wondering where her locket could be. She was confused now. Did she really have it on last night and leave it on the bureau? Or had she lost it during the day and not missed it? She couldn't figure out what to do next.

As they entered the parlor, Mandie spotted her grandmother sitting alone on the far side of the room. The other adults were carrying on conversations among one another. And the only one missing was Senator Morton, so evidently Mrs. Taft was waiting for him.

"Grandmother," Mandie said, rushing across the room before someone else joined her, "I have something to tell you." She quickly pulled up a stool next to Mrs. Taft's chair and sat down.

"Yes, what is it, dear?" Mrs. Taft asked. "What are you so upset about?"

Mandie smiled at her. Mrs. Taft seemed to be able to read her mind sometimes. "Grandmother, I've lost my locket with my father's picture in it," she explained. "We've searched our room, and it is definitely not in there. And now I don't know what to do next."

Mrs. Taft reached to pat Mandie's hand as she said, "Amanda, I've repeatedly told you that you need to take that picture out of the locket and have a photographer enlarge it enough to hang up. That way you would have two copies of the picture in case one got lost."

"I know, Grandmother, but I never seem to get everything done that I should. I'm sorry. If I can only find it this time I will give it to you to keep until I can get it done," Mandie replied, squeezing her grandmother's hand.

Senator Morton came into the parlor as Mandie looked up, and he headed straight for Mrs. Taft. Mandie quickly glanced at her grandmother and asked, "Have you figured out how we could go visit Lily?"

By that time the senator was standing by Mrs. Taft's chair. He smiled down at Mandie and said, "I hear you heard from Miss Masterson, that nice young lady on the ship to Europe."

Mandie rose to go join her friends as she said, "Yes, sir, she and her little sister are back home in Fountain Inn."

"And you would like to visit them, of course," the senator said with a big smile. "Perhaps we can work something out."

Mandie grinned up at the tall, white-haired, distinguished-looking man and said, "Yes, sir, I would be most grateful if you could work something out so we could visit them."

"We'll see," Senator Morton replied, still smiling.

"Thank you, thank you," Mandie said and quickly went to join her friends as the adults were beginning to leave for the breakfast room. She had not thought of enlisting the senator's help in getting to visit Lily. Now that he was behind it, she was sure it would be accomplished.

When the young people had been seated at the breakfast table with their food, Tommy looked around the group and said, "I think I should say something to my mother to delay our visit to the beach house until we can find out if that is Josephine at the Bedfords' house. What do y'all think?"

Everyone nodded in agreement.

"Yes," Mandie said. "However, I don't know what you can say

to your mother unless you tell her about the other girl at the Bedfords' house."

"I've been trying to think up something," Tommy said, looking around the group. "Does anyone have any ideas? I just don't want to tell my mother about our being at the Bedfords' house, not just yet. Believe me, it would be very unsettling if she found out about that."

"I could always say I just don't want to go to the beach house," Jonathan volunteered.

"I have a better idea," Joe said. "You could just tell her Mandie has lost her locket and we want to have time to look for it before we go to the beach house." He looked at Mandie and smiled.

Mandie smiled back and said, "Yes, I believe that would be a good excuse. It is the truth anyway. I'd rather find my locket before we move on to another house."

Tommy looked around the group and asked, "Is that acceptable to everyone?"

Everyone nodded in agreement.

"Then I will catch my mother after breakfast and speak to her," Tommy said. "I believe she was thinking of our going out there tomorrow."

"Thank you, Tommy," Mandie said. "I really do want to search for my locket, and I do hope I find it."

"And I hope you find it. We'll all be on the lookout to help," Tommy told her.

"I had a chance to speak to my grandmother before we came in here, and Senator Morton joined her and said he would be trying to find a way for us to visit Lily," Mandie told her friends.

"Don't count me in, because I will be leaving before the rest of you do to go home and spend some time with my parents before I go back to college," Joe reminded Mandie.

Robert looked across the table at Joe and said, "Perhaps we can get the same train, because I will also be going home before I return to school."

"Yes, that would be nice," Joe agreed.

Tommy looked back at Mandie and said, "Of course I won't be going with you to visit the girl. I've never met her anyhow. After all you people leave I will be going to Savannah to visit my grandmother for a few days."

Mandie looked at Tommy and said, "Now I suppose we will have to find out whether that is Josephine at the Bedfords' house or not so we can make plans for the rest of our visit here."

"Yes, and I would appreciate any suggestions anyone might have," Tommy told them.

"We could watch the house after dark. Then no one would see us," Jonathan suggested.

"I think we ought to just walk right up to the door and ask if your sister is there," Mandie said.

"But if that same man came to the door, you would never be able to make him understand what you want. Remember I told you he was a little foggy," Joe said.

"We could watch for someone else to come out of the house and ask them about Josephine," Celia said.

"Don't forget. Their gate is locked and you would have to jump the wall to get to the front door," Robert said.

"While we are doing all this thinking, please help me think up what to do next about my locket," Mandie reminded her friends.

"Yes, that is very important," Joe agreed.

"We need to retrace your movements yesterday," Tommy said. "And then search every place you've been."

"That will be quite a job, considering what all we did yesterday," Celia said.

"With all of us searching I hope we will find it," Tommy said.

Mandie looked at the adults at the other end of the table. They were beginning to get up. "I believe all the others are finished with breakfast," she said. "When are you going to speak to your mother, Tommy?"

Tommy quickly stood up and said, "I'll try right now." He hurried to join the adults as they began leaving the breakfast room.

Mandie watched as he caught up with his mother and walked with her out of the room as they talked. Then she looked around the table at her friends. "We had not even thought about the possibility that Mrs. Patton might want to go on to the beach house anyway," she said.

"Yes, she might," Joe agreed.

"In that case do you think we might be able to stay here while the adults go out there?" Mandie asked, looking around at her friends.

"I don't see why not," Jonathan spoke up. "We do things like that all the time at our house, some of the guests going different places and some staying home."

"But what about the servants?" Celia asked. "Do they take all the servants with them to the beach house?"

"I'm not sure," Robert said. "I've been here lots of times and we have all gone on to the beach house. I really don't know how many servants they have."

"As long as we had someone left here to cook for us we'd be all right," Mandie said.

"And they would probably insist that we have at least one adult here as a chaperone," Joe added.

"Here comes Tommy, and he doesn't look very happy," Jonathan said, looking across the room as Tommy came back to the table.

Tommy pulled out his chair and sat down. Looking around the table he said, "We almost lost that battle." He frowned and added, "My mother wanted to insist that we all go to the beach house tomorrow. She said that ought to give us enough time to find your locket, Mandie."

"And do we have to go then?" Mandie asked.

"No, I was able to win one day more to stay here, so we will have to go the day after tomorrow. My mother said that is final," Tommy explained.

"Does she have plans for us today and tomorrow?" Joe asked.

"No, the adults will go ahead with plans on their own, but we will have to be ready to move to the beach house the day after tomorrow, so we had better get busy and figure out what we are going to do about the Bedfords and also about searching for Mandie's locket," Tommy replied. "Let's go sit in the back parlor and formulate some kind of plan." He stood up.

As the group left the breakfast room Mandie had an idea. "I know that my grandmother is not too happy with hot beaches and that," she said. "I might be able to persuade her to stay here with us if we haven't yet solved the mystery of that other girl at the Bedfords' and have not found my locket."

Tommy looked down at her and said, "That's a good idea, Mandie. We'll see what happens."

Mandie was more worried about her locket than she was about who that girl at the Bedfords' might be. It was going to take some searching to find her locket. She wouldn't even think of the possibility of never finding the locket. She was determined to get it back.

# CHAPTER NINE

# SEARCHING

"Today is Friday, so your mother expects us to move to the beach house on Sunday, then?" Mandie asked as the young people sat in the back parlor.

"Yes, it will be Sunday. I wonder if she has thought about that," Tommy said. "I'm sure we will all be going to church Sunday, and that won't leave much time after we eat and all that to get moved out to the beach house."

"What are we going to do about that second girl at the Bedfords'?" Jonathan asked. "Are we going to just walk up and knock on the door? Or what?" He looked around the room at the others.

"I suppose I should be the one who goes to the house, much as I hate to," Tommy said. "Because I'm not sure any of y'all could positively identify Josephine if she is at the Bedfords'."

"But if that is Josephine there and she gets a glimpse of you, she will quickly hide and you won't be able to find her," Mandie reminded him.

"You are right," Tommy agreed and looked around the room at the others. "What do y'all suggest?"

"She wouldn't know me," Jonathan said. "I've never been here before. I could go to the door."

."But you wouldn't be able to identify Josephine, either," Mandie reminded him.

"Why don't we all go over the wall and surround the house?" Robert asked.

"Yes," Celia quickly agreed. "And we might be able to see through the windows whoever is in the house."

"When Jonathan and I went around the house before, most of the shutters were closed," Joe told them.

"Maybe we could go through a window and get into the house rather than knocking on the front door," Jonathan suggested.

"Oh no, Jonathan, they could press charges against us," Tommy quickly told him.

"Looks to me like the only way we can do it is just for everybody to walk up to the front door and knock," Joe decided.

"Yes," the others chorused.

Tommy stood up and said, "Let's go, then, before the sun gets too hot." He started for the door to the hall and stopped to say, "And let's go out the back door so we don't have to pass the parlor. My mother and the others are probably in there, and I don't want someone to ask where we're going."

"Good idea," Mandie said, following right behind him, and all her friends agreed.

When they got to the Bedfords' house they found the gate locked.

"Mandie, we can't just climb up there over the wall," Celia declared as the group stood there looking up at the wall.

"Yes, we can," Mandie told her.

Celia bent and tried to whisper to her, "But it would be indecent."

"Indecent?" Mandie loudly repeated and then covered her mouth as she saw the boys listening to them.

Joe grinned at Mandie and said, "Y'all just stay right here in the shade of that tree over there and we'll be right back."

"Oh, shucks!" Mandie said, stomping her foot.

"Come over in the shade, Mandie," Celia told her as she walked a couple of steps to the tree. "If only that gate was unlocked, we could follow the boys, but I think we'd better wait for them."

Mandie adjusted her straw hat brim so she could see the top of the wall as she joined Celia in the shade. She watched as the boys quickly went over the wall and disappeared into the overgrown front yard.

"I'm going back to the gate. Maybe I can hear what goes on in there," Mandie decided as she went back to attempt to see through the lacy ironwork of the gate.

She heard the knocker on the front door and knew the boys were finally knocking. Then there was a jumble of voices in low tones that she couldn't understand at all.

"Oh, why don't they talk loud enough for me to understand what they're saying?" she grumbled to herself.

She heard the door close and then there was silence. They must have all gone inside the house.

Celia came back over to join her. "Have you heard anything?" she asked.

"Just some mumbling and then the door closed," Mandie told her. She walked in circles in front of the gate as she became impatient for her friends to return. And she was beginning to feel the heat. Why were they taking so long? She could have been in and out of there half a dozen times by now. If only she had been able to get over the wall.

"Mandie, where are we going to look next for your locket?" Celia asked.

Mandie's attention immediately came back. "I suppose everywhere I've been since I came here," Mandie replied, looking down at the ground she was walking on. "Including around here." She began searching the ground as she moved around.

"This sand shifts so much when we walk on it, something could be just completely covered up with it," Celia said as she, too, looked around.

"Yes, and if I dropped my locket in sand like this I probably won't ever find it," Mandie said in a worried voice. She straightened up and looked at Celia. "But, Celia, I'm so sure I had it on last night. I've been thinking about what I did when I got ready for bed. I'm sure I can remember putting it on the bureau."

"If you did, then someone must have come into our room during the night and taken it," Celia decided.

"But who would do such a thing? And why didn't we hear them?" Mandie asked.

"I was awfully tired and went straight to sleep and didn't wake up all night," Celia said.

"I didn't wake up all night, either," Mandie said. She stopped to attempt to look through the gate. "These people really have everything grown up so you can't see into the yard, don't they?"

Celia joined her and put her face up near an open piece of ironwork. "Yes, and you know, I've been wondering whether they ever have anyone come to see them. If you tried knocking on this gate, no one in the house would hear you."

"I wonder who all lives in that big house, anyway," Mandie said, looking up where she could see the top of the mansion. "I certainly wouldn't like to live in a place all locked up like this one."

"Shh! Someone's in the yard," Celia whispered as she peered through a tiny opening in the ironwork.

Mandie moved up next to her. "I see someone," she whispered. "It's a girl, coming around the corner of the house." She reached to squeeze Celia's hand. "It's Josephine. It's Josephine."

"Josephine!" Celia whispered.

"She's coming this way," Mandie said, stepping back by the wall so the girl would not be able to see her.

Celia moved back with her, and they waited. Suddenly there was a click at the gate and the girls watched as it began to slowly move open.

Just as they started to move forward, Josephine saw them and quickly ran back into the yard, trying to slam the gate behind her, but it didn't shut.

"This way!" Mandie told Celia as she went through the gateway and followed Josephine around the house. "Hurry!"

But Josephine was too quick for them. She managed to open the door to the house, get inside, and slam it before they could get there.

"We can at least make some racket," Mandie said, beating on the door.

Celia stepped over to a window on the porch and began knocking on it. "Maybe the boys will hear us," she said.

"Joe was right. Josephine is here," Mandie said, pausing to rub her fists, which were beginning to feel bruised from the knocking.

"And she was probably coming out the gate to go home when we saw her," Celia added.

"Where are those boys?" Mandie moaned. "If they'd just come out right now they might be able to find her before she goes out the back door or somewhere else."

Finally the door opened, causing Mandie to almost fall inside as she raised her fist to knock. She looked up. It was Joe, followed by the other boys.

"Josephine is here," she quickly told them. "She came outside and was going through the gate when we caught up with her, but she ran back inside the house and shut the door," Mandie told him without taking a breath.

Joe quickly turned back into the house and the other boys followed him. Mandie and Celia stepped inside the huge foyer. Joe looked back and said, "Wait here." He hurried through a doorway, and Jonathan, Tommy, and Robert ran after him.

Mandie, afraid she would get lost in the big house or run into one of its occupants, stayed in the foyer with Celia. She could faintly hear the boys racing through the house, but no one came into the foyer.

In a few minutes they came back and Tommy said, "Maybe Josephine went home. I don't believe she's still in this house."

"Then let's go find out if she's home before she disappears again," Mandie said, going back to the front door.

As they all hurried back toward the Pattons' house, the boys tried to explain what they had found.

"The old man Joe saw was the grandfather and he's hard of hearing," Tommy explained. "He opened the door and let us in and couldn't understand what we wanted."

"And he insisted that we have coffee with him," Joe added.

"A manservant came down the hall with coffee and put it in the parlor," Jonathan explained.

"We heard someone talking in the next room, and when we went to see who it was they just vanished right quick," Robert said. "It was a girl, but it wasn't Josephine."

"That was Josephine we saw open the gate," Mandie said.

When they got to the Pattons' house, Tizzy informed them that all the adults had gone visiting somewhere and wouldn't return until afternoon.

"Did Josephine come home?" Tommy asked her as they all stood in the front hallway.

"No, ain't seen her at all," Tizzy said.

Tommy looked at his friends and said, "She could have come into the house without anyone seeing her. We can look in her room, but I doubt if she's there because she knows that's the first place we would go."

He was right. When they went upstairs to her room there was no sign of her.

"Let's just forget about Josephine for the time being," Tommy said as they went back down the hallway. "I'm tired of playing tricks with her. But we do know she is here and not at the beach, so I can tell my mother when she returns."

"Let's look for my locket," Mandie told him.

"Yes, we need to find your locket," Tommy agreed. "Now, let's think about where you've been in this house so we can search for it."

"We were all up on the third floor," Jonathan said. "Let's go up there and take a look from the widow's walk. We might see Josephine if she is in the yard."

"That's a good idea," Mandie agreed. Even though she didn't like the widow's walk, stuck high up there in the sky, she knew she should search for her locket on the third floor, and while they were at it they might as well look for Josephine, too.

Joe stayed right behind her going up the narrow steps to the roof. "Just don't look back," he told her. "I'm right behind you in case you slip."

"Thank you," she replied, finally stepping out onto the roof. Joe came along with her and held her hand.

Tommy walked around explaining what the sights were that they could see.

"We can see right down on other people's roofs," Jonathan remarked.

"Yes, and in some of the windows, too," Tommy said.

Mandie, holding tightly to Joe's hand, stopped to look at an open place in the distance. "Is that a park?" she asked. "Aren't those people playing music and dancing?" She could see quite a few people down there.

Tommy turned to look at her and replied, "That's a band of gypsies. They show up every now and then and stay a few days and then move on."

Mandie kept staring at the scene. "Real gypsies?" she repeated.

Tommy laughed, looked at her, and said, "Yes, real gypsies. Is there any other kind?"

Mandie looked at him and smiled back. "Come to think of it, I suppose there isn't," she said.

They went back down to the third floor and began the search for Mandie's locket. It was a time-consuming job, and they finally stopped at noontime to freshen up and go downstairs for the noon meal, which Tizzy served in the breakfast room since the adults would not be present. Mandie brought Snowball down to the kitchen and Tizzy fed him.

As they sat at the table, Tommy sighed and said, "You know, all this detective work can really tire one out."

"It certainly can," Joe agreed with a grin at Mandie.

"That's because you don't enjoy it," Mandie said, smiling at them.

"I wonder where Josephine went," Celia said, taking a bite of potatoes.

"I wonder how she got to the Bedfords' when she was supposed to be at the beach with some friends," Tommy said, putting down his fork.

"That's nothing unusual for her," Robert remarked. "Nearly every time I've ever been here she has been missing or into something."

"Where do the people live that she was at the beach with?" Joe asked.

"They have a beach house not far from ours, and my parents know them from a long time ago," Tommy explained. "They have a daughter about the same age as Josephine."

"Are you going to remind your parents that the day after tomorrow is Sunday, in case they don't want to move to the beach house on Sunday, like we discussed?" Mandie asked.

"Yes, as soon as they come home," Tommy said.

Before they had finished their meal they were surprised to see Mrs. Taft and Senator Morton return. Mandie looked up to see them standing in the doorway.

"Grandmother, are the others back, too?" Mandie asked.

Tommy rose to pull out some chairs. "Please come and join us," he told them. "Have y'all had anything to eat?"

"Yes, thank you, Tommy, we have eaten," Mrs. Taft said. "However, we will have coffee with y'all." She sat down across the table from Mandie.

The senator sat next to Mrs. Taft. "Yes, I could use a hot cup of coffee," he said.

Tizzy had followed them into the room and quickly set cups of coffee in front of them. She looked around the table and said, "If y'all ready fo' it, we still has some of dat chocolate cake." She smiled at Joe.

"Chocolate cake, that's wonderful," Joe replied with a big grin.

"Yes, bring on the chocolate cake," Jonathan added.

After Tizzy had served the cake and coffee, Mandie asked her grandmother, "Didn't y'all go with the others this morning when they went visiting?"

"Yes, we did, dear, but those were rather stuffy people and we thought we'd just come back and visit with y'all for a little while," Mrs. Taft said with a big smile.

"Stuffy people? That must be the Lesesnes you went to see," Tommy said, grinning.

"Exactly," Senator Morton replied as he smiled at the group.

"Another reason we came back early," Mrs. Taft said, sipping her coffee, "I seem to have lost one of my diamond earbobs and I need to look for it."

"Your diamond earbobs?" Mandie repeated. She knew those earbobs must be worth a fortune, and also that her grandfather had given them to her grandmother when they were young.

"Yes, dear, and you're such a good detective I thought perhaps you could help us look for it," Mrs. Taft replied, smiling at Mandie.

"We've been looking for my locket. Remember I told you it was missing," Mandie replied.

"Yes, you did, and I certainly hope you find it," Mrs. Taft told her.

"We haven't found it yet," Mandie said.

"We've actually been looking for my sister, Josephine, too," Tommy told them. "She is supposed to be at the beach with friends, but here she turns up out at the Bedfords' house and we can't catch up with her."

"Oh dear, how did she get out there from the beach?" Senator Morton asked.

"That's what we want to find out," Tommy said. "When my mother comes home and catches up with Josephine, she'll straighten things out."

Mandie looked at her grandmother and said, "You know Tommy's mother wants us to all go to the beach house day after tomorrow and that's Sunday, and I wanted to stay here until I can find my locket. And since you have something missing that we need to look for, maybe you could stay here with us until we find my locket and your earbob."

"Of course, dear," Mrs. Taft replied. "I had already made up my mind that I wouldn't leave here until I find that earbob. The others can go ahead. The senator and I will stay and help you find these things."

Mandie grinned and said, "Thank you, Grandmother."

"I'll ask my mother to leave Tizzy's sister, Mixie, here to cook for us until we join them at the beach," Tommy said.

"I knew everything would work out," Mandie said, smiling at Tommy.

"Now hold on a minute. My mother will have to agree to our plans," Tommy reminded her. "But since Mrs. Taft is involved I'm sure she will."

Mandie smiled and turned back to her grandmother. "Grandmother, would you like for us to search your room for the earbob?"

Mrs. Taft looked up from her coffee and said, "Why, yes, dear, that is a good idea. I tried looking for it, but I am not as young and nimble as you, so I'm sure you will do a more thorough job."

"We will," Mandie promised.

Mandie didn't want to discuss it in front of Tommy for fear he would be insulted, but she wondered if someone in the house had taken her locket and her grandmother's earbob. It was really strange that they both had jewelry missing. And then she wondered if anyone else had anything missing.

This was one mystery she definitely had to solve. It was important.

# CHAPTER TEN

# A SCARY DISCOVERY

As soon as the young people had finished their meal, Mrs. Taft told them, "Now, y'all go right ahead and look for my earbob in my room, or wherever, and I believe Senator Morton and I will just relax in the parlor. It has been a busy day." She rose from the table.

"We'll let you know when we finish," Mandie promised her as Mrs. Taft and Senator Morton left the room.

"Now, I suppose we have to get busy looking for that locket, too," Joe said as all the young people stood up.

"Maybe we'll find it and it won't take long," Mandie said, smiling at him as everyone left the breakfast room.

"If I remember correctly, your mystery solutions usually take a long time," Joe teased.

"But I have all this help this time," Mandie replied. As they continued down the hallway toward the main staircase, she suddenly stopped, stomped her foot, and said, "I had Grandmother right there where I could talk to her and I forgot to ask her if she had figured out how we could visit Lily. Oh, shucks."

"Well, if we hurry maybe she will still be in the parlor when we finish with her room," Joe replied.

"That's true because she won't be able to relax in her room while we are in it," Mandie said. "Yes, let's hurry."

They hurried through the search of Mrs. Taft's room as fast as they could, but it seemed that she had brought an awful lot of luggage. And the trunk was locked.

Mandie stood back and looked at the trunk. "I wonder what she has in there to cause her to lock it up," she said.

"Probably her expensive jewelry," Celia said.

"And maybe private papers," Jonathan added.

"Do you think her earbobs were in that trunk?" Mandie asked her friends. "She didn't say where they were supposed to be, did she?"

"We haven't seen a jewelry case, have we? So it's probably in that trunk," Celia surmised.

"Then the trunk must not have been locked all the time she's been here. How could anyone steal an earbob out of a locked trunk?" Mandie wondered.

"Now, just a minute, Mandie," Tommy quickly told her. "I don't believe your grandmother said someone *stole* her earbob, did she? As far as I remember, she said she couldn't find the other earbob."

"You are right, Tommy. I have a bad habit of assuming that whatever is missing that I am looking for has been stolen," Mandie answered. She looked around the room. "I believe we have finished. And the earbob is not in the room, unless it is in the trunk."

"I'd say we did a very thorough job," Robert said.

"Are you going down to the parlor and let your grandmother know that we have finished, just in case she is wanting to rest in her room awhile?" Celia asked.

"Yes, I suppose I should," Mandie replied as they went into the hall.

"While you go do that, Mandie, I think I will have a look around for my sister," Tommy said. "Anyone want to come with me?"

When all the others said they would, Mandie told them, "Maybe I can find out whether Grandmother has any plans yet about visiting Lily."

"Shall we meet back here in about thirty minutes, then?" Tommy asked. "Down in the alcove there." He pointed to where a group of chairs were placed at the far end of the hall.

"Yes, I'll be there," Mandie said, hurrying toward the main staircase as the others went in the opposite direction.

When she got to the front parlor, Mrs. Taft and Senator Morton were still there. She went across the room and pulled a stool near her grandmother and sat down.

"Grandmother, I'm sorry, but we couldn't find it," she told her. "Unless you have it in the trunk, which is locked, it is not in your room."

"No, it's not in the trunk. I've already checked inside it," Mrs. Taft replied. She frowned and said, "I don't understand how I lost just one of them. I put the set on my bureau last night and this morning one of them was missing."

"That is strange," Senator Morton said.

"But where is the one you didn't lose?" Mandie asked.

"Oh dear, I put it in the trunk immediately when I discovered that one was missing, and I also locked up my jewelry case in the trunk," Mrs. Taft explained.

"Grandmother, I wouldn't say this to anyone else, but I believe someone stole my locket and your earbob," Mandie said and then waited for her grandmother's reaction.

Mrs. Taft looked around the parlor, lowered her voice, and said, "You know, dear, I have been thinking the same thing. They have quite a few servants here and they seem to move around all over the house."

Mandie looked at the senator and asked, "Senator Morton, have you missed anything personal?"

"No, Miss Amanda, I'm glad to say I haven't," he replied. "However, that may be because I always keep things locked up no matter where I am staying. I've traveled so much in my life I've just made that a habit."

"That is a good habit and if I can ever find my locket I'll never leave it out on a bureau again," Mandie said. "And, Grandmother, Tommy's sister, Josephine, was staying at the Bedfords' house and we saw her there."

Mrs. Taft quickly looked at Mandie and asked, "Now, when were you at the Bedfords' house?"

Mandie quickly explained about Snowball jumping over the wall and Joe rescuing him and seeing the girl he thought was Josephine. "So we went back this morning and found out it was Josephine. She started out the gate and saw us and went back into the house. But Tommy is sure she came home and is hiding from us somewhere in the house here."

"Have you told her mother about this?" Mrs. Taft asked.

"No, ma'am," Mandie replied. "Tommy wanted to be sure it was Josephine, and now that he knows he will speak to his mother when she comes home. I didn't tell Tommy, but I'm wondering if Josephine could be the one who took my locket and your earbob."

"Do you really think the girl might do such a thing?" Mrs. Taft asked.

"Yes, ma'am, she's a strange girl," Mandie replied.

"I'm terribly sorry about your locket, dear," Mrs. Taft said. "I know it can't be replaced. But I can get another earbob made to match the one I have left."

"I'm glad you can, Grandmother, because I know my grandfather gave those to you many years ago," Mandie said.

"If you think Josephine may have taken your locket, have you looked in her room for it?" Mrs. Taft asked.

"No, I haven't, Grandmother," Mandie replied. "If she took it I don't imagine she would leave it out where I could find it. And then, too, I haven't had a chance yet." She cleared her throat and asked, "What about Lily, Grandmother? Have you decided what we can do about visiting her?"

"No, Amanda, but I plan to inquire about the train route when I speak to the Pattons tonight," Mrs. Taft said, smiling at Mandie. "I'll let you know as soon as I can look into the possibility of visiting her, dear."

Mandie stood up and smiled back. "Thank you, Grandmother," she said. "I have to go back and meet my friends now. We are going to search my room for my locket again even though we've already done that. And we'll also be looking for Josephine."

"All right, dear," Mrs. Taft said. "If I happen to see that girl I will most certainly let you know."

"Thank you, Grandmother," Mandie said as she left the parlor.

She hurried down the hall to the stairs and went up to meet her friends. But when she got to the designated meeting place, no one was there. She walked around in circles, looking down each end of the hallway and going to the intersection of the cross hall, but the place seemed deserted.

"I wonder how long I've been gone," she mumbled to herself as she finally stopped and sat down on a chair where she could see if anyone was coming.

She waited and waited and no one came. Finally she decided to go to her room and get Snowball. He needed some fresh air and exercise. Maybe by the time she picked him up the others would have returned.

"At least my room isn't far away," she said to herself as she went down the other end of the hall and came to the door to her room.

Pushing open the door, she found Snowball curled up in the middle of the big bed. He opened his eyes, stood up, yawned, and stretched and purred loudly.

"Snowball, come on, let's go," she told him as she reached for his red leash on a nearby chair. He wanted to play and kept trying to roll over as she attached it.

"Be still, Snowball, if you want to get out of this room," she told him. "You aren't going anyplace without this leash."

Out of the corner of her eye Mandie suddenly saw something move past the half-open door to the next room. She had not left that door open. She ran to push it back and look into the other room. She couldn't see anyone. But she was certain something had moved.

Snowball protested and tried to pull away from her. She quickly reached down and picked him up. He suddenly spit and growled. His fur stood up on his back. Mandie became frightened, but she made herself step into the other room and look around, holding Snowball tightly in her arms.

A door on the far side of the room seemed to be partly open. She went over to investigate and found it to be the doorway to an outside balcony. There was no one out there. She stepped back inside and pulled the door closed. Then hurriedly looking around the room, she went back into her room and firmly closed the door between them.

Snowball had relaxed and his fur was smoothed back down. Mandie stood in the middle of her room, thinking. Could that have been Josephine? Considering Snowball's reaction, it had to be someone he didn't like.

Then, remembering her friends, she went out into the hall, closing the door to her room, and hurried back to their meeting place. There was still no one there.

"Oh, where is everybody?" she mumbled to herself as she paced in circles, still holding Snowball. She shivered all over when she thought about that room next to hers. Who had been in there? And how did they get away so fast?

She looked down the hallway and saw Celia coming toward her from the other end. She hurried to meet her.

"Where have y'all been?" she asked.

"Chasing Josephine," Celia said, out of breath from walking so fast. "I told them I'd come and look for you because we were supposed to have already come back down here."

"Where are the boys? On the third floor?" Mandie asked.

"Yes, and we got a glimpse of Josephine in one of the rooms up there and then she disappeared," Celia explained.

"Come back to our room with me," Mandie said, walking in the other direction. Celia went along with her.

"I went in our room a while ago to get Snowball, and there is bound to have been someone in it," Mandie explained, pushing open the door to their room.

"Someone in our room?" Celia repeated as Mandie led the way in.

"This door over here," Mandie said, going over to the other door, "was partly open. I was putting on Snowball's leash and I got a glimpse of the door moving."

"Oh, Mandie, it couldn't have been Josephine because she is on the third floor," Celia said. "Who could it have been?"

"I don't know," Mandie said, pushing the door open. "I came in here and that other door there was open. There's a balcony outside it."

Celia stood there in the middle of the floor, looking at Mandie and then at the outside door. "Mandie, this is scary," she said. "I didn't know we had a door connecting to a room with an outside exit like this." She looked around. "Can we lock our door?" She went to examine the door.

Mandie said, "No, I've already looked and there isn't a key in any of these doors. Remember Tommy said they never lock doors around here."

They stepped back into their room and Mandie closed the connecting door.

"I'm going to be afraid to sleep in here tonight," Celia said, rubbing her arms.

"But, Celia, who could it have been?" Mandie asked. "I was holding Snowball and he bristled up. That means it was someone he didn't like. Maybe Josephine?" She looked at her friend.

"No, Mandie, I just told you. Josephine is on the third floor. It couldn't have been her," Celia replied.

"I think there's a possibility it was her. She gets around awfully fast, you know. And she knows every crack and corner of this house. I know that from the last time I visited here," Mandie said.

"Come on, Mandie. I was supposed to come down here and get you," Celia said, walking over to the hall door and opening it.

Mandie followed her into the hall and firmly closed the door to their room. She put Snowball down and grasped the end of his leash.

"Snowball, you can walk for exercise, but you had better not try to run, you hear?" she said, straightening up to follow Celia.

"The boys are in the hallway by the door to the tower," Celia told her. "At least they were when I left. We should be able to find them somewhere around there."

"And where is Josephine?" Mandie asked.

"We saw her go in one of those rooms off that circular hall there, and Tommy says she has to come back out one of those doors because there is no other way," Celia explained.

"If he finally comes face-to-face with her, what does he plan on doing?" Mandie asked. "She could still run away. Besides, what good will it do to catch up with her? I thought he only wanted to be sure she was in the house and was then going to tell his mother about her being at the Bedfords' house."

"I'm not sure," Celia said. "I know he wants to speak to her just for a moment, he said."

"Their mother is not home right now unless they came back after I left Grandmother in the parlor," Mandie said. "So Josephine could be long gone again before her parents return."

They found the boys where Celia had left them.

"Celia said you found Josephine," Mandie told Tommy.

"Yes, she's in there," he said, pointing to a closed door on his right. "And that's the only door out of that room."

"Why don't you just open the door and go in and talk to her?" Mandie asked, holding tightly to Snowball's leash as he prowled around.

"Because she would just run out and disappear somewhere again," Tommy said. "If I wait for her to come out, she can't get a head start on me and I'll just follow her and tell her a few things at the same time. And I'll also see where she goes and can tell my mother when she returns."

"I don't understand why she runs away all the time and won't listen to anyone," Mandie said.

"Her explanation for that has always been, 'No one listens to me and I'm not going to listen to you.' It's something she's made up to avoid behaving like she should," Tommy said.

"Did you ask your grandmother about visiting Lily?" Jonathan asked.

"Yes, and she is going to talk to my mother tonight," Mandie said. "I think it all depends on whether the train goes through Fountain Inn or not."

"What did your grandmother say about the locked trunk?" Joe asked.

"She said she always keeps it locked wherever she goes because of business papers in it." Mandie hated lying to Tommy, but she didn't want to admit that she and her grandmother believed the housekeepers had something to do with the disappearing jewelry.

"Why don't y'all go help Mandie search her room again for the locket and I'll stay right here, at least for a while, and see if Josephine comes out," Tommy told the others.

"All right," Robert agreed.

"Yes, we can get that over with," Joe said.

As they started down the hallway, Tommy called to them, "Would someone please come and let me know if my mother comes home?"

"Yes," was chorused back.

Mandie let Snowball walk but she held firmly to the end of the leash. He tried to run ahead and then looked up at Mandie and fussed when he found he couldn't.

When they got to Mandie and Celia's room, Mandie stepped ahead to open the door. She went inside and quickly looked at the other door. It was still closed. She explained to the others about what had happened when she was in the room alone.

"Do you mean there's an outside door through there?" Joe asked, stepping over to open the door to the adjoining room.

"Yes," Mandie said, following him into the next room. She pointed to the outside door. "That one opens onto a balcony."

The boys went outside to look out from the balcony.

"I don't think anyone would be able to get up on that balcony from outside," Joe said, stepping back into the room. "It's a long way down to the ground and there aren't any steps that I can see."

"I plan on putting a big chair in front of our door tonight," Celia said.

Mandie looped Snowball's leash around the leg of a chair while they began searching every crack and corner of the room for her locket. She felt it was useless because they had already searched in here before.

And after a while when they finished she said, "Thank you all, but I didn't think we'd find it. I just feel that someone stole it because I know I put it on the bureau when I went to bed."

Everyone quickly looked at her. "But who would steal it?" Joe asked.

"No one in this household, of course, but since I found that outside door, I feel that somehow someone got in here from there and took it," she said.

Joe looked concerned and said, "Maybe Tommy can find a key to that door and lock it for you."

"Or maybe we could change rooms," Celia added.

"We can see what he has to say about it when we explain about that outside door," Mandie said.

She knew for sure that she was going to move all the furniture over in front of that adjoining room door tonight if no solution was worked out. And she doubted she would sleep a wink but would lie awake listening to every little sound all night long.

# CHAPTER ELEVEN

# PLANS ARE MADE

Just as Mandie and her friends were leaving her and Celia's room, Tommy came rushing down the hall to join them.

"Where's Josephine?" Mandie asked as she stepped back to allow Tommy to enter the room.

"She finally came out and of course she just ran away again," he replied. "I yelled at her that she had better not go off anywhere again, that I was going to tell our mother where she had been. She just ignored me and ran down the stairs back there. I'm tired of her so I just let her go."

"I want to show you something," Mandie said, picking up Snowball to carry him. She opened the door to the balcony and then looked at Tommy. "Did you know there is an outside balcony here? And none of these doors are locked and there are no keys in any of them?"

"Yes, I know about the balcony," Tommy said, looking beyond Mandie to the outside. Turning back to her he said, "But I told you we don't ever lock any doors. I've never even seen a key in a door that I can remember."

Mandie explained that she thought someone had been in the adjoining room.

"It might have been Cheechee. You know she's always snooping around," Tommy said.

"I'm not sure it could have been Cheechee, because Snowball hissed and ruffled up his fur like he does when there's someone around that he doesn't like," Mandie replied.

"Tommy, can you find a key to lock the door to that other room there?" Celia asked, pointing to the adjoining room.

Tommy shook his head and said, "I can ask my mother about a key. I wouldn't know where to even look for one."

Joe looked at Jonathan and said, "Let's move a big chair in front of that door. Since it opens in this way that ought to hold it shut if someone tries to open it."

"Sure," Jonathan replied, stepping over to a large chair near the window. Joe joined him and they placed it in front of the door.

"Here, there's another chair," Tommy said. "We can move it over there, too." He and Robert picked up the other chair and set it beside the one Joe had moved.

Stepping back, Joe looked at the girls and asked, "Now do you think y'all will be all right?"

Mandie nodded and said, "If anyone tries to come through that door, at least the noise of pushing against those chairs will wake me."

"Those two chairs may deter an intruder, but, Tommy, I still wish you would ask your mother about a key," Celia said.

"I will," Tommy promised. "Let's go sit down for a little while." He led the way to the alcove at the end of the hallway where there were plenty of chairs for the group.

"What are we going to do about those old books in that bureau drawer?" Mandie asked as everyone sat down. She held Snowball in her lap.

"Do about those old books?" Tommy asked. "I suppose there's nothing to be done about those books. I don't know where they came from and I wouldn't know where to move them to."

"I just think it is a shame they are hidden away in that drawer when they seem to be such interesting books," Mandie said.

"If I have a chance I will ask my father about them," Tommy promised.

Jonathan cleared his throat loudly to get everyone's attention and said, "I think we ought to go down to the parlor. Who knows? There could be coffee and cake down there." He grinned at Mandie.

"You are probably right," Tommy said, rising from his chair. "We should go see."

When they got to the parlor, Tizzy was bringing in the tea cart for Mrs. Taft and Senator Morton, who were still there. Looking at the young people, she said, "I brought 'nuff fo' y'all, too. I figured y'all would smell dat coffee and be right heah after it." She smiled as she looked around the room.

"Thank you, Tizzy," Tommy said.

The others thanked the maid as she passed plates of chocolate cake and cups of hot coffee around.

Mandie went to sit near her grandmother as she took the plate and cup. "Grandmother, has my mother come back yet?" she asked.

"No, dear, none of them have returned yet," Mrs. Taft replied. "I'm glad you young people came to join the senator and me for cake and coffee. Did you not bring Josephine with you?"

Mandie knew her grandmother was trying to find out whether they had caught up with Josephine or not. She shook her head and said, "No, ma'am, she's upstairs." Then she added, "Somewhere."

Just as Tizzy was preparing to leave the room, Mandie heard the front door open and the sound of voices. Her mother and the others had returned. Tizzy also heard them and waited until they came into the parlor.

"We're just in time," Mrs. Patton said as she looked around the room. "Tizzy, do you have enough for all of us here?" She glanced at the tea cart.

"Won't take but a minute to go git mo', Miz Patton," Tizzy replied, going to wheel the tea cart out of the room.

As everyone came in and sat down, Mandie moved across the room to join her friends. The adults exchanged greetings with the young people and then carried on their own conversation.

During all the talking Mandie faintly heard her grandmother ask Mrs. Patton, "Do you know if the train will stop in Fountain Inn on our way back?"

That question caught the adults' attention and they stopped talking to listen.

"Yes, I believe it does stop there if there is someone who wants on or off as it goes through. Were you thinking of going to Fountain Inn?" Mrs. Patton asked.

"Well, yes, I was," Mrs. Taft replied, and then, turning to Elizabeth, she said, "Did you know Amanda received a letter from Lily Masterson saying she and her sister are back in Fountain Inn?"

Elizabeth smiled at her mother and said, "Yes, Mother, I saw the letter on the hall table when we came home from New York."

"Amanda and I would like to stop over in Fountain Inn and see her on our way back to Franklin," Mrs. Taft said.

"Just you and Amanda?" Elizabeth asked, looking across the room at Mandie.

"Well, Amanda and I and whoever else would like to join us," Mrs. Taft said, smiling at the young people who were listening to every word.

"I would, Mother," Celia told her mother.

"I knew you would," Jane Hamilton said, smiling at her daughter. "We'll see what we can work out."

"Please include me," Jonathan said, glancing at his father across the room.

"And of course Senator Morton," Mrs. Taft said, turning to look at him. He nodded.

"I believe we are going to have to work out a plan here," John Shaw said.

"Definitely," Mr. Guyer agreed.

It took an hour to do it, but the adults finally came to an agreement.

"Now, you will only stay over one night to visit Lily," Elizabeth told Mandie.

"Yes, ma'am," Mandie replied with a big grin, happy that she would be able to visit her friend.

"And the rest of us will go back to Franklin," Mr. Guyer told his son. "I can wait one day for you to come back and join me to go home to New York and no longer. Is that understood?"

"Yes, sir, thank you," Jonathan replied.

"What about you, Joe?" John Shaw asked. "Are you stopping over with them, or are you going home early?"

"I don't know exactly how long y'all will be staying here, but I will leave next Tuesday and go home so I can spend some time with my parents before I return to college, sir," Joe replied.

"And I will be getting the train with Joe. I have to get back and visit other relatives," Robert added.

"Then I believe we have everything settled," John Shaw said.

After they finished the coffee and cake, everyone went to their rooms to relax and freshen up for the evening meal.

Mandie was excited about the prospect of seeing Lily and Violet Masterson. She and Celia sat in their room and discussed it for a while. Then Mandie decided she should take Snowball down to the kitchen and leave him so Tizzy could feed him.

"I won't be gone but a minute," Mandie told Celia as she picked up the white cat.

Celia followed her to the door. "I'll go with you," she said.

Mandie stopped and looked at her. "We forgot to ask Mrs. Patton about a key to that door," she said.

"That's why I'm going with you," Celia said. "I'm not staying in this room by myself."

"All right, let's go," Mandie replied, going out into the hall. Celia followed.

They found Cheechee in the kitchen, and she immediately took over Snowball.

"Will you please be sure he gets something to eat, Cheechee?" Mandie asked.

Cheechee never had much to say. She nodded her head and took Snowball over to the sandbox in the corner. Tizzy came into the room then. "I knows dat white cat be hungry now," she said. "Don't you go and worry 'bout him. We'se gwine feed him good."

"Thank you, Tizzy," Mandie said. "I'll get him later."

"No need, missy," Tizzy said. "After he eats I'll take him back to yo' room."

"Thank you, Tizzy," Mandie said.

She and Celia went back down the hall and up the stairs to their room. Just as they came around the corner from the cross hall, Mandie looked ahead. Josephine was coming out of their room. She raced ahead.

"Josephine!" Mandie said, stopping in front of her. "What were you doing in my room?"

Josephine frowned at her and said, "Not your room. The room belongs to the house and the house is mine." She started to move on.

Mandie stepped back and got in her way. "You took my locket off my bureau, didn't you? And Grandmother's diamond earbob? Didn't you? Admit it," she angrily accused the girl.

Josephine looked at her with her mouth open and said, "What would I want with that old locket of yours? Cheap thing? And I sure don't wear diamond earbobs." She started to move around Mandie.

Mandie kept stepping in her way. "I'm going to tell your mother that you took my locket and Grandmother's earbob," she said.

Josephine stopped and raised her hand as though to slap Mandie, but Mandie dodged. "And if you do you'll be telling a lie," she said and raced down the hallway.

"Come on, Mandie, let's go into our room," Celia said.

Mandie looked at the girl running down the corridor and then turned to enter the room with Celia. She plopped down in one of the big chairs. "She took them," she said. "I've felt all the time she did."

"But, Mandie, you don't have any proof of it," Celia reminded her as she sat in the other chair.

"She has never liked me and she's always up to some mischief or other," Mandie replied.

"I don't believe she likes anyone," Celia said.

"I'm going to search her room as soon as I get a chance," Mandie decided.

"I'm going to change clothes," Celia said, rising from her chair.

"And I am, too," Mandie said.

"We don't have much time," Celia said, glancing at the clock on the mantelpiece.

"I know," Mandie said, finally getting up to go to the wardrobe for another dress.

While they were changing clothes there was a knock on their door. Mandie quickly buttoned her dress and went to answer it.

Joe was standing outside, smiling. "Guess who is here?" he asked.

Mandie looked at him and couldn't imagine who he was talking about.

"Uncle Ned," Joe said with a big grin. "He's in the parlor when y'all get ready to go down." He turned back down the hallway.

"Tell him I'll be down shortly," Mandie said excitedly.

"So Uncle Ned is here," Celia said as Mandie turned back into the room.

"Yes, you know he always checks up on me wherever I go," Mandie said and then added sadly, "because he promised my father he would look after me when he died." She hurried over to the bureau to brush her hair.

"I know," Celia said, tying a ribbon in her hair. "I wish my father had had a friend like him when he died."

Uncle Ned was not related to Mandie. He had been a lifetime Cherokee friend of her father's and had helped her find her real Cherokee kinpeople. She had not known until Uncle Ned told her that her father was one-half Cherokee.

"Uncle Ned is your friend, too, Celia," Mandie reminded her. "I do believe he loves you as much as he does me. He's like a grandfather to both of us."

"Yes," Celia agreed. "I'm glad he came because I know you must want to discuss all the happenings here with him."

"I plan to as soon as I can get a chance," Mandie agreed.

They went down to the parlor and found Uncle Ned and all the boys there.

Mandie hurried across the room to embrace the old man. "How long are you going to be here, Uncle Ned?" she asked as he rose from his chair.

The old Indian looked down at her and said, "Not long. Need talk with John Shaw." He seemed worried.

Mandie looked up at him and asked, "Is something wrong?"

At that moment John Shaw came into the parlor. Crossing the room to shake hands with Uncle Ned, he said, "I'm glad you came down here to join us, Uncle Ned."

The two men sat down and the young people listened to their conversation.

"Not good news, John Shaw," Uncle Ned began, glancing at Mandie.

"You have bad news, Uncle Ned?" John Shaw quickly asked.

"Trouble back home," Uncle Ned explained. "Find trouble in secret tunnel in John Shaw's house."

Knowing she should not interrupt, Mandie was anxiously listening. Trouble in the secret tunnel? What could it be?

"In the tunnel, Uncle Ned," John Shaw said. He frowned as he asked, "What kind of trouble?"

Uncle Ned was always slow and thoughtful when explaining anything. He said, "Abraham find crack in wall in tunnel, big crack."

Everyone took a deep breath as they listened.

"A crack?" Mandie asked.

John Shaw looked at the old man and quickly asked, "A crack? What seems to be the problem? Do you have any idea as to what caused it?"

Uncle Ned quickly nodded his head and answered, "Tornado, must be tornado made crack, shook house."

A tornado had passed through Franklin, North Carolina, a few weeks ago while Mandie and her friends were home for spring holidays.

"Uncle Ned, is it serious? Is it a large crack?" John Shaw quickly asked, leaning forward and frowning in deep concern.

Uncle Ned nodded. "Must see. Must fix," he replied.

John Shaw took a deep breath, rose from his chair, and paced about the room. "Then I suppose we had better go home at once," he told the old man. "I just hope it is not serious."

Mandie and her friends listened to the conversation and looked at each other.

"Do all of us need to go home, Uncle John?" Mandie asked.

John Shaw stopped to look at her and replied, "Yes, I think that would be the best way. We'll all go at once as soon as we can get the train."

Then Mandie remembered Lily. She, Celia, Jonathan, Mrs. Taft, and the senator were supposed to stop off on the way and visit Lily. She quickly decided their plans would have to be cancelled. This situation seemed to be urgent, and besides, she wanted to get home and see for herself what was happening to their house.

All her friends immediately agreed it would be best if they all left together.

"We won't be able to get the train until tomorrow," John Shaw told Uncle Ned. "Did you come on the train?"

"Yes," Uncle Ned replied. "I go back with you on train tomorrow."

"I'll have to speak to Lindall Guyer. We came in his private car on the railroad," John Shaw said.

Mandie and her friends looked at each other and Mandie said, "Tommy, I hope you don't mind if we go home earlier than we planned. And, Joe, will you be going with us rather than waiting until next week to leave here?"

"Of course I understand, Mandie," Tommy replied.

Joe ran his long fingers through his unruly brown hair and said, "I suppose I might as well go on with y'all. That would give me a little more time with my parents before I return to college."

"I hope y'all don't mind, but I will stay on here until next week, as I had planned," Robert told them.

Celia quickly looked at him and asked, "You don't want to go when we go?"

Robert smiled at her and replied, "I wouldn't be any help in repairing a crack in the bottom of a house, so I'll just stay here a few more days in the nice beach weather with the Pattons when they go out there. Maybe I'll see you again before school starts back."

"That would be nice," Celia said with a shy smile. "Right now I don't know where my mother and I will be, but I'm sure we will go home with Mandie tomorrow."

"I'll find out," Robert promised.

Mandie wanted a chance to speak privately with Uncle Ned about the mysteries occurring in the Patton house. She wanted to get away from her friends to do this. Later that night after supper she finally got her chance to ask him if they could go for a walk and talk.

"Too late to walk tonight," Uncle Ned told her. "Early tomorrow morning we walk, talk, before train comes."

Mandie smiled up at him and agreed. "All right, Uncle Ned, I'll meet you down here before breakfast."

Mandie was tired from all the events and planning that had taken place. She was glad when she and Celia finally went to their room for the night.

"I'm plumb tuckered out," Mandie said, pushing open the door to their room. She plopped down in a chair nearby.

"Me too," Celia agreed, going over to the wardrobe. "But I think I'll get ready for bed before I relax."

"Yes, and I should, too," Mandie said, joining her.

After they had put on their nightclothes they decided to get in bed. Mandie shook Snowball off the counterpane and turned down the covers. The white cat curled up at the foot of the bed.

And once they were in bed they both dropped off to sleep.

Mandie was awakened by Snowball growling and hissing in her ear. She reached up to smack him and then came wide awake because his fur was ruffled up and he was acting strange. She raised up on her elbow and suddenly saw something shadowy moving by the chairs. She quickly pinched Celia.

Celia woke and before she could speak Mandie reached for her hand. That was always their signal for repeating their Bible verse.

" 'What time I am afraid, I will trust in thee,' " they said together.

Mandie tried to see through the darkness. Whatever had been in the room with them seemed to have suddenly vanished. She shakily reached for the lamp switch by the bed. When the light came on there was no one there.

"I know there was someone in this room," Mandie whispered, sitting up. "Snowball was acting like he did earlier today, hissing, and he woke me up."

Celia sat up and looked around. "I don't see anyone, Mandie."

Mandie looked at her cat. He had become quiet and was washing his face as he sat in the middle of the bed.

"There is something strange about this room," Mandie declared. "And I'm going to leave the light on for the rest of the night."

Celia pulled the covers around her shoulders and said, "Yes, leave the light on."

"I wonder if Josephine could have been in this room just now," Mandie said.

"She never did show up for supper," Celia reminded her.

"I noticed that, but she is friends with Cheechee and I'm sure Cheechee took her something to eat in her room. I would like to have a chance to search her room before we leave to go home."

"If she took your locket, Mandie, she probably put it someplace where you would never find it."

"She's so unreasonable in everything she does that you never know what she's up to next," Mandie said.

Celia dropped off to sleep. Mandie stayed awake for a long time thinking about everything that had happened since they had arrived at the Pattons' house. She needed to discuss this with someone and she was glad Uncle Ned had arrived. He was always ready to listen with advice.

# CHAPTER TWELVE

# THE THIEF

The next morning Uncle Ned was waiting for Mandie when she brought Snowball and came down to the kitchen. Tizzy was already there and had a pot of coffee made. She brought a cup to the table for Mandie to sit with Uncle Ned, who had just started drinking his. Snowball ran to a plate of food that Tizzy placed on the floor by the huge cookstove.

"Thank you, Tizzy," Mandie said as she sat down.

"Must hurry," the old man reminded her as he sipped his coffee.

Mandie took her spoon and began dipping it in and out of the coffee in an effort to cool it down enough to drink. "I know, Uncle Ned. I don't really want this whole cup of coffee, so I'll be ready whenever you are to take a walk outside," she replied.

Mandie didn't want to begin a discussion with Uncle Ned with Tizzy present to hear, so she hurriedly drank a little of the coffee, and as soon as Uncle Ned finished his, she said, "I'm ready." She rose from the table and reached for Snowball's leash, which she had hung on the back of a chair. "I want to take Snowball with us. He needs to walk." She quickly stooped down to fasten the cat's leash to his collar as he finished his food.

"Let's walk toward the water," Mandie suggested once they were out in the yard.

"Yes," the old man agreed.

As they walked, Mandie began relating the events that had taken place since they had come to the Pattons' house. When they got near the water they sat on a low wall and Mandie tied Snowball's leash around an iron stake nearby. He protested and tried to get loose.

"Uncle Ned, my locket was missing when I got up the other morning and Grandmother's diamond earbob was, too, and we've searched everywhere and can't find them," Mandie told him. "However, I know that Josephine must have taken them. I told her so and she got furious with me." She stopped and frowned.

"Must not judge unless know," the old man quickly told her. "Remember, think before act." He looked worried.

"But I know that she must have taken them," Mandie insisted.

"How know? See her take?" Uncle Ned asked.

Mandie looked up at him and said, "I didn't actually see her take them, but she has acted strange the whole time we've been here and she doesn't like me."

"Must not accuse without proof. I tell Papoose before, never judge without proof," Uncle Ned said firmly. "Must do what Big Book says, judge not." He frowned as he looked at her.

Mandie felt her temper flaring up and tried to control it but didn't succeed very well. "Oh, Uncle Ned, I just know Josephine took my locket and my grandmother's earbob. There's no one else who could have done it," she insisted.

Uncle Ned shook his head and said, "Must not accuse, not see. Not right to do that. Must ask her forgiveness."

"Never will I ask Josephine's forgiveness for anything," Mandie quickly replied, stomping her foot in the sand. "She needs to ask mine."

"Big Book say forgive," the old man said.

Mandie jumped up and pulled on Snowball's leash as she unhooked it. He protested by rolling over in the sand. "I have to go back now, Uncle Ned," she said, trying to keep her voice from shaking. "I have to get my things packed for the train." Uncle Ned was wrong this time. That girl had stolen the locket and the earbob, she was sure. No use arguing about it.

Uncle Ned rose and said, "Yes, we go."

They silently walked back to the Pattons' house. Mandie was angry with the old man, and she could tell he was angry with her.

There was no use in trying to discuss this with him. Snowball tried to run ahead. She held tightly to his leash.

At the house, Mandie quickly entered the front door and, without looking back at him, she said, "I'm going up to my room now."

"Think, Papoose, think," the old man told her as she picked up Snowball and rushed ahead for the staircase.

When she got to the top of the steps, she slowed down to take a deep breath. Snowball tried to wriggle loose, but she held him tightly.

When Mandie opened the door to her and Celia's room, Snowball hissed and bristled up as he managed to escape from her arms. He raced across the room toward the bureau. Mandie stopped in shock as she watched him jump up onto the bureau to chase what looked like a real live monkey sitting there holding Celia's red ribbon. The animal responded in his own language to the cat's growl and quickly leaped through the open window, taking Celia's ribbon with him. Snowball didn't slow down as he continued the chase.

Mandie ran over to the window to grab the cat, but he managed to go through right after the animal. She leaned over to look outside. The balcony by the room next door extended to the edge of her window and both animals had jumped onto it. The monkey dropped Celia's ribbon in one of the huge flowerpots sitting on the balcony and then rushed over the edge. Snowball jumped up after him and sat on the balcony rail and growled.

Without thinking of the danger, Mandie slipped through the open window and jumped down to the balcony, trying to rescue her cat.

"Snowball, come here," she demanded as the cat sat on the edge looking down after the monkey, who had disappeared from her sight.

She carefully moved over to reach Snowball when she noticed the red ribbon in the flowerpot. Stopping to pull it out of the sticky plant, she suddenly saw something shiny in the sunshine on the dirt in the pot. Reaching between the sharp leaves, she pulled it out. When she saw what it was, she sat down on the balcony floor and started crying as she held it tightly. It was her locket. Snowball turned back to see what was wrong with his mistress. He jumped down and came to try to sit on her lap.

"Oh, Snowball, it's my locket," Mandie cried, opening the locket to be sure her father's picture was still inside. She gazed into his beloved face and tears streamed down onto her cat.

Celia suddenly appeared in the window to their room. "Mandie, what are you doing down there?" she asked, leaning out to look.

Mandie held up the locket and couldn't speak because of tears as she stood.

"You found it!" Celia excitedly called to her.

Mandie nodded and looked around for a way to get back up through the window in their room.

"Wait," Celia told her. "I'll get one of the boys to help you back up. Wait right there." She disappeared from the window.

Mandie wiped her eyes on the hem of her long skirt and stepped over to the flowerpot to get Celia's red ribbon. And she again saw something shiny. Reaching into the pot she pulled it out. It was Mrs. Taft's diamond earbob.

"Grandmother, I've found it for you," Mandie muttered to herself as she rubbed the dirt off the earbob.

Then she suddenly wondered where the monkey had gone. Going to lean over the edge of the balcony, she saw a small boy in brightly colored clothes standing in the yard below. The monkey was making its way down the steep outside steps toward him. "The gypsies," Mandie said to herself. She wondered if the gypsies had taught that monkey to steal.

"Mandie!" She heard her name and looked up to see Joe climbing out of the window. "I'm coming down to get you." He jumped down and asked, "Mandie, how did you get down here?"

"The way you just did, Joe, and look here," she said, holding up her locket and her grandmother's earbob. Pointing over the edge of the balcony, she added, "The monkey down there stole them."

Together they looked over the edge. The monkey had made it down to the ground, and the little boy picked him up as he looked up at Mandie and Joe.

"Go home," Joe yelled at the boy.

Tommy appeared in the window and jumped down to join them. "Get going," he yelled at the boy below. "Right now, you hear? Go home."

The gypsy boy finally turned and started to walk away, carrying the monkey with him.

It took the help of both boys to get Mandie back into her room. She couldn't reach the windowsill. Joe boosted her up so that Tommy could stand in the window and get hold of her hands and pull her through into the room. Mandie collapsed on the floor as Joe sent Snowball through behind her.

Tommy knelt by her side and asked, "What happened? Why were you down there on that balcony?"

Joe stepped through the window into the room and bent to look at Mandie as he asked, "Are you all right?"

Celia reached and took her red ribbon that Mandie held out to her.

"I've never been so scared and so happy all at the same time," Mandie finally replied as she saw Jonathan and Robert come into the room. She showed everyone her locket and the earbob as she stood and shook her skirt. "I need to get cleaned up," she added.

"We'll wait for you on the landing of the main staircase," Joe said as all the boys left the room.

"Mandie, I'm so happy you found your locket," Celia said. "And I'm glad it wasn't Josephine who took it and your grandmother's earbob."

Mandie turned around to look at her and said, "Oh, Celia, I accused Josephine of taking them." And she also remembered arguing with Uncle Ned about it just a little while ago.

"I know," Celia replied, sitting on the bed. Snowball jumped up beside her and began washing his face.

"Celia, I've got to find Uncle Ned right away," Mandie said. "Just as soon as I get cleaned up."

The girls securely closed the window in their room, left Snowball on the bed, and went to meet the boys.

"I have to find Uncle Ned right away," Mandie told the boys. "I'll find y'all later."

"We'll be in the back parlor," Tommy told her.

Mandie held the locket and the earbob tightly in her hand as she hurried down the stairs and to the main parlor. There was no one there and no one in the hallway. She opened the front door. Mrs. Taft was walking about the yard with Senator Morton.

"Grandmother!" she called excitedly as she ran to her. She held out the earbob and her locket in her hand. "Look! I found them!"

"Where?" Mrs. Taft asked with a big smile as she took the earbob.

"Let's sit down on that bench over there and I'll explain."

As soon as they were seated beneath the palm tree, Mandie explained what had happened. She added, "And, Grandmother, I would like for you to lock up my locket in your jewelry case, please. I am not going to wear it anymore until I get the picture enlarged like you've always told me to."

Mrs. Taft took the locket and smiled at her. "I am so happy that these have been found. I'll go up to my room right now and lock them up where they'll be safe." She stood up.

Mandie rose, too, and said, "I need to find Uncle Ned. Have you seen him?"

"I believe he was in the barn with the other men looking after the horses just a little while ago," Senator Morton said.

"Thank you, Senator Morton, I'll go see," Mandie called back as she raced down the pathway to the back of the house.

She dreaded facing Uncle Ned and admitting she had been wrong about Josephine, but it had to be done, and the sooner the better to get it off her mind.

Uncle Ned came out of the barn as she got within sight of it, and he was alone. "Uncle Ned," she called to him as she hurried on. "Wait for me."

The old man stopped and looked at her. Mandie hurried up to his side and took his hand in hers as she said, "Uncle Ned, I am sorry. I was wrong about Josephine." She quickly explained about the monkey and then looked up at him as she asked, "Will you please forgive me? I'm sorry." Her voice choked up and she couldn't say another word.

Uncle Ned looked down at her, squeezed her hand, and said, "Yes, I forgive Papoose."

"Thank you, Uncle Ned," she said.

"Now Papoose must ask Josephine forgiveness," he said. "And must always stop to think before act."

"I know, Uncle Ned, and as soon as I can find Josephine I'll apologize," she said.

"Must hurry," the old man said. "Get train two hours."

"Two hours?" Mandie asked. "I have to pack my things, too."

Mandie went back inside the house to look for the girl, which was going to be an endless task, as Josephine always managed to disappear. Going up the main staircase, she kept watching for Josephine, but she was nowhere around. When she reached the hallway where her room was, she was amazed to see the girl coming out of her and Célia's room. She felt her anger rise. She took a deep breath and hurried forward. Josephine stopped to look at her.

"Josephine, I want you to know that I'm sorry I accused you of taking my locket and Grandmother's earbob, because I found them. The gypsies' monkey has been coming through the window in our room and I saw him today. I found the locket and earbob in a flowerpot on the balcony where he dropped Celia's red ribbon. I'm sorry." Mandie waited for a reply.

Josephine stood absolutely still for a moment and then she said, "I would like to play with your cat."

Mandie was always amazed by reactions from the girl. Her apology seemed to have floated off into the air, without Josephine even acknowledging it. Then Mandie realized Josephine must have been going into their room to play with Snowball.

Smiling, Mandie said, "You may play with Snowball anytime you like, Josephine, but please don't let him get outside."

Josephine looked at her, pushed the door back open, and went inside.

Mandie hurried back downstairs to join her friends. They were in the back parlor.

"I left Josephine playing with Snowball in our room," she said to Celia.

Everyone looked at her in surprise.

"It seems that must be the reason she has been going in our room, just to play with Snowball," Mandie said.

"What did you do with your locket?" Joe asked.

"I gave it to Grandmother to lock up in her jewelry case for me," Mandie replied.

"I'm certainly glad we've got that all settled," Tommy said.

"I have to pack my trunk because we are leaving in two hours, in case no one has told you," Mandie said. "But first I'd like to go outside and see if that little boy really left."

Her friends already knew they had two hours to get ready to leave for the train.

"Your Uncle John came and told us," Celia explained.

"Come on if we are going outside," Joe said. "We don't have much time."

They went out the front door and walked around to the outside staircase.

Mandie looked up but there was no sign of the monkey or the boy. Then she thought she saw something on a step above.

"Do you see something up there?" she asked her friends.

Tommy squinted his eyes and said, "I do believe there is something up there. I'll go see." He hurried up the steep steps.

The others watched as he stooped and picked up something.

"Someone's handkerchief," Tommy said, holding up a lacy square of linen as he came back down.

"Oh, that's mine," Mandie said, reaching out to take it. "I must have lost it while I was on the balcony." She remembered that she had reached in the pocket of her skirt for her handkerchief and it was not there. She had rubbed her eyes on the hem of her skirt.

"Let's get our things packed," Jonathan reminded the others as he led the way back into the house. "My father's railroad car is ready."

"Yes, let's hurry. The sooner we get back to my house and find out what is wrong, the better," Mandie said as she rushed behind him, and the others followed.

Mandie was anxious to go home because she was also anxious to leave the Pattons and Josephine, especially, while nothing else was happening. Their visit to Charleston had had too many problems this time.

Then she began thinking of the crack in the secret tunnel at home. Had the tornado caused it? And what could be done about it? It all sounded like a big mystery to her. She could hardly wait to get home to solve it.

Mandie was sorry to miss seeing Lily Masterson on her way back to Franklin. Maybe she would be able to persuade her grandmother to make the journey back down on the train one day soon for a visit.

However, the crack in the secret tunnel was more important.

# MANDIE

## AND THE
## HIDDEN PAST

With love to a special little reader—

KAHLA ERICKSON

# CONTENTS

## MANDIE AND THE HIDDEN PAST

"Trust no future, howe'er pleasant!
Let the dead Past bury its dead!
Act, act in the living present!
Heart within, and God o'erhead!"

—HENRY WADSWORTH LONGFELLOW

# CHAPTER ONE

# *HOME AGAIN*

"Let's walk to the house," Mandie told her friends as everyone stood on the depot platform.

John Shaw overheard this remark and said, "That would save Abraham and Mr. Bond from having to make two trips for us and our luggage."

"Yes, sir," Mandie said with a smile, holding on to Snowball's red leash and looking at Celia, Joe, and Jonathan.

They had all just arrived in Franklin, North Carolina, from the Pattons' house in Charleston, South Carolina. And the adults, John Shaw and Elizabeth, Mrs. Taft and Senator Morton, Lindall Guyer and Celia Hamilton's mother, Jane, and Uncle Ned, would be able to squeeze into the Shaws' rig, which Mr. Bond had brought to the depot to pick them up. Abraham was driving the Shaws' wagon, and it would be filled with trunks and other baggage.

Joe looked at Mandie, smiled, and said, "I imagine you have a reason for offering to walk."

Mandie wasn't about to reveal that reason, either. She was anxious to get to the Shaws' house ahead of the adults so she could get into the secret tunnel to inspect the crack in the wall, which Uncle Ned had come to Charleston to tell John Shaw about.

"Come on, let's go," Mandie said to her friends.

"Amanda," Elizabeth Shaw called to her, "no stops along the way. Go straight home."

"Yes, ma'am, we'll hurry," Mandie replied with a grin as she looked at Joe.

The young people hastened down the street from the depot. Mandie set the pace, and she was in a hurry. Even Jonathan, a New Yorker used to fast walking, had trouble keeping up with her.

"Mandie, do you have to walk so fast?" Jonathan asked as he kept by her side.

Mandie slowed just a little to look at him as she replied, "I can't explain right now, but I want to get to the house before my mother and the others do. So we have to hurry." She walked even faster.

"I think you should go on ahead and we'll catch up with you," Celia said, blowing out her breath.

"That's a good idea," Joe agreed, slowing down to Celia's side.

Mandie glanced back and said, "All right, y'all know the way to my house." With that remark, she started practically running down the street. Jonathan, however, stayed right with her, determined not to let her get ahead. At the next corner Mandie and Jonathan cut through a back street, while Joe and Celia continued down the main thoroughfare. Snowball forged ahead at the end of his leash.

Within ten minutes, Mandie was opening the gate to the long walkway in front of the Shaws' house.

Between gasps for breath, she said, "I hope no one sees us come in."

Jonathan, close by her side, asked as he, too, tried to get his breath, "Why do you not want anyone to see us?"

"Just because I don't," Mandie managed to say. She picked up her long skirts and ran up the front steps onto the long veranda. Pulling open the screen door, she quickly unfastened Snowball's leash and let him run ahead down the main hall.

"Let's go upstairs to Uncle John's office," she told Jonathan as she hurried for the main staircase.

Suddenly Aunt Lou, the housekeeper, came hurrying toward them from the back hall. "I knowed my chile be home when dat white cat showed up," the old woman was saying with a big smile.

"Oh, shucks!" Mandie said under her breath to Jonathan.

As Aunt Lou caught up with them, she said, "I see you done brought dat Yankee boy home wid you." She reached for Mandie and gave her a quick hug.

"Yes, ma'am, I'm that Yankee boy come to visit awhile," Jonathan said with a big grin as the woman patted him on the shoulder.

"The rig wouldn't hold all of us, so we walked," Mandie explained. "So did Joe and Celia, but we were in a hurry and left them behind." She was about to explain to Aunt Lou the reason she had rushed ahead of the others when Liza, the young maid, came rushing down the hallway to greet them.

"Oh, Missy 'Manda, I'se right glad you got home 'fo' dis heah house fall down," Liza said. She danced around the hallway.

"Liza, hush yo' mouth," Aunt Lou said. "Ain't nuthin' but a li'l crack in de wall downstairs. Ain't about to fall in." Turning back to Mandie, she asked, "Who all be comin' wid you?"

"Everyone," Mandie said. "Joe, Celia and her mother, Grandmother and Senator Morton, Jonathan's father, and Uncle Ned. And my mother and Uncle John, of course. We all came home so Uncle John could have something done about that crack. And I was glad to leave the Pattons' house because so many strange things kept happening."

"What kinda strange thangs?" Liza asked as she stood still and looked at Mandie.

"I'll tell you about it later, Liza. Right now I want to go down and see the crack in the wall of the tunnel before everyone else gets here," Mandie said.

"So that's why you were practically running all the way home," Jonathan said with a big grin.

"Cain't see de crack," Liza said. "Mistuh Jason Bond he locked de do' and totes de key wid him."

Mandie was surprised. "Why does he do that?" she asked.

"So's dat if part of de house fall in de other part won't," Liza said. "Or sumpin' like dat, I guess."

Mandie and Jonathan smiled at the girl.

Aunt Lou scolded Liza. "Liza, git back in de kitchen and git dem potatoes peeled," she said, shaking her large white apron at the girl.

Liza quickly started down the hallway toward the kitchen door. She turned back to say, "When y'all git to see dat crack, don't stay in there too long. Might fall in."

"All right, Liza," Mandie replied as the girl opened the kitchen door. Looking at Aunt Lou, Mandie asked, "Did Mr. Bond really lock the tunnel up?"

"Dat he did, my chile, till we sees if it be dangerous," the old woman replied. "Now dat Mistuh John come home we find out."

Joe Woodard and Celia Hamilton came in the front door and down the hallway to join them.

"Glad you young'uns got here safe. Now I has to go see 'bout de food," Aunt Lou greeted Joe and Celia. As she started toward the kitchen door, she looked back and smiled as she said, "I do believe Jenny's bakin' a cake, a chocolate one."

"But you didn't know I was coming," Joe teased.

"No matter, I knows all you young'uns like chocolate cake," she replied and disappeared into the kitchen.

Mandie explained to Joe and Celia why she was in such a hurry to get home as they all sat down on the bottom step of the huge staircase. "And now I find out Mr. Jason has it locked up and I can't get into the tunnel," she added with a sigh.

The kitchen door opened down the hallway, and Liza stepped out and called to them, "Abraham, he be in de backyard wid de luggage. Say he need help."

Joe and Jonathan quickly rose and started for the kitchen door. Mandie and Celia followed.

The boys helped carry in the trunks and put them in the appropriate rooms. The girls brought in the handbags and smaller things.

As they came inside with the last load, Mandie said, "Let's all go to our rooms and get cleaned up. Mother and the others ought to be here shortly."

"They must have taken a detour," Joe remarked as they all started for the staircase.

"Yes, Abraham said my father had to see to his railcar being put on the side rail, and then he wanted to go by one of the stores," Jonathan explained.

"I'll see y'all back down here by the steps in ten minutes," Mandie told the boys as they climbed the steps.

"Ten minutes? I don't believe two girls can get changed that fast," Jonathan teased.

Joe grinned at him and said loudly, "It all depends on what they are planning to do."

Mandie, a few steps above the boys, paused to look down on them and said, "You know very well what I am planning to do. I'm going to see the crack in the tunnel as soon as it is possible."

Everyone laughed and continued up the stairs and to their rooms.

Mandie and Celia quickly opened their trunks, hung up their dresses, and then changed clothes.

As she was buttoning up the front of her gingham dress, Mandie said suddenly, "Oh, Celia, I'm wondering if the outside entrance to the tunnel is locked. Do you want to go with me to find out? I'd only take a couple of minutes." She finished the last button and hurried to the bureau to brush back her long blond hair. She tied it back with a ribbon to match her red dress.

Celia tied her sash around her waist and smoothed the full skirt of her green dress. "But, Mandie, even if it is open we wouldn't have time to go into the tunnel. Your mother and the others will be here any minute," she replied.

Mandie started for the door. "Come on, Celia," she said as she opened the door. "If you don't want to go with me, I'll go by myself."

Celia, following, reluctantly agreed. "Well, all right, but we'll have to practically run down there and back."

Joe and Jonathan were waiting by the staircase. Jonathan pulled out his pocket watch, opened the cover, and said, "Nine minutes. You made it."

"And you can be sure they are up to something," Joe said teasingly.

"We're going to see if the outside entrance to the tunnel is locked," Mandie replied, going on down the hallway toward the back door.

"I was wondering when you would think about that," Joe teased as he and Jonathan followed the girls out the back door.

They hurried down the hill, through the trees, to a secret door that opened into the tunnel. Mandie got there first and gave a push on the door. It opened so suddenly she almost fell inside.

"It's unlocked," she exclaimed as she got her balance and tried to see into the tunnel.

"Yes, but I don't see any lanterns around here, and you know very well it is too dark to see your hand in front of your face in that tunnel," Joe reminded her as he and the others stopped outside the door.

"Oh, shucks!" Mandie exclaimed, stomping her foot as she stood just inside the doorway. "We can go back and get a lantern," she decided and came outside in a hurry.

"We do not have time for that, Mandie," Celia said.

Mandie turned to start back up the hill. "Maybe if we hurry," she said and began practically running, holding up the skirt of her dress.

When they arrived at the back door they were all out of breath.

Jonathan collapsed on the steps and said, "Whew! I'm not used to such fast living."

Celia stopped to lean against the rail around the back porch.

Joe plopped down beside Jonathan and said, "Neither am I."

"I'll be right back. I'll get a lantern out of the pantry," Mandie told them as she went on inside the back door.

"Oh, shucks!" Mandie whispered to herself as she saw the front door open at the other end of the hall. Her mother and all the other adults came inside. She didn't have time to get the lantern and go back to the tunnel entrance.

Jonathan, Joe, and Celia came in the back door.

"I don't believe we can go back down there right now," Joe said to Mandie as they watched the adults go into the parlor at the front of the hall.

"You are right," Mandie agreed, blowing out her breath.

"Let's have a conference," Jonathan said, leading the way to the staircase, where he and Joe sat on the bottom step and the girls sat on the bench by the stairs.

"It seems we have to make other plans," Joe said.

"I don't think they will stay in the parlor long, because they will want to change clothes after that long train ride," Celia remarked.

Liza came out of the kitchen. She was rolling the tea cart, and as she passed them, she said, "Miz Lizbeth she tell Mistuh Bond to tell Aunt Lou to tell me to bring de coffee to de parlor. I'se jes' sayin' dis jes' in case y'all want some." She grinned as she went on toward the parlor.

"She didn't say what she had to eat on that cart," Joe said with a big grin.

"Let's just go and find out," Jonathan said as he stood up.

"That's a good idea," Celia said, also rising.

Mandie stood up and said, "Hope it's chocolate cake." She grinned at her friends as they all hurried down the hallway to the parlor.

The adults were busy with their own conversation. The young people sat on the other side of the parlor and waited for Liza to finish with the others.

As Liza rolled the cart over to them, she smiled and said, "I knowed y'all gwine come after me. I sho' did. Ain't got no choc'late cake on heah, but we sho' got some good choc'late cookies." She winked at them and added, "I knows 'cause I done et one."

Mandie and her friends laughed and helped themselves to the coffee and chocolate cookies.

"Now I has to put dis heah cart back over dere near Miz 'Lizbeth 'cause Aunt Lou said so, and I has to go back and help wid de food," Liza told them. She rolled the cart to the other side of the room and then passed by the young people on her way out. "Don't y'all eat too many of dem cookies," she said. "Save some room for dat choc'late cake what we's gwine have fo' supper." She hurried out into the hallway.

Joe looked at the others, grinned, and said, "Well, now we know what we're going to have for supper—chocolate cake."

"Yes," Jonathan responded.

Mandie tried to listen to the adults' conversation on the other side of the room, but as far as she could tell, they weren't discussing the crack in the tunnel. They were talking about their visit with the Pattons in Charleston.

Then in a few minutes, Mrs. Taft stood up and said, "I need to go to my room and rest a little before supper."

Jane Hamilton rose from her chair and said, "And I need to clean up and change clothes."

All the other adults also stood up and prepared to leave the parlor. Mandie decided to speak to Uncle John. She hurried to catch him as he started toward the door to the hall. He was talking to Lindall Guyer, and Mandie had to step in front of him to get his attention.

"Uncle John, could I—" she began to ask, when he quickly interrupted.

"The answer is no, Amanda," John Shaw said. "I know your curiosity has got the best of you, but you will not be allowed in the tunnel until I have inspected the crack and decided what to do about it."

As he walked on, Mandie quickly said, "But couldn't I—"

"I said no, Amanda," John Shaw firmly told her. "Now, I don't want to hear any more about it. I'll let you know when you may go into the tunnel." He quickly followed the other adults out of the room.

Mandie just stood there and stomped her foot. "I don't see why I can't go into the tunnel with him," she mumbled to herself as she walked back across the room to her friends.

"If that crack caused the support beams to shift or break, it really could be dangerous, Mandie," Joe told her as she sat down.

"Your uncle is thinking of your safety," Jonathan added.

"Well, if that crack is dangerous, then, just like Liza said, the house could fall in," Mandie grumbled. "But we are all in the house."

"Remember, Mandie, Uncle Ned has seen the crack, and he has probably told your uncle John how bad it is," Celia reminded her.

"I imagine that's where all the men have gone right now," Mandie said. "Therefore, I can't get the lantern and go in from the outside entrance to see the crack."

Joe frowned at her and said, "Mandie, you are not planning on going into that tunnel before your uncle gives you permission to, are you? Remember, he said you were not to go into the tunnel until he said you could."

Mandie blew out her breath and rose and walked around the room. "I know what he said. But what difference would it make if

I went in from the outside entrance? No one would really know it," she argued.

"Mandie! Mandie!" Celia exclaimed. "You are talking about disobeying him. You know you shouldn't do that."

Mandie looked at her and didn't reply as she continued walking about the room.

"This is one mystery that I refuse to take part in," Jonathan said. "I certainly don't want to get in trouble with your uncle."

"Neither will I," Celia said.

"Remember what Uncle Ned always tells you: think before you act," Joe reminded her.

"All right, all right, we won't talk about it anymore," Mandie quickly told him. Taking a deep breath, Mandie straightened up and headed for the door. "I'm going to my room to rest until it's time for supper. I'll see y'all then." She quickly went out into the hallway.

She mumbled to herself as she went up the staircase two steps at a time. None of her friends said anything, and none of them followed her.

"That's all right," she said to herself. "I'll find a way to get to see the crack."

The door to her room was partly open, and she found Snowball curled up in the middle of her bed. She reached for his leash and gave him a push to wake him up.

"Come on, Snowball, let's go outside," she told the cat.

Snowball meowed and sat up to wash his face.

She fastened on his leash but picked him up and carried him down the hall to the back stairs. No one was in sight as she pushed open the back door and went outside.

She walked around the back of the house and went down the hill to the creek, where the old house had stood that was blown away by the tornado in the spring.

Snowball pulled forward on his leash and managed to get to the edge of the water, where minnows were swimming around. He stuck a paw in the creek and tried to catch one. He got excited as the minnows quickly evaded him.

Mandie sat down on a huge boulder at the edge of the water and watched the cat. She thought about what had transpired in the parlor and realized she had been very rude with her friends. She would have to ask their forgiveness. She was truly sorry about that, but she wouldn't change her mind about finding a way to see the crack in the tunnel. Somehow she would accomplish that.

# CHAPTER TWO

# A TIRING DAY

Mandie reentered the house through the back door. She removed Snowball's leash and set him down. He raced down the hallway out of sight. She walked on down to the parlor door and looked into the room. All her friends were still there, quietly talking among themselves, but she could not understand what they were talking about.

Suddenly Joe looked up and saw her in the doorway. He grinned at her and said, "That was a quick rest. We were just trying to decide whether we should go for a walk." He stood up. "Come on in," he added and then teasingly said, "We might even let you go with us."

Mandie felt tears come into her blue eyes and quickly took a few deep breaths before she entered the parlor and replied, "I appreciate the friendship of all of you. And I apologize for my rude behavior. I am sorry from the bottom of my heart. Will y'all forgive me?" She stood in the middle of the room as she looked at each one.

Everyone tried to talk at one time.

"You don't have to apologize to me for anything, Mandie," Celia quickly said. "We are all tired after that long trip."

"She is right," Jonathan agreed. "We are all a little out of sorts."

"And you know that includes me," Joe said. "Now come on, let's all go outside."

"We can't go far. It's almost time for supper," Mandie reminded him.

"We could go sit in the rose arbor. They must be blooming now and would smell so good," Celia suggested.

"Yes, the roses are blooming," Mandie said.

"Then, let's go," Joe said, leading the way out of the parlor and out the back door.

As they walked down the hill toward the rose arbor, Mandie was surprised to see her uncle John, Jonathan's father, and Uncle Ned coming up the hill.

"Look, there's Uncle John coming from down toward the creek." Mandie stopped to look ahead as she spoke to her friends. "And Uncle Ned and your father, Jonathan."

"And they are carrying lanterns," Jonathan said.

"Which means they probably came out of the outside entrance to the tunnel," Joe added.

"Yes," Mandie agreed.

The young people waited until the men came up to where they were standing on the pathway.

"That is some tunnel. I hadn't been all the way through it before," Lindall Guyer told his son, Jonathan.

"Yes, sir, it is," Jonathan agreed. "It must have taken a lot of time and work."

"My father had it built, you know," John Shaw explained to Jonathan. "I always think of how many Cherokee people were saved from the white soldiers, who were slaughtering every Indian they could find during the Removal."

"Yes, your father saved many Cherokee lives," Uncle Ned added.

"Is the crack dangerous, Uncle John?" Mandie quickly asked.

"We are not sure yet. We need to do a little more investigating," John Shaw told her. "We'll let y'all know when you can go in the tunnel and look at it. Now we've got to get cleaned up for supper." He started to walk on, and the other two men followed.

"Come on," Celia said, going ahead. "I've got to at least smell the roses."

"I can smell them from here," Jonathan said as they all began following Celia down the hill.

When they came within sight of the arbor, they all stopped to gaze at the beautiful climbing pink roses adorning the framework.

"Oh, how beautiful!" Celia said with a loud intake of breath.

"I believe roses are my favorite flowers," Joe remarked as he went toward the blooming mass and bent to smell the flowers.

"Roses are beautiful, but I prefer pansies," Jonathan said. "They are small and dainty and orderly."

"And they won't stick you," Mandie added with a smile.

"Well, if you don't touch the roses, they won't stick you, either," Celia argued.

Mandie was still thinking of the crack in the tunnel and wondering how she could get inside to see it. Since Uncle John and the others had come out from the outside entrance, she was pretty sure they had locked the door. So now both ends of the tunnel were locked up. She would have to find a way to check the entrances, and she didn't want to discuss the tunnel anymore with her friends. She would have to explore alone.

Suddenly she wondered how long her friends would be here. Looking at Joe, she asked, "Is your father coming to get you?"

"He had said he would be making calls around this area and would check to see when I got back from Charleston with y'all," Joe explained. He sat down on the bench under the arbor, and the others joined him.

"Since our plans got changed and we didn't stop off to see Lily on our way back here, I don't know when my mother will want to go home," Celia said.

"It would have been nice seeing Lily," Jonathan said. "But I know your uncle was worried about that crack in the tunnel, so it's better we came straight back here, Mandie. However, I do know my father has to get back to work in a day or two."

"A day or two?" Mandie asked. "Maybe he'll let you stay a few more days with us. We do have quite a bit of our vacation time still left."

"Just think, this is our last vacation from school, Mandie. Next summer we will be graduating," Celia said.

"Yes, and then going to college," Mandie said. "And we've got to decide which college we are going to soon."

"And that is going to be a problem," Celia said. "What if we don't agree on the same college?"

"The same college? Celia Hamilton, you have to go to the same college with me," Mandie quickly told her.

"Why don't you both just come down to New Orleans to the college where I go?" Joe asked.

"No, come up to New York to college with me," Jonathan quickly said.

Mandie glanced up the hill and saw Liza hurrying down it.

"Suppertime! Suppertime!" Liza was screaming.

Everyone stood up as she approached.

"We heard you," Mandie yelled back at the girl. "We're coming right now."

"Miz 'Lizbeth say to make it quick," Liza told her as she came to stand by the arbor.

"All right, Liza. How about going back and telling her we're on the way?" Mandie said.

Liza started back and then stopped, looked at Mandie, and said, "Bettuh hurry. Dey talkin' 'bout dat crack."

"All right, we'll hurry," Mandie said, glancing at her friends as she started up the hill behind Liza.

The young people went straight to the parlor, where Mandie knew everyone gathered before a meal. They silently entered the room and found seats as near the adults as possible.

John Shaw was saying, "I don't want to bring in any local help to repair the crack because I don't want outsiders going into the tunnel. It has always been kept private. There are still people around today who would frown on the fact that my father built it just to protect his Cherokee friends."

"I'm sure we men here could do the work," Lindall Guyer said.

"But don't you have to get back to New York in a day or two?" John Shaw asked.

Lindall Guyer glanced at his son, Jonathan, and then back at John Shaw and said, "I can take a few days longer. I'll just have to send a message to New York."

"That's fine. I appreciate that," John Shaw said.

Senator Morton, sitting by Mrs. Taft nearby, said, "John, you know I'm an old hand at repairing concrete since I'm from Florida, where we have lots of that kind of structure. I'd certainly be glad to pitch in and help. And I'm in no hurry to leave here."

"That's very kind of you, Senator," John Shaw said. "We can certainly use your knowledge on this."

Mandie leaned toward her friends on the settee and whispered, "Seems no one is going home anytime soon."

"As soon as this other man Uncle Ned has contacted comes to take a look, we'll see what can be done to close the crack," John Shaw said.

Liza came to the doorway and announced loudly, "Miz 'Lizbeth, de supper be on de table." And she quickly went on down the hallway.

"Shall we go eat?" Elizabeth Shaw said, rising from her chair.

"Don't forget we're going to have chocolate cake," Joe whispered to the other young people as they followed the adults into the dining room.

"Yes," Mandie said.

The young people were seated together at one end of the long table, with the adults at the other end. Therefore, private conversations could be carried on by either group. Sometimes Mandie was glad for this opportunity to talk to her friends, but at other times she was frustrated because she couldn't hear what was being said at the other end of the table.

She tried to listen in on the adults' discussion of the crack in the secret tunnel but couldn't hear enough of anything to know what they were saying. She wondered if Uncle John had asked the adults to keep the information on the crack confidential.

"Why are you so quiet, Mandie? What are you thinking about?" Celia asked.

"It's easy to know what she's thinking about. The crack in the tunnel, of course," Joe said teasingly.

Mandie laid down her fork, looked at each of her friends, and said, "I am quiet because I am trying to hear what Uncle John is talking about. And so far I haven't been able to understand a thing that is being said. I believe the people at that end of the table are in a conspiracy of some kind."

Her friends all laughed. Mandie ignored them as she tried to concentrate on the discussion at the other end of the table. However, she was not able to pick up a single bit of conversation. So she decided to follow them into the parlor when the meal was over.

As everyone rose from the table later, Mandie turned to her friends and said, "I know, of course, that we had the chocolate cake here at the table tonight, but I thought we might go into the parlor for a little while and find out if there is any more information on the crack in the tunnel." Then, looking at the three, she added, "Of course, if y'all would rather do something else, we can."

"Oh no," Jonathan said.

"Whatever you want to do is fine with me," Joe said.

"Me too, Mandie," Celia added.

Mandie smiled at them and led the way behind the adults to the parlor. After everyone was seated, Liza brought coffee on the tea cart, but the young people didn't take any. And the adults seemed to have nothing to talk about but their visit to the Pattons.

Finally Mandie straightened up in her chair and said to her friends, "If there is anything else y'all would like to do, we could do it, whatever. I don't think they are even going to mention the tunnel." She blew out her breath.

"Well," began Celia, "we could—" she stopped as John Shaw spoke.

"Now, the man to inspect the tunnel should be here tomorrow, and then we can decide on a schedule for repairs," John Shaw was saying to the other men.

"Then I won't send the message to my office until we figure out how long I should stay to help with the work," Lindall Guyer replied.

At that moment Mandie heard a loud knock on the front door, which was just outside the parlor at the end of the hallway. She looked at her friends and said, "I wonder who that is."

They could hear Liza answering the door, and she was saying, "Dey all be in de parlor."

Mandie heard their next-door neighbor, Mrs. Cornwallis, reply, "Thank you, Liza. We'll just go right in."

"Oh no!" Mandie muttered under her breath. The visitors were Mrs. Cornwallis and her daughter, Polly, who always seemed to chase after Joe when he was visiting the Shaws.

Mrs. Cornwallis and Polly appeared in the doorway. Elizabeth Shaw saw them and rose to say, "Y'all come right in."

The men all rose to speak and then sat back down.

"We thought we'd just drop in for a few minutes," Mrs. Cornwallis said as she took a seat near the men. "We heard that Mr. Guyer and Jane Hamilton were here. I do hope we are not interrupting anything."

"Oh no, of course not," Elizabeth Shaw replied.

Then Polly found a seat between Jonathan and Joe. "Did y'all have a nice visit in Charleston with the Pattons?" she asked, looking around the group.

Mandie didn't reply. Celia, however, looked at the girl and said with a smile, "Of course. We always do when we go to their house."

"Where have you been since school let out for the summer?" Mandie asked the girl.

"Mother and I went to Atlanta to see some friends," Polly replied. Then turning to Joe, she asked, "How long are you going to be here?"

Joe frowned as he replied, "I'm not sure. I have to wait for my father."

"It must be awfully inconvenient having a doctor for a father and never being able to keep a schedule because of his calls," Polly replied, smiling at Joe and tossing back her long dark hair.

"No, it isn't inconvenient for me. I'm used to it, and I'm proud of my father being a doctor and helping sick people," Joe said with a little smile.

"But you are not going to be a doctor," Polly said. "At least, the last time I heard, you weren't."

"No, I am not," Joe answered.

"Are you staying home the rest of the summer?" Mandie asked. She wanted to know in order to try to avoid the girl. Polly usually caused trouble and was very inquisitive about other people's affairs.

"I think so, but I am not positive yet," Polly said. "Mother and I may go to New York to shop." Turning to Jonathan, she asked, "When are you and your father going home to New York?"

"I have no idea. My father will decide that," Jonathan replied.

"The Shaws' cook told our cook that y'all were here, and we thought we'd come over and find out if you would be home in New York in a few days, just in case we go up there," Polly said.

"Like I said, I do not know," Jonathan repeated.

"Have you decided what college you will be going to when we graduate next spring?" Celia asked.

"Mother has decided that we should go down and look at the one Joe goes to in New Orleans and then to New York to look at one there," Polly replied. "Where are you and Mandie going?"

"We don't know yet. We have not come to an agreement, and therefore we may go to different colleges," Celia said.

Mandie quickly said, "Oh no, Celia. We are going to the same college, somewhere."

"But we haven't come up with a mutually agreeable place," Celia said.

"We will soon," Mandie insisted. "I am not going to a college where I don't know a single soul. I remember how awful it was when I started at the Heathwoods' School because I had no friends there, and then I met you." She was trying to listen to the adults' conversation while they talked, and as far as she could tell, her uncle had not mentioned the crack in the tunnel to Mrs. Cornwallis. He knew how the lady and her daughter could meddle in other people's affairs.

"Did y'all buy anything in Charleston while y'all were at the Pattons' house?" Polly asked, glancing at all of the young people.

"We didn't go shopping, no," Mandie replied.

"I picked up a couple of shells down by the water," Jonathan said.

Mandie was relieved to see Mrs. Cornwallis rise from her chair. They were going home. Polly also stood up.

"We have to go now," Polly said. "Will y'all be home tomorrow? I could come back."

"I have no idea as to what we will be doing tomorrow, Polly," Mandie said. "But you could come back over and see." She added this last remark for fear of being too abrupt with the girl, but she hoped Polly would find somewhere else to go.

As soon as Mrs. Cornwallis and Polly left, with Elizabeth seeing them out the front door, John Shaw looked across the parlor at the young people and said, "I didn't have time to warn you all, but I don't want anyone outside this house to know about the crack in the tunnel. This is a private family matter, and I want to keep it that way."

"I didn't mention it," Mandie quickly told him.

"Neither did I," Joe said.

"And I didn't, either. That girl, Polly, asks so many questions you wouldn't have time to tell her anything," Jonathan said with a big grin.

"I didn't say anything about it, either," Celia said.

"That's good," John Shaw said.

"Uncle John, do you know yet what time the man will come tomorrow to look at the crack?" Mandie asked.

"No, I do not," he said. "And I've already told you I'd let you know when y'all may go in the tunnel."

Mandie was tired and decided she might as well go to bed. Her friends agreed with the idea. It had been a long, tiring day.

She lay awake a long time, though, wondering what the crack looked like and whether the house could be in danger of caving in from the tunnel. It was a scary thought, and when she finally did go to sleep, she had a bad dream about it. She and her friends were in the tunnel inspecting the crack, when suddenly it popped wide open with a loud roar.

She gasped for breath and woke up to find Snowball curled up, purring in her ear. She pushed him away and pulled the cover over her head, wishing for the morning to come.

# CHAPTER THREE

# UNEXPECTED HAPPENINGS

Mandie woke just as the sun peeped over the dark horizon. She decided to get up. Slipping quietly out of bed to keep from waking Celia, she quickly put on her clothes, picked up Snowball, who was sitting up on the bed washing his face, and quietly left the room, softly pulling the door behind her.

As she walked softly down the hallway to the staircase, she didn't hear a sound. No one seemed to be up. She carried Snowball downstairs, went out the back hall door, and set him down in the yard. The white cat rubbed around her ankles and followed her as she walked around the house to the pathway down the hill.

"Now would be a good time to check the outside entrance to the tunnel," she said to herself.

She left the pathway and cut through the wooded part of the property. Snowball ran ahead of her as he found a squirrel to chase. Then suddenly the squirrel ran up a tree, and Snowball followed and stopped at the base of the tree. He looked back at Mandie and meowed.

"Don't you go up that tree," Mandie yelled at him. "I know you. Once you get up a tree, someone has to go up and get you down. You come here, you hear?"

Snowball sat still and looked at her. Mandie caught up with him, but when she reached down to pick him up, he quickly ran up the tree trunk and sat on the lower limb, out of her reach.

Mandie stomped her foot as she stood and looked up at him. "Snowball, I think I'll just leave you up there," she said.

Snowball looked down at her and meowed. Mandie moved directly under where he was sitting and tried to reach him, but the limb was too high. And Snowball just sat there and meowed.

"I think you are just going to have to stay there until Joe or Jonathan comes to get you down," Mandie said.

Suddenly a voice behind her said, "I get cat down, Papoose," and she turned to see Uncle Ned standing there. He smiled and quickly jumped up to catch the limb on which the cat was sitting. Holding on with one hand, the old man grabbed the white cat with his other hand. Snowball wriggled out of his grasp, landed on his four feet, and ran off into the woods, meowing like he was angry.

"Thank you, Uncle Ned," Mandie said as she watched the white fur disappear in the brush. She smiled and said, "I don't know why he has to run up trees and then can't seem to figure out how to get down."

"White cat knows how to get down, just playing tricks with Papoose," the old man said. "Next time leave him up there. When he gets hungry he will come down." He frowned and asked, "Why Papoose up so early?"

Mandie shuffled her feet in the underbrush and replied, "I woke up early and thought I might as well get up and get some fresh air before breakfast." She paused to look up at the tall man and then added, "I had a bad dream last night."

"Dream about crack?" Uncle Ned asked.

"Yes, sir," Mandie replied, hugging her arms together. "It was roaring something awful, and I woke up to find Snowball purring in my ear." She shivered as she remembered the dream.

"We walk, Papoose," Uncle Ned said, leading the way on through the trees. He looked down at Mandie at his side and added, "Crack does not roar. Little size crack."

"Do you think the tornado caused the crack?" Mandie asked. The storm had not seemed to do any damage to the house at the time it went through.

"Yes, must have," Uncle Ned replied.

"What does the crack look like, Uncle Ned?" Mandie asked as they came out into the clearing.

Uncle Ned shrugged his shoulders and said, "Like crack."

Mandie smiled up at him and said, "What I meant was, is it a wide crack like this," and she held her two hands apart in front of her, then put them closer together and said, "Or like this?"

The old man frowned and said, "Like this," and he drew a crooked vertical line in the air in front of him.

Mandie smiled and said, "Then it's not a straight line of a crack, and it goes up and down and not crossways."

Uncle Ned bent, picked up a stick, and traced a crooked line in the dirt. "That way, that size," he said. He straightened up and added, "About six feet tall."

Mandie smiled at his description and said, "I understand. Can you see through the crack, Uncle Ned?"

He looked puzzled.

"Is the crack split open enough to see through it into whatever is behind it?" she added.

Uncle Ned nodded and said, "Dark behind crack."

"I suppose it would be, since that would be under the house," Mandie said. Then, looking up at the old man, she asked, "Do you have the key to the outside tunnel entrance? We're close to it; it's over there behind those trees." She pointed to their left.

"No key, Papoose. John Shaw keep key," he told her. Then glancing up at the sun in the sky, he added, "Time to go eat."

"Yes, sir," Mandie agreed, and they turned back toward the house. As they walked along, she thought to herself, *It wouldn't have done any good to go on to check the outside entrance to the tunnel. It would have been locked.*

When they got back to the kitchen, Aunt Lou, Jenny, the cook, and Liza were all there getting the morning meal ready.

Aunt Lou greeted them as they came in the back door. "Y'all jes' sit down right dere at de table. I bring coffee," she said.

"Oh, thank you, Aunt Lou," Mandie said as she and Uncle Ned sat where the old woman indicated.

Aunt Lou got two cups from the sideboard, took them to the huge iron cookstove, and picked up the percolator, steaming with coffee. She filled the cups and set them in front of Mandie and Uncle Ned. "Fresh made, good and strong," she said. "Git yo' minds to workin'."

The door opened, and Joe, Jonathan, and Celia came into the kitchen.

"Morning, everybody," Jonathan mumbled as though he were still half asleep.

Greetings were exchanged, and the three came to sit at the table with Mandie and Uncle Ned. Aunt Lou brought them cups of coffee.

"What time did you get up, Mandie? I didn't hear you," Celia said.

"About an hour ago, I think," Mandie said. "I woke up and decided to go out for a walk."

"Jonathan and I waited on the landing for you two, and then finally Celia came out of your room," Joe said. "Where have you been?" He looked directly at Mandie.

"Just for a walk in the woods with Snowball, and then he decided to chase a squirrel up a tree. Uncle Ned happened to come along, and he got him down for me," Mandie explained. She looked directly at him and added, "That's all." She knew he would understand that she had not been to the outside entrance of the tunnel as he had suspected.

"What are the plans for today?" Jonathan asked, sipping the hot coffee in his cup.

"Plans?" Mandie repeated. She looked at Uncle Ned and asked, "Do you know what plans Uncle John has for today?"

Uncle Ned shook his head and said, "Man come before noon sun to look at crack. Then we make plans."

"Plans to repair the crack," Jonathan said, nodding his head.

"Yes," Uncle Ned replied.

Mandie quickly looked at her friends and said, "Then we can go look at the crack this afternoon. Uncle John said after the man inspected it he would let us go in and look."

"Yes," Jonathan said with a big grin.

"I'm not sure I want to go in that dark tunnel just to look at a crack," Celia said.

"But we always take lanterns with us. It won't be dark in there," Mandie assured her.

"Remember, Mandie, if your uncle thinks the crack is dangerous, he said he would not allow anyone in there," Joe reminded her.

"Well, we'll know about that when Uncle Ned's friend inspects it," Mandie replied.

Liza, listening to the conversation from the other side of the room, spoke up. "Lawsy mercy, Missy 'Manda, don't see why you wants to look at dat ol' crack. I ain't gwine down dere. Might crack wide open."

Everyone laughed.

"And it ain't no laughin' matter," Liza said quickly. "Dis heah house might be 'bout to fall in."

"Liza, you jes' hush dat crazy talk now, you heah?" Aunt Lou told the girl. "Git a move on now and git de dining room table set, right now."

"Yes'm," Liza said, going to the cupboard to get dishes.

By the time Aunt Lou got the food on the sideboard in the dining room, all the adults had come down, and everyone went in to eat. Mandie didn't dare ask Uncle John any more questions about the crack, but she listened to all the conversations at the table that she could hear. Not a word was said about the crack until the meal was finished and everyone stood up to go into the parlor for coffee.

Then she overheard John Shaw as he spoke to Uncle Ned. "Your friend should be here any minute now, shouldn't he?" he asked.

"Yes, any time now," Uncle Ned agreed.

Mandie whispered to her friends as they followed the adults into the parlor, "Did you hear that? The man will be here any time now."

All her friends nodded, and everyone found a seat in the parlor. Liza brought the coffee on the tea cart since there were so many people present. As soon as everyone had their coffee, there was a loud knock on the front door. Liza was still in the room, and she went to answer it.

Mandie heard her saying, "Dey all in de parlor."

Then Polly Cornwallis appeared in the doorway. "I thought I'd see what y'all are doing today," she said as she came on into the room and sat down on a chair near Joe.

"We have no idea as to what we'll be doing today, Polly," Mandie said, and she saw her mother glance at her from across the room.

Mrs. Taft, Mandie's grandmother, was sitting next to Senator Morton near Mandie's mother, Elizabeth. Mandie saw the two ladies speak to each other but couldn't hear what was said. Then Mrs. Taft spoke across the room. "Amanda, I thought we could go for a ride out into the countryside. The senator has never really seen the area around here."

Before Mandie could answer, Elizabeth said, "Oh yes, Amanda, you should go with Mother and take your friends along. The rest of us will be busy today."

"But, Mother, I'm not sure they want to go," Mandie replied.

Then Jonathan spoke up. "Yes, let's do go. I'd love to see the country." He looked at the other young people.

John Shaw was listening to the conversation, and he said, "Joe, if you would be good enough to drive the rig, I'd appreciate it. Abraham is going to be busy with other things today."

Joe grinned at Mandie, then looked at John Shaw and said, "Yes, sir, I'd be glad to drive the rig."

"Then I'll put everything in your hands," John Shaw said.

Mrs. Taft rose from her chair and said, "Then let's get started. I just need to go to my room for a few minutes and then I'll be ready."

Mandie finally figured out what was going on. Evidently her mother was trying to get Polly out of the house before the man came to inspect the crack in the tunnel. Everyone knew Polly was always telling everything she heard, and John Shaw had already cautioned the young people not to talk about the secret tunnel.

"Oh well," Mandie said as all her friends stood up. "Let me find Snowball so I can take him with us and I'll be ready." Turning to Polly, she asked, "Are you coming with us, Polly?"

Polly looked at everyone and asked, "How long will y'all be gone?"

Mrs. Taft was walking across the room, and she said, "A few hours, Polly. We're taking our noon meal with us. If you want to go, you are welcome."

"Well, I'll have to go ask my mother," Polly said.

"Then hurry," Mandie told her.

Polly rushed out of the room as Mrs. Taft went into the hallway to go to her room.

Mandie turned to her friends and said, "I'll be right back with Snowball." Then under her breath, she added, "This must have been planned beforehand."

All her friends smiled and nodded.

Joe drove the rig down the winding roads into the countryside. Mandie, with Snowball, sat beside him. Celia, Polly, and Jonathan were right behind them. Mrs. Taft and Senator Morton sat on the backseat and carried on their own conversation.

Aunt Lou had quickly prepared a basket of food to send with them. Mandie knew they would be gone for a while and that the man coming to look at the crack would have been there and gone by the time they returned.

Even though Joe did not live near Franklin, he was familiar with the countryside because of having been with his father making his rounds many times. Mrs. Taft didn't give him any instructions, so he drove toward the mountain. And he knew who lived in practically every house they passed because, some time or other, most of the people had had to have his father doctor them.

"This is better than sitting around the house, isn't it?" Jonathan remarked, turning to the others.

"I suppose," Polly said.

"Yes," Celia said. "I knew the adults would be busy today, and I had been wondering what we would do."

"We could always have sat in the arbor or walked around town," Mandie said. Mrs. Taft and Senator Morton were not listening but were deep in a conversation of their own, in voices too low to understand over the rattle of the rig as they rode along.

After a long while, Mrs. Taft finally did speak up. "Joe, I believe we should stop to eat now whenever you find a suitable place," she said.

Joe glanced back and said, "Yes, ma'am. I know where there's a waterfall not far from here."

"Fine," Mrs. Taft said.

When Joe finally pulled the rig off the road beside a glistening waterfall, Snowball suddenly decided he wanted free. He managed to pull away from Mandie and jump down. Jonathan instantly went after him and barely caught his leash before he got away in the direction of the water.

"Please don't let that cat get away," Mrs. Taft told Mandie as everyone left the rig and the boys brought the basket of food to a rough log table with benches near the water.

"I won't," Mandie promised as she tied Snowball's leash to a bush near the water so he could drink from the pond.

As everyone sat around the table eating, Senator Morton said, "This is certainly beautiful country. I've never really been out this way before. I'm usually just in and out on the train."

"It's certainly different from your countryside in Florida," Mrs. Taft said as she ate a piece of fried chicken.

Mandie noticed that Aunt Lou had even put in linen napkins and a tablecloth, probably because it was for Mrs. Taft.

Turning to the young people, Mrs. Taft asked, "What do you all plan to do for the rest of your summer vacation?" She looked at Mandie.

Mandie instantly knew Mrs. Taft had something in mind for them to do. She quickly tried to think up an answer of some kind that would make her grandmother believe they already had plans, but she was not fast enough.

"My father and I will be going home as soon as he and Mr. Shaw get their little job done," Jonathan said.

"But that won't take long," Mrs. Taft said. "How would you all like to come visit with me back in Asheville? Hilda will be home, and it has been a while since y'all saw her."

Hilda was the girl Mandie and Celia had found living in the attic of their boarding school in Asheville, North Carolina. Mrs. Taft had taken the girl in to live with her. However, Hilda didn't talk and was hard to communicate with.

Celia glanced at Mandie. Mandie blew out her breath and said, "Grandmother, let us think about it."

Polly spoke up. "Am I invited, too, Mrs. Taft?"

Mrs. Taft looked at her and smiled as she said, "Of course, Polly, but you know you will have to ask your mother."

"Yes, ma'am, I will," Polly said. "She has been wanting to visit some friends over in Asheville, so maybe she could go, too. And we would all be back in Asheville to go back to school when it opens."

"Yes, your mother would be welcome, too, Polly," Mrs. Taft said.

Mandie turned her head to keep anyone from seeing her smile. Mrs. Taft had just become involved with Polly for the rest of the summer if they all agreed to go to her house. She couldn't imagine her grandmother being around Polly that long. Polly always seemed to get into messes of some kind every time she went anywhere with Mandie and her friends.

"My father will be coming for me any day," Joe said. "I want to go home and spend some time before I go back to college. And I plan to return in about two more weeks to take some special classes that I need to catch up with my class. But I thank you for asking me, Mrs. Taft."

"Just in case your plans are changed, Joe, you will be most welcome to come visit with the others," Mrs. Taft told him.

Mandie had already been thinking about what she should do with the rest of her summer vacation. All her friends seemed to have to go home, and she wasn't certain she wanted to go to her grandmother's house to stay before school opened. Maybe she would just stay home with her mother and Uncle John.

Mrs. Taft opened the lid on the little watch she wore on a chain around her neck and said, "Well, now, I believe we ought to be getting back. It's later than I thought."

Mandie and Celia quickly packed up what was left of the food into the basket. Joe put it in the rig.

"Shall I drive faster going back, Mrs. Taft? I mean, did we stay too long or something?" Joe asked as Senator Taft helped the lady back into the rig.

"Oh no, Joe, we're not late for anything that I know of," Mrs. Taft told him as she once again sat on the backseat with the senator.

Mandie held tightly to Snowball as her friends climbed back in and Joe drove out into the road.

"It was nice of you young people to take us out like this," Senator Morton said.

"Yes, I've enjoyed it, too," Mrs. Taft added.

"Grandmother, are you and all our parents planning anything for tonight?" Mandie asked as they rode along.

"Why, no, Amanda, not that I know of. Now, your mother could have made some plans while we were gone," Mrs. Taft said.

Mandie was secretly hoping the grown-ups would be going out somewhere late that day because if Uncle John didn't let them go into the tunnel when they got back, she was going to figure out how to get her grandmother on her side to allow them in the tunnel. She just had to see that crack. And she hoped she would not dream about it again tonight.

# CHAPTER FOUR

# SNOWBALL CREATES A MYSTERY

Whey they got back to the Shaws' house, there was no one home. Mandie went to the kitchen to ask Aunt Lou where everyone was. Polly went home.

"My chile, yo' mama and all dem other grown-ups dey done went off wid Miz Cornwallis in her rig," Aunt Lou explained.

"Did they say where they were going?" Mandie asked.

"No. Miz 'Lizbeth, she say dey be back in time fo' suppuh and to set four extry places," the old woman explained as she stirred a pot of green beans on the stove.

"Four extra places?" Mandie said. "I wonder who is going to have supper with us."

"I hears huh ask Miz Cornwallis to eat, and she say she will, she and dat daughter of hers," Aunt Lou replied. "But I don't be knowin' who de other people gwine be. Now, where yo' grandmother, chile, and dat senator? Do dey be wantin' coffee in de parlor?"

"Everybody is in the parlor that went with me, and I know they'd like coffee, Aunt Lou, especially if you have any of that chocolate cake left," Mandie said, smiling up at the woman.

"Oh, my chile, you gwine turn to chocolate one o' dese days," Aunt Lou replied with a big smile. "But I'se got plenty of dat cake in de cupboard. Jes' go tell Miz Taft de coffee and cake will be right in."

"Yes, ma'am, thank you," Mandie replied with a loving pat on Aunt Lou's shoulder.

Mrs. Taft and the senator were sitting on the far side of the parlor, and Mandie's friends were seated near the door. She went over to her grandmother.

"Everybody went off with Mrs. Cornwallis in her rig, and Aunt Lou said my mother told her to set places for four more people for supper tonight—Mrs. Cornwallis and Polly, and she didn't know who the other two would be. Do you?"

"Why, no, Amanda. I have no idea," Mrs. Taft said. "I hope you asked for coffee."

"Yes, ma'am, and chocolate cake," Mandie replied with a smile.

"I believe I could eat a piece of that cake this time," Senator Morton said.

Liza came in with the tea cart, and Mandie went over to sit with her friends. After Liza served Mrs. Taft and Senator Morton, she came over to the young people to pour their coffee and hand out the little plates of chocolate cake.

"Did the man come to look at the crack in the tunnel, Liza?" Jonathan asked as he set his coffee down on the end table by the settee.

"Oh, shucks!" Mandie suddenly said, blowing out her breath. "How could I forget to ask Aunt Lou about that? Did he come, Liza?"

"Some man come and went down in de tunnel wid all de men, but he didn't stay long, said he be in a hurry. And he got on his horse and hurried off down de road," the girl explained.

"Did you hear anything my uncle said about the crack in the tunnel?" Mandie asked.

"He jes' tell dat man we gotta fix it right quick 'fo' it falls in," Liza said. She danced around the room, hugging herself, and added, "I done told evybody dis heah house might fall in."

"Did Uncle John say it was dangerous?" Mandie asked.

Liza stopped in front of Mandie and replied, "He say befo' dis heah house fall in. Don't dat mean dis heah house might be gwine fall in?"

"Maybe," Mandie said.

"Did you go down and look at the crack, Liza?" Jonathan asked, sipping his coffee.

"No siree, ain't gwine down in dat place, no I ain't," the girl replied. "I'se gotta go now 'fo' Aunt Lou come lookin' fo' me." She quickly left the parlor.

Mandie looked at her friends and said, "I can't imagine who the other two people are for supper tonight, unless maybe one of them is the man who came to look at the crack."

"It might be," Celia agreed.

"I hope he does come back. Maybe we could hear what he says about the tunnel," Jonathan said.

"Liza said the man left in a hurry," Joe reminded them.

"I'd like to know exactly who he is, where he came from," Mandie said, sipping her coffee.

Joe hastily swallowed a mouthful of chocolate cake and said, "Remember, Mr. Shaw said the man was a friend of Uncle Ned's. He may be Cherokee."

"Yes," Mandie agreed, squishing the chocolate icing on her cake. "Anyhow, the adults are bound to discuss the man's visit tonight, and if we stay around them we can listen."

Mrs. Taft spoke from the other side of the parlor as she and the senator rose from their chairs. "Amanda, I am going to my room to rest for a little while, if your mother gets back and asks for me."

"And I am going to take a walk around the yard," Senator Morton said.

"Yes, ma'am, yes, sir," Mandie replied as the two left the room.

"Let's go sit in the kitchen," Jonathan suggested.

"Sit in the kitchen? Now, why do you want to do that?" Joe asked.

"Because I am not allowed to sit in our kitchen at home, and I love to talk to Aunt Lou," Jonathan explained with a big grin.

Mandie shrugged her shoulders and said, "Oh well, I suppose

we could. Only I thought if we stayed in here we would know when my mother and the others return, and maybe they'll have those other two people with them who are coming to supper."

"Doesn't your mother always let Aunt Lou know when she returns from being out somewhere?" Celia asked.

Mandie nodded and said, "Most of the time." She rose. "Come on, let's go." She picked up her cake plate and coffee cup and saucer. "I might as well take these."

Her friends picked up their dishes.

"I'll just get those over there that Mrs. Taft and Senator Morton left, and we'll save Liza a trip from the kitchen," Joe said, going to the other side of the room and getting the dishes.

When the four young people opened the door and entered the kitchen with all the dishes, Aunt Lou shook her head at them and said, "Now, whut fo' are y'all a-doin' dat? We gits paid to do dat." She stepped forward to take some of the dishes and said to Liza, "Come heah and git dese heah dishes, Liza."

When the two had taken all the dishes from the young people, Jonathan asked with a big grin, "Aunt Lou, may we have permission to sit at your table for a little while?"

Aunt Lou reached to pat him on the shoulder as she crossed the room and said, "Since you be one of dem Yankee boys and don't know no better, I suppose it'd be all right for a few minutes, but mind you, we's busy in heah gittin' supper ready."

Jonathan, still grinning, replied, "Thank you, Aunt Lou, for the privilege."

"Oh, come on, Jonathan, and sit down," Mandie told him as she and the others pulled out chairs at the long table.

"Aunt Lou, did you see the man who came to look at the crack in the tunnel?" Mandie asked.

"I sho' did," Aunt Lou said, stirring several pots of food on the big iron cookstove. "He come right heah through my kitchen."

"What did he look like? Was he Cherokee? He's Uncle Ned's friend, you know," Mandie said.

"He sho' is Cherokee, and young and good-looking, too," the old woman replied, turning and wiping her hands on her large white apron.

"I wonder if I've ever met him, if he lives anywhere near Uncle Ned," Mandie said.

Aunt Lou shook her head and said, "Don't think so. He says he has to hurry back home to Asheville. And he was wearin' white man's clothes, not dressed like Uncle Ned."

Mandie frowned as she and her friends looked at each other. "Asheville," she said. "I wonder if he has ever been around our school there."

"Probably not, Mandie," Celia said. "I don't remember ever seeing any Cherokee workmen around there."

"He's comin' back," Aunt Lou told her as she turned once again to stir the contents of the pots on the stove. "I hears him say he's comin' back."

"When is he coming back?" Mandie asked.

"I don't know, my chile. He went out de door about dat time," Aunt Lou replied. "Now, where dat Polly girl whut went wid y'all this afternoon?"

"She went home as soon as we got back," Mandie told her. "She said she was tired and dirty." She grinned at the thought.

"Well, I s'pects she'll be back tonight wid her mama," Aunt Lou said.

Liza was peeling potatoes at the sideboard and listening to the conversation. "She sho' will, wid two boys heah now," she said with a big grin.

Everyone laughed.

"Maybe the other two people expected for supper will be girls," Jonathan said, grinning at the others.

"That would make things interesting," Joe agreed, glancing at Mandie with a mischievous smile.

"Or they could be boys," Mandie said, grinning back.

"Or they could be older people," Celia added.

Aunt Lou was listening to their conversation. "Y'all jes' seem bound and determined to decide who's coming to eat tonight, but I thinks y'all just gwine hafta wait and see." She smiled at them.

Mandie instantly had the idea that Aunt Lou knew but didn't want to tell them who was expected. "Aunt Lou, why don't you tell us who is coming?" she asked with a big smile.

"Now, my chile, I ain't said I knows," Aunt Lou replied. "Now why don't y'all git out of my kitchen so I kin git supper ready? Shoo now."

Mandie and her friends laughed as they stood up.

"Yes, ma'am," Mandie said with a big grin. "We'll just go outside and find the senator and see what he is doing."

"Yes," Joe agreed. "He went out alone."

"Come on, then," Jonathan said, starting for the door.

Celia caught up with Mandie as they stepped into the hallway. "Mandie, I'll need to change clothes for supper," she said. "I feel dirty after that trip into the country."

"Yes, and I'll have to change, too," Mandie agreed. "But we have plenty of time for that."

The four went out the back door and looked around the yard, but there was no sign of Senator Morton.

"Maybe he came back inside and went to his room," Joe suggested.

"Let's walk down to the outside entrance to the tunnel," Mandie said, leading the way without looking to see whether her friends were following or not.

"It won't be unlocked," Joe reminded her as he followed.

Celia and Jonathan straggled behind.

When Mandie got to the outside entrance, hidden by vines, bushes, and trees, she was surprised to find Senator Morton sitting on a log nearby. He looked up as she approached.

"Is the door unlocked, Senator Morton?" Mandie asked, hurrying to investigate. The door was closed.

"No. I thought perhaps it would be, but no, it's locked," the senator replied. "So I thought I'd just sit here awhile and watch the birds and the squirrels. Your white cat has been chasing them." He smiled at her.

Mandie quickly looked around and saw Snowball crouched in the bushes, intently watching something hidden from her view. Her friends caught up with her.

"Oh, shucks, I was hoping the door would be unlocked," Mandie said, blowing out her breath.

"Yes, I thought the men might have left it open," Senator Morton said. "I wanted to have a look at the crack and see what could be done to repair it since I offered to help."

"Aunt Lou said the man was coming back, but she didn't know when," Mandie told him. "And she also said we are having two unidentified guests at supper tonight. Maybe one will be that man."

The four young people sat down on a nearby log.

"Have y'all decided to go home with Mrs. Taft for a visit?" the senator asked.

"No, sir, I haven't decided," Mandie said, glancing at her friends.

They all shook their heads.

"I have to wait and see what my mother wants to do," Celia said.

Suddenly Snowball quickly backed out of the bushes where he had been sitting. He growled and hit at something he was pulling along with his paw.

Mandie leaned forward to see what the cat was doing. "Snowball, what have you got there?" she asked.

The cat continued batting at something in the grass. Mandie got up to look. "Snowball, where did you get that?" she asked in surprise. He had a red velvet pincushion with several pins in it. She took it from him and examined it.

"A pincushion?" Celia said.

"Now, what would a cat want with a pincushion?" Jonathan teased as he watched Mandie turning it over in her hand.

"Maybe that cat has learned to sew," Joe added with a big grin.

Mandie was puzzled. "Yes, it is a pincushion, but where did it come from?" she said.

Snowball reached up to get his toy back from her as he meowed loudly.

"No, Snowball, you cannot have this back. In the first place, it has pins in it, and besides, it doesn't look dirty, so someone must have dropped it here recently." She turned it over and held it up for her friends to see.

"Aha, we have another mystery to solve," Jonathan said, grinning at her as he looked at the pincushion.

"Senator Morton, has Snowball been there in that bush the whole time you've been here?" Mandie asked.

"I believe so," he replied. "I remember seeing him through the bushes and wondering what he was doing down here without you."

"He does wander off without me when we're at home, like now," Mandie explained. "This morning he ran up a tree over there, and Uncle Ned happened to come by and got him down for me. But I would like to know where this pincushion came from. It's not dirty, and it doesn't look like it's been out here long."

"It doesn't look familiar to me," Celia said. "I don't believe I have seen it in your house."

"It doesn't belong to me," Mandie said. She bent over to fan the bushes aside where Snowball had found the pincushion. "I don't see anything else around here."

"Maybe someone in the house will recognize it," Joe suggested.

"But I can't imagine how a pincushion got down here," Mandie said.

"Maybe Snowball got it somewhere in the house and brought it down here," Jonathan said.

Mandie shook her head. "No, I imagine someone in the house would have seen him with it and taken it away. He must have just found it right here in the bushes."

"Do you know who it could possibly belong to?" Jonathan asked.

"No," Mandie replied. "I'll ask Liza if she has seen it before."

"Mandie, remember we have to clean up for supper, and it must be getting late," Celia reminded her.

"Yes, let's go back to the house," Mandie agreed. Looking down at her white cat, she said, "Come on, Snowball, let's go." She held the pincushion down just out of his reach, and he went with her up the path.

Senator Morton and the other young people followed Mandie back into the house.

"I shall see you all at supper. I must also get freshened up," the senator told them as he went on toward the staircase, and Mandie and her friends went to open the kitchen door.

Snowball darted ahead of everyone as soon as the door was opened.

Aunt Lou called to them from the stove, where she was still

stirring pots of food. "Now, I done tol' y'all to git out 'cause I gotta git de supper done."

"We are not staying," Mandie replied as she held up the pincushion. "I only want to show you this and ask if you've seen it before."

Liza was getting dishes down from the cupboard. She turned to look. "I ain't seen it before," she said as she glanced at the pincushion.

"No, I don't believe I have, either," Aunt Lou said. "What are you a-doin' totin' a pincushion around?"

Mandie explained where she had found it. "I thought maybe y'all might know where it came from," she added.

"Skiddoo," Aunt Lou said. "Y'all has to git outta heah so I can finish gittin' de supper ready now."

"All right, all right, we're going," Mandie quickly replied and followed her friends out into the hallway. Then she remembered her mother and the others who had gone off somewhere that day. Stopping to step back and push the door open, she asked, "Do y'all know if my mother and the others have come back yet?"

"Ain't seen 'em. Now git goin', my chile, 'fo' I burns up de supper," Aunt Lou told her.

Mandie quickly stepped back into the hallway and followed her friends to the main staircase, where they all paused for a few minutes.

"Let's meet back here in twenty minutes," Mandie told her friends.

They all agreed and everyone went on to their rooms.

Mandie laid the pincushion on her bureau. "I'm going to leave this here, but I'm also going to ask my mother and grandmother whether they are missing a pincushion," she said as she went over to the wardrobe to take down a dress.

"It probably does belong to someone in your house here," Celia agreed, reaching for a fresh dress, also. "Things are getting complicated. Now we have two mysteries, the crack and the pincushion."

"Actually, we have three mysteries unsolved, those two and the identity of who is coming to supper tonight," Mandie reminded her. She quickly removed her dress and slipped into the fresh one.

"At least we ought to be able to solve that one when everyone goes in to supper," Celia said, buttoning up the front of her new dress.

"Maybe we will find out before if we hurry and go down and wait in the parlor," Mandie said. "That is, if whoever it is comes back with my mother and the others."

The girls hurried and were back on the steps before the boys.

# CHAPTER FIVE

# *ONE MYSTERY SOLVED*

"Let's go sit in the parlor," Mandie told her friends at the staircase. "My mother and the others have to come home before supper, and maybe they will have the two extra guests with them."

As they walked down the hallway, Joe asked, "Suppose these two extra people are ones you don't like?"

Mandie paused to look up at him and ask, "Someone I don't like? I don't believe my mother would invite someone like that."

"You never know. It might be for business purposes," Jonathan reminded her as he, too, stopped in the hallway.

"If y'all aren't coming to the parlor, I am. I want to sit down and relax for a while," Celia told the others. She continued toward the parlor door. The others followed.

As soon as they sat down in the parlor, Mandie looked across the room at the doorway and saw Snowball rush in carrying the red pincushion. She jumped up to take it away from him.

"Snowball, how did you get that pincushion back so fast?" she said to him as he protested losing the pincushion to her.

"He must have followed us up to your room, Mandie," Celia said.

Mandie sat down, holding the pincushion as she turned it over and over. "Probably," she agreed. "I don't really remember where he went when we got back to the house."

"What are you going to do with that thing?" Jonathan asked.

"I want to find out where it came from," Mandie replied. "And who it belongs to."

"That may be hard to do since you found it all the way down by the outside entrance to the tunnel," Joe reminded her.

Mandie grinned at him and said, "Don't you understand? If I can find out who this belongs to, then I will know who was poking around the tunnel entrance."

"And what good will that do you?" Jonathan asked.

"Jonathan, I just don't like things to be unexplained," Mandie said. "Whoever dropped this pincushion down there was on our property and may have been trying to get into the tunnel. And I would like to know why."

Mrs. Taft and Senator Morton came into the parlor and looked around as they took seats across the room from the young people.

"I suppose your mother and the others are not back yet, Amanda," Mrs. Taft said.

"No, ma'am, we've been waiting in here for them," Mandie replied. She held up the red pincushion as she got up and walked over to her grandmother's chair. "Have you ever seen this red pincushion before, Grandmother?"

Mrs. Taft looked puzzled as she glanced at the pincushion and then at Mandie. "Why, no, I don't believe I have. Is there something wrong with it?"

"No, ma'am," Mandie replied. "Snowball was playing with it at the outside entrance to the tunnel when we walked down there, and I was wondering where it came from."

"Snowball was playing with a pincushion? It's a wonder he didn't get injured on it," Mrs. Taft said, frowning as she looked at the red object.

"Yes, ma'am, but I suppose I caught him in time," Mandie agreed. She had started back across the room to her chair when someone knocked on the front door. She immediately went out into the hallway to answer it.

When Mandie opened the front door, Polly was standing there. "Well, come on in, Polly," she said to the girl.

Polly fluffed her full skirt with one hand as she followed Mandie into the parlor. She immediately sat down in an empty chair next to Joe.

"My mother hasn't returned yet, so I thought I'd just come on over and wait since she and I will be having supper with y'all," Polly said to Mandie.

"Surely they will be back anytime now. It's almost suppertime," Mandie said.

"Do you know yet how much longer you will be here, Joe?" Polly asked.

"I'm waiting for my father so I don't know exactly," Joe replied, straightening up in his chair as Polly leaned over.

Polly looked across at Jonathan and asked him, "How about you, Jonathan? Will you be staying here awhile yet?"

Jonathan shrugged his shoulders and said, "I have no idea. It all depends on my father."

"It must be nice to have a father to make all those decisions for y'all," Polly said. "I haven't had a father since I was a baby. In fact, I'm not even sure I can remember him. I always wanted my mother to get married again after my father died, but she has no plans for that."

"You ought to be glad your mother hasn't remarried, because she might marry someone you don't like," Jonathan told her.

Mandie was turning the pincushion over and over in her hands as she listened, and then she became aware of Polly watching her.

"What are you doing with that pincushion, Mandie?" Polly asked.

"Nothing, really," Mandie replied. "I found it. Snowball was playing with it."

"He was?" Polly asked in surprise. "Where did Snowball get it?"

"Down by the outside entrance to the tunnel," Mandie said.

"Oh, have y'all been in the tunnel?" Polly asked, looking around at the four young people.

As everyone shook their heads, Mandie said, "No, it's locked and we don't have the key."

"Where is the key?" Polly asked. "Why don't y'all have it?"

Mandie became exasperated with the questions. "We don't have the key because Uncle John has it," she said, frowning at the girl.

There was another knock on the front door, and Mandie heard

Liza, who was evidently in the hall, open it. She couldn't hear what was being said.

Then everyone looked up to see Dr. and Mrs. Woodard standing in the doorway of the parlor.

"Dad! Mother!" Joe said in surprise as he stood up. "I'm glad you came so I can go back home before returning to school."

Mrs. Taft had also stood up, and she said, "Welcome. Elizabeth and all the others are out somewhere, so come on in and make yourselves at home."

Mrs. Woodard went over to sit by Mrs. Taft and Senator Morton. Dr. Woodard pulled an envelope out of his inside coat pocket and handed it to Joe. "You have a letter here from your college," he said as he sat down.

Joe took it and quickly tore it open. He scanned the one page and looked up at his father with a big grin. "I don't have to go back to college early. They have scheduled the extra classes I need to catch up during the afternoons, when we normally have breaks."

"That's wonderful, son," Dr. Woodard said, smiling.

"Yes, Joe, I'm so glad your vacation won't be cut short," his mother said across the room.

Joe looked around at his friends. "What a relief! Now I can have a whole vacation," he told them.

"Then you should all come home with me and spend at least a few days," Mrs. Taft said across the room.

The young people all looked at each other and didn't reply. Mandie said, "Grandmother, we'll discuss it and let you know what our plans are now that Joe is free for the summer."

"All right, Amanda, but you are all welcome at my house," Mrs. Taft replied.

Mrs. Woodard spoke up. "You could all just come home with us and visit for a while," she said, then turned to Mrs. Taft and added, "And of course that includes you and Senator Morton."

Mandie laughed and said, "Since people want us all to go different places, it might be better if we all just stayed here at my house for the rest of the summer."

"We'll see, Amanda," Mrs. Taft said.

"Yes, we can decide later after we talk to your mother, Amanda," Mrs. Woodard said.

Then Mandie heard the front door open and close and all the other adults came into the room—her mother; Uncle John; Jonathan's father; Uncle Ned; Polly's mother, Mrs. Cornwallis; Celia's mother, Jane Hamilton; and John Shaw's caretaker, Jason Bond.

As greetings were being exchanged, Liza came to the doorway and announced loudly, "Miz 'Lizbeth, suppah be ready."

Elizabeth turned and said, "Thank you, Liza. Please ask Aunt Lou to give us about fifteen minutes to freshen up, and we'll be in."

"Yes'm," Liza replied and disappeared down the hallway.

Elizabeth said, "I need to clean up a little. How about y'all?"

All the people who had been with her agreed and immediately left the room, with a promise to return in fifteen minutes.

Mandie sighed and said, "Oh, shucks, we won't have time to talk to any of them before we eat."

Then suddenly Jonathan spoke up. "Now we know who the two other guests are, Joe's parents." He grinned at Mandie.

"Yes," Mandie and her friends all agreed.

"And I'm glad it was them, because they brought me good news," Joe said.

As soon as everyone returned to the parlor, Elizabeth Shaw led the way to the dining room. Mandie was pleased to notice that because of the many adults present, the seating allowed the young people to sit closer to them and, therefore, to hear at least part of their conversation.

Mandie was still carrying the pincushion, and not knowing what else to do with it, she placed it on the table by her plate. Elizabeth Shaw noticed this and spoke from the other end of the table. "Why, Amanda, what are you doing with a pincushion at the table?"

Mandie frowned and reached to pick it up. "I just had it in my hand and forgot to leave it in the parlor while we eat," she explained.

"Where did you get it in the first place?" Elizabeth asked.

All the adults had turned to look at the pincushion.

"I found it," Mandie replied.

Mrs. Cornwallis spoke up. "That looks like one that belongs to

Polly." And glancing toward her daughter, she asked, "Is it yours, Polly?"

Polly stuttered with her answer, looking at the pincushion as she spoke. "Ah, no, ma'am, uh, that is, I don't think so."

The adults turned their attention to their own conversation. But Mandie had immediately noticed Polly's discomfort with the question from her mother. "It does belong to you, doesn't it, Polly?" she asked, holding it out to the girl across the table.

Polly took it, shook her head, and said, "I—I don't—uh—really know." She laid it down on the table.

"And you lost it at the outside entrance to our tunnel," Mandie said, low enough that the adults could not hear her. "What were you doing down there, Polly?"

Polly frowned, bit her lip, and said, "What do you mean, what was I doing down there? I didn't say I had been down there."

"We'll talk about it later," Mandie told her. She planned to get Polly away from the adults and ask her some questions.

Polly shrugged her shoulders and began eating.

Mandie was determined she was going to find out what the girl had been doing, but she heard her uncle mention the tunnel and she quit talking to listen.

"Uncle Ned's friend will return the first thing tomorrow morning, and we can go to work on that crack then," John Shaw was saying to the other adults.

"And according to him it shouldn't take more than a day to repair it," Lindall Guyer added.

Senator Morton laid down his fork and said, "I'm sorry I missed out on the plans, but I would like to help in any way I can."

"Thank you, Senator," John Shaw said. "Cliff, Uncle Ned's friend, examined the place and thought we could just add mortar to close it up and that it would be all right. In other words, he didn't seem to think it was dangerous."

"I see," Senator Morton replied. "Is this a crack with empty space behind it, or is it up against a wall?"

"We couldn't really tell, but we assumed the stairway where it's located was dug out just for the steps," John Shaw replied. "Therefore it would be solid dirt behind it."

"I would suggest you make sure of that," Senator Morton told him. "If there is a hollow space behind it, the crack could reopen after a while."

"I thought when we start work on it we could open a place in it just enough to see what's behind it," John Shaw replied.

"That's an intelligent decision," the senator agreed.

The young people were all listening to the conversation.

Suddenly Mandie remembered her uncle telling them to keep this problem secret, just within the family, and here he was talking about it in front of Mrs. Cornwallis and Polly and also Dr. and Mrs. Woodard. The Woodards were like kinpeople, but the Cornwallises were not. Polly loved to tote tales of anything she heard.

"Maybe they will allow us to look at the crack when they start to repair it," Jonathan said, looking around at the young people.

"Yes, I would like to see that crack," Polly spoke up.

"You would?" Mandie asked, watching her closely.

"Yes, wouldn't you?" Polly replied. "I heard your cook telling our cook about it yesterday, and I told my mother."

"You did?" Mandie said.

"Yes, and she said she didn't care to go down in that tunnel and look at it, but I would," Polly explained.

Mandie sighed and looked at her friends.

"Maybe we can all go down there together and look," Joe suggested.

"We will have to ask Uncle John," Mandie reminded him.

"Yes, of course," Joe agreed.

"If they get the crack repaired tomorrow, does that mean you and your father will be leaving the next day, Jonathan?" Mandie asked.

"I'll have to speak to him and find out," Jonathan replied.

As soon as the meal was over, everyone returned to the parlor for coffee. Mandie and her friends followed, hoping to hear more conversation regarding the crack in the tunnel. However, the adults were talking mainly about the friends they had been to visit that day.

After a while, Liza came to the parlor doorway and held up the red pincushion. "Somebody forgit dis heah thang?" she asked as she looked around at the young people.

Mandie waited for Polly to claim it, but she just looked at Liza and didn't say a word.

"I think it belongs to Polly," Mandie said.

Liza stepped inside the room and dropped it on the table next to where Polly was sitting. Then she turned and left the parlor.

When Polly didn't pick it up, Mandie said, "Take it, Polly; it must be yours."

Polly looked at it and finally picked it up as she said, "I'm not sure it's mine." She turned it over and over.

"You can take it home with you and see if yours is missing," Mandie said. She was positive it did belong to Polly, but she couldn't figure out how it came to be at the entrance of the tunnel.

"What are you girls planning on doing after you graduate next summer?" Jonathan asked.

"I'm not sure," Mandie told him. "Grandmother never has said whether she will give us all a trip to Europe for graduation or not. I imagine she will, but she will probably wait until the last minute to let us know. You know how she is about wanting to run everything, and she would want this to look like she had come up with the idea of a European trip herself." Mandie smiled at her friends.

"Are you going home with her for a visit before your school opens?" Joe asked.

"No, I don't think I want to," Mandie said. "What would we do for the rest of the summer at her house in Asheville?"

"Oh, you always find a mystery wherever you go," Jonathan told her with a big grin.

"Do you think your father might allow you to stay here for a while after he goes home?" Mandie asked.

"I'm not sure what he is planning. I know he has to go back to work, so he won't be home to do anything," Jonathan replied. Then in a whisper he added, "I thought maybe your grandmother and my father might become friends again."

Mandie smiled and said, "I thought so, too. However, the senator is here, and he takes up all her time. Maybe if the senator had not come, it would have happened."

Polly overheard the conversation, and she quickly asked,

"Do y'all mean Mrs. Taft and Mr. Guyer don't like each other or something?"

"Oh goodness," Mandie said.

"They are not exactly close friends," Jonathan said.

"Did they have a quarrel or something?" Polly asked.

"Oh, Polly, they used to be friends when they were young," Mandie said. "Does your mother have any men friends from long ago like that?"

Polly thought for a moment and said, "She has had lots of men friends over the years I've been growing up, but I don't think there was any special one."

Mandie was relieved to see Mrs. Cornwallis rise and announce, "I believe we had better be getting back home now. We greatly enjoyed your company today." Looking across the room, she said, "Polly, we must go now."

Polly stood up and said, "Yes, ma'am."

Mandie blew out her breath in relief. Polly was not going to ask to stay longer.

After Polly and her mother had departed, Mandie said, "I just know that pincushion must belong to Polly, but I can't figure out how it happened to get to the entrance of our tunnel."

"I agree that it must be hers, but I have no idea as to why she would be carrying a pincushion around with her," Celia said.

"We may never know," Joe said.

"She is a strange girl, so there was probably some strange reason why she had it down there by the tunnel entrance," Jonathan said.

"She was probably snooping to see if the tunnel was locked after she heard about the crack, but I don't think she would go inside the tunnel by herself, and besides, what would a pincushion have to do with it, anyway?" Mandie said.

———

After Mandie went to bed that night she thought about Polly and the pincushion for a long time but never could get the slightest idea of what the girl was doing with it.

She also thought about the crack in the tunnel and wondered if her uncle would allow them inside to look at it before the men covered it up. She intended being up early the next morning before the man arrived. Maybe if she asked Uncle John, he would allow her and her friends to go inside.

And then there was another thing that she thought about. Although her grandmother and Jonathan's father had seemed to forget their differences and become friends again while they were visiting Jonathan's house, the two didn't seem to ever even speak to each other now. Had something else happened to cause a break in their friendship?

So many problems to solve.

# CHAPTER SIX

# *THE INTRUDER*

Mandie quietly slipped out of bed the next morning, trying not to wake Celia, but Celia awoke anyway.

"Is it time to get up?" Celia asked as Mandie put on her dress.

Mandie turned to look at her. "It's early, but I wanted to get downstairs before the man comes to repair the crack," she told Celia. "Maybe Uncle John will allow us to go in the tunnel with him."

"Oh yes," Celia said, quickly getting out of bed, upsetting Snowball, who was curled up at the foot. He rose, stretched, and began washing his face.

The girls weren't the first to come down to the kitchen. John Shaw, Jonathan, and Joe were sitting at the table, drinking coffee.

"Good afternoon," Jonathan teased the girls when they came into the room.

"Y'all must have stayed up all night," Mandie replied. She and Celia went to the stove to fill cups of coffee and bring them to the table, where they sat down.

"Not all night, just half of it," Joe said, grinning at the girls as he sipped his coffee.

"The coffee tastes like you made it, Uncle John," Mandie said, drinking from her cup. "Good."

John Shaw smiled at her and said, "Don't let Aunt Lou hear you say that. She might refuse to ever make any more coffee for us."

"Is anyone else up?" Celia asked.

"Yes, Uncle Ned and Lindall have gone for a walk," John Shaw replied. He looked across the room at the door, which was being opened. "And here is Senator Morton. Good morning, sir. Come join us for a cup of coffee."

Mandie jumped up to get another cup. "Sit down, Senator Morton; I'll get your coffee," she said, filling the cup and bringing it to the table.

"I thought I'd better come on down and see if the man had arrived for the repairs," Senator Morton said, sitting down and picking up the cup of coffee. Turning to Mandie, he added, "Thank you, ma'am."

"Not yet, but he should be here shortly. Uncle Ned and Lindall are outside and will let us know when he arrives," John Shaw explained.

Mandie sat down at the side of the table next to her friends, and they listened to the conversation between her uncle and the senator.

"Will this man, Cliff, be able to do the job alone, or will he need some help?" Senator Morton asked.

"He seemed to think he could do it all," John Shaw said. "He's bringing his own supplies and equipment."

Senator Morton cleared his throat and then asked, "Do you think it would be possible for me to see this crack before the man gets the place tied up?"

"Oh yes, of course, I'm sorry, sir," John Shaw replied. "I didn't realize you were interested in seeing the place." He turned to look at Joe and said, "Joe, do you think you could get some lanterns and take the senator down to see the damage? I need to stay here and watch for the repairman."

"Yes, sir," Joe replied with a big grin as he quickly stood up.

Mandie also rose as she asked, "Uncle John, could—"

"Yes," John Shaw quickly interrupted her. "You may all go look, but mind you, don't stay too long." He handed Joe the key, which he had had in his pocket.

All the young people had started to rush out of the kitchen when Mandie stopped, looked back, and asked, "Uncle John, whereabouts is this crack? How far up in the tunnel is it? How do we find it?"

John Shaw laughed and replied, "Yes, I suppose I'd better give you some idea as to where to look. The crack is under the house, so you'll need to go all the way up from the outside entrance to the last set of steps, which go under the foundation of the house. Understand?"

Mandie nodded. She had been in the tunnel many times and knew the pathway it took.

"It's in the wall on the right just as you get to those last steps, and it extends from the step several feet up," John Shaw explained.

"Yes, sir, I understand. I can find it," Mandie replied, turning to rush on out with her friends.

"Remember, just go look and come right back," John Shaw reminded them. "The repairman will be here anytime now, and you should all be out of his way."

Senator Morton stood up and said, "I suppose I'd better get along, too, and follow them." He smiled as he hurried after the young people.

Joe knew where the lanterns were kept in the closet in the hallway by the back door. He opened the door and stepped inside.

Mandie and her other friends stood watching and waiting as Joe handed a lantern to Mandie and reached for the matches on a shelf.

"How about giving me a lantern, too?" Jonathan asked. "Just in case one goes out."

"Yes, the more lanterns the better," Celia said. "I know how dark it can get in there without a lantern, like the time Mandie and I lost the matches and the lantern went out."

Senator Morton, standing by and waiting, said, "Perhaps you, too, should take one."

"Yes, sir," Joe agreed and took a lantern for himself. He looked around and said, "All right, we have three lanterns between us. That ought to be enough." He stepped back into the hallway and closed the closet door.

As the group left the house and started down the hill, Senator Morton said, "You know, this is quite an adventure for me. I've never been in the tunnel."

Mandie, walking along by his side, said, "It's good the door wasn't unlocked when you were down here before, because if you had gone in there without a lantern, you wouldn't have been able to see your way back out, Senator Morton."

"Yes, I realize that now," the senator agreed. "But then, if I had taken a few steps inside and seen how dark it was, I probably wouldn't have gone any farther."

"Do you know the history of the tunnel?" Mandie asked, looking up at the tall man as the group hurried on down the hill.

"Yes, I believe I have heard enough bits and pieces to put it all together," Senator Morton replied. "John Shaw's grandfather, who was your great-grandfather, built the tunnel to hide his Cherokee friends from the white soldiers who were forcing all the Indian people to leave the country around here during the Removal in 1838."

"Yes, sir," Mandie agreed, smiling up at him. "And my grandmother was full-blooded Cherokee. That's Uncle John's mother."

Joe was walking ahead. He paused to look back and asked, "Am I walking too fast? Mr. Shaw said we should hurry."

Everyone else hurried to catch up with him.

"Not too fast for me," Senator Morton said. "He's right. We should get this over with so we are not in the way of the workman."

Everyone was silent as they neared the entrance to the tunnel. Mandie quickly looked around the area. She thought she had heard a rustle and also believed she saw a flash of something moving into the trees and bushes. The entrance to the tunnel was kept overgrown with such in order to hide it from anyone passing through. Although it was on John Shaw's property, sometimes other people cut through the area and came out on the main road a few hundred yards ahead.

"Oh well," she said to herself, "I don't have time to investigate." She moved up with Joe as he unlocked the door and pushed it open.

"Senator, since you have not been in here before, I should warn you," Joe explained. "The corridor is very rough and uneven, and there are lots of steps now and then." He passed out matches, and Mandie and Jonathan lit their lanterns as he also put a match to his.

"Thank you for the warning, Joe," Senator Morton replied.

"Why don't you walk along with me?" Jonathan said. "I have a lantern to light the way."

"Yes, that is a good idea. Thanks," the senator said, stepping inside behind Mandie and Celia, who were staying close to Joe. He looked around the interior. "Yes, this is quite a dark place and very interesting, the way it was cut out under the hill."

"One day when we have time I'll take you down into this tunnel from the other end. There is a secret door in Uncle John's office," Mandie told him, glancing back as she held her long skirts up with one hand and carried the lantern in the other.

As they made their way up the rough steps, Mandie thought about the something or someone she had heard outside at the entrance. Then she remembered that Uncle John had said Mr. Guyer and Uncle Ned were out walking somewhere. It was probably them going through the woods. But on the other hand, why didn't they stop to wave or speak to them? No, maybe it wasn't them. But who?

Joe slowed down as he began searching for the place where John Shaw had said the crack was. Mandie flashed her lantern up and down the walls. John Shaw had said it was in the wall on the right.

"Here it is," Joe said, a few steps ahead of her. "Look." He flashed his lantern on a large crack in the cement wall. Everyone crowded close to look. The crack was wide at the steps and narrowed off up the wall.

"That is a serious crack, I'd say," Senator Morton said, bending to run his hand down part of it.

Mandie quickly looked at the senator and asked, "Do you mean it could be dangerous?"

"No, not exactly, that is if it is repaired right away," the senator explained. "It's serious due to the fact that it is open and will take a lot of mortar to close it up. However, I don't think the house is in any danger."

Mandie got closer, flashed her lantern on it, and tried to see through the crack. The others crowded behind her.

"It's not wide enough to see through," Joe remarked.

Mandie tried to poke her finger through, but the crack was not wide enough. Her finger almost got stuck.

"Miss Amanda, I don't believe I'd do that," the senator warned her as he watched. "If your finger got stuck, we'd have to break part of the wall open to get it out."

"Yes, sir," Mandie said, quickly rubbing her finger down the back of her dress. The edges of the crack had slightly scratched it.

"How would you go about repairing this, Senator?" Joe asked.

Senator Morton cleared his throat and said, "First of all, you will have to remove any loose pieces of mortar, then press new mortar as far through the crack as you can and, of course, add more to smooth it off on the outside here. It is not a really big job. It will just take time. The first mortar should be allowed to dry a little before adding more, so that it will be firm through and through."

"You don't think the house is in danger, then," Mandie said.

"I would say it isn't. Look at all the other walls here that are holding up the house," Senator Morton replied.

"Do you think it was caused by the tornado we had in the spring?" Mandie asked.

"Possibly," the senator answered. "As old as this tunnel is, probably from the year 1838, since there evidently hasn't been any damage to it before in the sixty-something years since it was built, I'd say it was the result of the tornado."

"I wonder if your uncle has inspected the whole tunnel and foundation of the house," Jonathan said to Mandie as he listened.

"Jonathan, that's scary," Mandie said. "If it was the tornado and it did this much damage, it could have done something else under here." She quickly looked around.

Senator Morton spoke up. "Don't worry about it. I'm sure your uncle has made a thorough inspection of the whole area."

"I hope so," Celia muttered as she wrapped her arms around herself and glanced around in the faint rays of light from the lantern in the underground depths.

Mandie held her lantern up close to the crack in an effort to see through it. She squinted and leaned over to look. "I just wish I could see what's behind this crack," she said.

"When the workman removes the loose mortar, you might be able to see through the crack," Senator Morton said.

"Do you mean he has to make the crack bigger in order to repair it?" Mandie asked in surprise.

"Not exactly," Senator Morton explained. "If there is any loose mortar along the edges of the crack, he may have to remove it, but that wouldn't be enough to open up the crack."

"I wish I could watch him do the work," Mandie said.

"I think we'd better be getting back now," Joe said. "Mr. Shaw told us not to stay too long."

"Yes, you are right," Senator Morton agreed as he turned to go back down the passageway.

Joe led the way ahead of the senator in order to light up the steps as they went.

Mandie, coming along with her lantern, asked, "Do y'all think Uncle John might allow us to watch from a distance as the man does the repair work?"

Joe glanced back at her as they all descended the steps in the tunnel and said, "No, Mandie, I'm sure he won't."

"Well, it wouldn't hurt to ask," Mandie said.

"Oh, Mandie, what if the wall decided to cave in when the man starts clearing the crack to repair it?" Celia asked.

"You think up the worst things sometimes, Celia," Mandie told her.

Senator Morton spoke up. "There is a possibility of a little of the wall falling when he begins on it, but it's not very likely if he knows how to do the job correctly."

"And he must know, because Uncle Ned recommended him," Mandie said, flashing her lantern along the way as they continued.

"As far as watching the man do the repair, one other problem would be that the space is not large enough to hold other people," Senator Morton reminded her. "The repairman has to have space enough to work."

"But I could stay a few steps down from the crack and look up and watch him," Mandie said.

"Your uncle is not going to agree to that, and you know it, Mandie," Joe said.

"I see the outside door ahead. Let's hurry and get out of here," Celia told the others.

"Don't get in too big a hurry. You could fall down these steps. They are steep, you know," Jonathan said.

"I don't think I want to come back and watch the man work," Celia said, shivering with fright.

Everyone silently moved ahead, down the steps, and toward the open outside door.

As they neared the bottom, Mandie thought she heard something outside. "I believe someone is out there," she said. "The man is probably here already to do the work." She tried to see past Joe and Senator Morton, who were ahead of her.

"Possibly," the senator agreed.

Just as she stepped outside behind Joe and the senator, she was sure she saw another flash through the woods. She set down her lantern, raised her long skirts, and hurried off into the thicket in that direction.

"Mandie, where are you going?" Joe called after her.

She didn't answer. Suddenly she met up with Polly Cornwallis, who finally stopped when she realized she had been seen.

"Polly, what are you doing down here?" Mandie asked.

Polly wouldn't look at her but kept glancing off to her left. "Looking for you," she said.

The others had followed Mandie and were now listening to the conversation.

"How did you know I was down here?" Mandie asked.

"Well, I didn't really," Polly said. "You see, a—friend—of mine wanted to see your tunnel."

"A friend of yours wanted to see our tunnel?" Mandie asked. "You know the tunnel is kept locked." She looked around and said, "And where is this friend of yours? Who is it?"

"He's from Raleigh," Polly said, quickly moving back out into the open.

"From Raleigh?" Mandie asked.

"Who is this friend from Raleigh?" Joe asked. "Do we know him?"

"He is actually my cousin and just happened to come visit us," Polly replied.

Suddenly a tall young man walked out into the open from the cluster of bushes nearby. "I'm Chester Wardell from Raleigh. Polly had offered to show me your tunnel," he said, holding his hand out to Mandie.

Mandie stepped back without shaking hands and looked at him. "I haven't heard of any cousin of Polly's from Raleigh."

The young man shuffled his feet and said, "Well, you see—"

Joe suddenly straightened up, stepped forward, and said, "Now I recognize your name. You are a reporter for the newspaper in Raleigh. Just what are you doing here? This is private property."

"I really am Polly's cousin, and I only wanted—" the young man started to say.

Mandie cut in angrily, facing him, "A newspaper reporter? I don't care if you are Polly's cousin. You get off our property this very minute, and don't you dare ever come back here, you understand? Now get going."

The young people looked at Mandie and instantly understood why she was angry. They joined in the assault of words.

Finally Senator Morton said loudly, "I would warn you, young man, that you must leave this property immediately, or I'm sure Mr. Shaw will take legal action."

"I wasn't doing anything. I only wanted to see your tunnel," he argued.

"Yes, so you can print our personal business in your newspaper and tell the world about it," Mandie argued. Turning to Polly, she added, "And I don't think you had better show your face at our house anytime soon. You know that this is private family business."

Polly turned and fled through the woods. The young man took one last look at Mandie and followed her.

Mandie just stood there, stomping her foot. "Uncle John told us to keep all this about the tunnel private. I knew Polly would get hold of it and tell everyone everything she knew," she said angrily.

"At least it's not your fault," Joe said, stepping over to her. "Come on. Let's get back to the house."

"Yes, let's get back to the house so I can tell Uncle John what's happened," Mandie said, starting up the hill.

A newspaperman from Raleigh! How did the news get that far that fast? Mandie was sure Polly had contacted him and asked him to come down. Somehow, she was going to get to the bottom of this.

# CHAPTER SEVEN

# INVESTIGATIONS

When they got back to the house, Mandie rushed into the kitchen ahead of her friends and Senator Morton. John Shaw was still sitting at the table, drinking coffee.

"Uncle John, Polly told a newspaperman from Raleigh about the tunnel, and—" she began in a loud, excited voice.

John Shaw interrupted, "What are you talking about, Amanda?" He frowned at her outburst.

"We caught Polly and this reporter—" Mandie began to explain.

Suddenly Uncle Ned, her father's old Cherokee Indian friend, who had promised to look after her when her father died, came in from outside and stepped forward to put a hand on Mandie's shoulder. "Calm down, Papoose," he told her.

Mandie pulled away from his hand and continued, "Uncle John, you told us not to talk about the tunnel, but then Polly found out about it and went and told a newspaper reporter from Raleigh, and then—"

"A newspaper reporter from Raleigh?" John Shaw quickly cut in as he stood up. "I asked, Amanda, what are you talking about?"

"There's a reporter from the Raleigh newspaper with Polly, and she told him about the tunnel, and he tried to get us to let him in the tunnel, and we ran him off," Mandie said in one big breath.

There was complete silence in the room until John finally said, "Who is this reporter?"

"Polly said he's her cousin. Uncle John, Polly tells everything she knows and even adds to it most of the time," Mandie said.

"Where is this reporter? Where did he go?" John Shaw asked as he paced about the kitchen.

"We ran him and Polly off. They left together, so I suppose he's at Polly's house," Mandie said.

"I'm glad at least that he didn't get inside the tunnel," John Shaw said. Looking over at Uncle Ned, he said, "Uncle Ned, we need to post a guard at the door while the man is repairing the crack to be sure no one goes inside."

The old Indian nodded and said, "Two braves come with Cliff. Wait now for us to go to tunnel."

"Oh, they are already here," John Shaw said. "Then let's go get started." He walked toward the open back door.

Mandie and her friends followed the adults out into the yard. Three young Cherokee men were standing by a wagon. The eldest of the three stepped forward to shake hands with John Shaw.

"We are ready to begin work, sir," the man said.

"We'll go down with you and open up the tunnel," John Shaw told him.

Joe held up the key. "Here is the key, Mr. Shaw," he said, "and do you want to use the lanterns we have?" He looked at the young Cherokee man.

"No, we have plenty of lanterns, thank you," the young man replied.

"Then we'll just put them back where we found them," Joe said.

John Shaw took the key, and the men started down the hill for the tunnel entrance. Senator Morton and Uncle Ned went with them.

"Jonathan, I just noticed your father was with the Cherokee men," Mandie said, watching the wagon roll on in the direction of the entrance to the tunnel.

"Yes, I saw him talking to one of the Cherokee men," Jonathan said. "I wonder if he and all the other men are going to stay down there with the repair crew while they work."

"I doubt it," Mandie said. "For one thing, they haven't even had their breakfast yet, and neither have we. Let's go see if Aunt Lou is cooking it yet."

All the young people went back inside to the kitchen. Aunt Lou had just come into the room and was beginning preparations for the morning meal.

"Oh, Aunt Lou, we are all starving," Jonathan told the woman with a big grin. "One of your great big biscuits and bacon and eggs would help that situation a lot."

Aunt Lou grinned at him and said, "Oh, you quit dat now. You knows we'se gwine have all dat and more cooked in two shakes of a sheep's tail. And if y'all behave nice, I'll even allow y'all to eat it at my table over dere." She went over to the cookstove and started moving pots and pans about.

"Oh, thank you, Aunt Lou. We really appreciate your kindness," Jonathan said as he continued teasing the woman.

"Oh, Jonathan, if you don't stop that you may cause Aunt Lou to change her mind," Mandie said, going to sit at the table.

Liza came into the kitchen to help Aunt Lou prepare the meal, and it was soon on the table.

While they ate, the young people discussed the events at the tunnel.

"Do you think that reporter may come back and try to get into the tunnel?" Jonathan asked, looking at the others around the table.

"I doubt it, because if Polly sees Uncle John down there, she won't dare come near him," Mandie said, drinking her coffee.

"Liza, go check on dat parlor. See who done got up," Aunt Lou told the girl.

Liza left the kitchen.

"I imagine everyone else is up by now," Mandie said, and looking at Aunt Lou, she asked, "Do you think we could have coffee or something in the dining room with my mother and the others?"

Aunt Lou grinned at her and said, "Sho' 'nuff, my chile. I knows you wants to hear what dey all sayin' when dey gits together. We fix it."

Liza came back into the kitchen and reported, "Everybody be in de parlor. And dey all hungry."

"We's got de food ready, Liza; just he'p me take it to de sideboard in de dinin' room. And, my chile, finish yo' food, and we take de coffee in dere."

Mandie and her friends were already finished with the food. Liza set dishes in the dining room, and when the adults were called to breakfast, Mandie and her friends went to join them.

Mandie noticed that her uncle John, Mr. Guyer, the senator, and Uncle Ned had all returned without coming through the kitchen and were in the dining room for their breakfast with Dr. and Mrs. Woodard, Mandie's mother, Celia's mother, and Mrs. Taft. No one was talking about the tunnel. They were all discussing a dinner to which they had been invited for that night.

Jonathan said in a loud whisper to the other young people, "They are all going out tonight. What can we do that's exciting?"

"We could watch the tunnel to see if Polly and that reporter come back," Mandie said.

"Couldn't we think up something else to do?" Celia asked. "I don't think I want to go down there in the dark tonight."

"I don't suppose it would be a good idea to go down there at night," Mandie replied.

"We could play checkers," Joe suggested.

"But this is just breakfast time. We have all day to do something before tonight when they all go out," Celia reminded them.

"You're right," Jonathan agreed.

"So while it's still daytime we could always check on Polly and that reporter," Mandie told them.

"And how do you plan to do that?" Jonathan asked.

"We could just walk around all over our property and go over to the line where our land joins the Cornwallises' and watch for them. They are bound to be moving around somewhere or other. That man won't just sit still now that he has come all the way from Raleigh," Mandie explained.

"But he might have gone on back to Raleigh when he couldn't get in the tunnel," Joe said.

"Maybe your uncle would let us go look when the men finish repairing the crack in the tunnel," Jonathan suggested.

The adults were finishing their meal and were getting up to

leave the room. Mandie looked at them and told her friends, "Let's go out in the yard."

The young people left the table quickly as everyone got up, and Mandie led the way out into the backyard. They sat down on a bench under a huge chestnut tree.

"From here we can see everyone going and coming from the house," Mandie explained. "I'd like to know when the men have finished repairing the tunnel wall. Somehow we might get a chance to look at it."

As she was talking, one of the young Cherokee workmen came hurrying up the hill toward the house. She watched to see where he was going and was surprised when he came toward them and spoke to her.

"We need to speak with Mr. Shaw," he said. "We have some unexpected problems in the tunnel. Do you know where he is?"

Mandie quickly stood up and said, "Yes, he's in the house. Come on. I'll get him." She hurried toward the back door.

John Shaw, Lindall Guyer, Uncle Ned, Senator Morton, and Dr. Woodard all came out onto the back porch as they approached.

"Uncle John, this man wants to speak to you," she called to her uncle.

The men stopped and waited until Mandie and the Cherokee workman got to the porch.

"Sir, Cliff has sent me to tell you we have a problem with the crack in the tunnel and need for you to come look," the young fellow said.

John Shaw looked alarmed and said quickly, "Of course. I'll be right there."

The young fellow hurried back down the hill and disappeared in the trees toward the entrance to the tunnel.

"Let me get an extra lantern in case we need one," John Shaw told the other men and went back inside the house.

Mandie watched while the other men waited on the porch, and John Shaw quickly rejoined them with a lantern in his hand. The group hurriedly walked down the hill toward the tunnel.

Mandie quickly motioned to her friends in the yard to follow. They stayed far enough behind that the men wouldn't notice them.

"What is wrong?" Joe asked.

"I don't know. Let's go find out," Mandie told him.

"I'll go with y'all to the entrance, but I don't want to go back inside that tunnel," Celia said.

"Oh, Celia, something exciting is happening. Don't you want to go see for yourself what it is?" Jonathan teased her as he walked by her side.

Mandie slowed down to give the men time to enter the tunnel; then she hurried forward and stopped at the entrance.

"Are we going inside?" Jonathan asked.

"Maybe, maybe not," Mandie replied, trying to see inside the dark tunnel from the doorway. She could hear voices in there but could not understand what they were saying.

The young people stayed there, listening for a long time and waiting for someone to come out. Finally the same young man who had come for John Shaw came outside to get something out of their wagon, which was parked near the entrance. He started back for the tunnel.

"Could you tell us what has happened?" Mandie quickly asked him as he walked by her.

He stopped, frowned, and looked at her. "The crack got much larger when we tried to clean it for the mortar," he said. "I am sorry, but we are in a hurry."

As the young fellow quickly reentered the tunnel, Mandie turned to her friends and asked, "Did y'all hear that? That crack got bigger."

"Let's sit down over there," Joe suggested, pointing to a log bench under a tree at the edge of the woods. He led the way to it.

As they sat down, Jonathan said, "If that crack is opening up, it could be dangerous."

"But it could have been just mortar that was already loose," Mandie said. "Remember, Senator Morton said the loose mortar around it would have to be cleared away."

"But that fellow seemed excited, as though something was definitely wrong," Celia said.

"Maybe if we just sit and wait and listen we can find out exactly what is going on in there," Joe told them.

They waited and waited, and it seemed as though no one was ever going to come out of the tunnel. Finally Dr. Woodard came out alone.

Joe jumped up and hurried over to his father and asked, "What is wrong inside? Is the tunnel cracking open more than it was?"

"Yes, I suppose you'd say that's what it's doing," Dr. Woodard replied as the others gathered around him to listen. "I have to go make a round of calls and can't stay to see what happens. However, it seems the crack is widening, and from what we could see, there must be some kind of door or wall behind the tunnel wall."

"A door? Or wall?" Mandie repeated in excitement.

"Now, you young people stay out here. I don't think Mr. Shaw would want you in the way in there," Dr. Woodard said, turning to walk on. "I'll be back later this afternoon. I have to go up the mountain to see old Mrs. Fortner. And while I'm up there, I'll check on another two or three older folk." He continued up the hill toward the house.

The young people looked at each other and excitedly discussed the new situation in the tunnel.

"I hope Uncle John investigates whatever is behind the crack and doesn't just fill up the crack and close it," Mandie said.

"But what if it's too dangerous to open it up enough to look inside?" Celia asked.

"They must not think it's dangerous to the house foundation, or they would be having everyone leave the house," Jonathan said.

"I wish I could see it," Joe said.

"Yes, I'd like to see it, too," Mandie said. "Whenever Uncle John does come back out, I'm going to ask him all about it."

"And he's going to tell us we can't go inside the tunnel," Celia reminded her.

"At least he could explain what's going on," Mandie replied.

There was a sudden sound of something going through the brush behind them. The four quickly turned to stare at the woods.

"I believe there's someone in there," Mandie said under her breath.

"Yes, it sounded like someone running through there," Joe agreed.

"Come on, Joe, let's go look," Jonathan told him and then added,

"You girls stay here and watch the door of the tunnel and see that no one goes inside." He hurried off through the woods.

"Be sure you stay alert," Joe told the girls as he rushed off after Jonathan.

Mandie and Celia looked at each other.

As soon as the boys were out of sight, Mandie heard something in the bushes again. She became very still and waited and watched. The noise moved on and grew dimmer and disappeared altogether.

"Do you think that was someone, then?" Celia asked.

"Yes, it didn't sound like an animal," Mandie decided, "but I was afraid to go investigate because Uncle John and the others might come out of the tunnel and I'd miss them."

"Maybe Joe and Jonathan will find whoever it was," Celia said, shivering slightly. "I don't like scary things like that."

It seemed to Mandie that everything was moving awfully slowly. The boys should have returned by now. She got up and walked around. And someone inside the tunnel should have come out for some reason by now. Everything was at a standstill, and there was really nothing she could do about it.

"Do you think Joe and Jonathan got lost?" Celia finally asked.

Mandie stopped walking to look at her. "I don't think so," she said. "They are probably chasing someone around and around in the woods and haven't been able to catch up with them."

Then the girls finally saw some of the men coming out of the tunnel. John Shaw was walking along with the senator, Mr. Guyer, and Uncle Ned as they talked.

"I'll go on with Cliff to get the supplies and will see y'all later at the house," John Shaw said as Cliff came out and got in his wagon. John Shaw got in with him.

The other men walked on up the hill toward the house.

"All those men came out and didn't even see us," Mandie said, blowing out her breath. She stopped and looked at Celia and asked, "Want to go inside the tunnel while they're gone?"

"There are two more Cherokee men who didn't come out, Mandie," Celia reminded her.

"I know," she replied. "That's why I am not afraid to go inside. They are there. Are you coming?"

"No, I believe I'll just stay here and watch for Joe and Jonathan," Celia said. "They won't know where you are."

"All right. I won't be but a few minutes," Mandie promised as she hurried toward the entrance of the tunnel.

Someone had left a lighted lantern inside not very far from the door. Mandie hurriedly picked it up and continued up the passageway in the tunnel. She couldn't hear a sound, but she knew the two workmen had not come out. Therefore, they must still be inside somewhere.

She finally heard a slight metallic noise, like tools being moved around, and as she got farther inside she saw lighted lanterns ahead, revealing the two workmen mixing something in buckets. Not wanting to startle them, she called ahead, "I came to see the crack," she said. "I won't disturb your work. It'll only take a few minutes to look."

She hurried on forward and came up to the two men. They looked at her in surprise and didn't say anything.

"Is there some new problem with the crack?" she asked them.

One of the men was the one she had spoken to before. He shrugged his shoulders and replied, "It may not be a problem. We maybe can fix it."

"Would you please show me what you are talking about?" Mandie asked as she slowly continued toward them.

"Yes, here, look," the man said. "The crack gets wider and wider." The man walked over to the wall and flashed his lantern on it.

Mandie gasped in surprise. The crack was indeed much wider than it had been when she saw it before. She leaned to look closely. And there did seem to be something behind it. She reached her hand out to stick her finger in the crack and then remembered that she had almost got it stuck before. So she leaned closer and held the lantern up where it would shine into the crack.

"What do you think it is in there?" she turned to ask the man.

"Perhaps a door, or another wall," the man said. "Mr. Shaw must decide whether to open it and investigate or close it up for good."

"Oh, I hope he opens it to see what's back there," Mandie told the man.

"Mr. Shaw also said we were not to let anyone come in here, so we must ask you to go back outside," the man said.

"All right. I just wanted to see what things looked like now that you had begun work on it," Mandie replied. "Thank you." She turned and started back out of the tunnel.

She would love to talk to Uncle John about the crack and tell him that he must open it up to see what was behind it or whatever it was would be lost forever. However, she knew she was not supposed to go inside the tunnel. So what could she do about it? She would discuss it with her friends and see what they thought about the situation. She rushed back outside to find them.

# CHAPTER EIGHT

# *DELAYS*

When Mandie came out of the tunnel, she saw that Joe and Jonathan had returned and were talking to Celia. She hurried to join them and sat down.

"You went in the tunnel?" Joe asked in surprise.

"There are two of the workmen in there, and all I did was look," Mandie replied. Then she excitedly added, "The crack is getting bigger. I could probably have stuck my finger through it, but I was afraid it would get stuck—"

"You didn't, I hope," Celia interrupted.

"Could you see through the crack?" Jonathan asked.

"Yes, a little, enough to tell there is something behind it, either another wall or a door, or something, anyhow," Mandie told her friends. "And Uncle John has just got to open the crack up and see what it is behind it. If he seals over it, we will never know what it is on the other side."

"What is he planning on doing?" Joe asked.

"I don't know," Mandie said. "The man inside told me Uncle John had to let them know what to do further on the crack, open it up and see what's behind it or go ahead and seal it up."

"Did the man say when your uncle would let them know?" Jonathan asked.

"Celia told us your uncle went off with Cliff to get some supplies. Do you know when he will return?" Joe asked.

"No, I didn't ask the man inside," Mandie said. "But they are stopping work until he does return, so I imagine he won't be gone long." Then she remembered that the boys had gone investigating a noise they had heard in the woods. "Did y'all find anyone in the woods?"

"No, not even an animal," Joe replied. "And we didn't hear a sound, either."

"I wonder where that reporter went," Mandie said. "Did y'all see Polly anywhere while y'all were searching the woods? Did you go near her house?"

"We went across the back line of their property, but we didn't see anyone there," Joe said.

Cliff returned in his wagon with John Shaw. The young people watched as they unloaded two large croker sacks full of something and carried them into the tunnel. Mandie and her friends were far enough away in the trees that the men did not see them.

"I wonder what they had in those sacks," Mandie said.

"Whatever it was, it was heavy," Celia added.

In a few minutes John Shaw and Cliff came back out of the tunnel and stood at the entrance talking until the other workmen came outside. Then John locked the door and started up the hill as the others went to the wagon.

"I'll see you bright and early tomorrow morning," John Shaw said, waving to Cliff as the man drove up the hill to the road.

As soon as everyone was out of sight, Mandie said, "Well, we might as well leave, too."

"It's probably time to eat," Jonathan said, grinning at her.

"Probably," Mandie agreed as they all started up the hill toward the house.

"I wonder why they quit work," Joe remarked as they walked along.

Mandie stopped and looked at him, "Maybe Uncle John is going to open the crack and they wouldn't have had time to do it today and close it back up because the workmen were only supposed to seal up the crack when they came."

"You are probably right," Joe agreed.

"But how are we going to find out what they are planning to do?" Mandie asked.

"Just ask," Jonathan told her.

"No, we can't do that because then Uncle John would know that we have been talking to the workmen," Mandie replied.

"I suppose we'll just have to listen to their conversations, then," Jonathan said.

When they got to the back of the house, Liza was coming out the back door. She was carrying a bucket of water, which she poured on plants growing nearby.

"Liza, is everybody ready to eat?" Mandie asked.

"Lawsy mercy, no, Missy Amanda," Liza replied. "Ain't got it all cooked yet. Lots of people to feed." She turned to go back in the door.

Mandie turned to her friends and said, "Let's go sit in the arbor."

"That would be a nice restful place after all those weeds and bushes we've been in this morning," Celia said.

The four young people sat down under the arbor and were silent for a while. Then suddenly Celia whispered, "Look, there's your grandmother, Mandie, with Jonathan's father." She motioned down the pathway.

Mandie straightened up and looked. Her grandmother and Mr. Guyer were walking slowly up the path, pausing now and then to talk. When they came to a bench on the other side of the walkway, they sat down.

Mandie held her breath, hoping the two didn't see her and her friends. She couldn't hear everything they were saying, and she didn't want to eavesdrop, but it was too late to make her presence known.

Mrs. Taft was saying, "No, Lin, it's too late to pick up where we left off years and years ago."

"I disagree. It's never too late if you love someone," Lindall Guyer replied.

The young people couldn't see them because of shrubbery down the pathway, but they could hear most of what was said.

"Would you please tell me one thing?" Lindall Guyer said. "Do you plan on marrying the senator?"

Mandie caught her breath and strained to listen.

"To be rude to a rude question, Lindall, that is none of your business," Mrs. Taft replied.

Mandie saw Jonathan grinning at her.

"But I don't consider that a rude question," Mr. Guyer replied. "The answer is very important to me because if you don't have serious plans with Senator Morton, then I can keep trying," Lindall Guyer said with a little laugh.

"But you won't have much chance to do that," Mrs. Taft said. "Because I doubt if I'll ever go to your house again. I only went this time to get things settled in my mind once and for all."

"But we're still friends; therefore I can come visit at your house," Mr. Guyer told her.

"It wouldn't do you any good, Lin," Mrs. Taft said. "You should find some nice young woman and get married again yourself."

"I don't want a nice young woman," he said. "I'm not young myself, and I certainly don't want to get involved with a young woman." He cleared his throat loudly. "We used to have a lot in common, and I believe we still do. Maybe you are thinking about my work. I am gone for long periods of time, and I am sometimes involved in danger for the government. However, I am planning to retire soon. And if you would marry me, I would retire immediately."

"Maybe I've become so used to my freedom without a husband that I don't want to get tied down again," Mrs. Taft said.

"Oh, so then you are not planning on marrying the senator," Mr. Guyer quickly said with a loud chuckle. "Maybe I have a chance."

"Oh, let's discontinue this silly conversation. I need to get back to the house and freshen up before the meal is served," Mrs. Taft said.

The young people quickly and silently darted behind the rose-bushes as Mrs. Taft and Mr. Guyer came within sight on their way up the pathway.

As soon as they were gone, Mandie told her friends, "Oh, I feel absolutely, positively terrible, listening to all that private conversation."

The four came back out of the bushes and sat down.

"I thought that was an exciting conversation," Jonathan said with a big grin. "Now we know my father is still in love with your grandmother, Mandie."

"Maybe he just thinks he is. It has been a long time since they were young," Mandie reminded him.

"Ah, but true love never dies," Jonathan said, dramatically placing his hand over his heart.

Mandie laughed and looked at her friends when they didn't.

"I believe that," Joe said seriously. "True love never dies."

"I do, too," Celia quickly added.

"You see," Jonathan said, "I must be right about that."

"Anyhow, if my grandmother is going to get married again, I would prefer she marry the senator," Mandie said with a smirk.

Jonathan looked at her with his mouth open. "You don't like my father? And here I thought we might get to be kinpeople one day," he said.

"I didn't say I don't like your father, Jonathan," Mandie replied. "It's just that my grandmother always has to be the boss, and Senator Morton lets her do that. So if she married him she would have someone to boss around, and maybe she would stop trying to plan everything in my life."

"But, Mandie," Celia said, "I'd think she would be able to boss Jonathan's father around, because he is the one begging right now."

"Maybe, but I've never known anyone who could just take over with my father," Jonathan said.

Joe cleared his throat and said, "You are all forgetting. A real marriage should be a two-sided affair, not one a boss and the other a follower."

Mandie looked at him thoughtfully and said, "I never had thought about marriage that way. I always thought one or the other was the boss."

"My mother and father get along just fine. Neither one bosses the other," Joe explained.

"Jonathan, your father married your mother, and he must have loved her. He didn't pursue my grandmother then," Mandie said.

"I suppose so, but you know I can't remember her, and their love, or whatever it was, didn't last long because she died," Jonathan said.

"Anyhow, I don't think my grandmother will marry your father, Jonathan," Mandie decided as she stood up. "Let's go back to the house now."

"You may be wrong," Jonathan told her as the four started uphill toward the house.

When the four young people went inside the house, there was no one in sight. They looked in the parlor and found it empty.

Then they went to their rooms to freshen up, with agreement among them to meet back at the top of the main staircase in fifteen minutes.

"I suppose everyone else has gone to their rooms, too," Celia remarked as she brushed her long auburn hair and tied it back with a ribbon.

"I reckon," Mandie absentmindedly replied. She quickly brushed her blond hair. "You know, I've always wondered what my grandfather Taft was like, whether Grandmother was able to boss him around."

"I wouldn't think so, Mandie. After all, he was a United States senator," Celia reminded her. "I imagine he exuded a lot of bossy power himself. She did say down there by the arbor that she enjoyed being free without a husband."

"I suppose I'm a lot like my grandmother. I don't want someone bossing me around," Mandie replied, stepping over to the floor-length mirror in the corner to look at herself. Shaking out the folds in her long skirt, she flipped around to look at Celia and added, "Therefore, I don't think I ever want to get married."

Celia turned to look at her and said with a grin, "But Joe said neither one should be the boss, which means that he wouldn't try to boss you around if you married him."

Mandie stomped her foot and said, "Celia, stop that. We are too young to be talking about getting married. We'd better be talking about what college we are going to next year." She gave her long skirt a swish and started toward the door. "Come on, let's go."

Joe and Jonathan were sitting on the bench at the top of the staircase.

The boys stood up as the girls approached.

"My, my," Jonathan said with a grin. "What took you girls so long? I can't see a thing different about you."

Snowball came running down the hallway and jumped upon the top of the banister along the steps.

"Snowball, get down from there before you fall and break your neck," Mandie yelled at the white cat.

Snowball stopped and looked at his mistress. Mandie stepped over and quickly picked him up. Turning to her friends, she said, "Come on, I'm going to take him to the kitchen, which will give us an excuse to see if Aunt Lou knows anything about what Uncle John is planning to do with that crack in the wall." She started down the steps. The others followed.

"Do you have to have an excuse to go to the kitchen?" Jonathan asked.

Mandie looked back at him and replied, "Yes, right now I do because Aunt Lou is busy getting the food ready for all our company, and that's about a dozen people, which is a big job." She went on down the staircase and waited for her friends to catch up with her.

"Mandie, I haven't seen Jenny, your cook, today," Celia remarked.

"She has gone to visit her sister down in Georgia, who is recovering from a bad fall, but she'll be back soon," Mandie told her.

"Isn't she Abraham's wife?" Jonathan asked.

"Yes, and they have their own house on the property behind here," Mandie replied.

"With Aunt Lou short of help and all these people here, maybe we shouldn't bother her right now," Celia suggested.

"We won't bother her. I'll just leave Snowball in the kitchen and ask a question while I'm doing it," Mandie said.

"Maybe we could help with something or other," Joe suggested.

"That's a good idea," Jonathan said with a big grin. "But what can we do? I don't know how to cook."

Celia quickly looked at the others and said, "We could set the table. We know how to do that."

"I don't think Aunt Lou would allow it," Mandie said. "She's real bossy about her work."

Celia smiled and said, "We don't have to tell her. I know y'all keep the dishes in the china closet in the dining room, and we could slip in there and get them down and set the table. Surprise."

Mandie looked at her and then at the boys and said, "Yes, let's do that. But let me put Snowball in the kitchen first." She started on down the hallway toward the kitchen.

As soon as she pushed the door open, she set Snowball down, and he ran for his plate, which was kept near the woodbox by the big iron cookstove. Aunt Lou was putting something in the oven, and she glanced back at Mandie and her friends, who had stopped at the door. As she straightened up she said, "Now, my chile, de food not ready yet, and we busy right now."

Liza was chopping something on the cook table. "And we ain't got no time fo' y'all," she said.

"I just wanted to bring Snowball to eat. I didn't know whether he had even had his breakfast or not," Mandie said, smiling. "Did you see the men who were working in the tunnel when they left, Aunt Lou?"

"No, I ain't had time to see nobody," Aunt Lou replied. "And I ain't got time to see y'all, either, right now, so git. We'se busy." She fanned her big white apron in their direction.

Mandie's friends quickly backed out into the hallway. Mandie followed them as she said, "Yes, ma'am, we're going."

Outside in the hallway, and with the kitchen door closed, Mandie turned to her friends and said, "All right, we'll have to be quiet so Aunt Lou won't hear us." She pushed open the door to the dining room down the hall.

With all four of the young people helping, it didn't take long to get dishes down and set on the long table, and then the silverware and napkins. Mandie carefully straightened everything and stood back to look over their work.

"Aunt Lou is going to be surprised," Celia said.

"Yes, and we'd better make ourselves scarce, as she says, when she finds out what we've done. Let's go see if anyone is in the parlor," Mandie said, opening the door to the hall.

The parlor was empty, but by the time they had all sat down, the adults began coming in. Mandie tried to listen to the conversation around the room, hoping the adults would discuss the crack in the tunnel, but there seemed to be several different subjects being discussed, and it was hard to hear most of it.

"Your grandmother is not having much to say," Jonathan whispered to Mandie.

Mandie smiled as she looked at Mrs. Taft, who was seated across the room on a settee between Senator Morton and Mr. Guyer. The two men seemed to be talking to each other without any input from her.

Glancing at her mother, Elizabeth Shaw, who was talking with Mrs. Woodard and Jane Hamilton, Mandie distinctly heard her say, "Yes, I'm going to have to insist that Amanda make a decision about college soon."

"It would be nice if the girls would go to Joe's school. We could all visit there together," Mrs. Woodard said.

"I think Celia is going to decide on the one near us," Jane Hamilton told them.

Mandie quickly looked at Celia, who had also been listening to the conversation.

Celia said, "Now, Mandie, I have not made any decision. Mother would like for me to go to school near home."

"Celia Hamilton, you can't desert me where I have to go to a strange school all by myself," Mandie told her.

"The very solution would be to go to my school," Joe reminded the girls.

"Now, we could settle the whole dispute without any hard feelings if you girls would just come up to New York to school," Jonathan said with a big grin.

At that moment Liza appeared in the doorway and said loudly, "Miz 'Lizbeth, de food on de table." Then, stepping inside to look at Mandie and her friends, she added with a big grin, "And de dishes done been put on de table, too."

Mandie tried to keep a sober face as she replied, "Really? How did they get there?"

"One of dem li'l fairies musta done it," Liza replied and danced on out of the room.

Elizabeth rose and led the way to the dining room. The young people followed.

Aunt Lou was in the dining room, placing food on the sideboard. She turned to whisper to Mandie as she passed by her, "I'se gwine to spank you where you sits down if you don't stay outta my business, my chile."

Mandie grinned at her and said, "Then you will have to spank all four of us, and I don't think you would be able to manage that."

"You'd be surprised whut I kin do; you'd be surprised," the old woman replied as she left the room, shaking her head.

Everyone seemed to be hungry, and they were all eating instead of talking. The only conversation Mandie could overhear was about the adults' dinner that night with the Campbells, friends of the Shaws.

Mandie whispered to her friends, "I wish Uncle John would discuss the crack in the tunnel."

Joe whispered back, "He's not doing that because he knows you are listening." He grinned at her.

Mandie smiled at him and said, as she blew out her breath, "Oh well, I'll find out what's going on sooner or later."

And she meant it. She just had to know what was behind that crack in the tunnel.

# CHAPTER NINE

# *UNDECIDED*

The afternoon dragged for Mandie and her friends. The women stayed in their rooms most of the afternoon, getting ready for the night's visit out to supper. The men sat around in the backyard, talking about everything but the tunnel, from what Mandie and her friends could overhear as they constantly walked in and out of the house in an effort to eavesdrop.

Then Dr. Woodard returned from visiting his patients. Mandie and Celia were sitting on the back porch steps. Joe and Jonathan were leaning against the posts.

"I'm glad to find you all here together," Dr. Woodard said as he stopped his buggy in the driveway near the men. He stepped down and went over to join the men.

"I'm glad you have returned, Dr. Woodard," John Shaw told him. "Sit down." He indicated a bench nearby.

Dr. Woodard sat down and continued, "I've been over to see old Mrs. Fortner, and I think she's going to be all right, just the sniffles, really. But she has a problem. The fence around her chicken yard is down. Some of the posts look like they've rotted. And she lives alone, a long way from any neighbors, and her chickens have all got out and scattered through the woods."

John Shaw quickly said, "Do you think we might be able to redo her fence?"

"Yes, that's exactly what I was going to suggest," Dr. Woodard replied. He looked around at the other men, Senator Morton, Lindall Guyer, and Uncle Ned. "Would any of you like to run back over there with me and see what we can do about that fence?"

"Of course," Senator Morton replied.

"Yes," Uncle Ned said, nodding.

"I'm ready right now," Mr. Guyer told him.

They all stood up as John Shaw said, "Let's get some tools out of the barn." Then, turning back to Dr. Woodard, he asked, "Is the fence wire useable?"

"Oh, yes, it's fine for a while at least," Dr. Woodard said. "It's the posts that have rotted down and fallen."

"Then we'll load up some wood and take it with us," John Shaw said, walking on back toward the barn.

The other men followed.

Mandie and her friends had overheard the conversation.

Joe looked at the others and said, "I think perhaps I ought to volunteer to help."

"I will, too," Jonathan added.

"I can do something," Mandie said, standing up.

"I'll go, too, then, if you are all going," Celia said as she rose from the steps.

Mandie frowned at her friends and said, "We will have to get Uncle John's permission to go, you know."

"Yes," Celia said.

The boys nodded in agreement.

The four walked over to the door of the barn, where the men were getting supplies ready.

"Uncle John," Mandie began, "do you think we could go, too? Maybe there is something we can do."

John Shaw looked up from the boards he was stacking and shook his head as he replied, "No, Amanda, thank you, but we men can take care of this. Just remember to tell your mother where we have gone if she comes downstairs before we return."

"Yes, we shouldn't be gone long," Dr. Woodard added, picking up a bag of nails from a shelf.

Joe looked at his father and said, "Dad, I would be glad to help."

"I know, son, but we have plenty of help here," Dr. Woodard told him. "And I'll depend on you to explain to your mother where we've gone."

"Yes, sir," Joe replied. He looked at the other three young people and said, "I don't think we are needed. Let's find something else to do." He left the barn, and the others followed.

The four stood around on the back porch until the men loaded their supplies into John Shaw's wagon and drove off.

"Let's go sit in the parlor," Mandie suggested.

"That's a good idea," Jonathan said with a big grin. "Because when the ladies come down, Aunt Lou will probably serve coffee, won't she?"

Mandie nodded in the affirmative and added, "And something sweet, perhaps chocolate cake."

"Then, let's hurry in there. I wouldn't want to miss that chocolate cake," Joe said.

There was no one in the parlor. Snowball was curled up on a footstool.

As they all sat down, Jonathan said, "Perhaps we should let Aunt Lou know that we are in here so she could get that coffee started."

Mandie smiled at him and said, "That coffeepot stays full at all times on Aunt Lou's stove."

"And does she keep chocolate cake made all the time?" Joe asked with a grin.

"Just about all the time, especially when she knows you are here," Mandie replied.

Liza appeared in the doorway. "Jis' checkin' to see who all's in heah," she said as she glanced around the room.

"Are you going to bring coffee, Liza?" Mandie asked.

"And chocolate cake," Jonathan added.

Liza grinned at them and said, "I has to go ask Aunt Lou." She turned to leave.

"Just tell her everyone is here who would like chocolate cake," Jonathan told her.

"All the men went off to Mrs. Fortner's, Liza, and won't be back for a while," Mandie explained.

"And where de ladies at?" Liza asked.

"As far as we know, they are all in their rooms," Mandie replied.

"Gittin' dolled up to go out tonight," Liza added with a grin and turned to go back down the hallway.

"Do you think she'll bring it?" Jonathan asked.

"Yes, Aunt Lou will send us chocolate cake and coffee," Mandie replied. "And I'm sure she knows we will be the only ones home for supper tonight."

"Since there are only four of us, do you think Aunt Lou would allow us to eat at her table in the kitchen?" Jonathan asked.

"Oh, Jonathan, that's the table she uses for her meals with Liza and the other servants," Mandie said.

"Couldn't we just eat with them, then?" Jonathan asked.

Mandie laughed and said, "No, Aunt Lou wouldn't allow it. She likes to keep everything separate between us and the servants. Besides, there wouldn't be enough room for the four of us, since there are four of them when Jenny is home."

"Where is Mr. Bond? Where does he eat when everyone goes out?" Jonathan asked. "Since he's not a servant, not a relative, but the caretaker."

"He's not here right now," Mandie said. "Uncle John sent him over to Asheville for something, and I doubt he will get back before tomorrow. I heard them talking in the hallway this morning."

In a few minutes Liza came back with the tea cart, loaded with coffee and chocolate cake. "Aunt Lou, she done tole me to bring dis heah choc'late cake, but she say fo' y'all to be in de dinin' room at six fo' suppuh, and she say don't be late," Liza explained as she poured cups of coffee and distributed them.

"Thank you, Liza," Mandie said. "Tell Aunt Lou we'll be there."

Liza finished serving the cake and coffee and left the room.

"If we eat supper at six o'clock, it will still be daylight," Jonathan said. "We could go out for a walk or something." He sipped his coffee.

"Yes, that's a good idea," Joe agreed. "I need some exercise." He took a bite of his cake.

"Is there any special place y'all want to walk to?" Celia asked.

"Just walk, I suppose," Jonathan said.

"No place in particular," Joe added.

"We could go down and check the outside entrance to the tunnel," Mandie suggested.

"Now, Mandie, you know your uncle keeps that door locked," Joe reminded her.

"There's always a possibility that he might forget to sometime," Mandie said. "And we still don't know what Uncle John is going to do about that crack. I haven't heard a single word about it."

"Why don't you just ask him, in a nice way, of course?" Jonathan suggested.

Mandie quickly looked at him and said, "I don't want to irritate him. And then, too, he may not ever let us look at the crack, especially now that it is opening up and could be dangerous."

The men weren't gone long. When they returned they went to their rooms, changed clothes, and returned to the parlor, where Liza was again serving coffee.

"Did y'all get the fence back up?" Joe asked his father.

"Yes, it didn't take long with all of us working on it, and I believe it will stay awhile now," Dr. Woodard told him. "We weren't able to find all the chickens, though. We rounded up twenty-three, and Mrs. Fortner said there should have been about fifty."

"Yes, it's too bad that many got away, but like I told her, I'll take more to her as soon as I find someone who has some for sale," John Shaw added.

"What plans do you young people have for tonight while we older ones are out?" Lindall Guyer asked Jonathan.

Jonathan shrugged his shoulders and replied, "Nothing in particular. We are going for a walk." Glancing at John Shaw, he added, "We would like to see the crack in the tunnel if Mr. Shaw would allow it."

Mandie quickly held her breath as she watched her uncle.

John Shaw quickly spoke up. "No, not unless I'm with y'all. It could be dangerous because it is getting wider."

Jonathan cleared his throat and said, "Well, then, Mr. Shaw, do you think we might be able to see it tomorrow when you have time?"

"We'll see," John Shaw said, and turning to Dr. Woodard, he said, "Cliff will be back early tomorrow morning, and I'll have to decide by then whether to seal it up or open the crack and see what's behind it."

"Any idea as to what you might decide?" Dr. Woodard asked.

"Well, it would be much easier to just seal it up, which wouldn't take long," John Shaw said. "However, not knowing what's behind it, I'm not sure it would be a good idea to do that. We probably need to see what's back there. And, of course, that would take a lot more time and a lot more work, depending on what we would find."

Dr. Woodard cleared his throat and said, "If it were my house, I wouldn't be satisfied until I found out what is behind it. There could be some faulty foundation work in there that needs repairing. We just don't know what that tornado did when it went through here."

"Yes, I suppose I'd always worry about it if I don't find out what's back there," John Shaw said thoughtfully.

Mandie waited to hear more, but John Shaw changed the topic of the conversation. She looked at Jonathan and grinned. He had some nerve, asking her uncle about seeing the crack.

The men's conversation had come back around to the chickens for Mrs. Fortner.

"I know where chickens can be bought," Uncle Ned spoke up.

"You do, Uncle Ned?" John Shaw replied.

"Yes, Cherokee man over mountain sell chickens," the old man said.

"I can't go over there tomorrow because the workmen are coming back and I need to be here whenever they continue work on the crack," John Shaw said. "But when they finish, and it may take them several days, then I can go with you to see about the chickens."

Dr. Woodard looked at the young people and then back at John Shaw as he said, "I will be busy making more calls tomorrow, but perhaps Joe could go with Uncle Ned to get the chickens."

"I'd be glad to go," Joe spoke up.

"But then we will have to take them up to Mrs. Fortner, and that will take time," John Shaw said.

"If Uncle Ned wants to deliver them to the lady, I'll go with him up there," Joe said.

John Shaw turned to Uncle Ned and asked, "Where is this place located? Is it anywhere near Mrs. Fortner?"

"No, other side of mountain," the old man replied. "Make two trips, one to get chickens and one to take to Mrs. Fortner."

"Unless we are going home tomorrow, I have plenty of time to do that," Joe told his father.

"I thought we'd stay until that crack is safely taken care of just in case I'm needed here," Dr. Woodard said. "Go ahead and plan this with Uncle Ned if you want to."

Mandie listened as Uncle Ned and Joe made plans to leave early the next morning, get the chickens, and go on over to the other side of the mountain to deliver them to Mrs. Fortner. It would probably take all day since Uncle Ned said it was a long ways to get them.

The ladies finally came down to the parlor, and by then John Shaw said it was time for them to all leave for the Campbells'.

"I don't know how late we will be, Amanda, but don't stay up too late," Elizabeth Shaw told her.

"Yes, ma'am," Mandie replied. "We aren't doing anything in particular, anyhow."

Jane Hamilton also cautioned Celia not to sit up waiting for them to return. They would not be in a hurry to get back.

As soon as all the adults had left, the young people discussed the crack in the tunnel.

"Uncle John must think it is dangerous," Mandie decided. "I could tell he was worried about closing it up without investigating behind it, and, Joe, your father seemed to think it should be opened up."

"Yes, I listened to what they were saying," Joe agreed.

"I would say your uncle is going to look into it and not just seal it up," Jonathan said.

"I don't think I want to be in this house if they open that crack up," Celia said. "It could damage the foundation, and the house could sink or something."

"Yes, it could," Joe agreed. "However, I don't believe it would damage the whole house. This is a well-built house, even though it's old, and I don't believe that tornado did much, if any, damage to the foundation or the house would have shown signs of it somewhere before now. Also, the tunnel only runs under part of the house. The rest of the house is sitting on firm ground."

"I suppose if we just go and sit where we were today, we could watch and see them coming in and out tomorrow and maybe overhear something about the crack," Mandie told her friends.

"As long as they don't see us," Celia said. "Otherwise Mr. Shaw might ask us to leave or stop hanging around the tunnel."

Liza came to the door of the parlor and announced, "Y'all's supper be on de table. Aunt Lou say git a move on now."

"We're coming right now, Liza, thank you," Mandie said as she quickly rose from her chair.

Her friends joined her, and they all went into the dining room, where the meal was set out.

"If we don't waste too much time eating, we'll have more time before dark to go for a walk," Celia told the others as they all sat down together at the end of the table.

"Right," Jonathan agreed. "I can always eat in a hurry."

Mandie asked Joe, "Will you and Uncle Ned be gone all day tomorrow?"

Joe replied, "I'm not sure. I have no idea how long it will take us to get the chickens and deliver them to Mrs. Fortner."

"Just how are you going to pick up all those chickens and deliver them to that woman? What do you put them in or whatever? I've never hauled chickens before," Jonathan said with a grin.

"Oh, that will be easy," Joe said. "We'll just take some cages with us if Mr. Shaw has any, and if he doesn't we'll get them from the people we are getting the chickens from. Uncle Ned's wagon will hold enough."

"No such problems in the city of New York, where I live," Jonathan said, grinning, as he shook his head.

"You get an education every time you leave that great big city, don't you?" Joe asked him.

"Sometimes," Jonathan agreed. "Life down here is so different from ours in New York. And I've never lived in a small place like this. All the boarding schools I've been to were in large cities."

Mandie quickly sipped her coffee and said, "I just can't imagine my grandmother ever living in New York, but evidently she did when she was young, because that was where she knew your father, Jonathan."

Jonathan grinned at her and said, "I still think they should get back together, your grandmother and my father. I wouldn't mind having your grandmother for a stepmother."

"You wouldn't?" Mandie asked in surprise. "You just don't know my grandmother, then. She can really take over everybody and everything when she wants to."

"You know that she even bought the school Mandie and I go to in Asheville, don't you?" Celia asked.

"I remember hearing something mentioned about that. But wasn't it because the old lady sisters who own it, the Misses Heathwood, were in money trouble and about to close it up?" Jonathan asked.

"Well, that was one reason, wasn't it, Mandie?" Celia replied and looked to Mandie to explain.

"It was a good excuse for her to buy it and become the boss as the new owner," Mandie explained. "She hasn't made a whole lot of changes. Miss Hope and Miss Prudence still run it, but I'm sure they consult my grandmother on every move they make."

"After this next year, you girls will be finished with that school, and then where will you all be going to college? You have to make up your minds in time to get enrolled somewhere, you know," Joe said. "And I would highly recommend my college, where I go in New Orleans."

"Before we get into all that, let's hurry and finish our food and get outside before it gets dark," Mandie suggested, hastily eating the potatoes on her plate.

"Good idea," Jonathan agreed.

Once they were finished with their supper and outside in the yard, Joe asked, "Which way shall we walk?"

"Down to the entrance of the tunnel first, before it gets dark," Mandie quickly told him.

"Mandie, you know that the door down there is locked, so what good will it do you to walk down there?" Jonathan asked.

"We can sit down for a few minutes when we get down there and plan out what we will do tomorrow while they are working on the tunnel, where we will sit so we can watch the entrance, and all that," Mandie quickly explained as she led the way down the hill.

She secretly never gave up the hope of finding the tunnel unlocked. She would never know until she went down and checked.

# CHAPTER TEN

# A VISITOR

When Mandie and her friends opened the front door and went outside, Snowball had come running down the hall and slipped out with them.

Jonathan saw him and said, "Mandie, there is that white cat. Will he run away or get lost?"

Mandie smiled at him and replied, "No way. That cat knows every crack and corner of this property. And he may disappear for a while, but he always comes home. This is not like New York, where you have to keep your pets on a leash." She watched as Snowball ran ahead of them and disappeared down the hill.

"Now, Mandie, he has been lost a couple of times that I remember," Joe told her with a big smile.

"Yes, but that was unusual," Mandie said.

Celia suddenly stopped and said, "Oh, for goodness' sake, I've caught my skirt on that rosebush." She was trying to reach the back of her dress, where it was stuck to a thorny branch.

"Hold still, I'll get it loose," Mandie told her and quickly came to remove the rosebush's thorns.

Celia tried to see the spot on the back of her skirt where it had stuck. "I can't see. Did it damage my skirt?" she asked.

Mandie fluffed the material and stood back to look. "No, I can't even see where it was," she replied.

"Those big fluffy skirts you girls wear don't mix too well with rosebushes, do they?" Jonathan remarked.

"I shouldn't have been taking a shortcut through the rosebushes," Celia told him.

"Let's get back out on the main path," Mandie said, leading the way down the hill.

"Joe, you won't be here tomorrow because you are going off with Uncle Ned," Mandie remarked as they came out within sight of the bushes and trees hiding the entrance to the tunnel. "You may miss some excitement, depending on whether Uncle John opens up the crack or not."

"I realize that, but we need to get those chickens to Mrs. Fortner while we are here," Joe replied, walking beside her. "If he opens the crack, maybe we will get back in time to see what's behind it."

"But Mr. Shaw has not promised that we could go in and see whatever they find if they do open it," Jonathan said.

"Yes, and it could be something so dangerous that we won't be allowed in there at all," Celia added.

They came to the bushes, and Mandie quickly slipped through them to check the tunnel door. It was locked. She had known it would be. But then, you could never tell when someone might leave it unlocked. Stepping back to her friends, she said, "It's locked."

There was a slight crashing noise in the woods nearby, and they all glanced at one another.

"Did you hear something?" Mandie asked as she quickly turned to look around toward the thicket nearby.

Joe and Jonathan pushed bushes back and ran in to search. They made a loud noise as they did.

"Whatever it was, y'all have scared it away with your racket," Mandie called to them as she watched to see if anything came out.

The boys returned to the clearing. Joe said, "Yes, we probably did. It might have been a squirrel or another animal."

"And those animals are always quicker than we are," Jonathan decided, stomping his feet to shake off the leaves that stuck to his pants.

"So are some human beings," Mandie added with a thoughtful frown.

"Anyhow, the tunnel door is locked, and if it was something or someone trying to get in there, they wouldn't have been able to," Celia reminded them.

"Oh well, let's go over here," Mandie said, leading the way through rhododendron bushes to the place where they had sat before.

When they were all seated, Joe looked in front of them and said, "You really can't see much from here except the door to the tunnel."

"And that means no one can see us if we just sit still and look and listen," Mandie reminded him.

"Do you think these workmen will come after breakfast?" Jonathan asked.

"We can get up early and eat breakfast in the kitchen before the others come downstairs," Mandie said.

"I imagine all the men will plan on doing that, because I would think they will all go to the tunnel with Mr. Shaw," Celia said.

"That would clutter up Aunt Lou's kitchen. What do you think she would have to say about that?" Jonathan asked with a grin.

Mandie looked at him and said, "She may not even be up early like we will."

"Now, how are we going to eat breakfast if there isn't any because Aunt Lou is not there to prepare it?" Jonathan asked.

"Oh, Jonathan, my uncle knows how to cook breakfast, and so do I," Mandie said and then added sadly, "I used to get up early when my father was living and we lived at Charley Gap. He always had the coffee made, and when I came down we would cook breakfast. He even knew how to make biscuits." Her eyes misted over as she remembered her father, Jim Shaw.

"What did your cook say about that?" Jonathan asked.

Everyone laughed at that remark. Mandie smiled at him and said, "We didn't have a cook, or any servants at all, and we lived in a log cabin, which, as you know, I still own. Those were happy days." She swallowed to keep her voice from shaking.

"Now, that would be wonderful, to be able to live without all those servants around, bossing everything all the time," Jonathan said with a big grin. "I think I'll marry you, Mandie Shaw, and live with you in that log cabin."

"Now, hold on just a minute," Joe quickly said. "That's taken care of already."

Mandie quickly stood up and said, "Let's walk back up the hill." Everyone followed without a word. She didn't want to get into the subject of marriage. Lifting her long skirts as she climbed uphill, she looked back at her friends and said, "Let's go out on the main road and walk for a while."

"Yes," they all agreed.

Once they were on the main road, they walked down into the business district. Most of the stores were closed for the night, but lots of people were strolling along the streets.

As they came to an intersection on Main Street, Mandie looked at Jonathan, laughed, and said, "And now here is Broadway."

Jonathan glanced around and said, "I don't believe New York's Broadway could have ever looked like this."

Different kinds of stores stood next to each other, with open parks here and there and benches in those. The structures were of a variety, some brick, some wooden, and some part mortar, some very old, some old, and some not so old. And most of the benches were unoccupied.

"Let's sit down over here for a few minutes," Mandie suggested as they came to a bench.

"I thought you wanted to walk," Joe said as he sat next to her and Jonathan and Celia joined them.

"I do, I did, and we will be walking back, and you know that involves some steep hills," Mandie replied. "I just thought we could catch our breath before doing that."

"Why, Mandie, you sound like you're getting old," Celia teased her.

"Oh no, not old, just curious about who is out for a walk besides us," Mandie said.

"You probably know everyone in town, don't you?" Jonathan asked. "After all, there aren't a whole lot of people living in Franklin."

"No, I don't know everyone in town," Mandie replied. "You

know I have only been living in Franklin for about three years, and most of that time I've been away to school in Asheville."

"Oh yes, I keep forgetting you lived over in Swain County near Joe when your father was living," Jonathan said.

Suddenly Mandie heard someone calling, "Missy 'Manda, Missy 'Manda, where you at?"

Mandie smiled at her friends as they all rose from the bench. "It's Liza." The girl had finally spotted her and was coming down the hill. "Here I am, Liza. What's wrong?"

"Aunt Lou, she send me to find you. Man at house wants to see you," Liza explained as soon as she could get her breath from running.

"A man at the house wants to see me?" Mandie questioned. "Who is it, Liza?"

"Lawsy mercy, Missy 'Manda, I disremember who dat man is," Liza replied. "Aunt Lou she say git a move on and git right back to de house. Come on now." She turned to go back up the road.

Mandie and her friends hurried after Liza.

"Must be a stranger if Liza doesn't know who he is," Joe remarked.

"Liza never is good at remembering people's names," Mandie said as they climbed the hill toward the house. Liza was way ahead of them and had disappeared into the house.

When they came within view of the house, Mandie saw a man sitting on the steps. The sun was fading, and she squinted to see who he was.

"Oh, it's Mr. Jacob Smith," she said excitedly.

"Yes, it is," Joe agreed.

"Who is Mr. Jacob Smith?" Jonathan asked as they hurried on.

"He lives in my father's house at Charley Gap," Mandie quickly explained.

As she came to the steps, the huge, burly, gray-haired man stood up and reached to embrace her with a tight squeeze. "And how is Jim Shaw's little daughter?" he asked.

"Oh, Mr. Jacob, I'm so glad to see you," Mandie told him as she held his hand. "You are like part of my past with my father." She blinked her eyes as she felt them mist over. Trying to control her feelings, she asked, "How are things with you, Mr. Jacob?"

"Just fine, just fine," he replied. "Got everything stocked up now to begin farming, thanks to the neighbors out there."

At that moment Liza pushed open the door, stuck her head out, and said loudly, "Aunt Lou say you git yo'selfs in dis heah house right now. She got coffee and choc'late cake awaitin'." She closed the door.

"Yes, ma'am," Mandie said with a big smile. Turning to her friends, she said, "We'd better get a move on, or Liza will be back."

When they went inside, Mandie went down the hall and opened the kitchen door and looked inside. Aunt Lou saw her and quickly said, "Now, y'all jes' take de comp'ny to de parlor. Liza gwine bring coffee and cake. Shoo now."

"But I thought maybe we could eat in here with you," Mandie protested.

"Dat ain't no way to treat dat friend of yo' pa's," Aunt Lou replied. She shook her white apron at Mandie and said, "Git now."

"Yes, ma'am, I'm going," Mandie said, and turning to her friends behind her, she said, "We have to go to the parlor and let Liza bring the coffee in there." She led the way to the parlor, where they sat down by the windows.

"Aunt Lou told me everyone was gone out to visit some friends and wouldn't be back until late," Jacob Smith said to Mandie.

"Yes, sir, they all went out together," Mandie explained. "And my mother didn't know when they'd be back, probably late, but you're going to spend the night, aren't you?"

"Well, I suppose I'll have to in order to see your uncle John," Mr. Smith replied.

Liza came in with the tea cart and began passing out the chocolate cake and coffee.

"You probably haven't heard, because Uncle John didn't want us to talk to people about it, but we have a crack in the wall of the tunnel under the house," Mandie told him.

Liza heard that remark and began grumbling as she finished serving the coffee. "Dis heah house might be gwine fall right down, might be," she said, just loud enough for everyone to hear.

"Now, Liza, this house is not going to fall in from that little crack in the tunnel," Jonathan said teasingly.

"Jes' you wait and see, wait and see," the girl replied as she left the room.

"A crack in the wall of the tunnel?" Mr. Smith questioned, drinking his coffee.

Mandie explained how they had all been in Charleston at the Pattons' house and Uncle Ned had come to tell Uncle John that he must go home to investigate the crack.

"But a crack in the wall of the tunnel wouldn't really be serious, would it?" Jacob Smith asked.

"I don't know how serious it is, but I saw it and there is something behind the crack, either a door or a wall," Mandie replied. "And I hope Uncle John finds out what it is before he seals up the crack."

"There's a possibility the crack was caused by the tornado that came through here back in the spring," Joe said. "So there could be more damage down there somewhere else."

Mandie quickly looked at Joe and said, "But Uncle John never mentioned anything like that. If there is more damage, then it could be awfully serious, couldn't it, Mr. Jacob?" She looked at Mr. Smith.

"Now, I couldn't rightly express any opinion on it because I have not seen the crack you are talking about. And I would have to make a thorough investigation of the whole tunnel to look for more damage," Mr. Smith told her.

"But Uncle John hasn't mentioned anything else down there. I don't know whether he has inspected the whole tunnel or not," Mandie said, looking at her friends. "Have y'all heard anyone mention doing that?"

"No, Mandie, I haven't heard anything," Celia said.

"Neither have I, but then, I haven't discussed it with my father and he has been down there with your uncle, Mandie," Jonathan told her.

Joe shrugged his shoulders and said, "I don't know any more than you do."

"The workmen have been going in and out the outside entrance to the tunnel, and we've been watching, but I don't know what my uncle will do about it," Mandie said and then added, "Would you like to see the outside entrance to the tunnel before it gets too dark, Mr. Jacob?"

"I could use a little walk," Mr. Smith said. "Been riding horse-back nearly all day."

"Then let's walk down to the tunnel entrance," Mandie said, glancing at her friends.

Mandie knew her friends were tired of her going down to the tunnel entrance to check the door every time they went outside, so she was silent as they walked down the hill. Everyone else was quiet, too.

Just as they got within sight of the bushes hiding the tunnel door, Mandie heard someone talking, and she put up her hand and whispered to her friends, "Sh-h-h-h!" She crept forward, trying not to make a sound.

Everyone stopped where they were. As she got close enough to peek through the bushes, she was astonished to see Polly Cornwallis and that newspaperman messing with the lock on the door.

"I told you you couldn't unlock that door with pins. What a stupid idea," the reporter was saying.

"If I stick enough of them in the hole in the lock, it might work," Polly replied as she continued messing with the lock.

Mandie instantly hurried forward, pulled the bushes back, and confronted the two. "Just what are you doing, Polly Cornwallis? And you, reporter or cousin or whoever you are, my uncle has forbidden you to come on our property."

Mandie's friends and Jacob Smith had rushed forward when they heard the conversation between Mandie and the intruders.

"I was not doing anything," Polly argued, but then when she looked up and saw Mr. Smith, she quickly ran off into the bushes.

The reporter didn't budge. "I don't know why you have to try to keep all this a secret, because it will surely be put in all the papers," he said.

"Don't you dare trespass on our property," Mandie said, walking up close to him.

Jacob Smith moved closer with her and asked, "Who are you, fella? This is private property."

Mandie looked up at him and explained, "He's that newspaper reporter that has been snooping around here. Uncle John told him never to come back."

"Then you had better get off this property immediately," Mr. Smith told him.

The reporter continued standing there as he said, "I'm not sure this is private property right here or that it belongs to the Shaws. Polly said it wasn't."

"I can guarantee you, buddy, this property does belong to the Shaws, and I myself will remove you if you don't get off it," Jacob Smith insisted, stepping nearer to the man.

The reporter drew in a long breath and then turned and ran off into the bushes.

"Shall we chase him, sir, to be sure he has gone?" Jonathan asked.

"I don't think he will return so long as he knows I am here," Mr. Smith replied.

Mandie walked over to the door of the tunnel and looked at the lock. "The lock is full of straight pins," she exclaimed as the others crowded around. "Polly has put straight pins in the lock."

"Let me see what I can do about this," Jacob Smith said, taking his pocketknife out of his pocket.

Mandie moved aside and watched as he carefully picked out the straight pins from the hole in the lock. Her friends joined her.

"What a dumb idea," Jonathan said, "thinking she could unlock the door by sticking pins in the lock."

"All those pins could jam up the lock to where you couldn't unlock it with the key," Joe said.

"I figured all the time the pincushion belonged to Polly, but I had no idea she was using it for such a thing as this," Mandie remarked.

Mr. Smith got the last of the pins out and turned to ask, "Do you have the key? We could see if it works all right now or whether a pin or two might have slipped on down inside the lock."

Mandie shook her head and said, "No, Mr. Jacob, Uncle John has the key."

"Well, I don't think those two could open this lock without the key, so I'd say it's safe for now," Mr. Smith said.

They went back to the house and sat in the parlor until midnight, at which time the adults had still not returned and at which time everyone decided to go to bed. Aunt Lou showed Mr. Smith to a bedroom upstairs, and the young people went to their own rooms.

When Mandie and Celia got in bed, Celia immediately went to sleep. Mandie stayed awake thinking about the tunnel and about Polly and that reporter. She wanted to be up bright and early to tell her uncle about those two.

# CHAPTER ELEVEN

# *PREPARATIONS*

Celia woke first the next morning. She leaned up on her elbow and shook Mandie. "You wanted to get downstairs early, didn't you, Mandie?" she asked.

"Mmmmm," Mandie grunted as she sat up in bed. And then remembering her reason, she quickly slid out of bed and hurried to get dressed. "Yes, I want to speak to Uncle John about Polly and that reporter."

Celia put on her clothes, and the two went down to the kitchen. There was no one there. The coffee was not made, either.

"Everybody must have overslept," Mandie said, going to pick up the percolator. "I'll get the coffee going." She took the can of coffee out of the cupboard and measured the amount to use. Dumping it into the coffeepot, she filled the pot with water and put it back on the stove.

"Mandie, the stove is hot. Someone must have been in here before us," Celia remarked as she held her hands near the hot iron stove door.

"You're right. It's hot enough to make the coffee," Mandie agreed. "But I wonder who built the fire in it? I don't think it could have been Uncle John or Aunt Lou, because they would have made the coffee. But who could it have been?" She thought about it for a minute.

At that moment Uncle Ned came in the back door. "Good morning," he greeted them with a big smile. "I went for walk and came back to make coffee. You make coffee."

"Yes, sir, Uncle Ned, I just made it, and it ought to be ready by the time we get the cups," Mandie replied, going over to the cupboard and getting down cups and saucers.

John Shaw came into the kitchen from the hallway and said, "Now, that's nice of you, Amanda, to make the coffee."

Before she could reply, Joe and Jonathan also entered the room.

Mandie waited until everyone had coffee and they were seated at the table before she told John Shaw about Polly and the reporter.

"They both ran away when we caught them," she concluded.

Jacob Smith came in through the door from the hallway and joined them.

"Good morning. I didn't realize you were here," John Shaw greeted the man. "Pull out a chair and have some coffee."

"Thank you, that would be invigorating," Mr. Smith replied as he sat down and Mandie hurried to fill a cup with coffee for him.

"Oh, and Uncle John, I forgot to mention that Mr. Jacob was with us when we found Polly and that reporter down at the tunnel entrance," she said.

"I'm glad you were there," John Shaw told Jacob Smith. "Otherwise, Amanda and her friends might have had trouble with the two. I just don't know what I am going to do about them. Since Polly is a neighbor, I can't be too rude to her, but that reporter is absolutely trespassing. On the other hand, if I try to use legal means to keep him off the property, there's no telling what he might write in his newspaper about us. And I certainly don't want that tunnel publicized."

"That is a touchy situation," Jacob Smith agreed.

"We get braves watch property," Uncle Ned suggested. "Stop them from coming to tunnel."

"That would be a good solution, Uncle Ned," John Shaw told him. "Would you be able to get some young fellows over here today while we work on the crack?"

"Need go get chickens today," the old man said. "For Mrs. Fortner."

"I wonder if we could wait another day for that, Uncle Ned," John

Shaw said. "I don't think it's real urgent, because she has plenty of chickens for the time being. In fact, it might be a couple more days before we could get the chickens, because I have decided to open up the crack, and that will take a much longer time than just repairing it."

Mandie grinned at her friends when they heard this.

Uncle Ned smiled at John Shaw and said, "Yes, right thing to open up crack. Chickens can wait. Braves coming today to help with filling crack. I tell them stand watch instead."

"Thank you, Uncle Ned, that will solve that problem, I believe," John Shaw said.

Jacob Smith spoke up. "I need to speak to you confidentially, John. I have a message to deliver."

John Shaw looked at him in surprise and asked, "You do?" He stood up and said, "Suppose we step out in the yard, then, for a few minutes. The workmen will be here soon."

Mandie was listening, and she looked at her friends and saw they also had heard what Mr. Smith had to say. Now, what kind of a message did he have? And who was it from? she wondered as the two men left the room.

Joe grinned at her and said, "You will never hear what the message is."

"Maybe not now but later," Mandie answered. "He didn't tell us when he came last night that he had a message."

"But, Mandie, it was not a message for us. It was for your uncle," Celia reminded her.

"So why should he tell us that he had a message?" Jonathan asked.

"Well, I would like to know what the message is since it is considered so confidential," Mandie argued.

Uncle Ned spoke up. "Message not for Papoose," he said. "Must not pry."

Mandie took a deep breath and remained silent. She didn't want to argue with Uncle Ned. If John Shaw didn't allow the young people in the tunnel, she might be able to get some information about the crack from Uncle Ned.

John Shaw and Jacob Smith came back into the kitchen and sat down at the table. John Shaw told Mandie, "Whenever your grand-mother comes downstairs, I need to speak to her, Amanda."

Now, this was getting to be a mystery. Whatever had been said between her uncle and Jacob Smith must concern her grandmother.

Jacob Smith drank up his coffee and said, "I must be getting on the road home." He stood up.

"Do you have to leave now? We'll have some breakfast soon," John Shaw told him.

"No, I'd better not stay for breakfast. I usually don't eat much in the morning anyway. Besides, it won't take me long to get back to Charley Gap since I rode my horse and didn't bring the wagon," Jacob Smith replied. He looked down at Mandie and said, "Don't forget to come to see me, young lady."

"I'll come over one day before I go back to school," Mandie promised. "But I wish you could stay awhile."

"I've got work to do," he replied. "Maybe next time I can stay longer."

John Shaw walked out the back door with Jacob Smith as he went to get his horse from the barn. Uncle Ned followed.

Aunt Lou came into the kitchen from the hall door. She stopped, looked at everybody, and said, "Now, why didn't y'all let me know y'all up dis bright and early?" Going over to the stove, she opened the door to the firebox and added another piece of wood from the woodbox sitting behind the stove.

"We didn't want to bother you, Aunt Lou. I made the coffee," Mandie told her.

Aunt Lou looked at her and then opened the lid of the coffeepot. "Is it fittin' to be drunk?" she asked, bending to look inside the pot. She picked up the pot and carried it to the sink.

"Aunt Lou, don't pour it out. It tasted fine to me," Joe objected.

Aunt Lou looked at him and replied, "It mighta been, but it ain't now. Y'all done drunk it all up. Gotta make more." She dumped the coffee grounds into a can under the sink and began preparing another pot of coffee.

Liza came into the kitchen, rubbing her eyes and yawning.

Aunt Lou looked at Mandie and her friends. "Y'all drink up dat coffee in a hurry now and git out of heah," she said. "We'se got to git breakfast a-goin'."

"Yes, ma'am," Mandie said, finishing the last of the coffee in her cup and standing up. Her friends joined her. "We'll leave now."

As the young people started for the back door, Mandie turned back to say, "Aunt Lou, if my grandmother comes down, Uncle John said he needs to speak to her."

"All right, git out of heah now," Aunt Lou replied.

The young people hurried out the back door. Mandie stopped on the back porch to look around. No one was in sight. Mr. Smith must have left, and Uncle John and Uncle Ned had probably gone down to the tunnel entrance.

"If we sit out there on the bench under that chestnut tree, we can see everybody going and coming to the tunnel entrance," she told her friends.

"And we won't be too far away to know when breakfast is ready," Jonathan added.

"Yes, that's important," Joe agreed.

"We couldn't go sit down near the tunnel entrance right now anyway because all the men are probably down there," Celia said.

Just as they got to the log bench and sat down, Uncle Ned came from around the front of the house. He had two young Cherokee men with him. They were speaking quickly in the Cherokee language and went on down the lane to the tunnel entrance without noticing Mandie and her friends.

"They must be the ones Uncle Ned said he would get to keep that reporter and Polly off our property," Mandie remarked.

"Probably," Joe said. "What I'd like to know is how they are going to do that. They certainly can't touch Polly, and y'all know she won't do anything she doesn't want to do."

"Yes, since she's a girl that's a problem," Jonathan said.

"Well, I'm a girl, too, and I'll help those Indians keep her away," Mandie told them.

"How, Mandie?" Celia asked.

Mandie thought for a minute and then said, "By scaring her. I'll tell her the house might fall in."

"And then she'll go tell that reporter and he'll put it in his paper that your house is in dangerous shape," Joe warned her.

"But his paper is all the way up in Raleigh," Mandie protested.

"And a lot of the people living here buy that Raleigh newspaper since that is the state capital," Joe replied.

"And your local newspaper would probably pick it up from the Raleigh paper," Celia added.

"I doubt that. Anyhow, we'll have the crack repaired before word could be circulated around about it," Mandie told them.

It wasn't long before John Shaw and Uncle Ned came up the hill from the tunnel entrance and went in the back door of the house. And then Liza came to get them for breakfast.

Mandie looked around the table. Everyone was present except her grandmother. Where could she be? She had hoped to hear whatever it was Uncle John was going to tell Mrs. Taft, but she wasn't there and no one mentioned her name. Senator Morton was there. He was sitting next to Jane Hamilton.

"Have you noticed?" Mandie whispered to her friends at the table. "My grandmother isn't here."

"Probably just sleeping late," Jonathan decided.

"Maybe she'll be along shortly," Joe suggested.

"I hope she isn't sick," Celia said.

"Sick?" Mandie questioned. She had not even thought of such a thing. Her grandmother was never sick. She could outdo everyone else when she wanted to.

Then suddenly the door opened, and Mrs. Taft came hurrying into the room and took a seat on the other side of Senator Morton.

"I apologize for being late," she said, looking around the table. "I had to do some things before I came downstairs."

Liza immediately came to Mrs. Taft's side with the coffeepot and filled her cup. "Would you like fo' me to fill up dat plate fo' you?" Liza asked.

"Oh yes, that would be nice, Liza, please," Mrs. Taft replied. "Just give me a dab of grits and a little bacon and eggs. That would be fine."

"Yessum," Liza said, picking up Mrs. Taft's plate and taking it to the sideboard, where she proceeded to pile it high with food.

When she brought it back, Mrs. Taft looked at it in surprise, frowned, and then smiled. "Thank you, Liza," she said as she picked up her fork and began eating.

"I don't think my grandmother will eat all that food," Mandie told her friends, almost giggling behind her hand.

"Liza must have figured she was hungry," Jonathan whispered.

John Shaw was seated across the table from Mrs. Taft. He laid down his fork and spoke to her. "After we finish the meal, Mrs. Taft, may I have a word with you?"

Mrs. Taft looked at him in surprise and replied, "Of course, John."

Mandie whispered behind her hand to her friends, "Uncle John hasn't told her whatever it is yet."

Her friends shook their heads and looked at Mrs. Taft.

Mandie tried to listen to the grown-ups' conversation, but she could only hear snatches of it now and then.

"It will be after noontime before we can tell," John Shaw told Jane Hamilton in answer to a question that Mandie could not understand.

"Please be careful down there, John," Elizabeth cautioned him.

"I am not involved in the work myself. Those young Cherokee men are doing most of it, with Cliff supervising," John Shaw replied.

"You are not allowing anyone else in there, are you?" Elizabeth asked, slightly glancing at Mandie and her friends.

Mandie immediately dropped her eyes and hurriedly forked up her food, pretending she had not heard a word.

"Of course not. Everyone has been warned not to go inside the tunnel," John replied.

Dr. and Mrs. Woodard were seated next to Elizabeth, and Mandie saw the doctor glance down the table at them.

"I think everyone realizes how dangerous it could be if that wall caves in when they open the crack," Dr. Woodard said.

After that the adults' conversation turned to other things.

Finally the meal was over, and everyone began leaving the room. Mandie noticed Uncle John motioning to Mrs. Taft to follow him into the hallway and tried to follow closely behind them. Her uncle walked on down the hallway, though, and waited for Mrs. Taft to catch up with him.

"Come on, Mandie," Celia said as Mandie stopped outside the dining room door and watched. "You can't follow them."

"No, but I can watch from here," Mandie whispered to her friends as she moved slowly across the hall. They followed.

The other adults moved on down the hallway to the parlor. Mandie and her friends stood there, whispering to each other, with Mandie looking down the corridor at her grandmother and John Shaw.

Whatever her uncle was telling her grandmother seemed to be a surprise to the lady. She threw up her hands as she quickly replied and shook her head. Then she hurried down the hallway to the parlor and went in. John Shaw followed her.

"Come on," Mandie told her friends and hurried after the adults.

When she and her friends entered the parlor, Mandie saw her grandmother talking to her mother. But she couldn't get close enough to overhear the conversation. The young people sat down as near to the adults as they could find seats, but it was too far away in the huge room to overhear conversations.

Liza had brought the tea cart in and was serving the coffee. As she passed Mandie, she whispered, "Yo' grandma she gwine home, ain't she?"

Mandie looked at her in surprise and replied, "I don't know. Did something happen to cause her to have to go home?"

"Now, dat's whut I'm askin' you, Missy 'Manda," Liza said. "I only hears her say she's gwine git packed and be ready to leave tomorrow. Now, don't dat sound like she be gwine home?"

"Yes, Liza, it does, but I don't know anything about it," Mandie said. "Who did she say that to?"

"She be tellin' yo' ma," Liza replied, hurriedly leaving the room.

Mandie looked at her friends, who had overheard the conversation with Liza. "Something must be wrong at her home," she told them.

"She will probably tell you all about it before she leaves," Joe said.

"And I suppose the senator will go with her," Jonathan said. "Looks like no chance for my father there."

Mandie grinned at him and said, "That's right."

Mandie was anxious to walk down to the tunnel entrance and

watch from there to see what was going on, but she also wanted to know what was happening with her grandmother, and she couldn't be in two places at one time.

Finally Mandie heard Mrs. Taft suggest to Senator Morton that they go for a walk. And she couldn't follow them, so she decided to go on down to the tunnel entrance.

"Let's go sit in our special place down at the tunnel and watch what goes on down there," Mandie told her friends.

"I'll go, but I don't think we will be able to see anything that goes on because all the activity will be inside the tunnel," Joe told her.

"You never know what might happen, though," Mandie replied.

"We might be able to ask the workmen some questions," Jonathan said.

"They may not speak English," Joe told him.

"Let's go find out," Mandie said.

They would sit there near the tunnel entrance and try to find out what was going on inside the tunnel.

# CHAPTER TWELVE

# *THE PAST*

Mandie and her friends watched and managed to get down near the tunnel without the adults seeing them. They sat in the place half hidden by the bushes, where no one could walk by them but from where they could see people going in and out of the tunnel.

"I don't see Uncle Ned's friends who are supposed to be watching the tunnel," Joe said, looking around the area.

"Oh, they are never seen but they can see you. You know how secretive they are about things like that," Mandie told him.

"There are some men in the tunnel working, I suppose," Jonathan said.

"There should be," Mandie agreed.

"Too bad we didn't get down here in time to see who all went in there," Jonathan said.

"I think the only people working in there are the Cherokee man, Cliff, and his Cherokee friends," Mandie said.

"I'd like to know what they are doing," Jonathan remarked.

"Yes, and I'd also like to know what is going on with my grandmother," Mandie said. "Something is going on, and I haven't figured out yet what it is." She frowned as she thought about the conversation between Mrs. Taft and John Shaw, the part that she could hear. And what did Jacob Smith have to do with it all? He had been her father's friend, and she didn't believe her grandmother had even known him.

Joe looked at Mandie and said, "I know what you are thinking. What is the connection between Mrs. Taft and Mr. Jacob Smith?"

Mandie looked at him in surprise. "Why, yes, I can't imagine what happened this morning. Evidently Mr. Jacob gave Uncle John a message for my grandmother, but what message was it? Not only that, how did Mr. Jacob know my grandmother was here?"

"Knowing Mandie Shaw, I'd say we'll have that mystery solved sooner or later," Jonathan said with a big grin.

"It must be something awfully important for Mr. Smith to come all the way over here to tell her whatever it is," Celia remarked.

"What do y'all plan on doing the rest of the summer? My grandmother wants us to go home with her, but I'm not sure I want to," Mandie said.

"I suppose I'll leave it up to my mother about what I should do," Celia said.

Snowball, Mandie's white cat, came running down the hill and went straight to them and jumped up in Mandie's lap.

"Well, Snowball, what's the hurry?" Mandie asked as she stroked his fur. "Something must have scared him."

"Like a dog?" Jonathan asked.

"No, not a dog. Snowball chases dogs, believe it or not," Mandie replied. Snowball jumped back down and ran off through the bushes. "He may be playing around with a squirrel."

"Squirrels can hurt," Celia said. "They have sharp teeth."

"I hear someone coming down the hill," Mandie whispered.

The four sat silently waiting to see who would appear through the bushes as the footsteps came closer.

"Sh-h-h-h! It's Uncle John and Uncle Ned," Mandie whispered.

The four sat completely still, waiting and watching.

"I just want to be sure the men don't need anything before I leave," John Shaw was saying. "I won't be gone long, but in case anyone shows up around here, be sure your men get rid of them, Uncle Ned."

"Braves watch; no one come near," the old Indian said.

The two men entered the tunnel. Mandie couldn't hear anything after that. But then, the workmen were a long distance up in the tunnel, and it would be impossible to hear them from the entrance.

The young people waited silently. Finally John Shaw and Uncle Ned came back out of the tunnel.

"Looks like it will be quite a while before they get enough of the wall out to see what's behind the crack. I'll be back by then," John Shaw said as they started to walk up the hill.

"Yes, go slow so wall not fall in," Uncle Ned said as they went on.

Once they were out of sight, Mandie said, "I wish I could see what's going on in there."

The four sat there engrossed with their own thoughts for a long time. Snowball didn't return, and there was no sound coming from the tunnel. No one came down the hill. Everything was silent.

Suddenly there was loud talking in the tunnel, and Cliff and the two young Cherokee men came rushing outside, speaking loudly in Cherokee. The two young men ran up the hill, and Cliff went after them.

"They must be having some kind of argument," Mandie said.

"It certainly sounded like it," Jonathan said.

"Their language sounds so much different from ours that it's hard to figure out what they are saying," Joe remarked.

"They were the only ones in the tunnel, weren't they?" Celia asked.

Mandie sat up straight and said, "Yes, they were. I am going to look while they are gone." She stood up.

"And I'll go with you," Jonathan said, also rising.

"Mandie, I don't think you ought to go inside. Your uncle will be furious if you are caught in there," Joe reminded her.

"Yes, Mandie, I wouldn't go in there," Celia added.

"It will only take me a couple of minutes to run down the tunnel and see what they've done," Mandie insisted.

She hurried off into the entrance of the tunnel. Jonathan followed.

The men had left lanterns sitting here and there along the way so it was not dark. She could see nothing unusual as she went along, inspecting the walls as she got deeper inside the tunnel. Then up ahead she could see a whole lot of lanterns lighting up the place and knew instantly that was where the crack was.

"Here's the crack," she whispered to Jonathan, who was following. She saw when she got closer that the crack was a lot wider than when she had seen it before. Debris was piled up nearby.

"They have started widening it," she told Jonathan.

Jonathan got close to the wall to try and see what was on the other side. Mandie picked up one of the lanterns and flashed it along the wall. The light faintly illuminated the opening.

"Jonathan, there is something behind this crack," she said excitedly. She pressed her face against the mortar. Then she stood back and looked at the crack. "You know, Jonathan, I believe I can get through that crack and see what is on the other side if you will hold the lantern for me."

"Mandie, you are not going through that small space," Jonathan said. "You might get stuck, and I don't know how I would get you out."

"If I can get through without getting stuck, then I can get back out without getting stuck," she insisted, handing him the lantern. "Hold this up close for me so it won't be so dark in there when I get through. And, Jonathan, don't you dare run off and leave me in there."

"I won't, Mandie, but I still don't think you ought to try it," Jonathan replied, holding the lantern up close to inspect the crack. "The wall could start crumbling because they have been working on it and have probably loosened a lot of mortar."

"Just hold the lantern still and let me see if I can get through," Mandie insisted as she quickly wrapped her full skirt around her tightly and put one foot through the crack. She turned sideways and practically held her breath as she managed to squeeze her torso, her head, and finally her other foot through the crack.

"Mandie, please be careful," Jonathan told her. "There could be some creatures living in there."

"Jonathan, don't say that," Mandie screeched back to him. "I'm in here now, anyway. Hold the lantern up to the crack and let me see if I can figure out what's in here."

Jonathan held the lantern against the crack and waited.

Mandie squinted her eyes to see better and then told Jonathan, "This is a room, a real room, Jonathan, and—" Suddenly she tried to scream and couldn't, and in a hoarse whisper she told him, "There's a grave in here, Jonathan. Help me to get out. Quick!" She backed away from the nearby mound of dirt with a head marker and tried to put her foot back through the crack. She was trembling with fright so badly she couldn't manage to squeeze back through.

"Come on, Mandie," Jonathan told her excitedly. "Put your foot through or something; come on and get out of there." He tried to reach through the small opening.

Mandie was shaking so hard she couldn't concentrate on what she was doing. Finally Jonathan gave up. "Mandie, I'll leave the lantern right here next to the crack," he said. "I'm going to get Joe to help."

"Don't leave me alone in here," Mandie cried as he ran off down the tunnel.

He came back with Joe and Celia in a few minutes that seemed like hours to Mandie.

"Mandie, where are you?" Joe asked as he picked up the lantern and flashed its light through the crack.

"Mandie, come on out," Celia called to her.

"Joe, help me," Mandie called out from the other side of the wall. "There's a grave in here." Her voice broke.

Joe stooped down, picked up a chisel the men had been using, and started to work trying to widen the crack.

"I'll help," Jonathan said, picking up another chisel and hammering on the crack with it.

Mortar began to fall everywhere as the boys pounded, and the crack gradually grew wider.

"Mandie, try it now. I think you can squeeze through," Joe told her. "Reach through and give me your hand."

Mandie reached for his hand and said, "Everybody, our verse." All four friends instantly joined hands as they repeated their favorite Bible verse, " 'What time I am afraid I will put my trust in Thee.' "

"Now," Mandie said and began pushing through the crack. The release was so sudden she practically fell into the arms of Joe and Jonathan, who kept her from ending up on the rough cement floor. She sat down, shaking with fright.

"Mandie, are you all right?" Joe asked as he stooped by her side.

"Come on, Mandie, let's get out of here," Celia told her.

Jonathan flashed the lantern light through the crack, which was much wider now, and excitedly said, "Mandie was right. There is a grave in there."

Joe bent forward from Mandie's side to look. "Yes, there is," he said.

Mandie got to her feet and said, "Let's get the crack open enough to see exactly what is in there."

"Sit back down there. Jonathan and I will widen it if we can," Joe told her.

Mandie collapsed again on the cement floor, and Celia sat by her. The two boys chipped and hammered at the crack, and it suddenly gave way in large chunks, exposing the room behind it. The boys stood back and looked.

Mandie got to her feet and said, "See, I told you there was a grave in there." She pointed through the large opening.

Joe stepped through and inspected the grave. There was a post for the head marker, with an army cap hanging on it. He stooped to pick it up and examine it. A folded paper fell out of it.

"Look, Mandie, there is a piece of paper in this hat," he said, holding the paper out to her as she stood watching.

Taking the paper, Mandie's trembling hands managed to unfold it. She squinted in the light of the lantern to read the contents. The others crowded close by and held lanterns to illuminate.

She read, " 'Here lies Corporal Albert McKinnon from Washington, who attempted to kill me because I would not give up my Cherokee friends to be removed from their land to Oklahoma. My dear friend, Wirt Pindar, shot him and saved my life. May the Lord have mercy on this soldier's soul. Signed, John Shaw, Senior.' "

Mandie was completely still and silent for a moment as the importance of what she held finally soaked through to her. Her friends waited and watched.

"This is signed by my father's father, my grandfather. And Uncle Wirt shot this man," she managed to say as the paper shook in her hands.

Joe reached over, took the paper, folded it, and put it in his pocket. "Come on, Mandie, we need to get out of here," he said.

"Yes, let's hurry," Celia added, shivering all over.

Jonathan moved over to hold Celia's hand. "It's all over now. It's just a grave in there. Let's go."

Celia allowed Jonathan to move her along the tunnel toward the entrance. Joe and Mandie followed.

They were about one-third of the way out when John Shaw and Uncle Ned came rushing in and almost knocked them down before they saw them.

"Amanda! What are you doing in here?" John Shaw demanded.

Mandie looked up through tears and couldn't reply. Joe pulled out the paper and handed it to John Shaw.

"What is this?" the man asked as he quickly unfolded it. Then as he read it, he exclaimed, "So there is a grave in there, and my father must have had it sealed up to protect his friends." He hurried on down the tunnel toward the crack after he explained to Uncle Ned what the paper said.

The young people turned and came along behind him and Uncle Ned. The two men were conversing in the Cherokee language, and Mandie and her friends couldn't understand a word they were saying. She remembered that her uncle's mother had been full-blooded Cherokee. Therefore, he would know the language.

John Shaw and Uncle Ned took several lanterns into the hidden room and explored the walls.

"Look here, Uncle Ned," John Shaw said, pointing to a wall where he stood. "There's a dumbwaiter here, and it has been sealed off upstairs." He pointed overhead. "See that patching on the ceiling there?"

"Yes," the old Indian said. "What do now, John Shaw?"

John Shaw thought for a moment and then said, "My father said Uncle Wirt shot this man and saved his life by doing so, but I think we need to keep this quiet and just seal the room back up, the way he had done it. What do you think?"

"Yes, we tell Wirt but we tell no one else," Uncle Ned said.

"We will go back to the house now, Amanda, and none of this is to ever be discussed with anyone outside the family by any of you," John Shaw said, looking at Mandie and her friends.

"No, sir," Joe said instantly.

Jonathan nodded his head. "I won't talk about it."

"I certainly won't," Celia added.

"Let's get the men back in here and close it," John Shaw said as they walked down the tunnel toward the exit.

When they got back to the house, John Shaw called everyone together in the parlor and told them the story.

"I trust no one will ever repeat this outside of this room," he ended up saying. "That's mainly to protect Uncle Wirt, and it is our own private business."

Senator Morton, Mrs. Taft, Mr. Guyer, Jane Hamilton, Dr. and Mrs. Woodard, Jason Bond, the caretaker, who had just returned from his errand for John Shaw, Uncle Ned, Elizabeth Shaw, and the four young people all listened and agreed.

"The men will reseal the crack with something stronger than what's there and repair it so it will not be noticeable. Therefore future generations of Shaws who live in this house will have no reason to suspect there's a room back there," John Shaw explained. "And Uncle Ned has the workmen sworn to secrecy because of Uncle Wirt."

When the meeting was over, Mandie said to her friends, "Let's sit on the back porch for a little while." She needed some fresh air badly.

After they had all sat down, the door opened and Mandie looked up to see her grandmother standing there.

"Are you going to join us, Grandmother?" Mandie asked.

"No, dear, I thought perhaps you all would join me," Mrs. Taft said. She stopped and looked at each one.

"Join you? Where?" Mandie asked.

"At my house in Asheville, dear," Mrs. Taft said. "Before you decide, I must tell you the news."

The four young people instantly straightened up to listen.

"You all know Mr. Jacob Smith, I'm sure," Mrs. Taft said as she looked directly at Mandie.

"Yes, ma'am," replied the four.

"Well, Mr. Smith brought me a message," Mrs. Taft continued and then paused.

Mandie quickly smiled and thought, *She's going to tell us what it was.*

"It seems that we have an awfully big mystery back in Asheville,"

Mrs. Taft said. "And several people there had to trace me down. Mr. Smith happened to be in Asheville and knew where I was."

Mandie thought, *Oh, please hurry up and tell us what the mystery is.*

"Girls, Miss Hope at your school has completely disappeared, not a sign of her anywhere now for three days before Mr. Smith came," Mrs. Taft explained.

The four drew in their breath.

"Miss Hope missing?" Mandie said. "Oh, I hope nothing has happened to her."

"Yes, Miss Hope is nice," Celia added.

"And it's the other one, her sister, Miss Prudence, who is so tough on you girls, isn't it?" Joe asked.

The girls nodded.

"Now, since I own the school, Miss Prudence has sent me this news and asked if I could launch a search for her sister, and I thought perhaps you young people might want to help," she said, looking around the group.

"Oh, yes, ma'am, Grandmother," Mandie instantly replied.

"Yes," Celia agreed. "That is, if my mother will allow me to go to Asheville with y'all."

"And I want to go, also, but I'll have to clear it with my father," Jonathan said.

"I'll go with you," Joe promised.

"I thank you all," Mrs. Taft said. "Now, we need to get that train out of here tomorrow, so please be ready." She went back inside.

The young people discussed the newest mystery. Where was Miss Hope? She was shy, and it wasn't like her to just disappear without letting anyone know where she was going.

Mandie thought, *But we'll find you, Miss Hope. I know we will.*

So they were all going home to Asheville with Mrs. Taft after all.